Polyphony

VOLUME 4

Polyphony

VOLUME 4

DEBORAH LAYNE
EDITOR

JAY LAKE
EDITOR

 **Wheatland Press**
http://www.wheatlandpress.com

Polyphony, Volume 4

Published by

🌱 Wheatland Press

http://www.wheatlandpress.com

P. O. Box 1818

Wilsonville, OR 97070

Anthology copyright © 2004 by Wheatland Press

Introduction and headnotes copyright © 2004 by Wheatland Press
The Girl With the Sun in Her Head by Jeremiah Tolbert copyright © 2004 by Jeremiah Tolbert
Down in the Fog-Shrouded City by Alex Irvine copyright © 2004 by Alex Irvine
Black Dog At Work by Steven Mohan copyright © 2004 by Steven Mohan
Blackpool Ascensions by Lucius Shepard copyright © 2004 by Lucius Shepard
The Mud Fork Cottonmouth Expedition by Eric Witchey copyright © 2004 by Eric Witchey
When They Came by Don Webb copyright © 2004 by Don Webb
Over Alsace by Forrest Aguirre copyright © 2004 by Forrest Aguirre
State Change by Ken Liu copyright © 2004 by Ken Liu
High Rise High by Kit Reed copyright © 2004 by Kit Reed
The Storyteller's Story by Gavin Grant copyright © 2004 by Gavin Grant
Memree by Jenn Reese copyright © 2004 by Jenn Reese
The Eye by Eliot Fintushel copyright © 2004 by Eliot Fintushel
The Train There's No Getting Off by Bruce Holland Rogers, Ray Vukcevich and Holly Arrow copyright © 2004
Baby Love by Michael Bishop copyright © 2004 by Michael Bishop
Psyche and Eros by Diana Sherman copyright © 2004 by Diana Sherman
Hart and Boot by Tim Pratt copyright © 2004 by Tim Pratt
Life in the Movies by Mikal Trimm copyright © 2004 by Mikal Trimm
Bagging the Peak by Jerry Oltion copyright © 2004 by Jerry Oltion
The Journal of Philip Schuyler by Robert Wexler copyright © 2004 by Robert Wexler
Ataxia, The Wooden Continent by Stepan Chapman copyright © 2004 by Stepan Chapman
Tales From the City of Seams by Greg van Eekhout copyright © 2004 by Greg van Eekout
The Wings of Meister Wilhelm by Theodora Goss copyright © 2004 by Theodora Goss
Crazy Rain by Piper Selden copyright © 2004 by Piper Selden
Three Days in a Border Town by Jeff VanderMeer copyright © 2004 by Jeff VanderMeer

Library of Congress Cataloging-in-Publication data is available upon request.

ISBN 0-9720547-6-6

Printed in the United States of America

Layout and cover design by Deborah Layne.

Cover photograph by Jay Lake.

INTRODUCTION

It's been a long, strange road since the original volume of *Polyphony* was conceived by the dashboard lights along the lonely miles of I-5 in the Willamette Valley. Two and a half years have gone by, three volumes have been published in the series, markets have changed, production technology has evolved, and somehow, our book has found a home in genre.

When *Polyphony* first took off, it was on a wing and a prayer, with the help of a few dozen supporters and a lot of hope. New Weird was not the topic of the hour, the definition of slipstream was even more arguable than it is now. The phrase "interstitial" hadn't crept into the critical lexicon, let alone spawned a foundation or a conference. *We* weren't even sure whether to call *Polyphony* "cross-genre" or "slipstream" or "literary with a genre sensibility" (the last being the least elegant but most descriptive). As Supreme Court Justice Potter Stewart once said in another context, "We know it when we see it."

We weren't the first. *Lady Churchill's Rosebud Wristlet, Leviathan* and *Strange Horizons*, to name several, had charted this oh-so-literate genre territory before us. We haven't necessarily been the best—only the years will tell that. But we have been privileged to make a mark, and perhaps even set a standard, for a kind of fiction that many wanted to write, and many more wanted to read.

We could fill this book thanking all the mentors, authors, publishers, reviewers, critics, booksellers, friends, fans, and family members that have helped us along the way.

Instead we thought we'd fill this book with stories.

Curl up and read. That's what we'll be doing because we *still* love short fiction.

Jay Lake and Deborah Layne
Portland, Oregon
July, 2004

CONTENTS

THE GIRL WITH THE SUN IN HER HEAD

JEREMIAH TOLBERT

Emelia's home is in a city where only children are allowed to draw graffiti on the crumbling walls. The old bricks and stones are covered in crude pictographs and stick figures, smoking chimney houses and bicycles with four wheels and two seats. Chalk is a penny a piece, any color to be had. A little old lady with gnarled fingers and crooked eyes sells the sticks out of cigar boxes on street corners, even in the rain.

Emelia lives with her father and twin brothers, Blanco and Negro. Negro is very nice to Emelia and buys her sweets. Blanco steals and hides them underneath his mattress. In the spring, the flies are drawn to the sugar, and Blanco spends the night swatting at them without much success. The flies never bother Emelia or Negro, or their father who sleeps in the rocking chair in the living room beside the fireplace. Ever since robbers came down the chimney to steal and carried away Emelia's mother instead, her father has stood watch over the sooty tunnel. He lost his job years ago.

Negro and Blanco work on the waterfront unloading exotic goods from far away lands. When no one is looking, Blanco stashes a bolt of spun silk or a bag of spices under his shirt. He sells these things on the underground market and uses the money to buy dirty comic books and tickets to the movies for his girlfriend, a prostitute twice his age named Consuela. Sometimes, Blanco brings Consuela home with him and takes her into the bedroom.

To Emelia, Consuela is a sour-smelling monster with long, red-painted talons and ragged dresses in garish colors. Her skin seems permanently colored by the red glare of the lantern that hangs from her window above the cobblestone streets.

When Consuela comes to visit, Emelia takes a penny from her hiding place in the flour jar below the kitchen sink and runs down the stone steps from her family's apartment, down the streets between buildings built from blocks of pink and grey corals, through the green-grassed Tommy-Gaul Park and past the dolphins dancing fountain, until she reaches the little lady with the gnarled knuckles and the box full of chalks.

"I will take one stick of yellow," she says to the lady, and the lady nods and grins, staring over Emelia's shoulder down the street and out over the endless waves of water. The old woman is blind, but she can feel the colors of the chalks through her weathered fingers.

Many children have tried to steal from the chalk seller, but she can always hear them sneaking up, no matter how softly their footsteps. Emelia always buys her chalk, and always buys yellow. When the woman has no more yellow, Emelia comes back another day, and another, until finally the yellow is there again. Nobody, especially not Emelia, knows where the woman gets her chalk. The art store that caters to the rich and lonely artists who rent small rooms in the hotels along the waterfront sells its chalk for three times the price, sometimes more.

Once, Consuela brought Emelia a piece a blue chalk. "When I was a little girl, I would draw on the walls," Consuela said. "I drew the waves of the ocean, and tall masts disappearing over the horizon." Emelia said nothing. She gave the chalk to Mariana, the little girl who lived next door. Consuela never gave Emelia anything again.

"Here's your yellow, dear," says the chalk seller with a toothless smile. The stick of chalk is perfectly round and as long as Emelia's finger, but brittle and frail. Emelia cups the palm of her hand, and the chalk seller lets the stick roll gently off her fingertips and into Emelia's hand.

Emelia closes her hand carefully and then runs, pretending that monsters from the sewers have slunk out of the foul stink and wish to make her their princess. She runs around the bend, past the bakery and the smells of fresh croissants and the window full of ginger cookies, around the men playing obscure games of dice and checkered board games on the street corner outside the tannery, over the wall of the cemetery, past the collapsing church with more holes in the roof than statues of saints within, and down the alleyway, always uphill, always higher into the city and away from the smell of brine and drying fish, until she stops, huffing and holding her stretched sides.

When she looks up, she is surrounded by stuccoed walls and dark windows. These nicer neighborhoods pay their children to wash the walls each day, unlike her part of the city where the graffiti piles up and piles up, and only the rain ever washes the walls clean.

Here she sets to work, chalk piece held gently in her hand, pressing ever so softly against the stucco. She draws in quick and furtive motions, only half looking at the chalk. Mostly she looks above and below and all around, like a mouse in the open, afraid of getting caught. Her work is not against the law but the people in this neighborhood would like it to be. The children are paid to clean the walls, but they're paid even better to keep away the children from the streets below. Emelia knows that they play games in the forest after their lunches, but sometimes they come home early, especially when someone scrapes a knee or twists an ankle.

She sketches quick circles that are nearly perfect. Her circles can and have made the artists on the waterfront weep when they stumble across them, knowing because of the law that they must be the work of a child. She throws circles from her quick wrists, and then fast, perfectly straight lines radiating out from the circle.

In the middle of drawing, she switches hands, and without thinking, wipes away the wet, sweat-soaked yellow chalk across the front of her white dress. She leans in so close that she can see the fine gritty pattern of the stucco, even in the shadow of the buildings with the sky-sun obscured. She draws his face, each time differently, but the features are almost always the same. It is only the expressions that change.

This time, Emelia draws him smiling, an expression like that of St. Lucius on the statue she found locked away in the cellar of the church among spare pews and boxes of books filled with hymns that she had never heard sung in all her life. It was a knowing smile, a smile that that said the wearer held a secret mystery within.

She draws the sun's face as if it were a middle-aged man, his eyes lined with wrinkles, his lips full and plump, with the nose of hawk, sharp and beaked, but bent a little to the left. When she finishes, the chalk stick is little more than a nub, barely able to be held between her tiny fingers and touch the wall at the same time. She tosses the nub to the ground, grinds it under her bare feet, and then runs as if the harpies from the mountain have come to take her for their stew.

On this afternoon in the late spring when the winds are changing direction and windows are left open more often in the evenings to catch the sea breeze, she glances back at a sound from an alley as she passes and catches a glimpse of a long-necked aristocratic animal, a cat of indeterminable grace and wisdom, as it leaps from a windowsill and down into the street. When she turns back to the direction she is running, it is too late; she runs headlong into the black-coated figure of a man who eyes are shocked, his mouth an O of surprise. Then the collision, and all the bones in Emelia's small body are jarred and she falls, as does the man in the black coat. They land in a jumbled heap on the warm, smooth stones below.

Emelia lies for a moment, shocked by the impact, and surprised at the coolness of the black cloth beneath her. The coat should be hot and uncomfortable, but instead the touch is soothing, like a damp rag across her forehead. She remembers suffering from a fever, a cool cloth held by an almost forgotten mother who had almond eyes and straight black hair. Black like the man's coat. She lies motionless and holds her breath.

The man groans and stirs, then freezes when he realizes that Emelia does not move. Gently, he slips out from underneath her, and Emelia could swear that he becomes as thin as a shadow and half as there when he does so. She doesn't move from the stones and keeps her eyes looking downward. She pretends to be dead.

"Little miss, please get up," the man whispers. His voice reminds her of the taste of grapes, wet and tart, the consonants like small pops in her ears. She cannot help but roll over to look up at him, even though she is ashamed for her inattention. He offers her a hand twice the size of hers. It is covered in thin black lines that swirl and coil back on themselves. A labyrinth of lines crisscrosses his hand, and her gaze is trapped on the path, chasing an exit that isn't there.

He coughs politely, and she looks up, the spell broken. He wears a broad hat made of green felt with a peacock feather in the band. Emelia has never seen a peacock feather so close before. Staring at the feather and the delicate whorls of color, she takes his hand, and he lifts her effortlessly to her feet.

"I—I'm sorry, master, I should have been looking where I was going," she says, her voice cracking like dropped china. She doesn't want to cry, but the man is being too nice. If she ran into a man on the waterfront, he would whip her silly for her stupidity.

"What thing scares you so that you run like a frightened rabbit?" He asks in his grape voice. His eyes are as green as his hat, and his hair is white, though his face looks young and unwrinkled.

"Nothing, sir. I always run this fast," she answers.

He shakes his head. "You run as if something chases you. I know about such things, you see."

"I pretend that things chase me, so that I run faster. Each time, I run a little faster. One day, I will run faster than the setting sun, and then I will see him in his slumber."

"Oh ho," the man says. "You wish to see the sun resting his head upon his bed? That is an odd thing for a child to wish."

She holds her head low. "I'm sorry, master."

"It is nothing to be sorry for," he says, smiling and reaching out to tilt her head. His eyes are the color of seaweed, she thinks. "Maybe you will, one day."

"Thank you, master," she says, and then dodges past him, her heart fluttering, and this time she runs, afraid that the strange man in the black coat and the green hat will follow her. When she looks back, he is not, and part of her is sad, but she does not know why.

The next day, a fierce storm blows in from the sea, and Blanco and Negro stay home. They sit in the chairs from the kitchen table beside their father and listen to the wailing wind, getting up only occasionally to refasten a shutter. Emelia lies on her bed and stares at the ceiling. She wonders if the sun takes naps on days where the rain clouds blanket the earth. What else would he do, besides nap or stare at the clouds below? When he wakes up, he glares and frowns, and the clouds boil away, she thinks.

When Emelia was too little to walk, she remembers being left in the park on a blanket under a clear blue sky with the sun in his noon perch. She remembers staring deeply at the yellow orb until it became all that she could see. All she could see for weeks afterwards was the sun's face, his curious half-smile and his sad eyes. It does not seem strange to her that she could remember things from when she was so young. She remembers more.

Doctors feared she had gone blind, and her mother sobbed every night above her cradle; her mother blamed herself. They took Emelia to see the old healer who lives in the abandoned lighthouse where the rocks used to be until heavy man-o-wars came and blasted them away with cannons and made the waters safe. She was blessed in the church with cool water sprinkled on her brow. A few weeks later, her sight slowly drifted back, but the image of the sun stayed. He was always there, except at night or on a cloudy day.

She wonders often what the sun is thinking, to accompany his odd facial expressions, but everyone knows that the sun can not speak to people. So this she sets aside, and does not allow it to trouble her. When the sun sets, he is no longer in her mind, no longer her ever-present and silent companion. Where does he go, and most importantly, what look rests upon his face while he sleeps in the dark night's sky?

And so she runs every day, from home to the little school when the bells ring and the teacher is sober, to church on Sundays, to take her brothers lunch in the afternoons, and on her chalking excursions up the hill and down the rich streets.

It rains for three days after she met the man in the green hat. In the rain, the sun is away from her mind as it is at night, and she grows lonely for the sight of his kind face. The sun is never fierce to her, not even in the hottest days of summer; in fact, he seems most joyous on those days.

Finally, she wakes with the sunrise on the fourth day, and the sun beams across the sea on her city into the open window of her bedroom. Roosters call from below in the streets. The sun is happy, but weary and exhausted. Emelia smiles; she also feels that way when she has slept too long.

She creeps out of the house, past her snoring father, and down to the street. She runs to the waterfront, swinging her arms like she is hammering nails. This time, Black Legionnaires are onto her and will sell her as a concubine overseas if she doesn't escape. Emelia doesn't know what a concubine is, except that it is a very bad thing for a young girl to become, and it happens often in the stories that are told by old sailors from the bows of their ships to the laborers.

Today, she will earn a penny running errands, she decides, and then she will draw the face better than she ever has. Sometimes, she wishes that her drawings could remain longer than the chalk; she dreams of buying canvas and paint and putting the sun down in all his magnificence. Maybe then she will get it right, and truly capture him in a way that she can share with her family. Blanco once saw her drawing the sun and only laughed and shook his head. That was when she decided to move up onto the hill for her sketches. Negro seems to know about them, but he never speaks of them. Sometimes she wishes that he would. She almost wants someone to explain it to her as much as she wants to explain it to herself.

For most of the morning, Emelia delivers bread across town for the baker, whose son stepped on a shard of glass and would not be walking for the next several days. To and from the bakery, she is chased by goblins, wicked sea gulls, and sea spirits with sharp tridents that will jab her fiercely if she slows. Finally, there is no more bread to deliver, and the baker's wife pays her three pennies for the morning's work, promising that Emelia can make more if she comes back the next day. Everyone knows how fast Emelia can run, and often they vie for her to run their deliveries when their regular help is unavailable.

Emelia stops home and places two of the pennies in her father's lap. He nods always when she brings him money, but never looks her in the eye. She backs away, watching him for some other reaction, and then she is off, down the streets, only just avoiding the roof-bandits and their lassos tossed from above.

She comes to the chalk seller and gives the old woman her penny. "Yellow, please."

"Of course, dear." The old woman's hands fumbles within her box until she withdraws a green stick. "Here you are."

"Ma'am, I'm sorry. That stick is green," Emelia says, suddenly feeling a cold chill run down her neck. It is green like the man's hat.

The old woman frowns, but reaches back into her box and feels again. This time, her hands returns with Emelia's yellow.

"Stay away from him, little one," the old woman says, and does let go of the chalk. "He's been around; I can smell him." Then she drops the chalk into Emelia's hand.

"Thank you!" Emelia says when she is already halfway around the bend and to the bakery. She runs as if the man in the green hat is there behind her, following without taking a step, just floating in the air alongside, and she runs faster than she ever has before. When she glances back, she sees him and he waves to her with a grin. She runs faster.

When she reaches her spot for drawing, she nearly collapses from the strain of running. She pants and wipes sweat from her brow. She ties her long brown hair back behind her head in a loose knot, only to look into her hand and see that she has broken her chalk stick in two while running. Emelia has never broken her chalk before.

Tears well up in her eyes, but before she can let them loose a hand grips her shoulder from behind and shakes, then spins her around. A fat man in brightly colored, expensive clothing glares at her and begins to shout. His voice blasts her like a hurricane.

"So you're the useless thing that draws on walls nearly every day! It costs me a penny to have your pointless doodlings scrubbed away! What's this?" His sausage fingers pry open her hand and pluck the chalk from her. He throws the pieces to the ground and grinds them into dust.

"No more! It may not be against the law for you to draw here, but *I* won't have it! If I catch you drawing your sun here again, I'll have you sold to gypsies!"

Emelia is too frightened to say anything. The man is a rich banker, one her father owes money. She did not know that the walls she draws on nearly every day are the walls of his home.

"You look familiar," he says. He squints and turns her face upwards. "You're Marco's daughter, aren't you?"

Emelia is too terrified to admit that she is. What would he do if he knew? That look in his eyes, a greedy look she has seen in Blanco's eyes so many times. He looks at her and sees something valuable.

"If I catch you here again, I *will* have you sold to gypsies, girl. Go away."

Satisfied, the banker turns and enters his home, slamming the wooden door shut with a bang like a cannon shot. Emelia then begins to cry in great sobs that nearly shake her to pieces like the broken chalk.

If she doesn't have her drawings, what does she have? Brothers who barely know she's there and a father who has not spoken to her since her mother was taken away? Only the sun in her mind, and he is not always there. If he can leave her at sunset, he might leave her forever one day. He is the only one that cares for her anymore.

She wanders through the streets and alleyways, sniffing and sighing. The sun begins to set, the shadows grow longer, and the noises of the homes around her grow louder. She flops down on a coral stoop to rest her tired legs.

The man in the green hat is beside her, sitting with his feet crossed and his hands across his lap. The maze lines draw in her eyes again, hypnotizing them.

"There's very little for you here, Emelia. If you could run to him," he cocks his head to the west, "would you? Would you run as hard as you could?"

"I could only run that hard if something *really* chases me," she says with a sniff.

"Wherever you run, little miss, something will pursue you, even if it's ghosts of memory. But if you want to go to him, I'll help. I have seen how he looks in your drawings. He is lonely, don't you think?"

And that's it exactly, the reason that she has felt sad for so long. The sun looks at her, each day, whether smiling or frowning, grinning or grimacing, and he is sad, because he is all alone in the sky. The moon and the stars must fear him.

"I would run to him, if only I could," she whispers.

"Then look," the man in the green hat says, and he opens coat, dark as the approaching night. Inside, red eyes watch her. "The beasts will fall upon you and devour you if you do not run. Run to him. Only his light will save you." And then they flow out; the gargoyles, the demons, the spirits, the ghouls and ghasts. The creatures of the night, the terrible things that cannot be seen directly, they come and they chase.

Emelia runs. She turns to the west and stretches her legs as much as they can, and then some more. Each step goes a little further. The creatures behind her howl with anger and hunger. She bounds over the walls of the city and across the treetops of the forest on the mountain slopes. The creatures bounce along beneath her, leaping up. Their claws graze the soles of her feet, but they cannot grasp her now. She is too fast.

She runs until she is a speck in the distance. She runs until she disappears over the horizon. The creatures give up, and shuffle back to the home in the man with the green hat's coat.

When the sun rises in the morning, a tiny little star follows it closely, one that was not there the day before. And when the sun sets that night, the tiny little speck of light hurries to keep up with it.

Negro weeps when she does not come home. He goes into Emelia's room to collect her things to give away to the needy children. In the children's drawings, Negro occasionally sees the sun drawn as an old man, and he holds hands with fast-footed little girl who is always smiling.

Her father vanishes one night from his chair, and Blanco finds the floor around the chimney covered in soot and ash. The people of the city catch glimpses in the night of a pair running across the rooftops holding hands.

Consuela finds religion, but Blanco does not. She tricks him into marrying her after a late night of drunken revelry. They fight often over petty things, but especially Blanco's cheating. Soon they have three horrid little children that Blanco spoils, mostly to irritate his wife.

The man in the green hat hikes into the forest, continuing on his journey to the east. Anyone he meets gets what she wants, but not always what she deserves.

DOWN IN THE FOG-SHROUDED CITY

ALEX IRVINE

On one side of the City a mountain range leaps up. On the other yellow plains stretch out. In between, a river flows. The City is prone to fogs. At the change of seasons it rains, and the river strains against its banks. The reservoirs have to release water. Below the spillways, forgotten debris is churned up from the river bottom. When the weather has cleared, the garbage of the City—which in one way is its only memory—has returned to the riverbanks. Whatever you throw away, if the fish don't eat it and the hoboes don't steal it, finds a new life on the riverbanks after the rains.

Money circulates through the City, and magic. One is blood, one is lymph. If you think of the City as a body, you become amazed that it has survived its diseases and the depravity of its history.

Sometimes at night the City's buildings block stars where, standing in the same location, I remember stars shining on other nights. From this I deduce that the City's changes are not always zoned, financed, backed by bonds. Sometimes during the day I find myself in unfamiliar streets, when at other times I knew every street between the snaking tracks that wind tortuously out of the mountains and the ruler-straight country roads that reach that more distant horizon behind the plains.

I've traveled in all six directions, seen oceans and mountains, the stars and the shining phosphorescence of animals that live underground, arctic emptiness and the overwhelming presence of jungle. But I always return to the City, and often as not I have no memory of where I've been, or why, or what I did there. Agency Amnesia: we try to laugh about it. This is part of the deal when you work for the Agency. Many things leave your memory.

At first it upsets you. Later you become upset at the things you still remember, standing tall in what seems like a limitless ocean of featureless past. Agency Amnesia is selective, a little unpredictable. I have never yet forgotten my name, but they had effaced the name of my beloved. I had not forgotten the *delight* I took in her face, but that face itself was obscured. *Indelible*, I told myself. Her face is *indelible*. Something covers it only.

To resist the effects of the amnesia, I recited to myself a sing-songy phrase: *If I am who I am, this is what I'll do.* The rhythm of it comforted me, and I swear there are times when muttering this phrase over and over again under my breath brought back a memory. A simple assertion of Self, I guess, in a place where everything and everyone is so easily forgotten.

I've traveled within the City as well, from its wealthy suburbs to the railyard menace lit only when the moon breaks through the clouds. By trade I was a courier, and by avocation a wanderer. In my work, my natural inclinations found expression. Because of this I imagined myself to be happy.

I worked for the Agency. Often the Agency forgot this. I was usually able to remind them, but even when I could not, they recognized that I carry things. A thing carried is a thing valued, and the Agency values every thing that is valued. In this way the Agency was constantly forgetting me and then being reminded. In me it—they—saw. See. Sees. No longer in their employ, I am to the Agency a reminder, an abrupt and demanding recollection of the desires it has forgotten in the particularities of its immensity.

When I saw the magician catching peanuts between his teeth at a back table of McGuirk's Tavern, I knew eyes were on me.

Magicians have to do little tricks like that all the time. They don't know how to stop, or maybe it's that they don't know how they would start again. I used to have the same problem.

My primary job for the Agency is to carry Monkey-prose from the Warehouse to the Refinery. This is what I was doing when I found out that my love had been taken from me. This is why I was in McGuirk's Tavern, and why I had to talk to the wizard, and why I knew eyes were on me. Magic does its own things to the senses, and the people in the bar, wizards or not, could no more have looked away from me than they could have picked out which stars were missing from one City night to the next. We forget about the stars, we City-dwellers.

This wizard was named Wink, for a tic at the corner of his left eye. His razored salt-and-pepper hair formed a sharp widow's-peak, and he dressed like the miners and railroad workers who frequented McGuirk's. He threw peanuts into the air, and some of them hung there until a passerby on the way to the restroom plucked them out of the air. Others organized themselves into miniature solar systems, or gathered into formations that moved with a smooth unison like players in a soccer match or minnows twitching together in unanticipated directions. Some of them just fell back to his mouth, to crack between his molars. Wizards cannot stop.

"I need a spell," I said to Wink. "There's this to trade."

The satchel I dropped on the table in front of him whispered, blinked, stank, vibrated with magic. Magic crept from it and sank into the grain of the wood. Every peanut in Wink's constellation spiraled down to it and clung trembling to the leather flap. Magic has its own gravity.

Wink's habitual smirk wavered. "You're making me unpopular."

"With certain elements, sure. Others are casting your statue already." I wanted to sit, but didn't want to give Wink the ease. "I need a spell."

"Can't trade raw magic for finished spells," Wink said.

I knew Wink. I had never asked him to do something like this before, but if I hadn't been certain he'd assent, I would never have taken the risk. He would find some way to refine the raw spellemes in the satchel, and he would find some way to hide the excess product from the Agency. Whichever branch of the Agency he worked for.

Most of the wizards I knew earned their living in the Refinery. Each bit of Monkey-prose that produced a sensible effect in the Warehouse became a potential spell, a spelleme to be vetted and polished by magicians. Spells diverged into oeuvres, imprinted with the personalities of their wizards, idiosyncratic as accents or neighborhood pidgins. Different phyla of spells came to identify various adversarial offshoots of the Agency. Wink and I were in theory cohorts, accomplices. The fact of the situation, though, was that neither he nor I knew whether the Agency thought we were cohorts, and what the Agency thought was generally all that mattered. This day, though, I was hunting for myself. The Agency had kidnapped my beloved, and by doing so transformed my loyalty into implacable hostility. Do not mistake me, though; the moment a reunion was engineered, I would slip back into my previous loyal mold, and the Agency would let me. In its vastness, the Agency lost track of small duplicities; the fact that a small duplicity had first riven my beloved away from me does not contradict that general truth.

Wink grinned. Like all wizards, he had excellent teeth, and he had a wily exuberance that suffused the spells he created. I thought I would need it. "Where do you suppose I can take this raw stuff, assuming? I haven't heard what you want."

"I want a spell. What's here is more than enough to create it and leave you enough left over to fly to the moon."

"I'd want to be able to get back," he said.

"Let's go to the Refinery," I said. "They'll expect us there anyway."

The Refinery, a facility as ornate and luxurious as the Monkey Warehouse is forbidding and austere, occupied a gentle brushy slope on the mountain side of the river. The view out its windows was never less than spectacular, even when the City was cloaked in fog. Everything seemed a little clearer, a little nearer, seen from the windows of the Refinery. Magic had long ago seeped into its timbers and beams, saturated the glass of its windows and the slate of its roof, polished the marble of its floors until one's reflection became a window to the soul.

From the Refinery's genteel perspective, the Warehouse squatted in a sooty district northeast of the City's clustered downtown. A steady stream of traffic traveled between the two, primarily couriers like myself carrying raw magic in one direction and experimental results in the other; the wizards never quite trusted the Spotters to look out for the correct new manifestations. None of this laborious exchange would have been needed if the Refinery and Warehouse had been located nearer each other, but long practice had demonstrated that it was unhealthy to test spells too close to the pool of chaos defined by the Warehouse's walls. Spells, too, failed to thrive and acquire a distinctive power unless they were given room to breathe away from the crude forms in which they first appeared.

In the Monkey Warehouse, the chatter of typewriter keys drowns out all other sound. Up close, each keystroke sounds distinct and harsh. From farther away, the strokes merge together into a kind of clacking roar, and behind that is the white noise pouring in from the dim reaches of the building, beyond the range at which the eye can distinguish figure from machine. Those three levels of sound are constantly present, and when speaking with someone else, I often find that certain sounds leap out from the background, silhouetted as it were against the aural vanishing point, that conceptual space into which all of the levels of sound collapse. The monkeys never talk. They harvest language, these monkeys with cigarettes and glasses of whiskey, bad posture and the perpetual squint of disillusionment. They seem to hear the aural vanishing point, but they locate it in a different space than I do. There are howlers and spider monkeys, great mandrills and tiny marmosets, capuchins and colobuses.

People walk up and down the aisles between banks of typewriters. Their footfalls create a jagged and hesitant counterpoint to the chatter, the drone, the whicker of typewriter keys. Some of them walk in absolute silence, assassin's silence. Others wear shoes with heavy heels, to startle the monkeys with sudden booming footsteps precipitating out of the infinite background rattle. Every one of them wears some sort of apparatus to correct and enhance vision — monocles, eyeglasses, loupes, sometimes all three. At first this seems strange, since their job is often as not to hear, but among the Spotters superstition is more important than the perceptions of Blinks, which is what they call anyone who isn't a Spotter. Each of these Spotters is responsible for a certain carefully demarcated area of the Monkey Warehouse. Within that area, an individual Spotter bears the responsibility of noticing when a monkey has created a disturbance that might be magic. In the Monkey Warehouse, the monkeys type and magic happens.

From miniscule causes great events arise. I read that somewhere.

On the way to the Refinery, I remembered: I had known how to read. I hoped to know again, when the tides of amnesia slackened.

Once, breaking every relevant Agency rule, I escorted my beloved into the Warehouse when she was off duty. Off-duty Spotters are prohibited from the Warehouse, on the grounds that they might identify with one or more of the monkeys as a spectator, and that this identification will interfere with their ability to perform their evaluative function. While we were there, one of the monkeys typed something that spread in a fine mist above it, a gauzy prism. Filaments of this mist wafted over the monkeys' heads, touching them the way one might rest one's hand on the head of a dog, and as one the entire section of monkeys threw up their hands and screamed ecstatically, leaping from their chairs as if forgetting for a moment that they were cut off from the sun by concrete on five sides and steel on the sixth, many miles and more generations from the jungles whose images they still held behind their faces. She stood with shining eyes, watching their joy.

Sometimes magic is like that.

Like always, a brace of goons flanked the Refinery gate. They eyeballed me after letting Wink go on through. "Careful hanging around with wizards," one of them said.

I looked at his bald head, the thick fold of flesh under the line of his jaw. The pinstripes on his suit were too far apart. I get irritated when goons think they know my business. I get more irritated when I find out they're right.

"Courier," the goon said as I brushed past him. "People are watching. Eyes on you."

"Nothing to hide," I said, and waited for him to take his hand off my shoulder. When he did, I slipped a bill into his cuff. It pays to have the goons looking out for you. Not that I mistrusted Wink, but it rarely pays to have too much riding on the reliability of wizards.

Wink led me into his laboratory. He drew the shutters, lit a lamp, and spilled the magic from the satchel onto a granite-topped table. Most raw magic is inert when in contact with granite. Refining spells to attack igneous rock has been an intensive ongoing project of the Agency, and of its rebellious splinters.

The magic on the table lay in a jumble of creased corners and strikethroughs. Wink selected one spelleme and carried it to a burnished copper basin large enough to comfortably bathe in. Copper's electrical conductivity is surpassed only by its superlative suitability to magical propagation. In the basin, the spelleme began to spark, to throw off eyeball-sized orbs of plasma that left glowing oblong smears on the marble floor.

"Energy," Wink said. "Physical. Useful to the trades, with a little polish." He turned back to the table, leaving the spelleme to spit and crackle in the copper basin. I edged away from it, anxious to get moving, to be doing rather than waiting.

"Wink," I said.

"What sort of spell do you need?" He was using a pair of tongs to separate the sheaves of spellemes.

"I don't know," I said. "But once I do, I'll need it fast."

On the way out, the bald goon muttered a single word: *Haven.*

So the spell had to do with monkeys. Okay. Before I went back to the Refinery, though, I had to circulate through the expected channels.

Most Spotters are women. My beloved was a Spotter when I first saw her, and a Spotter until the Agency took her from me. This is the only thing I could remember about her. She roamed her area intently, stopping often to peer through a loupe at the air above a particular typewriter or the texture of a certain monkey's fur. When she reached to slip the paper from a carriage, she offered the monkey a piece of fruit in exchange. The monkeys, who have nothing else, grow possessive of their typewriters, their paper, their ashtrays and their melancholy. Like them, I who had only her—and the unstable benison of Agency employment—became desperately possessive of her. She withstood this, and saw me through it. In her I was able to find the strength to not wander, to look upon my surroundings and find them good.

Driving through the City, I kept to streets I was certain I knew. Too much flux already, without me straying to add to it. I stopped at a diner, walked in the door and left again thinking *Deli. Deli. Deli.* The word would not leave my head. I wanted eggs and toast, but the word *deli* drove me to a counter on the other side of the city, where I tried to remember to sit up straight while I worked my way through corned beef. *Delicious.* Bad posture bothers many Couriers, who spend too many hours slumped in broken-down seats. It takes a conscious effort for me to keep it out of my stable of problems, an effort I was glad to make since it reminded me of how my beloved would make sure I kept my chin up and shoulders back.

To stay awake, I started driving again. Sleep makes the amnesia worse, and I had gained enough memory that day to know I didn't want to lose any of it.

At the Prison I spoke to the Warden. "Let her go," I said without preamble. "I didn't do anything. Neither did she."

"We have reason," said the Warden, "to believe differently." He sat at a granite desk. I imagined all kinds of counterspells etched into the arms of his chair, the handset of his telephone, the soles of his shoes. The granite desk was a natural precaution, given the Warden's ever-growing number of enemies. He'd certainly added me to the list.

"Your reasons are wrong. Let her go."

"Courier," said the Warden, "there is one thing you can say that will induce me to free her. I suggest you figure out what it is during the next twenty-four hours."

The Warden had let slip more than he realized. I chewed over the implications as I crawled across town to the University to drop a package I'd picked up at the Prison. I had to keep working; the Agency would only tolerate my freelance investigations if I kept up my normal volume of deliveries.

What I figured out was this: the Warden wasn't sure whether I had done what he'd been told I'd done. He'd been told by someone higher up what he had to do. Perhaps he even felt whatever sympathy a Warden is capable of feeling. When he told me I had twenty-four hours to figure out what to say, he was telling me I had twenty-four hours to convince him that he'd been right in waiting twenty-four hours before doing whatever the higher-ups had told him to do.

It was clear that I also had twenty-four hours before the Agency cut their losses and disposed of both my beloved and me.

When I sneaked my beloved into the Monkey Warehouse, she did in fact point out one of the monkeys. "Look at him," she said. "He's got something figured out."

"He's in your area," I joked. "You're trying to make yourself look good."

"Is that so hard?" she said, flirting with me.

This monkey, her favorite, a small and stringy capuchin with bald patches on the back of its head, was the one I stole from the Monkey Haven that night, a night clear and glittering as an act of faith, a night that made me afraid to look at the stars. Stealing the monkey was a hunch born of careful paranoia, and I played it. I assumed that I'd been watched when my beloved and I went to the Warehouse, and I assumed that this monkey was at the center of whatever misunderstanding had led me to my extremity. I assumed, too, that they were watching me take it from its comfortable cage. The bald goon had heard something and passed it along to me; I hoped he hadn't been overheard in the hearing, or in the transmission of his single-word message.

Agency shadows were following me, then, as I made my meandering way to the Offices and took the capuchin through the front doors, feeling the air pressure shift against my eardrums. Then I'm sure they waited for me to come out. Even the slickest shadows are afraid to go into the Offices. In the Offices, where the Agency is most powerful and most densely concentrated, slips of memory are common. If you're forgotten there, nobody in the City can remember you again.

Once, in the mountains, from an overlook where I sat picnicking with my beloved, I looked down on the City and thought: I could get away. The Agency mistakes itself for the world, but it isn't. It can't be.

I was unable to make myself act on that moment, and after some time I stopped believing that there was any difference between the Agency and the world. Only when I remembered her, mouth open in unconscious mimicry of the monkeys' ecstatic forgetfulness, did I realize how wrong that was. I defied the Agency, and all of the methods I had learned to accommodate and avoid its irrationalities, at least partially to tell her that. If I had not been able to tell her that, I told myself, I would have had to believe that the Agency, in its violently paradoxical interaction with the world that both is and is not itself, had at last stumbled on the truth.

Since people use it to kill each other, magic is big business in the City, and its manufacturers and distillers enjoy the sort of deference accorded to economic linchpins. Numerologists, graphologists, mathematicians, statisticians, linguists — the production of magic employs all of these, and still no one knows exactly how it works except one monkey who isn't telling. One of the supervising Spotters in the warehouse once shouted to me over the clacking din, "It all happens here. The rest of it … you take them, the wizards tinker, the Agency shoots it out with whoever. Epiphenomena. The real event is here. Monkeys, typewriters, Spotters to find the magic."

"Right," I shouted back. I think he was disappointed when I didn't ask him to define *epiphenomena*.

I was on the periphery of all this. As a courier of spellemes, and occasionally of finished spells to prominent citizens, I stood in the penumbra of the magiconomy. That was more or less how I liked it. Too much attention means some of it will be bad. I didn't know for sure, but I was pretty sure that was why they had taken my beloved from me. Too many people had noticed me, or noticed her, or noticed the monkey I would name Mudflap, or noticed her noticing it. Something. Eyes on me. Eyes on her.

In the mountains, I remember thinking during this time, people would not watch us.

The air of the Offices sickens people who are accustomed to being outside. The reverse is true for the Office workers, who spend their lives within the Office Building's walls and gradually develop a powerful aversion to whatever lies without those stone and glass barriers. The monkey sagged in my arms as I waited for the elevator to take me — us — to the top floor, where the higher-ups were. Officials or Officers, I could never decide. Either was deducible from the fact of the Office.

I was sure that the shadows had let me go. The only danger I faced was a challenge from one of the mid-level Officials. Officers. One of the ones who seemed to demand the term Functionary. If challenged, I would have to muster all of my resolve not to answer the challenge as directly as it was put to me; I had a gun, but using it in the office would be a prayer for bodily dissolution. The only path of any safety lay in being as oblique and absurd in my answers as my prosecutor was in his accusations.

"You there."

So at least I wouldn't have to wait. I turned, shifting the drooping monkey's weight in my arms, and looked into the bearded face of a Functionary. He was officious without being an Officer.

"What?" I said.

"Your business here? You can't come in here."

I saw on the other side of the lobby several goons. Among them was the watchful goon who had passed on the word *Haven* to me as I left the Refinery.

"This monkey is very sick," I said. I wasn't feeling so well myself.

The Functionary drew himself up. "You can't just come in here," he said, his voice like the grinding of worn gears. "Do you know where you are? You could get lost."

He meant it as a threat. "A Courier is never lost," I said.

The elevator door opened. When the Functionary didn't summon goons, I got on it and pressed the button for the top floor. The monkey lost consciousness on the way up, and I started to hallucinate. It seemed at one point that the elevator shaft was transparent, and so was the building around it. People, hundreds of them, thousands perhaps, walked on invisible floors, leaned against invisible doorjambs, slipped notes over invisible transoms and plotted into invisible telephones. Beyond them, all of the stars were in exactly their correct places, and the mountains were just silhouetted against the last fading radiance of evening. Afraid, I looked between my feet, and saw the base of the elevator shaft receding faster than I could have imagined moving. At its bottom, her face half-lit by an emergency bulb set into the side of the shaft, my beloved looked up at me.

My finger stabbed into the Stop Elevator button before it had registered in my mind that I could see the button again. The elevator lurched to a halt, its pulleys squealing. Everything was visible again.

"Come on, monkey," I said. "Snap out of it."

The monkey's head lolled in the crook of my left arm.

"Come on, monkey!" I slapped the side of its face. Its eyes opened. I reached up and popped the elevator car's emergency hatch. The monkey made a half-hearted attempt to hold on when I thrust it toward the opening.

I shook it. Shrieking, it tried to bite me. I lifted it up again, and this time it hoisted itself up onto the roof of the car. I managed to wedge myself through after it.

A groove cut into one side of the elevator shaft, with curved iron rungs bolted into the recessed part of the wall. I let myself down over the edge of the dangling car and looked for the monkey. It was lying flat on the roof, mouth open and tongue hanging. I hauled it closer and draped it over my shoulder, where it hung drooling down my back. Strength started to leave my arms and legs, and I realized that the monkey was just demonstrating what would sooner or later happen to me.

Before it did, though, I had to get to the bottom and pick up the trail of my beloved.

To call the climb down arduous …. My fingers grew clumsy, barely able to hook over each successive rung, and after a while it seemed like even the soles of my shoes were tiring, slipping a little more with each step.

When this is over, I resolved, I will take her and we will leave the City and we will not come back. We will leave the Agency to its own internecine devices. I had just completed the thought when my fingers loosened and I fell down the elevator shaft, holding the monkey with one arm and reaching out with the other as if someone might throw me a lifeline.

Either the building was shorter than it looked from inside or I'd been descending faster than I'd thought. Whichever was the case, the fall didn't kill me.

Monkeys, as a general rule, hate Spotters. They even go to such extremes as to stage shit-throwing battles amongst themselves just so they can catch a particularly despised Spotter in the crossfire. The monkeys recognize that every Spotter is only a Spotter until she or he picks out something important and gets whisked away to the Offices, never to return to the foul-smelling dimness of the Warehouse. Knowing that the Spotters use them in this way, the monkeys grow resentful. Violence is not unknown.

Alone among Spotters, my beloved made herself welcome in that key-clacking immensity. This, I think, was what made me realize her transcendent worthiness. If the monkeys could shower her with affection instead of effluvium, what greater emotional heroism could I achieve?

This was before it became clear to me how very similar I was to many of the monkeys.

The fall did knock me unconscious, but I didn't realize that right away. At some point I had been struggling against the steady depletion of strength and coordination; at some later point I opened my eyes and squinted at the bottom of the elevator car that descended toward me with remarkable speed. I rolled over, noticed grinding pain in every joint on the right side of my body, and banged into a block and tackle bolted into the cement floor. Hanging onto the monkey, I scrambled to a crouch and looked for a way out.

A door, thoughtfully labeled EXIT, glowed in the cone of light from an emergency bulb. The same light, I realized as I limped to the door, that had cast the planes of my beloved's face into their moonscape palette of light and dark. I opened it and stepped through as the elevator groaned to a halt.

Then I stepped back, read the sign again. I could read. Getting closer, I thought.

The door opened into an office. The monkey stirred, whined, urinated down my left leg. "Hey," I said, and held it away from my body. It was heavy, and my right arm ached with the effort. Its eyes opened, and I said, "That's more like it. Which way did she go?" I wasn't actually asking the monkey, but it seemed to understand. It pointed over my shoulder and made typing motions with its fingers.

On the office desk, covered in dust, stood a typewriter. I put the monkey down, and it leapt onto the desk and typed *I have been here before.*

So that's what its spell had been.

"Holy smokes, monkey," I said, a little awed.

It looked at me with an expression of aggrieved patience. What a cruel imbecile I was for not recognizing its radical individuality.

"Don't be such a pansy," I said. "Where'd she go?" It started typing an answer. It occurred to me that I should name the monkey, and the first word that presented itself was *mudflap.* "Hurry up, Mudflap," I said.

The way I knew what was going on went something like this: the Agency had rules. The Agency broke the rules. The Agency was generally predictable, but sporadically responsible for actions that beggared belief. Putting all of this together with the knowledge that Mudflap was my beloved's favorite monkey, and that she was its favorite Spotter, and that she had been kidnapped out of a misunderstanding begun by a junior

Agency Functionary and perpetuated throughout the Agency hierarchy, I could only assume that my beloved and Mudflap the monkey had at some earlier time been present in the basement of the Office Building. Whatever had happened during this previous visit had somehow precipitated the misunderstanding that had brought events to the juncture where they now stood.

Simple deduction, possible even though I didn't really know a thing.

"Wait, Mudflap," I said. "Who is she?"

Mudflap had already begun typing. He (I had started thinking of him as male) shot me a poisonous glance, hit his carriage return twice, and typed five letters.

I looked: *They took her*, he had started, and when I'd revised the question he had typed *Delia*.

I could expand my lungs, but no oxygen made it into my brain. The venomous air of the Office, yes; but even more than that, it was the overpressure of returning memory that squeezed my diaphragm, stole the breath from my throat.

Delia. Yes. Delia.

Her face swam before me, diaphanous, her black hair falling out of her severe Spotter's braid. Something in her eyes frightened me, and I closed my own. At that moment another memory reawakened, and I realized that something in her eyes had always frightened me. Her mouth was slightly open, as if in this image — which must, I thought, be memory — she was drawing breath to speak.

Mudflap typed again, while I gaped like a fish at the mirage of my beloved Delia. When I did not respond to him, he pinched me hard on the earlobe.

"Dammit, monkey," I growled, slapping his fingers away. Mudflap waved a sheet of paper before me: *You took her to the Flats yesterday.*

"I," I said. "I took her?"

I tried to remember the previous day, but in my mind there was no sense of previous and next. A jumble of days piled on one another, and each of them caught my attention only if I could find Delia in my recollections of them. Delia laughing, Delia shining faintly, I imagined, in the light of my adoration. Each memory of her more comical in its caricature of devotion than the last. I began to wonder if she was real at all, or if the Agency had created her in my mind; I had heard of spells, had in fact transported spellemes, that could do exactly that, and it would be just like them to make me suffer transports of love for a magical apparition.

But no, not if Mudflap too remembered her. Monkeys were notoriously resistant to magic. If they were not, their crude typings would too often grow into real (and uncontrollable) spells, exhausting their energy before the Refinery had any chance to exert its influence. If Mudflap remembered Delia in my company, then in my company she had been.

It is a strange thing to place your trust in an ensorcelled capuchin.

"Why the Flats?" I asked Mudflap, although I knew before he had typed his first word.

The Flats lie between the Refinery and the Warehouse, somewhat downriver of the Offices. The Monkey Haven itself is just across the street from the Flats' outer boundary. In the Flats live those denizens of the City whose collective voice is not loud or persuasive enough to lift them from the river's floodplain. Light falls strangely there. The garbage left by the river's seasonal flood clutters the porches and, if they are unlucky, the basements of Flatplainers. As the river passes through the Flats, it grows broad and oxbowed, shallow and reedy and mucky of bank. The detritus of the City stands out of the muck and cattails like public art that has survived the ruin of civilization.

The only reason anyone ever takes anyone else to the Flats, unless one or the other of them lives there, is to commit murder. The squalor of the Flats suits the tableau of the kneeling victim and the single spell to the back of the head. Beatings, sex crimes, extortionate assignations all take place in other neighborhoods. In the Flats, people live and people die. Nothing in between.

But there I was, not killing anyone.

"Wink," I called to the wizard when I saw him leaning against the corner of a low cinder-block house. He looked up and down the potholed street as I pulled the car to a stop. In the Flatlight his face seemed pallid and unevenly whiskered.

He got into the car. "You didn't kill her," he said.

I had known that, but the confirmation came as a relief. "What are you doing down here?"

"Figured the monkey would talk sooner or later." In the back seat, Mudflap looked a little bleary. Carsick, I figured, or the lingering effects of the Office air. "And," Wink finished, "I knew you'd come looking for her."

"But she's not here. I didn't kill her."

I'd been shifting the car in and out of gear, feeling the thump in its transmission and hoping that my mind would clunk into drive soon. "We need to go to the Refinery," Wink said. "The spell you need is there." Grateful for the direction, I roared away from the curb and out of the Flats where I had not killed my beloved.

The Refinery steamed and groaned like it always did, and lights prismed in its many windows. But no goons waited at the door. Wink looked at me, and I made sure I had my gun. It was loaded with spells he himself had refined.

I left the car parked in an open Courier space in the circular part of the driveway, with Mudflap hiding under the rear seat. He'd been there since we left the Flats; I didn't know whether the Agency had been observing since I picked up Wink, and I wanted them a little uncertain about Mudflap's whereabouts.

Wink went into the building first, and I followed him up the stairs to his second-floor laboratory. Red light flared in the heating ducts as we walked down the hall, and I wondered what had gone wrong in the basement. The Refinery wasn't always a safe place to be.

Gunfire erupted as soon as we opened the door. I flinched and ducked behind the frame, but Wink had thrown up counterspells and each of the goons' shots deflected away from us. Several burned or broke through the walls on either side of the door; others left behind effects more subtle and frightening. An eye appeared in the laboratory wall near Wink's head, squinting as if the person it belonged to was peering into a microscope, and a rain of iridescent fish scales scattered about our feet.

I fired several shots around the door frame and heard a variety of sounds as a result. One of the goons wailed; smoke whooshed out through the doorway with a sound like falling water; glass broke; Wink coughed and disappeared into the room; an odd flat buzzing tickled my ears and there was a smell of cilantro.

The truth is, even wizards don't have a clear idea about what many spells do. When I duckwalked into the room, hiding in the smoke, I had no idea whether I had hit either of the goons or what any possible hits might have done to them. By the time the smoke had cleared, it was abundantly clear that both of them were dead. One lay on the floor, knees drawn in and both hands over his face. I couldn't tell what had happened to him. The other goon was gone, and appeared to have been replaced by a loose group of soap bubbles that drifted in the breeze from the broken window.

"Damn," said Wink. "I wish I knew which one that was." I guessed he had an idea. Wizards and their false modesty.

I should have worried about killing Agency goons, but I didn't, first of all because they were trying to kill me and second because I knew that if the Agency decided I was more valuable than the goons the killings wouldn't cause any trouble. And right then I was worried about getting my beloved out of the Offices where, despite my conversation with the Warden, I was sure she was hidden. To do that, though, I needed the spell Wink had saved for me here in his laboratory. I asked him where it was.

He opened a drawer. "Right here."

The spell looked like a feather, one of those long ones from the tails of bright tropical birds. I tucked it in my pocket.

"Damn, I wish I knew which one that was," Wink said again, watching the bubbles.

"What does it do?" I asked him.

"If you're going to get her," he said, "it'll do what you need."

I held my hand over the pocket where I'd secreted the spell. "Thanks."

"Welcome," Wink said. "But you know it's not free."

"What do you want, Wink?"

"They took your girl to get at me."

For the second time that day, I reeled under a volcanic flow of returning memories. Delia and Wink, together on the floor of the Monkey Warehouse, a place as forbidden to wizards as the Refinery was to Spotters. Why had they met?

There was only one answer. Delia was giving Wink a spelleme she'd gotten from a monkey, probably Mudflap. I was one of very few people in the Warehouse who would have recognized Wink, so I must have been the only one who knew he shouldn't have been there. I knew Wink embezzled spells; I had funneled a few his way myself. But what had been so important that he needed to violate Agency directive by going to the Warehouse to pinch it?

"You know that spell the monkey cast on itself?" Wink winked at me. "It was working on a special typewriter that day, if you get my meaning."

Another door in my mind burst open. The Warehouse, silent. In wavering cantrip-light Wink puts a typewriter on Mudflap's desk. I stand behind him holding Mudflap's old typewriter. I take it up to Delia's office; she will replace it later and I will return Wink's enchanted machine to him. *Take me to the Flats*, she says. *It will throw them off the track if they think you might have killed me.*

And if they catch you, she goes on, *tell them you know you've lost, tell them we just want one last moment of us alone together*. She catches my wrist. *Remember*, she says. *Remember.*

"Yours?" I stammered. "Your spell?"

Wink nodded. "I figured it out. I prepared it. I can cast it on a human now. On myself. On you. On anyone. I just had to see if it would work on a monkey first."

"What would it do to a human?" I asked. "We can already talk."

"You'd remember everything, Courier," he answered, looking me dead in the eye. "The monkey remembers the spell, so it keeps working on him. You'd remember all the things you've forgotten that you've forgotten. Anyone could remember anything. You tell me: what would that do to the Agency?"

It would do to everyone in the City, I thought, exactly what Wink is doing to me now. Everybody would know who their friends and enemies were. What the Agency was, where it began and ended. Everybody would know who they were.

"Who made me forget all this, Wink?"

"Delia had to protect you, Courier. She couldn't have you remembering that you'd seen us together. At least not until she knew if it would work."

Delia had taken my memories. She had taken my memories even of dropping her in the Flats. And she had taken my memory of her name, her face. I suffered with this knowledge. It hurt me so profoundly that it almost obscured the more basic truth that she had done it so I could rediscover her, and so that after that rediscovery I would never again be made to forget. She had risked clandestine interactions with a wizard. She had plotted the misappropriation of spellemes and, much more dangerously, tinkered with the monkeys' generation of those spellemes. And when Mudflap had brought down Wink's spell upon himself, she must have been standing right there not knowing until the event whether things would go off as planned. Anything could have gone wrong. Anything.

Magic is like that sometimes.

"If it would work, if it would work, if it would work," Wink was muttering to himself.

"It did work," I said.

He looked at me. "You remember everything?"

"Not yet. That's not what I mean."

What I meant was, I knew what to say to the Warden now. I knew how to play the wounded bird, fluttering my wing so they wouldn't notice Wink stealing away through the rushes with the memories of the City. I knew what the Agency had done to me, and I hated them for it, and I began to believe in the possibility that Wink might bring wholeness.

I had been abased so that I could be made whole. Unknowing, I had been transformed by love.

"Sure is a nice car," Wink said, looking out the broken window. "Too bad we'll have to hide behind it while they shoot at us." He was absently spinning a pen around his thumb and index finger while his counterspells foamed and sizzled around the doorjamb. The copper basins in which he analyzed spellemes had begun to glow a strange green-orange. Abruptly Wink flipped the pen over his shoulder and said, "Time to go. Best hit the ground running."

I didn't ask questions. When Wink went out the window, I did too. When he hit and rolled, I did too. And when he came to a panting halt against my car, leaning against the passenger door but not getting in, I squatted next to him and waited.

"Car's spelled," he wheezed. "Can't drive it now."

"They were here?" He nodded. "Shit," I said. "Mudflap."

Wink shook his head. "Magic can't find monkeys unless they cast it themselves. Even then it usually doesn't work. My spell wouldn't even have worked unless I'd calibrated the typewriter perfectly. No way some random goon with generic spells is going to find your monkey."

"So he's in there."

"He's in there."

"Let's get him then."

Just then a huge white burst of energy shattered every window on the second floor. Bits of glass and brick rained down around us. I jerked open the car's passenger door and hauled Mudflap up from the floorboards. He bit my arm and I belted him against the dashboard. "Goddammit, Mudflap! It's me!"

Gunshots crackled like miniature echoes of the explosion. I could hear something hitting the other side of the car, and the usual unpredictable side effects of large-scale magical discharge manifested themselves. Snow fell. A palm tree grew suddenly out of the car's engine compartment. The tires melted, reconstituted themselves as gaskets, galoshes, rubber bands.

"We need to get out of here," Wink said.

"So it would appear." I looked back toward the building, expecting more goons from that direction, but they must have cleared out in anticipation of the explosion. Soon, I figured, they'd be circling around.

"Go," Wink said. "Into the brush."

I did what he said. Spells came my way, one close enough to leave a trail of poison oak on the back of my leg. Then I was in the brush, Mudflap clinging to my back. I thrashed my way down to the shady flats along the river and waited for Wink to catch up.

He didn't.

I swore, made as if to go on, hesitated at the tug of my conscience. "Damn," I said. "Damn all magicians." I set Mudflap at the base of a tree. "Stay here," I said. He scampered up the tree and peered down at me. "Don't you go anywhere, monkey," I said.

When I got back to the edge of the Refinery's lawn, I saw that Wink was alive and surrounded by goons. One of them was the bald goon who had said *Haven* to me and then watched impassively as the Functionary in the Office nearly erased me from the City's memory.

In hindsight, of course, I knew nothing could have happened to me there. The Agency needed me, and in the Office there were no miscommunications. The bald goon had given me just enough information to make me lead the Agency to Wink—and through him to my beloved Delia. Only she knew which monkey had been enchanted, and only I knew which was her favorite. But the Agency would only know what the bald goon told them.

There would only be one chance. I gripped my gun in both hands, breathed deeply, and fired at the bald goon in the pause at the end of my exhalation.

The spell struck him just under the left collarbone. I was expecting something grand and eerie: I thought he might burst into flame, turn inside out, disappear entirely. Instead he stumbled backwards and sat down hard. There was no blood. Slowly he leaned to his left, and then he must have lost his balance. He fell onto his side and lay there. I was too far away to see if he was still breathing.

"Go, Courier!" Wink shouted. One of the goons kicked him to the ground, but still he shouted. "Go, go, go!"

I hesitated. Spells began to flicker and stink in the brush around me. I shot twice more, high, and then leaped back down the hillside toward the river.

In the Flats I stole a car and drove toward the Office. "Okay, Mudflap. Where is she? You were there. Help me out."

Mudflap shook his head. He pantomimed typing.

"Goddammit, monkey," I said. "Do not fool around. I just left an ally to die if he is lucky. I could just kill you and deal with the rest of it later. Tell me. Write it on a napkin or something." I found a parking ticket, threw it into the back seat with a pencil I had in my coat pocket.

Mudflap pantomimed typing. I screamed and crushed the brake pedal to the floor, came to a squealing halt in front of a real-estate office and dragged him inside. "You are not seeing this," I said to the receptionist as I grabbed the back of her chair and wheeled her away from her desk. "Repeat what I just said to you."

"I am not seeing this," she said, her shadowed eyes riveted on Mudflap, who climbed up onto the desk and painstakingly typed FIRST WE FREE THE MONKEYS FROM HAVEN.

When I could speak I said, as calmly as I could, "You spring this on me now?"

FREE THE MONKEYS, Mudflap typed again. With a growl, I tore the sheet from the typewriter.

"Shit shit shit shit," I said, and dragged him out of the office. In this way I became liberator of monkeys when all I wanted was to swashbuckle just enough to rescue my beloved Delia.

"How we do this," I said to him, "is simple. I go in with you on my back. You got lost and I'm returning you. If we're lucky, the guard loans me his keys. If not, I blast the locks and you screech in monkey-lingo. Fast, get it? I shoot, you yell jailbreak, and we're gone. Then you owe me. Clear?"

Mudflap nodded and pissed on the seat. I took that to mean that his anticipation had gotten the better of him. With him hanging on my back, I crept from the idling car around to the front door of the Monkey Haven. It was late at night, and the Warehouse was shut down. All of the Monkeys had been bused back to the Haven, fed, and separated into peaceful groups.

"Hey, Courier," the guard said as I entered. "Some important package you got there."

"Last time I take one," I groused. "You should see the inside of my car."

The guard got up. "No, take a load off," I said. "I'll put him back. Just tell me where."

He looked at Mudflap. "Capuchins are all on the right hand side, about two-thirds of the way down. Make sure you don't put him in with the baboons."

It occurred to me right then that I didn't want to still be in the building when the baboons were freed. I took the guard's keys and made sure to shut the outer door tightly behind me when I went into the kennel corridor. Right away I started opening doors. Mudflap was smart enough not to scream right away, and most of the monkeys were asleep, so I got most of the way down the hall without much of a racket. At the first capuchin cage, though, Mudflap lost all of his self-restraint and started screeching. "Shit," I said, as the chorus of answers began to echo up and down the hall. I started unlocking faster.

The outer door opened and the guard appeared, silhouetted in the bright office light. "What the hell," he said, and then he was overwhelmed by a surging tide of monkeys. The marmosets scampered under him, spider monkeys leaped over and around him, and when he saw the baboons coming he turned and fled out into the night.

I finished unlocking cages and found the door at the other end of the hall chained shut. Mudflap was still screeching, but something in his tone had changed, and when I looked over my shoulder I saw what seemed like every mandrill in the world rushing fang-first in my direction. They're monkeys, I thought to myself. They don't know the door doesn't open.

Before I could think about it I leveled my gun at the door and began firing. Spells clashed, and before my eyes the door rusted, started leaking water, played a strange kind of string music, and—just as the band of mandrills got within biting distance—turned to flour. Most of the rear wall collapsed in a great white cloud, and I lunged through it along with the frenzied mass of my primate brethren. Somewhere along the way I tripped and fell, skinning my palms on the sidewalk, and I looked up to see what must have been hundreds of monkeys dusted with white, disappearing into the quiet City night.

Mudflap cringed as we approached the front doors of the great Office tower. "Strength," I said. "One way or another, we won't be in there long." I took several deep breaths before entering.

"It's you," a Functionary said. I could not tell if it was the same one who had accosted me earlier. They all seem to have the same beard and the same voice.

"It is," I said. "Where is the Warden?"

"He won't see you."

"Well, he'll see this monkey," I said. "Where is he?"

"The Warden works at the Prison," sneered the Functionary.

"But he's here," I said. "Where?"

The Functionary glared. His beard trembled. His hands thrashed in his pockets.

"The elevator will take you," he spat at last, and turned away.

I got on the first elevator that opened its doors and didn't bother to push a button. When the doors opened again, I stepped out holding Mudflap in the crook of my arm. The Warden sat at a desk in a grandly featureless white room. I thought it was the same desk I'd seen in the Prison earlier in the day.

"One thing, right?" I said to him.

"One," he answered.

"All right. Here it is. I just want a minute with her. Just us. To understand. I know there's no more than that."

For a long moment he stared unblinking into my face. Then he gave Mudflap the same treatment. "So you do know where you stand," he said.

I nodded.

"You do know you were already forgotten when you came here this morning."

I nodded again. This was the moment when I discovered whether Delia had been right, whether Wink still survived, whether I had been forgotten permanently or only for a moment, the time it takes for a city to stir and shake Agency cobwebs from its mind.

"Get in the elevator," the Warden said. "It will go up. She will be there. In a few minutes others will arrive to keep you company." The Warden showed his teeth. "The Agency is not cruel."

In the elevator I grew dizzy, and Mudflap began to sag in my grasp. The Office miasma. I was glad to step out onto the roof. Even though I knew that my life would either end in the next few minutes or be transformed into something unrecognizable to me, I was glad. Wind blew the Office air out of my nose, and I looked out over the magnificent nighttime City, cottoned with fog made translucent by the corpuscular glow of headlights on the streets. Beyond the City the mountains were a vast absence of stars.

And Delia was there.

Neither of us spoke for several breaths. I looked into her face and saw that she knew me, and something loosened in my stomach. I had been afraid that while I was remembering, she—like the rest of the City—would be forgetting. But perhaps the Agency hadn't wanted to waste the magic on amnesia for an ex-Spotter who was already forgotten by the City. She knew me, and she smiled.

"Did it work?" she said.

"I think it did," I answered. "I remember our meeting with Wink, the typewriter, all the rest. And here's Mudflap."

She laughed at the name.

"I couldn't save Wink, though," I said sadly. "I had to leave him at the Refinery. There was nothing I could do."

"Don't worry," Delia said. "They can't touch Wink."

"What?"

"Who do you think brews up their amnesia for them?"

Another wrench, I thought. Another surprise. And so late in the day. Wink, brewer of amnesia, tinkerer with typewriters to give capuchins the gift of clacking speech. I began to believe everything might work, but my mouth, tired and City-cynical, contested the point. "But the goons don't know that."

"The Warden does. They need Wink for amnesia, but they don't know he's crafted memory as well. Wink will be okay. He is the downfall of the Agency, and he has made himself indispensable to it."

The elevator chimed. Delia turned to me. "Now we find out," she said, "if he came through for us."

I took the feather from my pocket.

In every spell is an element of pure wishfulness. This is why the numerologists and graphologists, statisticians and linguists have been unable to fathom magic's mysteries. At its heart the spell is an expression of desire for that which cannot be. What separates it from most such desires is that the spell makes the impossible ephemerally real.

Mountains, I thought. Mountains and Delia and never return, *and you forget us*.

Before the Agency took her from me, I said my beloved's name with great joy. Now I fear that the mention of her name will call their attention to her again. I remember to fear them; and I remember to love her, nameless and eyes shining, looking down at the fog-shrouded City. Sometimes we skirt close enough to the City that we can smell its musk of money and magic. Generally we keep a more careful distance. We make jokes about the imbecility and ineptitude of the Agency, but I still refrain from calling her by name. We have evolved a flirtatious matrix of nicknames.

Wink brings us news and supplies, occasionally spells. He has forgiven me, I think, for the damage I did to his laboratory. I said before that wizards cannot stop. This means that they have great difficulty holding grudges, and in any case my beloved was right. Wink alone can make the City forget, and for this the Agency needs him.

But there is an Awakening in the City. Fewer people are forgetting, Wink tells us with a glitter in his crow-footed eye. More are aware of themselves. There are still typewriters in the Warehouse and wizards in the Refinery, but more magic flows outside the Agency's field of vision. Wink believes that he has set in motion irreversible change. I think he is right.

New monkeys have replaced the old, who fled to the mountains and now populate the sloping forests. They fling shit on my beloved and me whenever we startle them. Even Mudflap, who I see now and again gazing at the towers of the City with what must be simian longing, joins in the flinging of excrement. Let it never be said that monkeys are grateful.

Their screaming and flinging is not limited to our intrusions, though. Every human is treated much the same. From time to time I hear a ruckus in one of the valleys below the cabin I share with my beloved. Invariably it is the monkeys, joined in pitched battle against interlopers who must, I think, be Agency Operatives. The Agency perpetuates itself and its spurious distinctions. Despite my faith in Wink's magic, the threat of the Agency denies me peace.

"Relax," Delia says. "We're out here. Leave them down there." And she is right.

Out here my memory is intact. I remember everything of my last day in the City, and every moment since, making allowances of course for normal frailty. That, and my reunion with the woman I love, makes me complete. I no longer wander as an avocation, and no longer need to. Love drove me to recapture my memory, and in my memory I find love. I am myself again. No, I am myself at last.

If I worry about the Agency, I hope it is only in the nature of reflex self-preservation. The truth of it is that I have enough of Wink's spells stockpiled to repel an armed expeditionary force—or to simply go somewhere else. As I said, I no longer wander as an avocation, but I haven't completely lost the desire to see new horizons, and with Delia …

Sometimes I slip. Thus far there have been no consequences. She assures me there will be none, and I believe she is right. The rest is superstition, an irrational persistence of Agency paranoia. But she is right. Leave them down in the fog-shrouded City. We are out here.

Whenever there is no work to be done and I tire of the stars and the plummeting slopes of the valley we have made our home, I put each sense to work absorbing and reveling in her presence. I am Delia-tropic. We learn how to provide for our needs, how not to fear the tendrils of the Agency. We watch, but we do not spend our lives watching, and we rely on Wink's Awakening, as we have begun to call it. It is good to be clear-eyed and have faith and be in love.

BLACK DOG AT WORK

STEVEN MOHAN, JR.

Bear was bitching me out for being ten minutes late, which always pissed me off because, Jeez, it's only ten minutes and four in the a.m. is way too early to be so retentive. Besides all he was going to do was go home and crack open a bottle of Johnny Walker and fall asleep with a copy of *Playboy's Nakedest Coeds* on his lap, and if all you had to look forward to was hard liquor and soft porn what difference did ten minutes make anyway?

"You know, Joe," he said, "you are—"

"Black Dog," I said.

Bear's middle-aged face crumpled like a side panel after a fender-bender. "What?"

"Call me Black Dog."

Joe shook his head. "You're not black."

"No," I admitted, "but I *am* one bad actor."

"No, you dumb ass, you're a bad worker. I think it's time I called Old Man Hagen."

Uh oh. Threatening to call Old Man Hagen was the Chicago Premier Parking equivalent of using tactical nuclear weapons.

"Roberto," I said using his real name in an attempt to shock him out of the kind of madness that leads to mutual assured destruction, "if he puts in an automatic system, we both lose our jobs."

Bear was a massive Mexican in his late fifties who stood nearly six feet tall. He'd probably gain another three inches if he ever stood up straight. He waved my words away with one giant paw. "He's not going to put in an automatic system."

I held up my hands. "All right, Bear. You want me to be a better worker. Help me out here." I pointed to a boxy black shape that sat in one corner of the dark lot. "Why is that Volvo still here?"

He squinted at the car. "Gee, Joe, I don't—"

I held up a hand to stop him. "Black Dog, all right? *Black. Dog.*" I pulled my black tee-shirt down so he could see it better. The white outline of a bull dog was emblazoned on the shirt. "Look, I remember that car. Came in yesterday about ten. Why's it still here?"

Bear scratched his head and I decided I needed to put the question in terms a dirty old man could understand. (Don't get me wrong, it's not like I'm a monk or anything. But I'm twenty-six. I'm *supposed* to be horny all the time.)

"Good looking chicka. Five four. She had nice—" I clicked my tongue twice.

He nodded eagerly. "Yeah, I remember. The tasty Mexican chicka."

I blinked. He *had* seen her. "Yeah. I'm not for sure about the Mexican part, but I'll go with tasty. Now follow closely, *compadre*. If she dropped the car off yesterday on Morning Shift and you saw her on Mids, *why is the car still here?*"

Bear shrugged. "Maybe she dropped something off at the car and went back out again."

Bingo. "Maybe," I agreed. "How come you don't know for sure? Did you lose her in the crowd of hot young things that usually pick up their cars between midnight and four?"

Bear didn't say anything.

"Now you weren't sleeping, were you, Roberto?"

Bear opened his mouth and then closed it again.

"A really good employee might feel compelled to call Old Man Hagen." I held up my hands in a gesture of generosity. "Me? I'm gonna let it go."

Bear's mouth tightened into a thin line and he shuffled off, but at least he understood.

And that was that. For the next five hours I sat in my little box, surveying my quarter-acre kingdom of blacktop and Chevy Suburbans. Cars came and cars went and I collected rent for the man, not thinking about the boxy Volvo sedan, or the fact that Bear had never really answered my question. I forgot all of it.

Until I saw the flies.

It was nine and I was walking the lot, making sure everything was kosher, when I passed the Volvo. Really, I wasn't being a good worker. I was just walking around hoping for a little breeze. August is hot and sticky in Chi-Town and it was about one-ten in my little aluminum box.

Anyway, a dozen fluorescent green bottle flies crawled across the Volvo's passenger side window and alighted on the car's dark blue paint job. There aren't many things that attract flies and none of them are good.

I thought of Flash Henderson, who was a legend among the city's parking lot attendants. Flash supposedly was checking out a Cadillac that had sat in his lot for a week and found two mil in coke (and not the trademarked kind) in the back seat and promptly lit off for greener pastures. It seems the car's driver had taken a bad meeting and wasn't never coming back.

I took a step toward the Volvo. I was coming at the car from the back and I could see a Northwestern University logo on the back window. Three light purple parking stickers mingled on her rear bumper with a white bumper sticker that said "National Organization For Women" in forest green letters.

The passenger side window was cracked open and flies buzzed in and out of the car. A thin film of fine, white powder coated the window's bottom, like someone had spilled laundry soap across the glass surface and it'd stuck.

I took another step forward and leaned over.

The pretty chicka lay slumped to one side in the driver's side seat. Crimson vomit covered her lower jaw and stained her pretty see-through blouse.

I fumbled with my phone and dialed 9-1-1 and then, wouldn't you know it, I actually did call Old Man Hagen and left a message on his machine.

Then I jimmied the door open and pulled her out. It's not that I didn't know what the fine white powder might be (hey, I watch the Discovery Channel as much as the next guy), but I just couldn't leave her in there. Part of it was that a quick check of her prone form revealed that her shapely chest was rising and falling, and part of it was that I felt a little bad about clicking my tongue at her boobs for Bear's amusement, but most of it was because the Black Dog is one bad actor.

Chicago PD Detective Bill Kauffman ran one pudgy hand through his stupid-looking buzz cut (some men just have no sense of style) and took off his ugly brown sports jacket. He was already sweating through the white shirt underneath. He leaned into the Volvo and popped open the glove compartment.

"I wouldn't do that, Bill," I said. "That white powder's got to be Ebola or some shit. Did the EMT's check to see if she was bleeding from all her orifices?"

"My name," said Kauffman between clenched teeth, "is Detective Kauffman. If you don't think you can remember that, I can guarantee you that *you'll* be bleeding from all your orifices."

"Sure thing, Bill," I said cheerfully.

Kauffman is built like a tank and has a temper to match. I'm sure he's done his fair share of non-Miranda interrogations and despite our long professional relationship (I've had to call the Chicago PD fourteen times in my parking career: nine DUI's, four assaults, and, I'm sorry to say, one rape) he's made it very clear he has no love of me.

Still, I was utterly certain he wasn't going to pound my face in. The pretty girl-child from the *Trib* who was watching the proceedings was good for that much at least.

A half-dozen beat cops were trying to keep lot customers away from the crime scene, carefully regulating who could come and who could go. I have to tell you honestly that the six of them were not doing nearly as good a job as I do each and every day.

I got to stand there (outside the yellow tape, of course) because I was a witness and the *Trib* girl got to stand next to me because she was press. The EMT's had already carried the victim off, but I didn't have much faith she would make it.

Kauffman extracted her registration, gave it a quick flick with his wrist to clear the white powder off, and said, "Israa al-Marzouqi."

"See," I said gleefully. "I told Bear she wasn't Mexican."

"That would be your associate, Roberto Ramirez," said the *Trib* girl. I nodded and she jotted something down in her little steno pad.

Her name was Nancy Something and she didn't look half-bad. She had shoulder-length dishwater blonde hair and pretty hazel eyes. Sadly, it took only a quick glance at her pale blue polo shirt to reveal that she was not nearly so well-endowed as the future former Ms. al-Marzouqi.

Plus she couldn't be much older than twenty. The *Trib* had obviously sent her down to my lot because they were under the mistaken impression that this was just another random Chicago homicide rather than a mega-dangerous terrorist strike at America's heart.

Chicago Premier Parking.

"And your name again?"

"Black Dog," I said, tugging my shirt bottom down for maximum effect.

Kauffman rolled his eyes. "His name is Joseph McNaught," he growled.

"My name is not 'naught.' Naught means nothing." I winked at Nancy Whatever-her-name-was. "And clearly I'm something."

"Clearly," she said unenthusiastically.

Kauffman did what any cop who was too stupid to breathe would do, he leaned into the car and pulled out a red backpack.

"Hey, Bill," I said.

He shot me a look.

"All right. Detective Kauffman. I really wouldn't do that. Maybe you should call the FBI."

Kauffman snorted. "The Feds can't even keep track of their own damn evidence lockers."

I frowned and glanced at the reporter.

"$1.2 million in seized drug money disappeared from the federal building two weeks ago," said Nancy. "It was in all the papers."

"Yeah," I said. "The papers. So the feds misplaced a million dollars. Hardly sounds like news to me. Bi—, er, Detective Kauffman, you need some help. I think this is a terrorist attack."

"Yeah, I'll get right on that."

"Why would any terrorist want to kill this woman?" asked Nancy.

"Maybe they're not after the woman," I said. "The way Bill's spreading powder around they could take out the whole lot."

"Will America ever be the same?" asked Kauffman sadly.

"Mr., uh—" She glanced at her notes, "McNaught. Why would terrorists want to hit a parking lot?"

"Black Dog, honey," I said, pointing at the shirt for emphasis. *"Black. Dog.* It's a soft target. Can you imagine the chaos if people had to drive into the city and didn't have anywhere to park?"

"I'm not sure I buy the analysis," said a new voice, "but he may actually be right."

I turned and saw a six-three man in a stylish gray suit with salt-and-pepper hair and a square jaw. He flashed a gold badge. "Assistant Special Agent in Charge Samuel Norton. Chicago Office of the Federal Bureau of Investigation."

"Looky, Bill," I said grinning from ear to ear, "the A-team's here."

Kauffman turned bright scarlet, but he stepped forward and shook Norton's hand. "I appreciate your input, but—"

Norton held up his hand. "Wait one." He turned to a blond woman in a blue windbreaker that said "FBI" in yellow letters on the back. "Margaret, get antibiotics for everyone on the crime scene. That includes the first responders. We'll want a biohazard team, of course. And check all the buildings in a one-block radius to make sure the terrorists didn't hit anywhere else. I'll meet with the press at noon."

"What the hell do you think you're doing," growled Kauffman.

"The federal government has jurisdiction in terrorist attacks, Officer, uh—"

"Kauffman. *Detective* Kauffman."

"Or Bill for short," I said.

Nancy covered a smirk with her hand and turned away. I liked her better and better all the time.

"I think this might be a hit by the Russian mob," snapped Kauffman.

Norton shook his head. "When was the last time the Russian mob hit someone and left them alive, Detective? Besides, she'd have to have some serious internal injuries to cause her to vomit blood. The Russians might slit a woman's throat or shoot her in the back of the head, but they wouldn't beat her. That's *nekulturny.*"

I thought Kauffman's eyes were going to bug right out of his head. "Nul—"

"*Nekulturny.* It means uncultured. I spent three years as the law enforcement attaché in Moscow."

A vein throbbed in Kauffman's forehead. "You can't just come in here barking orders and —"

Norton reached forward and pulled the backpack out of Kauffman's hands. He unzipped the bag and pulled out a textbook entitled *Microcellular Structure*. "Ms. al-Marzouqi was doing graduate work in Biomedical Engineering at Northwestern."

He handed the book and the bag to one of his windbreakered flunkies and opened the Volvo's rear door. Whatever al-Marzouqi's other virtues were she hadn't been a neat-freak. Papers and books littered the car's back seat.

Norton extended a telescoping pointer and started poking through the debris. "Here." He flicked aside a pile of papers revealing a square Tupperware container filled with some kind of white powder. "*Bacillus anthracis*. Weaponized anthrax. I'd bet anything." The container's warped lid didn't quite seal. "She was probably transporting the disease when some of it leaked out. We may have gotten lucky here."

"Wait," I said. "Are you saying the girl was the terrorist? That can't be right."

"She was a Qatari national."

"She *is* a Qatari national," said Kauffman petulantly. "The last word we had was that she was still alive."

Norton's face went perfectly blank. "Wonderful," he said. "Maybe if we're lucky, we'll have a chance to interview her. Margaret, make a note."

"But you're wrong," I shouted. "It couldn't have been her."

Norton turned and offered me a plastic smile. "Thank you for your help, sir. Margaret, please see to this gentlemen." He made a shooing motion.

So Eva Braun pulled me back from the police tape and left me in the care of the Chicago PD. I sat myself down on the curb and buried my head in my hands.

"Mr. McNaught? Joe?"

I looked up. Nancy Something was standing over me. "Black Dog," I said.

"Why did you say al-Marzouqi couldn't be the terrorist?"

"She was wearing a see-through blouse and a lacy white bra."

Nancy blushed. "Was she?"

"Believe me, I'm a man. We notice these things." I jerked my head toward the car. "Also, there's a NOW sticker on her bumper."

She turned to look.

"Radical Muslims and radical feminists are two free radicals that usually don't mix."

Nancy said nothing for a long moment. "If she didn't put the anthrax in her car, how did it get here?"

I shrugged helplessly. "I don't know. Where does the stuff come from?"

"Cows and deer mostly," she muttered. "The U.S. had an anthrax program in the sixties. So did Saddam before he went boom. Maybe Iran."

I remembered the expression on Norton's face when Kauffman told him that al-Marzouqi was still alive. "Russia?"

She nodded. "The former Soviet Union was big into bioweapons." She blinked and her eyes widened. "What are you saying?"

"The man always keeps ya' down. There's someone here who suddenly has more power than an alderman. And no one even voted for him. Not that it's that big of a deal in Chicago."

"Norton," she whispered. "He went right to the anthrax like he knew where it was. He has Russian contacts. And all that missing DEA money could buy a lot of bioweapons."

"What if he put it in her car and waited for it to take effect. Then he swoops in plays the hero."

She turned and my eyes followed her gaze. The blue-jacketed feds looked like a conquering army, pouring over the crime scene. Chicago cops stood all around Chicago Premier Parking with their heads down. Defeated.

"If he took command of the situation . . ." Nancy shook her head. "Imagine the news coverage. My God, he could be another Rudy Giuliani."

She glanced down at me and said, "Wait right here, I'm going to go talk to Bill."

I stood up and watched her push past a couple of Chicago beat cops who made a half-hearted attempt to stop her. She grabbed Kauffman by the shoulder and talked excitedly for a solid minute. I watched his ugly head jerk up.

He pulled out his cell phone and made a quick call. I stood there and watched him talk and talk and talk. Finally, Nancy ran over to me.

"What did Bill say?"

She smiled and her whole face lit up. Suddenly I didn't care how big her double tongue clicks were.

"He was talking to the mayor. Chicago PD's taking over the investigation. They're going to pull Norton off the investigation until they sort it out."

I felt the grin spread across my face. "Well, bitchin'. It all turned out. Even if I did have to help Bill out."

Her face fell. "Yeah, look. I'm sorry, but no one wanted to believe it was your idea." She held her hands out. "I wish there were some way to make it up to you."

"Maybe there is."

She blushed again.

"Hey, I just meant dinner."

She laughed and handed me her card. "I know that's all *you* meant. See you around, Black Dog." I watched her pull her steno pad out and walk back to the crime scene.

I told you I was a bad actor.

I put her card in my pocket and walked away from Chicago Premier Parking. I figure this was one day when even Old Man Hagen couldn't bitch at me for taking a few hours off. After all I caught the bad guy and got the girl which is all just in a day's work for the Black Dog.

THE BLACKPOOL ASCENSIONS

LUCIUS SHEPARD

Edward Pinney, a lovely old man, so everyone said, and kind as April after March, came walking at cold gray daybreak along the beach at Blackpool with nary a wobble nor a totter in his stride, cricket-thin and crooked in posture, yet still hale at seventy-six. His good right eye roamed the turvy tops of the waves and the slate-colored swells beyond the bar heaving thickly, ponderously, like liquefied stone. The wind, "the long ahhs of the world," his best friend Colin (singer and poet, long-dead, victim of the Sixties, loved his drugs oer'much) had once called these October blows, flung sand through the air and set crusts of foam to tumbling along the shingle and flapped the collar of Edward's pea coat and lashed up his hair, shoulder-length since youth, into white snakelings that snapped at his cheeks and madly framed his fallen-in face. He carved a straight line with his step, sloshing through tide pools, aiming for the city's famous tower, a Victorian skeleton of ruddy steel that sprouted from the Promenade, rising four hundred feet to an enclosed viewing platform, itself surmounted by a massive boxy structure of steel plates and beams, the entire thing topped off by a caged enclosure shaped rather like an ornament on the lid of a Chinese teakettle and flying the Union Jack above from a metal pole. Admirable bit of construction, that (so Edward countenanced it), albeit wholly confectionary and merely a half-pint version of *le Tour Eiffel* — thus, to his way of thinking, no more praiseworthy a feat than his own engineering masterwork, a footbridge carrying the Lancaster Canal tow-path over the confluence of the Ribble and the Savick, its concrete piers dressed with alternations of red Accrington brick and blue. Most decorous, people had told him.

Thoughts of this trivial order sleeted through Edward's brain, but his truest thought, the one that stayed firm in him, was an apprehension of joy both manifest and imminent. Although he understood neither its measure nor its source, an apprehension of it having flared up in him midway through his constitutional (two miles along the shore and back being the daily prescription), he was slave to it now, obedient to its every impulse. Time was short, that much he understood. A vague promise summoned him, as did a curious sense of necessity. He had to hurry, hurry, or else miss the tide of joy that he believed would lift him off the reef of loneliness and despondency upon which his life had foundered. With each step he felt an increase of vigor, a beautiful, youthful strength flowing through his limbs, and he wondered if this sudden renewal might presage an equally sudden decline, affecting a last surge of power before his battery lost its spark. So be it, he told himself. He'd had a good run. Yet even as he framed this self-judgment, he recognized its inaccuracy. His three-quarters of a century was a patch of time without significant memorial, defined by an indifferent childhood, a loveless listless marriage, and the dull pleasures of the public house, its character determined by missed opportunities and petty deceits. Oh, there had been moments, to be sure, when he'd caught a glimpse of life-as-it-should-be. Knocking boots with Mindy Whitsett, first and foremost. Hadn't she made him feel half-again the king in heaven? Things might have run different for them had not Mindy's Tory bastard boyfriend (next in line for a peerage), on learning of the affair, used Edward's schoolboy flirtation with communism to paint him red and have him bounced from his firm, thereby condemning him to a non-descript career. It wasn't that the Earl of Nothingness or whatever he now called himself had planned to marry a common sort like Mindy. He'd wound up with the usual inbred sprig of celery these pricks always married. No, he had ruined their lives simply because it pleased him. It would have made a better result, Edward thought, if he'd actually been a communist, if he'd spent his days blowing up churches and sniping at those proceedings during which they trotted out the royals to put a dignified stamp on the opening of a nuclear waste plant or the awarding of medals to schoolgirls' horticultural displays. Royals, my arse! he said to himself. Could there be a more unlovely bunch? Useless twats with lumpish faces like those sometimes produced on the surfaces of root vegetables. A thought of Mindy, a bubble of remembered sweetness, cut the potency of Edward's despairing anger, reducing it to self-pity, and his eyes watered. His book of regrets was too voluminous by far. Yet as he walked on, joy came again, a torrent washing through him, battering at the house of his dismaying memories, until it seemed all his dreary past had been sluiced away.

Something glittered in the sand up ahead. Odd, that. A reflection without a shred of sun to make it. Edward veered toward the spot. There, cupped in a depression, lay a jellyfish. Cast up by the storm, one would suppose. A smallish specimen sheathed in a film of mud and unexceptional in all particulars but one. Embedded within its gelatinous substance were spindly structures that pulsed many-hued, flickering gold to blue to violet, those colors repeating at regular intervals, suggesting some sort of digital process. He touched it gingerly and the surface of the thing shifted, morphing into a crystal disc upon which was incised a figure half-serpent, half-woman, bound about its circumference by a circlet of reddish iron. Instead of jerking back his hand, as would have been his natural instinct, he snatched the disc up, clutching it to his chest, and felt an intensification of joy, this accompanied by a confusion of names and images without apparent precedent or interrelation that sprayed into his mind as if from the bursting of a hidden conduit. Rosslyn, the sacred grove. Riddley and Bastock. The secret lineage, the holy conjoining. McCauley the builder. The cup. The princess in her coffin. The Melusine...That sinuous, mellifluous name darkened his mood, generating a dread. His jaw dropped, his eyelids fluttered down. With the tip of his forefinger, he began obsessively to trace the heraldic figure cut into the surface of the disc. He remained in this posture, dazed, unable to think, scarcely able to breathe, until, at length, the glitter that had drawn his eye seemed to penetrate his interior world, pointing every possibility with dancing light.

Having recovered his good spirits, Edward's attention came to be dominated by the Blackpool Tower and he gave scant thought to either the information that continued spraying into his brain (most of it, if not all, he realized, having some association with the tower), or to the miraculous transformation he had witnessed. The beach, the promenade stretching alongside it, mirroring the course of Bank Hey Road, and the tower itself comprised a geography with which he shared a considerable history. At sixteen, he had worked as a laborer, repairing the building that enclosed the base of the tower, lending the struts stability in a high wind — a five-layer Victorian cake so thoroughly representative of the Great Queen's middlebrow pomposity, it might have been one of her edicts hardened into red brick and fanciful white trim. While at university, as a student exercise, he had submitted plans for the renovation of the tower and a nearby hotel (the Butlins Metropole); during the heyday of his professional career, he had consulted upon the matter of tidal stress with the designers of the North Pier, one of the three piers that sectioned the Blackpool shore, extending hundreds of feet into the sea; and he had been among the contractors who bid on the job of enlarging the tower's viewing platform to accommodate a restaurant, a project that had been discarded. Yet looking along the Promenade and the beach, wide and brown, crossed with channels carved by the tide, he felt newly awakened to the area, as if for all these years he had somehow misperceived it, failing to grasp its signal importance. He did not fully grasp its importance now, but he suspected there might be a connection between the place — the tower, in particular — and the soaring sensation within him, the attendant desire to go up and up and up, to follow the push of that sensation. It must be, he decided, the tower to which he was being directed. A remnant of logic sought to muscle into his mental conversation, reminding him that the tower would be closed until ten. Did he think they would bend the rules, unlock the doors, and wave him in four hours early? And wasn't he acting the daft old thing to believe himself guided by unseen forces? But Edward, emotionally armored against such contraries, soldiered on in the cause of joy, still clutching the disc to his chest, moving at a quickened pace, trusting that the way would be opened.

Ronald Bajema, twenty-two years of pissed-off gutter boy, a shaven-headed, second-generation street monster barnacled with ear studs and sporting an iron cross, two prominently be-fanged serpents, a crux ansata, eleven diminutive skulls in a row, a red-eyed monkey trapped in a spider web, and arcana yet more cryptic inked upon his mesomorphic chest, neck and arms, kept a disreputable secret from his mates, this being the fact that he was a member in good standing of the Blackpool Model Yacht Club. It was in the service of this boyhood passion, then, and not of any motive allied with his usual guise of conscienceless thug, that he hiked down to the beach that same morning, carrying a bulky shopping sack that contained a vintage "Corbie" K938, built in 1954 by W. J. Daniels, sporting a mahogany hull, two genoas, two spinnakers, and two mainsails—a prize for which he had paid fifteen hundred pounds, monies earned by beatings-for-hire and the one-time-only ("I swear, baby! Just this once! I've got to have the cash!") pimping of his lady love, Delores DeNovo. With loving hands, young Ronald removed the craft from the sack and set it down in a channel gouged out by the waves. The blustery conditions were perfect for testing the controls and, as he twitched the sails, sending the yacht yawing and tacking across the mud-colored reach, he sank into a stuporous contentment, essentially a condition of non-being flecked with pleasure into which he commonly lapsed for hours, the universe reduced to what might have been an emblem of self, a tiny brown boat cleverly sailing nowhere.

On this occasion, barely a minute passed before a glinting from the far side of the channel penetrated Ronald's somnolent state and, without thought for his toy, he went splashing toward the opposite bank. "Fucking hell!" he said, bending to the disgusting bit of sea life that had distracted him. He brought up his boot to stomp it, but then, thinking it would be more interesting to dare being stung and squeeze the squishy thing, to feel its life break cold and runny over his knuckles, he seized it in his fist and was possessed by a rage such as he had never before experienced. Not that it was greater in scope or intensity than any of his previous rages. Thanks to the serial violences, physical and spiritual, visited upon him by his mum and dad, and by their friends and associates in addiction, Ronald was a very angry boy, prone to lash out at whoever or whatever fell to hand. Unlike his typical outbursts, however, this one was specifically focused, directed toward the Blackpool Tower. The way it tapered, abruptly widening at the viewing platform a hundred feet or so below the flagpole at its summit, it resembled a gigantic dog's prick. Ronald hated dogs, though he appreciated their meat savagery, and this association of their sexual weapon with the tower ignited his customary unfigured contempt for that piece of sky trash into full-blown detestation. He pictured it fallen, lying in sections, concrete dust rising up from broken steel webs, and the brick cozy that the jolly old farts back in century nineteen had fitted around its base, that was smashed flat, squiggles of life's blood eeling from beneath the rubble. Without conscious intent, he moved a couple of steps closer to the tower and the fires of his rage were banked into a fury. His mind movie grew increasingly detailed. He envisioned seaside hotels, shops, restaurants crushed by the fallen tower, collapsed into the street, ambulances and police cars beetling about, their lights flashing red blue orange, and politicians moving in for photo-ops, that little prig-tyrant, the Prime Blister, Tony B, foremost amongst them, his microphone squealing as he quoted William Blake and Bono (his secret bedmate, hinted *The Globe and Mail*), using their words for a balm to slime over the raw wounds of national tragedy and titillate the assembled proles who did jumping jacks every time he puked up another platitude, hoping in their hearts this would be the moment when his inner essence would burst forth, when he'd rip off the old wool-and-worsted and go prancing about in a sequined jockstrap, rendering lisping selections from the Boy George catalog. These images captivated Ronald. All his intentions for the morning — testing the boat, picking up coffee and buns, having a shag with Delores — were dismasted by the blustery notion that he might be capable of bringing such a carnival of devastation to pass. The idea would not have withstood even a superficial analysis, but Ronald's analytic powers were weak and largely untried. Registering that the object in his fist had hardened into a crystal disc, yet not wondering much about it, he jammed the thing into the pocket of his windbreaker and set forth to make his dreams come true, while at his back, a dream forsaken, the model yacht, with no hand to guide it, went over onto its side in a strong gust, its sails filling with water.

At twenty-eight, Jill Livingood, two years ahead of schedule in her quest for corporate domination ("corporate dominatrix," the board room apes whom she daily spanked might have essayed), knew the business value of a sexy body and so made a religion of fitness and a cult of plastic surgery. Nipped and tucked, augmented by silicon, her figure teetered on the edge of the voluptuous. When necessary, it could be employed as a distracting force, yet was not so exaggerated in its femininity that she was unable to muffle her charms beneath a conservative suit. Her features were ill-matched to her shape. Negligible gray eyes. Thin lips, a straight, sharp nose, and a broad, pale span of forehead implied a Thatcheresque severity and corresponding emotional moonscape. Standing nude in front of her mirror, it would appear to Jill (ever the violent self-critic) that the head of a harsh schoolmistress had been transplanted onto the neck of a lingerie model. She had considered making some further cosmetic changes, but came to realize that her physical dissonance was alluring to the powerful men with whom she worked. Princes of commerce, one of whom Jill intended eventually to mate. Mere beauty was too simple for their tastes, but a desirable woman whose visual presentation incorporated the idea of cruelty...such a woman appealed to the malformed lusts that power had bred in them.

Keeping up Jill's expensive improvements required, among other disciplines, a seven-mile run along a different course each morning, this variance being her strategy to alleviate boredom. Thursday's course conveyed her from south of the city center to the shore and thence past the Pleasure Beach amusement park toward the Blackpool Tower. A massive eyesore, or so Jill countenanced it. Prior to entering business school, she had dabbled in the arts and gained local notoriety with a grant proposal suggesting the tower be fitted for seasonally appropriate costumes intended to disguise it variously as Jesus, Sir Mick Jagger, Scrooge, and a lifelike phallus from which gouts of light would intermittently spray. Clad in a crimson running suit, her light brown hair clipped in a pony tail, she reached the sand that particular morning twenty-two seconds quicker than her previous best. Exhilarated by this, she felt but a shadow of the fear and revulsion that the heavy brine smell usually triggered in her. Nor was she disturbed, as was often the case, by the sight of the mucky ocher sand, populated at that early hour by a handful of strollers and seashell gatherers; the three piers in the distance, the centermost supporting a white dancehall at its seaward end; the park's jumble of decaying carnival rides and dead neon signs that, though garishly attractive by night, had by day the appearance of a child's misbegotten attempt at fabricating a toy city from a kit of wooden curves, metal sticks, and plastic turrets. Six years before, Jill had been assaulted at Pleasure Beach, dragged beneath the roller coaster, the Pepsi-Max Big One, and done rough by two men wearing Bradley Beaver masks, her cries so thoroughly muted by piped rock and roll and the roar and rattle of the cars, she herself had been unable to hear them. She chose to let the rape go unreported—being perceived as a victim would not have been an asset to her career—and shifted the emphasis of her workouts, developing her arms, shoulders, and back, and studying Muy Thai. When a second assault occurred four years later, she left her attacker face-down and bloody under the Central Pier with the incoming tide foaming over his unconscious form, a circumstance that prompted a half-inch item in the next morning's *Gazette* remarking on the demise by drowning beneath the pier of one Gerald Clote, 28, of Avonslea, following a beating by person or persons unknown. By way of acknowledging Gerald's discharge from the armies of predation, Jill drove to her gym and there established a personal record for chin-ups, 29, a standard she had not since surpassed.

Ordinarily, Jill allowed nothing to interrupt her routine. She had a schedule to keep. Home by seven. Self-gratified, showered, dressed and breakfasted by eight. A double espresso and the Times at a corner coffee bar; then into the office by nine or thereabouts, the exact hour dependent upon when she observed the arrival of a fellow executive. Being second to arrive suited her image—it never served for a woman to appear too assertive in her pursuit of excellence. But as she leaped over a tide pool, she glimpsed a bright something in the mud below and, after several strides, she turned back, stunned by a burst of mental clarity that, like a sun break, dispersed the endorphin-drenched high generated by the run. A fresh purpose shouldered aside worries about a corporate divestiture, a car lease, keeping an appointment with her psychic. She was uncertain regarding the character of this purpose, but knew that until it had been accomplished, she could not get on with her day. "Damn!" she said, reacting to this schedule-disrupting annoyance, and went to inspect the shiny item that had so disturbed her. Jellyfish. That was her initial impression. But even before she bent to pick it up, which she did after the briefest of hesitations, she observed that the translucent shape was flickering at its edges, giving evidence either that it was not what it seemed or that what it seemed was mutable. It fit perfectly in her palm. No longer in aspect a jellyfish, but a crystal disc with a curious figure—body of a snake, head and torso of a nude woman—carved into the surface, and an encircling iron band upon which were engraved a dozen symbols, among them a disembodied eye; a pyramid; several characters that might been letters in a lost alphabet, one of which—an A whose cross-stroke was broken in the middle—seemed familiar. It was, she realized, a symbol of Freemasonry. Not an actual A, but a geometer's compass, emblematic of spirituality. Always alert to new opportunities for networking, Jill had contemplated joining the Honorable Fraternity of Ancient Freemasons, the female co-order of the organization.

The membership of the Blackpool lodge included two prominent executives whose acquaintance she desired to make. To this end she had researched the order on the Internet, sifting through garbage relating to the Masonic alliance with Satan, their possession of sacred Jesus scrolls and the Holy Grail (buried, according to various screed, near Rosslyn Chapel in Scotland), and had ordered official pamphlets, all of which bore the compass symbol on their covers.

A puzzle having been presented her, Jill — who doted on puzzles — set to work at solving it. The sole clue: a jellyfish, likely washed up on the tide, that had turned into a crystal disc with marks of Freemasonry inscribed upon it. Or perhaps the disc had cast the illusion of being a jellyfish in order to avoid falling into the wrong hands. Which would mean that hers were the right hands and that she had been selected by means of some process to...What? To deliver the disc somewhere? That much seemed evident. It was further evident that whatever puzzle the disc was a piece of would not be solved by standing on the beach. Her eyes locked onto the tower. She wondered if the scrap of Victoriana in her palm might belong to its enormous cultural relative. It might not have come from the sea — it might have blown off the tower during the night. Or if it had come from the sea, the disc might wish to be brought to the tower in order to enable some function or another.

Had Jill been ensconced in her office (a corner office that afforded her a lordly view of the Blackpudlian sphere, one wall adorned with a framed letter penned by the late Princess Diana that acknowledged with saccharine formality Jill's cousin many-times-removed connection to the Spencer line, an artifact that prompted her in-house enemies to label her "Lady Die"), reading a report on her discovery of and mental reactions to the disc, she would have laughed at herself for indulging in such twee speculation. In truth, she was inclined to laugh at herself now, and would have but for the fact that an uncanny principle seemed to be in play. Having glanced toward the tower, she found she could not look away. The longer she stared, the more persuaded she became that it must be pivotal to the issue. She slipped the disc into her breast pocket and made for the tower at a jog, dubious that this would prove to be the most fruitful possibility, yet considering it sensible to eliminate the big ugly possibility first. The basic concept underlying that notion amused her: Eliminate The Big Ugly One First. Jill's desk did not have upon it, as did the desks of many junior executives in her firm, a nameplate engraved with an inspirational motto, but if ever she decided to go that route, she thought those six words would do quite well.

If Edward Pinney had been at Ronald's side as he approached the building that formed a brick skirt about the base of the tower, he might, in an effort to calm the lad, have informed him that his vision of mass destruction could never come to pass. Twenty-six hundred tons of steel had been utilized in raising the tower, the metal distributed so that should the structure be toppled, it would fall into the sea and the city would suffer no damage apart from the loss of its famous landmark. But Edward, his pace flagging, was still trudging along the beach, and Ronald, rather than being concerned with the tower itself, had fixed his arrows against the neon sign displayed on the building's facade that spelled out the legend: TOWER WORLD. His mum had loved the place. Whenever she could manage, she would drop acid and, dragging Ronald by his then-tiny hand, would bus down to Tower World and spend hours hallucinating in the aquarium that lay just beyond its doors, unmindful of her son's complaints. Often they were tossed out of the building after Mum vomited or spray painted her name on a tank or made some other sort of row, and these serial evictions had been a source of deep embarrassment to Ronald. Now, standing at the door, pounding on it, peering through the glass panel, the memories of those days, children with chocolate smeared on their faces, some staring at him aghast, some laughing; and Mum, strings of saliva swaying from her chin, bursting into fey song at the sight of some pretty sea roach; the reproving, pitying gazes of the security guards ...those memories were like gasoline thrown on a fire, turning the heat inside his head to scalding, and when a portly middle-aged guard ambled up to the door from within and told him to come back at ten, only the thought that he might set off an alarm stayed Ronald from smashing his fist through the glass, snagging the bastard by the shirtfront, hauling him through the newly created gap and beating him pulpy. He searched for a reason that would convince the guard to permit him entry and then dug into his jacket pocket and pulled out the crystal disc, which he had all but forgotten in his rage.

"Oi! This belong here?" he shouted, holding the disc up as the guard started to walk away. The crystal flickered prettily, as if doing its bit to help sell the con. By no definition, however loosely applied, could Ronald be described as intelligent, yet he was adept at street craft and recognized the sudden blankness that came over the guard's face to be a symptom of greed disguised.

"I found it on the beach," Ronald said, conjuring an earnest look. "Thought somebody might have nicked it, y'know."

The guard hesitated; then he unlocked the door and opened it a crack. "Yeah, might be ours. Gi'e us a look."

Ronald kicked the door inward and, after head-butting the guard, drove him to the floor. He straddled the man's chest and caught him by the throat and rendered him unconscious with three short right hands, each blow transmitting a delicious shock up into his shoulder. He was tempted to lay on a few extra, make a dish of meat-and-bones pudding, but acting with uncommon efficiency and restraint, he tied the guard's hands with his own belt, dragged him to a storage closet off the entrance, stuffed rags in his mouth and took his gun. Praise Jesus, he thought, for creating a terrorist threat and thus inspiring the powers-that-be to arm these fucking gits.

The aquarium, situated just off the lobby, was tarted up to resemble a fish dungeon, a cavern with walls of mossy stone in which the tanks were mounted, eerily illuminated by UV tubes. The place had daunted Ronald as a child, being full of shadowy corners from which he feared some claw-fingered terror might emerge. Now, fresh from conquest, gun in hand, he felt himself to be the terror of the place, the doom of the candy-colored fish floating in their chilly glass houses. He stopped beside a tank along whose bottom a good-sized lobster was crawling. Its mutant look annoyed him. He positioned himself to strike at the glass with the gun butt, prepared to dart out of the way; yet when he delivered the blow, the glass remained intact, yielding a *thunk*. "Fucking hell!" he said in frustration, denied the sight of water chuting forth, bright fish and glass chunks spewing, and the lobster monster scrabbling along the floor, continuing its tedious adventure, unaware of the boot poised above its spiny back. A harder blow achieved no more satisfying result. Determined to give the lobster what-for, he stuck the gun in his waistband and cast about for something heavier.

"Don't you fucking move!" said a reedy voice at his rear.

A security guard stood in a crouch by the entrance to the aquarium, pointing a gun at Ronald, shifting back-and-forth between a one- and two-handed grip, as if uncertain which of his favorite television detectives had demonstrated proper technique. He was young, a few years older than Ronald, with a face round and pale as an onion, and a startlingly red cherubic mouth. His uniform blouse was too small, stretched tightly over the softly disposed bulges of his potato-shaped torso.

"Here now!" he said less authoritatively as Ronald turned to him. "Put that gun on the floor!"

Ronald debated the plusses and minuses of a shoot-out. The guard's aim wavered, his eyes twitched to the side. His bullets probably had better chance of causing attrition among the fish-and-eel population than they did of striking that at which he aimed, yet once again Ronald was governed by restraint. Obeying the guard's instruction, holding the barrel with two fingers, he deposited his gun gently on the floor and kicked it away. It seemed at the same time that he kicked away a sizable portion of his anger. Though he would have enjoyed putting his hands on the guard, the urge was relatively subdued.

A lashing of swagger in his tone, the guard said, "That's the ticket. Keep being a good boy, you might just live to tell."

"You're a right menace, ain'tcha?" Ronald lifted his chin and gave his neck a scratch. "I'd never have suspected it of a mucousy twat like yourself."

The guard's cheeks flushed; he stiffened his gun arm; he bent his knees in imitation, doubtless, of some other prime time hero. "Suppose I do you here and now and save the coppers a bother? What you think about that, son?"

"You've got my full attention," Ronald said. "Wasn't for the piss dribbling down your leg, I'd be in fear for my life."

Movement behind the guard attracted Ronald's eye. A woman, hatchet-faced, wearing red running gear, was sneaking toward them, edging along the wall—she signaled to Ronald, cautioning him not to give away her presence. He forced himself to look at the guard and said, "'Course I may be doing you a disservice. Just 'cause you look like a terwilliger, that don't rule out the possibility you've the soul of Clint Eastwood lodged in your pasty flesh."

Scowling and adjusting his grip as if to imply that he was on the verge of firing, the guard said, "G'wan! Keep it up!"

The woman paused several feet to the guard's rear, adopting what appeared to be a fighter's stance, left leg back, hands up and open, and Ronald wondered why a rich trout like her...and she was rich, all right! She wore no rings, no jewelry of any sort, but he could tell she was the type wiped her arse with tenners. Why would she spring to his assistance?

"All right. Easy now, Clint," Ronald said. "I'm reaching into my pocket. Very slow, okay? If you're able to forestall your murderous impulses, maybe I can do you a favor." He withdrew the disc and offered it to the guard. "See what I got here for you?"

The guard squinted. "What is it?"

"Pardon me!" the woman said and, as the guard swung toward her, she kicked him in the jaw. He came unstrung and collapsed, the back of his head smacking against the floor.

"Oh, yeah! Lovely stuff!" said Ronald. "Fuck, yeah!"

The woman scooped up the guard's gun, an act that thinned Ronald's exuberance.

"What'cha doing?" he asked.

She sideswiped him with a glance that conveyed unmistakable loathing, yet Ronald derived from it as well a sense of community, a feeling that they were somehow aligned—judging by the way she studied him, he had the idea that she might have reached a similar conclusion.

"Something funny's going on here, ain't it?" he said.

This earned him a derisive laugh. She fingered an object out from the breast pocket of her running suit—a crystal disk similar to the one he had found. Spreading his hands to show he presented no danger, he approached and compared her disc to his own.

"They're the same," he said.

"Handsome *and* a genius! Who'd have thought?"

Her face would have scared crows from the corn, but the cow came equipped with a nice pair of Dolly Partons. Watching them strain against the shiny red fabric of her suit, Ronald ignored the insult. "Why'd you help me?" he asked.

The guard stirred, moaned. Ronald moved to him, preparing to give him a kick. The woman said, "Don't! We may need him."

"What the hell for?"

"Just leave him alone."

"Give us a reason, I might."

Throwing up her hands in exasperation, she turned her back to him. "If you must brutalize him...Fine! Satisfy yourself. But do it quietly, won't you! I have to think."

She seemed to tighten in frame, as if he had withdrawn a step or two. His fingers felt numb. In a cold, steady voice, he said, "You fucking cunt. Who do you think you're talking to?"

"Will you please not speak!"

Ronald gave a dry laugh. "I can see you're accustomed to ordering people about. And you've mistaken me for an employee. A servant, perhaps. We need to correct that impression before proceeding further with the relationship."

Every inch of her radiated contempt. She stared into a fish tank wherein rays glided low above a white sandy floor. In the greenish glow of the UV lamp, her features looked sharper and harder. Nice round ass, though. All in all, a juicy little cow once you got past the map of Switzerland on her face.

"Look here," he said. "Let's dial it down, shall we? I realize I'm not part of your usual program, but under the circumstances, we'd both be advised to be forthcoming. Where'd you find that bauble in your pocket? On the beach? It's where I found mine."

She maintained her silent contemplation of the rays.

"Why did you help me?" he asked again. "Was it the sight of my manly figger?"

She put a hand to her brow as if stricken by a headache. The guard produced another moan.

"Goddamn it!" Ronald spun her about—she knocked his arm aside and dropped into her fighting stance.

"No, no, no." He wagged a forefinger. "That kung fu shite may get results when you're dealing with Pig Boy there. Try kicking me in the face, you'll wind up in the tank with your brothers and sisters."

A flutter of uncertainty disturbed her martial focus.

"Don't you doubt it," he said. "I'm a terrible sinner."

Seconds slipped past, and she relaxed by a degree. "I found mine on the beach as well. We're supposed to do something with them...something related to the tower."

"Specifics, please."

She shook her head. "I don't have any."

"I want a straight answer or I'm gone."

"That's all the answer I've got."

The guard had rolled onto his side and was struggling to sit up.

"Keep out of the fray, Clint," Ronald warned him.

The woman made an amused noise. "I thought you were going. Did you change your mind?"

"Oh, I'm going, all right! You watch me." Ronald couldn't get his feet moving.

Her smile was thin and supercilious. "And what is it I should be watching for?"

Ronald commanded his body to carry him away from what was plainly a disaster in the making, but it was if the impulses sent by his brain were being deflected by a barrier south of his neck. Feeling foolish, he shuffled his feet, but went nowhere.

"Can't find the motivation?" the woman asked. "Is that the problem? I imagine that's been a problem most of your life."

"Do you mind? I can do without the bollixing."

"Simply making a point." She pointed to his disc. "These things are controlling us. It sounds mad, I know. But there's no other explanation I can think of."

Ronald examined the disc and was briefly mesmerized by its bright internal flickering. "Weird little dinkus! Is it a machine?"

"It does what it does," she said. "Whatever it is."

The guard managed to sit up. He stared groggily, perhaps at them. Difficult to say, since his eyes were wobbling about. It was plain he posed no threat.

"What should we do, then?" Ronald asked the woman. "Have you worked it out?"

"I was attempting to do precisely that. Since you don't appear equal to the task, perhaps you'll let me get back to it. I don't think we have much time."

"Too right," said the guard sluggishly. "My mates'll be 'round soon enough."

Ronald kicked him in the thigh. The guard cried out, squeezed his eyes shut, and pressed a hand to the injured spot.

"Wanker!" Ronald feigned another kick. "How many mates are we talking about?"

"Five! Jesus, you might have broke my hip!"

"Five including yourself?"

"No, six! Counting me, it's six. That's all, I swear!"

Ronald retrieved his gun. "I'll keep watch," he said to the woman. "Give a shout when you've thought things through."

She appeared disconcerted, as if she found his acceptance of their complicity unnerving.

"Astonishing, ain't it?" said Ronald, and winked. "Dead opposites, us. Napoleon brandy and a pint of bitters. Yet here we are, functioning as a team."

She made a gesture indicating that he should look behind him. A rickety old gent with windblown white hair stood in the doorway, beaming at them, clutching a crystal disc to his chest. "Hello," he said breezily, tripping forward in a manner that brought to Ronald's mind a comedy he'd once watched with his mum—a geriatric priest, his feminine side on full display, had gone poncing along a church aisle to greet a gaggle of dowdy hags in flowered dresses and wide-brimmed hats that each supported a miniature garden of fake flowers.

The old man offered his hand to the woman. "Delighted to meet you! Edward Pinney."

"Jill," the woman said with perplexity.

He aimed his smile at Ronald. "And you are...?"

"Ronald."

Pinney stooped to the guard, introduced himself a third time.

"Martin," the guard said, and winced when Pinney vigorously patted his shoulder.

"Well, then! Perhaps we should be getting along. Time is short!" Pinney glanced at each of them, as if seeking a consensus.

"Go where?" Jill asked.

"Up into the tower! Where else?"

She seemed to be mulling over his response; at length she said, "Where else, indeed."

"Hold on, now." Ronald took a stand between the two of them. "This puff of smoke strolls up and gives us a grin, now we're going to follow wherever he leads?"

"Excuse me," said Pinney sweetly. "Robert, is it?"

"Ronald!"

"Ah, yes. Far be it from me to impose my point of view, Ronald. But I believe if you take a moment's pause to examine what you're feeling...the joy, the anticipation. You'll find your answer there."

"It's not joy what I'm feeling...Edwin, is it? I say we get the fuck out and study on things. Whatever we're supposed to do, it can wait a bit."

"You've already had a go at leaving, haven't you?" said Jill.

In a merry, sing-songy voice, as if he were encouraging a child confronted by a difficult experience, Edward said, "She's right, you know! I'm afraid we've got no choice!"

Angry at them both, angrier yet at the tower, the ultimate source of irritation, Ronald revisited his vision of destruction. The upper levels held a distinct allure for the vandal in him, but the aquarium itself was target-rich, as was the ballroom where geezers like Edward took their spindly, liver-spotted spouses to listen to oldies played on the Wurlitzer and feel a last bit of giddy and tingle. Five floors full of potential damage awaited his pleasure. He had no need to venture into the tower, and the notion that something might be maneuvering him to do so made him skittish. Getting away from the tower and taking stock was the wise move. Any other would be insane. He remembered his model yacht, cursed himself for having left it on the beach. He visualized Delores waking in concupiscent glory, breasts lolling up like seal pups from beneath a grimy sheet, all noddy and eager to play. He had better to do than to hang about and maybe get himself dead with Kung Fu Woman and the Ghost of Christmas Past. Yet the thought of running wouldn't stay in his head.

"Fuck me!" he said.

"There's the lad!" said Pinney.

Jill took Martin's arm, told Ronald to come help, and when Ronald asked what was the point of dragging his fat ass along, she said, "Yes, of course! Let's leave him so he can alert the others."

Together they got Martin to his feet and guided him toward the lift, Pinney preceding them, keeping up a steady chatter about the glorious vantage that would soon be theirs.

"On a clear day," he said, "you'd be able to see a fat lady draining a pint in a Dublin pub! Even on a day like this, you'll have a view of Little Singleton to the west. That by design, I'm told. Sir Joshua Brickstaffe...He was instrumental in developing the tower project, and asked it be built to afford such a view. He'd a mistress in Little Singleton. Used a spyglass to keep watch on the traffic past her house."

Martin slumped, forcing Ronald to tighten his grip and prop him up with a shoulder.

"You seem to know quite a lot about the tower, Mister Pinney," Jill said, her voice exhibiting strain from her share of the burden.

"I was an engineer. Couldn't help but be fascinated by it. By all the towers. They built similar towers, you see, in a number of British coastal towns during the late nineteenth century. Something of a fad, I imagine. The Blackpool Tower became my particular passion. Indeed, it seems I know a few things more than once I did."

"Is that so? These new things, do they...?"

"Perhaps I misspoke. They're not new....not all of them, at any rate. Things I've forgotten, I imagine. Bits and pieces, dribs and drabs. All swirling about in here." Pinney put a forefinger to his temple, not quite touching it, an oddly delicate gesture, as if worried lest a spark jump the gap between the two surfaces. "Perhaps they'll come to something. Form a shape, a pattern. Or they may not be important at all. If they are, we'll know in due course. We're being shown what we need to be shown, don't you think?"

All this in that sing-song delivery—he might have been reciting a verse about bluebells and fairies riding bareback on dragonflies in a mystic grove and what little Tandy did 'pon straying there.

"We should back this down and have us a talk," Ronald said, peering over the top of Martin's head at Jill, still hoping to find an ally in doubt. With his free hand, he waved toward Pinney, who continued his burbling. "We're making a serious error, trusting to this one. He's lost the fucking plot, he has."

Edward, happy though he was, came near to being made unhappy by the lift ride, primarily because Martin, a pleasant enough sort, albeit not much of a talker, vomited all over himself during the ascent, and the others began yelling about the likelihood of a concussion, the need for a hospital, and who was to blame, the ruffian, Ronald, appearing to gain the upper hand in this debate with his insistence that Jill was responsible for injuring Martin's head. For the most part, the logic of their conversation eluded Edward, and its shrill tenor dismayed him. But since each of his emotions was at inception extruded through a virtual film of joy, coated with it, rather like a candy bar on a production line passing through a stream of chocolate, the effects of this negativity were short-lived. Of more lasting difficulty were the tidbits of knowledge relating to the architecture and history of the tower that were beaming into brain like bursts of informative static transmitted by a faulty radio. Number of light bulbs adorning the structure's exterior; percentage of steel replaced during the 1920s reconstruction; names of World War II military staff attached to the tower; lists of materiel; tonnages of concrete, etcetera and so on. There were so many! A shrapnel of factoids, a consciousness-perforating assault that tattered Edward's poise and cored his bliss with unease. He desperately embraced the idea that all would soon be made clear.

With an aerosol hiss, the lift doors slid open, revealing the glass-enclosed portion of the viewing platform, a surround of an overcast sky inland and, to seaward, a darkness of moiling clouds. Ronald sprang out, pointing his weapon in all directions, alert to the potential presence of a guard stationed there — Jill had interrogated Martin in regard to this possibility, but his responses had been sluggish and incoherent. There being no guard in evidence, the two of them locked the doors open and dragged Martin from the lift, leaving him sitting braced and semi-conscious against its outer wall. That done, Ronald went over to the Walk of Faith, a transparent section of the floor that offered a view of a rooftop four hundred feet below, and started jumping up and down on that surface, grinning hugely as if expecting their approval for his show of idiot bravado. Jill stood close to the glass along the east wall and stared off across the roofs and avenues of the town whose grayly orthodox declensions had from that height the aspect of an overcrowded cemetery. Edward, seating himself near Martin so as to engage a southerly view, an arc of sand and sea that blurred into bluish gray at the horizon, felt unduly diminished. Having heeded the unspoken instruction of the joyful current flowing through him, he had ascended the tower and, instead of the cresting emotion he'd been promised, a tide that would free him from his doldrums, he had been rewarded with the answers to a game of Trivial Pursuit. He considered the staircase that led upward to three open-air vantage points above the enclosed portion of the platform. Perhaps, he thought, he was meant to climb higher. But on seeing Jill and Ronald mount the stairs, he was not moved to follow. It appeared he had completed his ascension, although he was certain that the upper reaches of the tower were of significance to them all.

Faith, Edward counseled himself. One must keep the faith.

Confounded by a factual avalanche, a blizzarding of stress factors and volume displacements, old steel-engraved plaques bearing forgotten names, anecdotes involving priapic ironworkers and their hoisted-up-in-a-basket lollies, a grimoire of accidental death and mutilation, speeches given at various openings, reopenings, and consecrations...in a maelstrom of data gone viral, he hewed as best he could to the frail legend of faith. And when it seemed that he might lose his grip, fresh thoughts of Mindy came to steady him, yet these were not sweet thoughts of their time together, but bitterness regarding the earl, bitterness toward all the Tory pricks who cared more about the crispness of their bacon than they did about the tragedies of common folk, and how he wished he could hurt them! He should have done! He should have pounded the earl's skull with a rock until his brains ran out and laughed at the wooden tops when they arrived to cart him off...then a rumor in his mind, a female rumor, not Mindy, but an unfamiliar strain, a whisper of thought suggesting that vengeance was not beyond his reach, calming him with that promise, showing him the mechanisms by which it could be achieved, encouraging him to hang on a little longer. He was too damaged to retain much of what he had been shown, but he took the encouragement to heart, and so, when Ronald, returned from the open-air platform alone, put a hand to Martin's throat and, with unseemly jocularity, said, "I believe this pint of milk's gone bad!", and called out to Jill, still aloft, that she was done for now, it struck Edward as being only another piece of trivia to be taken on faith as an element of a newly comprehended joyful prospect. He failed to grasp a great deal of what was going on around him and inside him, but this much he did understand: Things truly did happen for a reason.

Learning that she had killed the guard was the primary factor in shaping Jill's eventual scheme, but it was prior to hearing this unfortunate news, while gazing at the sea from one of the open-air platforms, that she began to understand what in general needed to be done. Until then, despite her obedience to the impulses she had experienced since finding the crystal disc, she had not accepted that three unrelated people could have stumbled upon three discs and been moved by the mechanisms embedded within those artifacts to ascend the Blackpool Tower, there to perform some obscure duty...a duty that may have been assigned, however improbable it sounded, by Victorian-era Masons a century before. With acceptance no longer at issue, it was as if a mental portal had opened to admit new insights into their situation. The discs, she realized, could not have been cast up by the sea or blown off the tower. It was too random a design for a plan that had required more than a century to mature. They must have been there all the while, in fixed position...which would explain the usefulness of the illusion that had masked them. Who would pick up a jellyfish unless they were compelled to do so? This led her to wonder why the three of them been chosen from among the variety of joggers, strollers, and derelicts available. Pinney's knowledge concerning the tower imbued his selection with some rational basis. But Ronald? Was mere brutishness a qualifier for the task ahead? Perhaps he had already served his purpose by breaking into the building below. And what made her suitable for this great adventure? Leadership, she thought. She must have been chosen for her leadership qualities. Yet while this explanation satisfied on one level, she couldn't help feeling she was missing some more pertinent detail.

An ironwork fence, 12-feet-high and curved inward so as to discourage the suicidally inclined, bounded the open-air platform; an unsteady pour of wind came off the water and, above its rush, Jill could hear the Union Jack snapping far overhead. She pressed her face between the bars, doing toe-raises while she considered the situation. Toning the calves, freeing the mind through repetition. The sea edged the shore like a tattered gray blanket that just failed to cover a tawny sheet, lying rumpled to the horizon, from which dark clouds were towarding. Another storm headed their way. What Pinney had said about the Victorians building towers all along the coast...Might every one of them have had some purpose apart from the cosmetic? The same secret Masonic purpose? Coastal towers were traditionally built to detect danger from the sea, yet she could perceive no imminent threat from that quarter, none that might inspire the urgency she felt. The approaching storm promised a severe blow, but looked to be nothing out of the ordinary. At the left-hand verge of the platform, a stair led upward to a third open-air vantage. It was blocked by a padlocked gate. They were going to have to climb higher — that much she understood — and since the stair was the only path leading in that direction, she thought she might as well investigate it now. She angled the barrel of Martin's gun so that a ricochet would not be a menace, and shot off the lock. Ronald, who had left her minutes before, came vaulting up the stairs from the vantage below. Upon seeing what she had done, he said in a voice brushed with disappointment, "I thought you might've topped yourself off," and vanished down the stairs again.

The third open-air platform was also bounded by an ironwork fence. Unlike the first two, it was roofed by heavy wire netting. Above the wire lay the sixty-foot-high boxy structure of beams and steel plates that surmounted the enclosed portion of the viewing platform. Once the wire had been peeled back sufficiently to allow passage, it would be an easy climb to reach the structure. A minute or two. No more. If she were to slip, her fall would be broken by the wire after few feet. She would need Ronald's help with the wire, and this recognition dismissed the idea, freshly rooted in her mental soil, that it might be best to shoot him before they went any further. Mounted upon the platform were three satellite dishes and a camera bearing the BBC logo angled down toward the town; two more dishes were affixed to the bottom of the steel plating overhead. Jill kept beyond range of the camera, observing its slow repetitive sweep. She had an intimation that it might come in handy, though she could not imagine how.

The wind gusted, making her shiver, and the shiver seemed to dislodge a remnant scrap of doubt. Of the entire event thus far, the involvement of the Masonic Order was the most difficult thing to accept. The Masons she had met were stolid, unimaginative types who used the lodge's reputation for charitable works to color their acquisitive natures with a civic-minded gloss. They wore funny hats and gave puppet shows at children's hospitals. That they were in any wise connected with arcane rites or magical science or the Grail, the stuff of the rumors that had attached to the order since its beginning, was absurd. Of course, the contemporary order might have been cut off from its mystic roots. Hadn't she read somewhere that those in the outer circle were misled as to the deeper purposes of the order? The inner circle might consist of hoary old Merlins whose minds were hives of Byzantine abstraction and plotted the secret history of the word and lit cigars from the phosphor flashes that they conjured by snapping their fingers. Ridiculous. If such a group existed, why would they not themselves handle this piece of business? Why would she, Pinney, and Ronald have been drafted into its service? Easier to believe that the order had decayed (this, the impression she had gained from her researches), its venerable powers forgotten, fallen into disuse, and that the discs were a sort of back-up system employed to handle some emergency. Equally ridiculous, she told herself; yet it fit the facts as she knew them.

When Ronald called out to her, announcing Martin's passing, Jill hurried down the stairs, presuming that he had misconstrued unconsciousness for death; but in this instance his judgment proved unerring. Martin's skin was beginning to grow waxy; his eyes, partly open, were jellied. Understanding how tightly she was boxed in by circumstance caused her a spike of panic. They were bound to be apprehended and, though she might testify that it had been Ronald who killed the guard, if Pinney had been listening to their argument in the lift, he could bear witness to the contrary. As, of course, could Ronald, though his evidence would carry less weight by virtue of his class. Dutiful impulse overwhelmed her panic. First things first, she told herself. Finish whatever task had been assigned and do it right. That, she believed, was key—if she could successfully complete this elusive and nonsensical assignment, a means of evading guilt would fall to hand. Her certainty of this was unshaken by the fact that she perceived no cause for certainty. But one way or another, she could not risk Pinney's testimony. Although his blithe manner had eroded into senile distraction, his condition might improve, and, that being so, her determination having been made, she realized that she would do well to milk him for whatever information he might have. Now. Before the opportunity to kill him arose. Kneeling before him, she said, "Edward? Will you talk to me?"

Pinney muttered something under his breath; his eyes shifted to her.

"Do you recall a connection between Freemasonry and the tower," she asked. "Anything at all."

"Ain't you the cool one!" Ronald said behind her. "If it was me facing life in Bullworth Hall, I wouldn't be wasting my time having a chat with this old poofter."

"What *would* you be doing? Since I have no doubt the police will take you for my accomplice, I suspect the question's relevant."

Ronald's expression was so stunned as to seem comical.

"If you cooperate," Jill went on, "I imagine they might offer the possibility of parole, but..." She clicked her tongue against her teeth. "I assume you have a criminal record. They likely won't be disposed to great leniency."

He started to speak, but Jill drowned him out.

"Your best hope is to work with me," she said. "So you'd do well to let me talk to this man without interruption."

After a pause, grudgingly, he said, "Right. But I'm keeping my eye on you."

Jill addressed herself to Pinney, repeating her question, and repeating it a second time when he was slow to answer.

"Sir Matthew Ridley." Pinney licked his lips spasmodically. "A Thirty-third degree Mason, he was."

"This Ridley had something to do with the tower?"

"Oh, yes...yes. He was one of the movers-and-shakers behind the project." Before Jill could formulate another question, Pinney went on, "The crew Joshua McCauley brought from Rosslyn to reconstruct the tower...they were Masons. As was McCauley himself."

"Rosslyn? In Scotland, you mean?"

"Yes, they...."

"The tower was demolished and then rebuilt by Scotts Masons from Rosslyn?"

"Not demolished. Replaced. They'd never painted it, you understand. The entire structure was corroded and the city fathers made plans to tear it down. Would have been much simpler. But another of your Mason fellows, Michael Bastock, led the charge to preserve the tower and all the steel was replaced over a three-year period. Nineteen-twenty-one to 'twenty-four."

"This may sound odd," Jill said after a pause. "Have you ever heard the Holy Grail mentioned in context of the tower?"

"Yeah," Ronald said. "Superman flew it in from the Fortress of Solitude.

They buried it under the foundation along with the bones of Jack the Ripper. Made a lovely ceremony."

"The cup...yes. The cup's crucial!" Pinney said.

"How is it crucial?" Jill asked.

Agitated, he said, "In the tabernacle above, on the altar. It awaits the stones."

"The stones...You mean the discs?"

He appeared to nod.

"Okay, Edward. I want you to tell me if I'm wrong. The cup is up above us somewhere. In a tabernacle. We're supposed to take the discs to it. Am I right?"

"Yes, I think...yes."

"And how is the cup crucial?"

"It summons and repels. It conjures, it controls. Without it, she would not come; without it, she would not depart."

"Who are you talking about?"

"Diana knew her...knew her well. And perhaps knows her yet, even in the grave."

"Princess Diana?"

"Fucking Christ!" said Ronald.

"Will you shut up!" She shot him a scathing look, then turned again to Pinney. "What are you on about? Who does Diana know?"

"The Melusine."

Ronald snorted laughter and walked away.

"Tell me about the Melusine," Jill said. "What is it?"

His expression lapsed into a pitiable confusion. "She...she..."

"The Melusine is a she? Is that right? And she's the one who's compelled by the Grail."

"The tail," he said. "The heraldic tail is...emblematic of the...conjoining."

"I don't understand! Can..."

Lightning cracked, whitely illuminating the viewing platform, and a deafening peal of thunder followed. In that momentary glare she saw that his eyes were glistening.

"Can you explain more clearly, Edward?" she asked. "Please try!"

"Poor, poor girl!"

Jill's frustration mounted, but she tamped it down and said, "Are you referring to me?"

Edward made a forlorn noise and covered his face with both hands.

"Princess Di? Is she your 'poor girl.'"

He shook his head, but did so with such vigor and for such a long time she could not determine whether he was answering her or merely venting sorrow.

"All right. Go easy. Let's talk about something else, shall we? Why don't you tell me more about the tower? About the tabernacle. Can you tell me what the tabernacle is?"

The subject of the Melusine having been discarded, Pinney grew more fluent in his recital. The names of Freemasons, however casually associated with the tower, came spilling forth, accompanied by quotations that might have been excerpted from bland Masonic texts such as Jill recalled from her research (i.e. "...the Network, by the intimate connection of its several parts, denotes Unity..."). Of the Grail he kept repeating that "the cup" rested in the tabernacle on the altar high above and was awaiting the stones, and, further, that it summoned, repelled, etcetera; in response to an additional question about the Melusine, he mouthed gibberish about a "sacred lineage" and the "conjoining of holy bloodlines," and once again began to lose control, forcing her to turn him onto another track, more dithering about the refurbishing of the tower. After having absorbed as much of this as she could tolerate, half-listening as she might to a television set on in the next room, Jill confronted the problem of how to shift the blame for Martin's death to Ronald. It was essential that she manufacture a reasonable certainty of his guilt prior to their capture and she could think of but one way to achieve that end. Killing him would be less self-punitive than the stratagem she conceived, but she needed Ronald and, too, a second murder might be less persuasive of her innocence than would DNA evidence of rape. If Ronald were dead, although logic might suggest to the police that he was culpable, they might be frustrated by the lack of a live suspect and thus turn upon her a harsher and more demanding scrutiny. If, on the other hand, she was able to cast him as a rapist, his protestations that she had committed the murder would surely be perceived as the desperate manipulations of a guilty man with the IQ of paint. The prospect repelled her, but she had performed equally debasing acts for less of a return. This act, at least, would not take an entire weekend to consummate.

"You look tired, Edward." She put a hand on Pinney's shoulder.

"I am...a little. Yes. Actually, I'm quite tired."

"I have to talk to Ronald now. Why don't you close your eyes? Perhaps you can have a sleep? I'll wake you when we're ready to proceed.'

"This last bit's yours to manage," he said feebly. "I'll not be going higher."

Jill thought to congratulate him on his prescience, but only said, "There's a dear. Go to sleep. We'll have another chat before it's time to go."

Ronald had wandered to the opposite side of the lift and was gazing out to sea. The edge of the storm was lashing up the surf and rain spotted the glass. He waved at the masses of wild dark clouds as Jill came up. "If we're going, we should get on with it." He said this in a fatalistic tone and she wondered how he was coping with being controlled by a force whose effects he could not feel, whether his acceptance of the situation was as complete as her own, or if his stunted intellect prevented him from fully accepting any limitation whatsoever. Probably, she decided, he was used to being controlled by the exigencies of his life, albeit only marginally aware of it, and so had acquired a certain tolerance for the process. The red-eyed monkey tattooed on his neck, entwined in a badly inked spider web: she doubted that the statement it made was the one he'd imagined.

"This will be dangerous, you know," she said.

"Dangerous? Climbing about a steel tower four hundred feet high in the midst of a fucking storm? There's a revelation."

"What I'm attempting to communicate is, we might die."

"That's new for you? Thinking you might die in the pursuit of some ridiculous enterprise?"

"It is, rather."

"Welcome to the working class."

What she intended suddenly seemed inappropriate, and not merely because it would be degrading. She believed that the logical justification of the act was sound. The Blackpool police were more naive than their London cousins—they might think her capable of murder, but she doubted they would accept that she had offered herself to Ronald. Yet having acknowledged Ronald in human terms and, however minimal that consideration, it was more than she had rendered to anyone else in a very long time...Acknowledging him in that way reconnected her to her own humanity and she balked at manipulating him, at debasing herself, even in the interests of her survival. She'd had such moments before and knew her pragmatism would pave over any pothole caused by conscience; but she was seduced by the feeling of connection, by the uncommon sense of inclusion it visited upon her, and she exulted in it for as long as it would last.

The clouds bulled shoreward, shouldering one another aside in their windy haste, massive blackish gray animals without faces, their guts flickering with lightning, and Jill thought she saw—buried deep within them—a shifting, a vast serpentine shape whose slow torsions were responsible for their clumsy roiling, as if it were a spine and the clouds its attached muscles, and thought she heard a thunderous voice, a great maternal voice that made tender, rumbling remarks, instructing her to calm perseverance, and then, thus soothed and assured, she heard herself telling Ronald that she wanted sex before they risked themselves—when he expressed a swaggering, loutish amusement ("You want a shag, do you? So it *was* my manly figger!"), she said it was not him specifically that roused her interest, she was after a technical approximation of sex, a facsimile of passionate involvement, nothing more, and a shag *per se* was out of the question, as this was her time of month. His befuddled expression lapsed when she dropped to her knees, replaced by a buffoonish, gloating look; his hand went to the back of her head. She pushed the hand away and cautioned him not to touch her, not to speak, or else there might be an accident. As she pulled down his briefs, she imagined she heard the thunder's voice muttering advice, suggesting that this might be unnecessary, that Ronald carried within himself the seeds of his own destruction. But better safe than sorry was Jill's judgment, and thus she set herself to endure a voluntary rape, one that would free her as definitively as actual rape had imprisoned her, and, in the service of laboratory analysis, prepared to ruin a perfectly good running suit.

Ripping at the wire that roofed the third open-air platform, with the rain slashing down, the wind moaning through the tower struts, and the intermittent crack of thunder: it altogether made a symphony that restored a violent music to Ronald's soul and allowed him to cast off the shroud of bewilderment that had been muffling his nihilistic energies. His emotions were those of a man swinging a hammer, exultant, pointed toward the abolition of resistance and, while he had no vision of what was to come, he sensed the gathering of a destructive force and knew himself to be at its center. After ten minutes he succeeded in peeling back sufficient of the stiff wire to let him ascend to the base of the boxlike structure atop the viewing platform. Using rivets for finger holds, he scaled the side of a steel plate and straddled its edge, balanced against the wind, looking at the gray, dilapidated, toy-sized city below. It lacked something. A gigantic footprint, maybe. Christ, what a fucking sewer! Had it been a calm day, he would have seized the opportunity to have a piss on Blackpool and, if possible, on the whole of Jolly Old, that Dismal Rock Upon Which The Great Sky Monkey Wiped Its Arse. This godlike view inflated his sense of entitlement and he saw himself as an avenger, less citizen than denizen of the realm he surveyed. His hatred grew to such wide dimension, he wished he could be a bomb, preferably nuclear, capable of self-detonation.

Redirected by a change in the wind, the rain strafed his face. He swung his leg over the edge of the plate and ducked inside the structure. The interior was a maze of criss-crossing iron beams, vertical and perpendicular Xes. Far more than needed for support; so many you could scarcely take two steps in any direction before encountering an obstruction; and there were smaller Xes at the joins, spanning the angles between beams, like decorative touches. Suspended at their center, twenty feet above, fixed in position by a beam that appeared to penetrate one end and exit at the other, was a long coffin-shaped iron box with a considerably smaller box resting atop it; the underside of the larger box extended out into a shelf upon which it might be possible to stand. The design of the place seemed not at all utilitarian, but somehow celebratory, and Ronald was tempted to investigate, wondering what might be inside the boxes; however, the beams leading up to them were narrow and it would be a trick to keep his balance; furthermore, he had to stay put in order to help the trout make the climb. He peered over the side at the camera- and satellite dish-cluttered platform below. No sign of her. Why she'd felt the need to go back down and ask Pinney more questions, he hadn't the slightest. The garbage that old bastard was spewing wouldn't help them, at least not that Ronald could see. He was impatient to get on with things before the cops came swarming. By now, the guards must have discovered that they'd had a break-in; if it weren't for the storm, a helicopter filled with beefy detectives and their pet sniper might be already buzzing about the platform, yearning for fanatic Arabs to pot. And yet Ronald wasn't as worried as he should have been. Most likely, he told himself, the fucking trinket in his pocket was to blame for that. He hadn't been right since he had found the damn thing. Or else it was the trout and her wicked, wicked mouth. Thought she was sly, that one. She'd softened him up proper, but he was onto her. A woman who dropped to her knees without a curse or a beckon was a woman with a plan. He hoped she'd enjoyed that little episode of tug-and-guzzle, because it was all the benefit she'd ever reap from her association with Ronald Bajema.

A deafening crack, and the interior of the structure was lit by a white flash of such intensity that—in reflex—Ronald sank into a crouch. For some minutes thereafter he saw dazzling afterimages and smelled ozone. The sky churned, rushing clouds the color of crematory ash, their surfaces producing bulges that swelled like the muscles of a great snake swallowing. He apprehended their power as being something separate from the storm, as if they were nested inside it, and, though his heart pounded from the fearful shock of the lightning bolt, he was exhilarated, charged with a new strength. Whatever they were being driven to accomplish, the storm was part of it, and he was part of the storm, his anger merging with its anger, his outcry—an outcry drawn from him in sympathy with the storm—blending with the wind and thunder. It seemed it took him longer than usual to stand, his body telescoping upward, becoming a giant's body, rising among the maze of iron beams, inhabiting his rightful place, embracing the towering principle that encaged him and accepting his role as its defender, finally coming into his own.

Standing over Pinney, watching him twitch and mumble, still clutching the crystal disc to his chest, Jill felt a teaspoon of pity. Judging by his long hair, the poor old thing was a relic of the Sixties. Sensory overload and sexual fun. Even today, in her dotage, Jill's mum was still in the habit of lighting up a joint and listening to Procol Harum and the Moody Blues, the lugubrious musical trash she claimed was superior to today's glitzy musical trash. Doubtless Pinney had enjoyed his fair share of those antique pleasures, yet he wasn't having much fun now. She would be doing him a favor, she advised herself, by sparing him the indignities of physical infirmity, cutting him loose from a brain that was deteriorating appreciably from moment to moment. But although she had killed once before in self-defense, that had been an act of passion; this calculated act demanded a sterner commitment and would take more than a simplistic justification to support its essential motive. Either Ronald or Pinney had to die, that was dead clear. She was confident that she could successfully rebut one witness against her, but two...Albeit unreliable, they would confirm each other's testimony. If she were to spare Pinney, she would have to kill Ronald once he outlived his usefulness. That path held a singular advantage—Pinney would be incapable of offering coherent evidence that she had murdered Ronald (she no longer believed he would improve), whereas Ronald, alive, would be vociferous in his contention that she had murdered Pinney. On the other hand, she might not be up to killing Ronald, either because of his physical superiority or a lack of opportunity. Pinney, then, was the logical choice, the opportune choice. The only choice.

"Edward?" She hunkered down next to him. "I'll need your disc."

She had anticipated that he would be reluctant to part with it, but he opened his hand and let her take the disc without complaint. He blinked at her, a meaningless semaphore, then closed his eyes and turned his head to the side. She thought how to proceed. The thunder might be sufficient to drown out a gunshot, but if wasn't... She didn't want to stimulate Ronald. She prodded Pinney's shoulder and asked if there was anything else he could tell her. He opened his eyes, his lips moved soundlessly. He looked and acted years older than he had when he walked into the aquarium. All his color and brightness gone, broken capillaries on his cheeks standing out sharply against the ghastly white of his skin. She wondered if the disc were responsible, if—in using the three of them—it was draining them of energy, and Pinney, being oldest and most unfit, had had less energy to yield. That being the case, she would do well to quit mucking about. She stood and considered how best to dispatch him. She had no desire to cause him pain. He was so frail, one kick should do it, but she felt unsteady, concerned lest she botch the job. Resting her weight on her back foot, she prepared for the strike, and Pinney, his vague manner abruptly dissipated, said, "God! What a lovely face you have!"

Taken aback by the fact that he appeared to have regained his senses, and compelled by the tenor of the comment, which spoke to a central concern, the dissonance between her face and body, Jill relaxed from her stance.

"Lovely enough for a queen," he said.

Irritated, she said, "Don't be silly!"

"You can't see it yet, but you will! I promise you will!" His cheery tone restored, reminding her of a children's show host on BBC radio, he began to dither on about her beauty and bravery.

"Stop it!" she told him.

"No, no! I can see things now," he said, rushing his words. "Things you'll never see. You'll live them, yes, but you won't ever see them plainly like I do. Chances are, you won't recall enough of what's about to happen to make the connections. But you mustn't be afraid! There's no need! She's in your corner, and she'll help you through the change. You can count on her through thick and thin. You and her, you'll do for the pricks like I never could have. Stand firm in the face of fear and everything we've won will come to you. And we have won, you know. Yes, there's more to do! But we've done the hardest mile already. We've understood what needs to be accomplished. All that's left is for you to hold firm. After that..." His eyelids drooped as if he were experiencing an ecstatic peak. "Oh, the conquests that will be yours! There will be perils. Great perils. But men will look beneath your beauty to the heroic mask that provoked it and how they will be bedizened!"

"Damn you! Stop!" Jill wheeled about, not wanting to look at him, infuriated by her perception that he was mocking her, that the narrowing of some cerebral vessel had tweaked his brain chemistry in such a way, it permitted him to glimpse her insecurities and was squeezing from him these hurtful words.

"This is the transcendent moment of my life," Pinney went on. "To know you. To have this brief sight of you. To realize I've played a part in your ascension. Everything that's gone before, all the rant and scatter of my life, it was nothing. Like some old tin cans and a worn scrap of blanket ready to be tossed in the litter. But this... you..."

Jill shrieked at him wordlessly, but the piercing alarm of her cry fazed Pinney not in the least, and, in the instant before she launched her kick, an athletic movement that in its perfect balance and powerful delivery and mortal accuracy was identical in every respect to a kick she had delivered that long-ago night beneath the pier, when Gerald Clote, on his knees in the wet sand, holding his groin, had stared up at her with mute surprise and dismay...in that moment, fitting the words so precisely into that brief term, he spoke the last syllable of his declaration just as Jill's heel smashed into his temple, a blow from which he did not flinch, Pinney said sweetly, blissfully, "You've given it all meaning. You've brought me joy."

Standing beneath the coffin-shaped box, watching the trout maneuver along a cross-beam toward it, the three discs stuffed into her pockets, her figure illuminated by flickers of lightning, Ronald found himself once again admiring her tits and ass...though his admiration was not of such unalloyed prurience as it had previously been. Perhaps because the grandeur of the storm had orchestrated and refined his emotions, his view of her acquired the passion of a proletarian aesthete. Against the backdrop of enormous iron Xes, she looked like a performer in a mad heavy metal circus, engaged upon a mystical acrobatic errand. And neither was his admiration limited to the physical. He had come as well to admire aspects of her personality. Her coolness under fire, for one. Her cleverness, for another. He'd seen through her attempts to manipulate him, but acknowledged that this was an abnormal situation; he suspected that she was capable of greater subtlety. If things went well, and he had the sense that they would, it might be profitable to nourish their relationship. Not its sexual component, however. He wouldn't sneer at a tour of her soft bits if the offer were to be forthcoming, but he preferred partners of a more docile temperament and it was a commercial relationship he had in mind to explore. The idea of a connection between the street and the corridors of power posed intriguing possibilities.

A prodigious peal of thunder, and she wobbled on the beam. Ronald thought she might fall, but she caught herself and stood stockstill. Several seconds passed, then she fished the dead guard's pistol from her waistband and called out, "Here! Catch this!"

"I told you, you should leave it!" he shouted.

She released the gun and Ronald, gauging its speed incorrectly, succeeded in breaking its fall, but not in catching it. "Bollocks!" he said, kicking the gun aside in frustration. Idiot bitch! Trying to walk a fucking tightrope with a metal cock stuck up her drawers! She shouted something else—not, he imagined, a pleasantry—that was carried away by the wind and then continued along the beam. Once she reached the box and was standing on the lip that extended from its bottom, he called to her, asking what was up. She made no response, bending to the box, appearing to study its upper surface.

"Piss on you, then!" he said, but not so she could hear, having learned the value of letting her think.

He braced against a beam, standing legs crossed, arms folded, throwing an eye toward Jill every so often, but his attention mainly given to the storm. Dark as half-night, it was, and the clouds out to sea were darker yet. Slate gray with inky hearts. The wind came cold, moaning through the tower like the music drowned men hear, the warped, dolorous songs of old ghost whales punctuated by the booming of remembered cannons, the crack of foundering hulls. Lightning stitched the bellies of the clouds, bringing to sight the ugly specifics of their moiling as they tumbled landward, and Ronald, mesmerized by this bleak, confused majesty, dropped out of the moment and thought of his fifteen-hundred-pound investment, by now stolen or washed out to sea. He pictured the little ship sailing off on a rip tide, heading for the Irish coast, where it would be spotted among the rocks by some feckless 12-year-old scrote who would delight in it for a day, then trade it for a handful of pills that would make Ireland go away. He thought, too, of Delores, pacing the apartment, cursing him for his waywardness, becoming bored.

Suppose he didn't come back, suppose after this little adventure he went on the run and left her to stew. How long would it take for boredom to overcome her fear of reprisals and drive her out into the pubs, searching for a remedy? Three or four days, he figured. A week at most. She wasn't much for the long view. Not like the trout, there. No, the trout would weigh the issue many times over and exercise extreme caution. Of course, on Delores' side of the ledger, whenever she gave him a ride, he could be fairly certain that's what it was...a ride, not an element of her master plan. An old-fashioned girl in her nastily modern way, Delores. Butter her cake and put sugar in her tea, she'd add a smile to your life. That was the contract. The clouds caught his eye again. Weird, how they were pushing in directly at the tower, so low and fast it seemed that in a minute or two, he'd be among them. That would be cozy! Trapped in a steel cage; blind and swaddled in fog; with lightning playing Frankenstein-style over the the struts. What were the odds that him and the trout could avoid being fried? Probably not a winning number, but there was no use in worrying at this stage.

The edges of the clouds...Cloud, actually. It was a single bulky grayness, the edges of which appeared to be circulating in a curious manner, like a digital crawl around the outside of a building, an enclosing band, and, as it pushed nearer, he saw a yellow glow within. He had a glance up at the trout. She was doing something with the small box that sat atop the coffin-shaped one. Best not to disturb. But as the cloud closed down around the tower, encircling it, nary a shred of its substance penetrating the struts and beams, Ronald became more than a little anxious. This was no ordinary cloud, he told himself. It was a mutant cloud, a cloud such as might surround a spaceship, a cloud of mystical radiation that commonly heralded the manifestation of a movie god, only less glorious and markedly more menacing, a ton of dirty sludge avalanching toward them, a mass of grungy tissue flexing its muscles, constrained by that strangely circulating edge— and yet like those cinematic clouds, those time-lapsed roilings that typically surround super science mysteries and were, he now recognized, nothing like the real thing, the authentic model from which their images had been derived, it was a cloud's cloud, a cloud with style and personality, a cloud with a fucking purpose.

"Oy! Jill!" he shouted, his voice swallowed by the roar of the wind.

She remained hunched over the boxes.

Ronald aimed his pistol at the cloud, trying to track the gauzy yellow light that alternately appeared and vanished in its depths (or perhaps it was many lights, for it never materialized in the same general area). Where else shoot a cloud except in its golden eye? He fired a round into the toiling mass and, though it had no visible effect, the sound of the discharge suffering the same fate as his shout, it served to boost his spirits. He had a comic book flash and saw himself in dramatic frame, dwarfed by the iron intricacy around him, his heroic shadow thrown by lightning strikes, a muscular, tattooed baldy doing battle with the Cloud Beast, firing bullet after bullet into its flabby guts, seconds prior to receiving the wound that would infect him with unique superpowers and transform him into the Blackpool Giant.

The upper surface of the large iron box was inscribed with what Jill took to be Freemason symbols, dozens of them; on the sides and top of the smaller box, itself roughly the shape and about twice the size of a gift box containing a bottle of spirits, were three shallow circular depressions, each with a raised figure (half snake, half woman) at its center that looked as if it would fit nicely into the figures cut in the faces of the three discs. The box was welded shut. There was neither door nor handle, no suggestion that it could be opened; yet when she slotted the discs into place, she expected it to spring open and reveal the Grail. After listening to Pinney's drivel, despite her cynicism, she had carried away an image of herself holding the Grail high, defying some vile black shape by dint of its holy virtue. She ran a hand over the box and thought she detected a vibration within, but amid the fury of the storm and the stronger vibrations it stirred from the tower, she couldn't be certain. Was that the sum of it? Surely not. It made no sense that after all this rigmarole; their sole function had been to transport the discs to this iron box. Although the notion that Ronald could be right about anything seemed absurd, she thought now that perhaps he had been right—they should have paused to take stock of the situation.

She re-examined the box, seeking some clue as to what she should do next. With the discs in place, it was all but impossible to tell that the circular depressions had existed—they fit that neatly, faces inward, their iron bases an exact color match to that of the box. The symbols inscribed on the surface of the larger box drew her attention again. She bent down to inspect them, bracing both hands on the box. Though she had assumed they were Freemason symbols, she recognized none of them, and now, on second glance, they more closely resembled ideoforms, characters in the alphabet of an early language such as Sanskrit. Yet she supposed they might be related to Freemasonry. Her knowledge of the organization and its arcana was sketchy at best.

Movement at the periphery of her vision.

The three discs she had fitted to the smaller box were slowly— ominously, it seemed to Jill—revolving. It was such an uncanny thing to see, she was hypnotized by their fluid revolutions. On recovering her wits, she edged away along the lip, worried that she might have activated an explosive device, and discovered that her hands were stuck to the surface of the larger box. Panicked, she tried to wrench them free, but only succeeded in hurting her wrists. She screamed for Ronald, adding a piping note to the wind's howl, and twisted her head about, searching for him. He was nowhere in view. As the discs revolved, pinholes appeared in them, singly at first, then in great number, and from each of them issued golden light...or perhaps it wasn't true light, perhaps it was a radiant semi-solid of some kind, for it did not beam forth, but rather trickled outward like glowing smoke released into untroubled air, thousands of needle-thin columns that entwined and gathered and eventually bloomed into a golden volume that encompassed the boxes and the platform whereon she stood, its shape steadying around her, unaffected by the wind. She tried more fiercely to free herself and found that her hands were not stuck, but embedded an inch deep in the surface of the larger box, as if the iron had melted inward and sealed about her flesh. She managed an approximation of calm, seeking to attack the problem with logic, and was punished for this act of self-control by an awareness that her mind, too, had been captured by the golden light, by this production of an eccentric Victorian science, the union of a cup—an antique chalice steeped in the energies of a Hebrew magus—and scraps of alchemy, secrets passed down through the generations and guarded by the order, a knowledge that streamed into her brain accompanied by a multitude of equally foreign principles and truths and threads of history. One such thread impressed itself upon her...

...A desert place, a romance between a witch of common blood and a prince to whom, due to the difference in their stations, she was unsuitable as a bride. Betrayal, despair, and a vengeful female magic that delivered a painful death to the unfaithful prince and inadvertently transformed its mistress into a demon, a remnant sliver of her soul, most of it consumed by the creation of evil, now housed in the flesh of a dread creature of the air, who practiced her particular malice whenever opportunity arose...

...Blind to everything but the golden light, almost insensate, her intimate barriers overthrown, Jill had no will to resist the streams of imagery and emotional detail in which the narrative was couched, like unfamiliar memories colonizing the ground of her thought...

...A crusader knight with magic of his own came to the desert and warred against that ill-begotten spirit, a contest that achieved no clear cut resolution, yet left the knight depleted, and when he fled back to his green and pleasant land, bearing the cup in which the original magic had been

brewed, the demon followed and the war went on, the knight's descendants defending their shores with spells that kept the demon, whom they named the Melusine, at bay...

...Memories, Jill reckoned, might not be the correct word for the elements of this historical revelation. Except for a handful of fragments, the knowledge flooding her mind seemed to wash beyond the place of memory, receding from her consciousness and filling a reservoir into which she could not see, merging there with some fundamental darkness...

In time, the Melusine, afflicted by her exile, cut off from the nourishing heat and apocalyptic emptiness of the desert, grew mortally enfeebled and erratic, uncertain why she had abandoned her home, now all but forgotten, and come to this watery waste. The spells, too, weakened, as did the men and women who wove them. Over the centuries, the process of the war degraded into a desultory struggle between a demon who wandered aimless and dying above the Irish Sea, spending her powers in stormy tantrums, infrequently remembering the deep reason for her spite, then launching a foray against the hated coast, and a handful of old men unable to fathom the actions they performed, yet continuing to perform them, albeit less for duty's sake than for personal gain...

...She could not feel her body, handicapped by a tactile blindness as well as a literal one, yet Jill nonetheless had a sense of something huge snuffling around her, windy breath puffing from its nostrils...

With that perversion of duty, the devices and stratagems of the order had also been perverted, and their purpose, diluted by empty ritual and abracadabra, no longer served them, but had been turned to the purposes of the Melusine...

...sniffing at her, coiling around her so as to know her shape, tasting her with its flickering tongues...

...Thus their towers, their precious cup, their machines and mechanistic magic had, thanks to their ineptitude, been wrongly used, contriving not a defense against the Melusine, but a lure, a beacon, and, most significantly...

...judging the chemical subtleties of her taste to be suitable, but her shape imperfect, though that could be remedied. All in all, a better fit than that blonde simpering dishrag the order had flung at her the last time...

....an instrumentality that charged and revitalized the Melusine, causing her to reclaim her memories, to understand that what had been

offered here was not a trap in which she would expire, but a means of entry into realms forbidden her these long years...

...that pudding of a princess whom she had flung back at them and—by that rejection—influenced them to murder, though they'd nearly bungled the task, just as the princess had bungled her end, unable to exact a proper vengeance upon that dismal, pompous, tweedy prat, blood descendant of the knight, spiritual descendant of her own charmless prince...

...the realms of the senses, of the flesh...

...But this one, this rigid, violent, dark-haired bitch, though not wholly suitable, would suffice...

...of sweet breath and gentle touch, of burning need and the joys of satiety...

...her blood suitable to conjoin with a more protean chemistry, her station suitable to be a royal bride, her ruthlessness suitable to partner with greater ruthlessness, her body a more suitable weapon for contemporary war than was this more powerful yet dying body from which she must now separate, though not abandon...

...of England...

Ronald wished he'd known dying would be this much fun. If he had, he would have dragged that BBC camera up from the viewing platform so it could record his fate for the benefit of his mates, Roger and Arthur. He imagined them watching replays in the pub, remembering the row they'd had about death. How would you want to die? That was the question they'd debated over whiskey and lager one night. Roger said he would prefer to take his departure while shagging Angelina Jolie. Before or after you come? Arthur asked and, after a second's deliberation, Roger said, Right when, if you please, and they'd had a laugh at that and argued over whether Ms. Jolie would be preferable to Ms. Brittany Spears as an agent of the Grim Reaper. She's a cheap tart! Ronald said of Ms. Spears, and Arthur said, Right! And Angelina Jolie, what's she, then? Arthur's choice of exit was to go out in his sleep and, hearing this, Ronald said, You're cunts, the both of you! It's a blaze of glory for me. And when they laughed at him, well...under no circumstance did Ronald enjoy being derided. He stood up from his stool and said, Two of you don't want to know what's coming. That's why you're cunts. Me, if I see Godzilla stepping along the lane, smashing lorries with his tail and knocking buildings asunder, I'm walking straight up and taking a piss on him before he stomps me skinny. Roger said, Fuck off! Pissing yourself's what you'd be doing. And Ronald, giving him a shove with his elbow, said, You see, live or die, I don't care one way or the fucking other. That's the difference between us. That's what makes me free and what makes you a cunt! You'll be sucking your thumb and cuddling your nads when the devil collects your pimply arse. Roger removed a pistol from his jacket and said in a tone of cool menace, Since you don't care and all, suppose I just top you off this minute? Ronald chested the muzzle of the pistol, pushing at Roger, and said, Fuck you, you fucking vagina! I'm standing here telling you I don't fucking care! Voices of reason intervened, rough hands forced them apart, and, following an interval of stiff necks and injured feelings, the evening resumed. Yet there was a moment when blood was near. Roger was mad as a match and a can of petrol, death was a blank premise in his eyes, and Ronald thought he had pushed too far and felt a spot of cold fear behind his lungs. He had doubted himself, thinking he might not be so uncaring as he presumed. However, he doubted himself no longer.

Having emptied his pistol at the cloud, at the beast inside it (though no Godzilla, it was a nasty piece of business, nothing you'd want flying around your tower), Ronald expected it would have done with him and stood waiting to be eaten, torn apart or burned to a crisp—he assumed his fate would be brutal, yet could not be certain of its exact nature, because he never achieved a clear sight of the thing, every so often glimpsing an area of scaly skin, a pupil-less golden eye, the remainder of its body concealed by that confining cloud. When death failed to manifest, with the wind full-throated (and was that a savage, animal roaring he heard beneath the wind's roar, as of some mad imprisoned creature?) and the trout enveloped in bowl of golden flame, with crossed iron beams behind her and above, the whole reminiscent of a frame from one of the old *Conan* or *Dr. Strange* books that he kept in plastic covers, the priestess of Zabir'Nha communing with her god on the heights of a primitive futuristic temple...with all that lurid glory to consider, Ronald had no thought of running. He was transfixed, gleeful. Why do you call them "shite," he'd once asked Delores after she's teased him about his stacks of comics. Because when I walk out to do the laundry or pick up something at the market, I rarely happen to see a great bloody pyramid rising from the ruins of Blackpool, with alien spaceships circling 'round, she said, and Ronald replied, Well, maybe you ain't looked close! Maybe you haven't noticed what's going on behind the scenes, as it were! Maybe there's alien ships dashing hither and thither all the time, and you don't fucking know it! He'd been on the defensive, not really advancing a thesis concerning the complexity of reality, but he had been right. He'd suspected that there was more to life than met the eye, and here lay proof positive. It was amazing, even to him. It was astonishing, flabbergasting, and fucking mind-boggling. He had been right about everything.

The light around the trout grew murky. Strands of cloud were being drawn forth from the turbulent mass that encircled the tower, muddying the golden air, weaving a cocoon about her, and, as it thickened, gradually hiding her from view, the scaly patches and intimations of eyes that Ronald had observed within the cloud proper became visible beneath the surface of the cocoon, as if the beast had shrunk itself and was coiling around her. And once she had been completely obscured by a whirling gray spindle, then the cocoon, the golden light, the strands of cloud twisting within the light — it all vanished.

In an instant, the blink of an eye.

Gone.

Not dissipated, however. Not dispersed. He couldn't be sure, it had happened so swiftly, but he was of the distinct impression that it had been sucked inside her.

The tower height seemed a dim, dirty, and forsaken place by contrast to the radiant strangeness of a few seconds past, and, though Ronald had been entranced by the build-up to this event, he was sorely disappointed by its climax. It had happened too quickly. He wanted the movie to continue, he wanted to see it again. He wanted something more. More light, maybe an explosion or two, a burst of infernal energy from which there would emerge a crimson-skinned Satan flourishing a scimitar or a serene ivory-hued goddess naked but for a diadem of fire, her Miss Galaxy breasts tipped with tiny blue skulls that spoke riddles in trebly voices, and showing her filed teeth in a gloating smile.

The trout knees buckled and, making no attempt to right herself, fell, landing face-down on the roof of the platform with a thump so heavy,

Ronald heard it above the wind. Something of a comic afterthought, it seemed. Like a scene in a cartoon wherein a single bottle is left wobbling on a partially collapsed shelf and, after a second or two, it clunks down onto the head of the woozy fellow whose pratfall broke the shelf. He went toward her, thinking he should check her pulse, knowing this to be a formality—she'd be lights-out and halfway to Limbo by now. Then an arm twitched, a leg shifted. She lifted her head, heaved up to all-fours and looked at him. Nose smashed flat. One eye filled with blood; a cheekbone caved. Mouth a gash. A corpse by Pablo fucking Picasso, from his clown period, done all in red and white. And yet she got to her feet. On an aesthetic level, Ronald was pleased by the trout's improbable revival, but expiring in the grip of a mangled and possibly undead woman, one who exhibited unnatural strength, appealed less to his practical side than did a swift evisceration by an occult beast. He took a step backward. She swayed, gathered herself and started toward him; but instead of seizing him and tearing at him with her zombie mouth, she walked straight past, heading for the steel plates that fenced the platform roof. She must be alive, he decided. Out on her feet, obeying her instincts, going for medical assistance. He went after her, intending to help, but she made a pushing gesture with both hands—he took it for a signal that he should stay where he was. Confused, he watched her straddle the plating. She paused, her figure startlingly solid by contrast to the tumbling cloud against which she was superimposed, and performed a more complicated gesture from which he derived no meaning whatsoever. A sequence of graceful motions like those ornate Arab salutations offered to the highly respected, yet also reminiscent of a conductor's emphatic direction while guiding musicians through a treacherous stretch of Mozart, finishing with her arms outflung, a summoning pose that inspired Ronald to wonder whether she had orchestrated the sharp intensification of the wind that followed hard upon it. Then she lowered herself over the side of the steel plate, passing from view.

Ronald had precious little time for thought after that, no time even to doubt what was happening to him, and what thought he did manage was basic, the registering of urges and comprehensions. The cloud bulged inward, pushing toward him, squeezing through apertures between struts and beams like filthy cotton wadding, the ectoplasmic body of a great ghost that muttered thunderously, folding around him, immersing him in a warm, muffling thickness. He flailed his arms, panicked, yet in no real distress, and as the warmth pervaded him, dissolute warmth into which he seemed to melt, a process that involved an ample portion of pain, he realized he was not dying—the cloud was taking him unto itself, replacing the animating principle that had abandoned it with *his* principle, *his* force. There were further comprehensions and a short-lived flux of color and shape that might have been a rush of memory, but these he disregarded. The most important thing, the thing he cleaved to as he was stirred into the cloud, swirled through it like cream into tea, was the idea that he would continue and that he possessed the power to satisfy his every urge. Raw power was the medium into which he was being stirred. Yet as his dissolution progressed, as Ronald the man, the myth of self, dwindled to a curl of flavor and form in the vast unflavored formlessness of the cloud, his thoughts grew sluggish and few, and he found it impossible to hang onto all of his urges, a winnowing that reduced an interminable list of ill-wishes to two: the desire to destroy the iron cage that bound him and to locate a ship stolen from him, he believed, by an Irishman...though he could not have said with any certainty how this theft occurred or even how he knew it. No matter. Two granted wishes were likely more than he was due. He discovered that he could move again, that movement was no longer limited by the proscriptions of muscle and bone. He felt he if were to stand up, he would rise forever. He could go anywhere and do anything. The joy that accompanied this final comprehension overwhelmed all other concerns. He was ready to go boiling across the sky, soaring above fate, free to indulge the least whim that sprang to mind. And had he been more generous in his hatred, his fury less defined by the minute portion of humanity that survived enclouded. Who can say what calamities he might have engineered?

Those Blackpudlians who dared walk out in the storm that morning had not been looking at the tower when it exploded, but had been going with their heads down, shielded by umbrellas; a few dozen people, however, were gazing from hotel room and office windows, and many of them claimed that the cloud occluding the upper reaches of the tower had, at the moment of the explosion, appeared to acquire the shape of an enormous man —"man" was the word used by most, though half-a-dozen said "figure" and two chose "giant." They further claimed they had seen no sign of a fireball. Their reports were discounted for no other reason than that they could not be explained, as was the report that the storm, following the explosion, had veered abruptly off toward Ireland—yet another exporting of British violence to that oft-violated shore—where it savaged the coast, raging up and down it for a week before decaying into intemperate breezes and glum skies, obeying no known weather pattern. Mysteries abounded, but as often happens with mysteries, they faded from the public mind, which for some time thereafter was dominated by a more compelling image: Jill's bloody, broken face staring into the BBC camera on the upper viewing platform, begging silently for help.

That face, in alliance with proclamations of Jill's heroism, could be seen everywhere in the press and on television. The fact that neither of the two men (Edward Pinney and Martin Shay) whom she dragged from the tower had survived did not diminish her heroic cachet. As disoriented as she must have been with pain and shock resulting from her rape and beating at the hands of the terrorist, Ronald Bajema, she'd no way of knowing that both men were likely dead when she hauled them into the lift. Her effort was supremely heroic, everyone agreed. Medals and certificates of honor were readied for presentation, and when it was learned that Jill's bloodline was tributary to that of Saint Diana, still greater honors were discussed, and the royals, who were going through a bad patch, thanks mainly to Prince William's recent scandalous behavior, moved quickly to co-opt her heroic glow, sending the prince to visit her in hospital, where, it was said, he lingered long at her bedside.

The presentations had to be set aside, of course, awaiting that far-off day when Jill's surgeries and recuperation were done, and the media's attention turned to the destruction caused by the explosion and to the man who triggered it. The bulk of the tower had collapsed onto the beach, crushing the Central Pier, but the viewing platform and everything above it had been blown to pieces and flung inland, damaging buildings along the Promenade, killing forty-one people. Bajema's body could not be found, nor could the least evidence relating to the nature of the explosive device that, according to Jill, he had carried. Absent a villain, the police focused their investigation upon Bajema's associates; while they uncovered no terrorist plots, they did succeed in doing tremendous harm to Blackpool's criminal organizations. Bajema, it was concluded, had been a madman acting alone. His name was coming to occupy a pantheon inhabited by a special few, notably Jack the Ripper, and his legend was enlarged in countless interviews with his former lover, Delores DeNovo. She testified to his ravings, his vile use of women, painting herself as victim, and gained sufficient celebrity to attract the lustful eye of a pop star, whose child she later bore, thereafter living quite handsomely on a settlement.

The story dwindled to the occasional mention in the media and then, sixteen months after her ordeal, Jill emerged from her final bandages, displaying to the nation the face of an angel. The surgeons, who had been modestly hopeful in their prognoses, were amazed by the result. The tabloids dubbed her "England's New Rose." A television pundit enthused, "It's as though she is wearing the face of her deeds, not that of her birth," an opinion that was embraced by a mass audience of feeble-minded shopkeepers and housewives, royal-worshipping twits so desperate for evidence of God's blessing upon England and their own petty stake in the country, they were eager to accord Jill's transformation a miraculous weight, to view it as a heavenly reward. Their faith was given force when the conspirators in the murder of Princess Diana, including several fringe royals and members of the London lodge of the Freemasons, were brought before the bar. Coincidence? asked the tabloids. That the killers of England's Rose should be nabbed just at a time when the New Rose appears? I should think not! cried a demented populace. One tabloid floated the supposition that Jill had died in the tower and her body had been possessed by Diana's spirit, proposing as well that she had provided information leading to the arrests, a claim that hit closer to the mark than its editors knew. And when several of the conspirators accused Jill of being complicit in the crime, supporting their accusation with a tale that, so said the *Times*, deserved, at the least, to be "short-listed for the Booker Prize", the magical materials of that tale, though believed by no one, added to her mystic luster.

As for Jill herself, she returned to her corner office, letting it serve as a fortress against the brilliant light of publicity. There she learned that the men once enlivened by the plainness of her face were even more excited by the bloody mask they now saw beneath her sculpted features. But she had no interest in proceeding with her career. Great opportunities were opening to her and the office environment allowed her time to get her bearings. To say that she had scant recall of what had happened in the tower was not quite true. Her memories of the incident were fragmentary, to be sure, but she had an apprehension that she had been changed by it in some fundamental way. One indication of change made itself known on her first post-tower visit to her gym. She had done her best to maintain muscle tone while in hospital, yet she was nowhere near as fit as she'd been prior to the explosion. Nonetheless, she did fifty-four chin-ups and could have done more, breaking off the exercise upon noticing that her performance was attracting attention. Long before her workout, however, she recognized the change. When the police came to the hospital to question her, the disjointed story she told, focusing all guilt on Ronald, was more cleverly articulated than she should have been able to manage, given her disoriented state. And then there were the crumbs of memory, of information, that seemed to have been dropped by someone who had taken a stroll through her brain while eating a sandwich. Included among them were the names of eleven men that, acting on a powerful compulsion, she had communicated by anonymous means to the press, along with the suggestion of their connections to Diana's death. That her action had borne fruit implied that the other crumbs might someday be of value. Despite these inexplicable memories, despite everything she had endured, Jill was remarkably centered, eager to get on with life, yet no longer frantic in the pursuit of goals. She held firm to the conviction that an opportunity suitable to her needs would come to her. It was inevitability. That, too, seemed part of the change. That assurance, that self-confidence. Although she entertained moments of doubt, that portion of her being was unassailable. No matter how hard she tried to unearth some hint of weakness or overcompensation, it resisted her, and, one morning, a Thursday morning in the dead of winter, shortly after she had returned to work, a man wearing a dark blue suit of expensive cut entered her office, bringing proof that her conviction had been justified.

Except for his suit, the man, Paul Osteen, was unprepossessing. Short and thickish; in his thirties; his blond hairline receding from a doughy, small-featured face. He maintained such an erect bearing, Jill suspected on first glimpse that he was in service. The envelope he handed her contained a note handwritten on heavy vellum that began, "My Dear Cousin..." and was signed, "...W.O.W," the initials standing for William of Wales. Between salutation and signature were a few chatty lines and an invitation to meet the prince at his retreat in Switzerland two weeks hence for the purpose of getting to know each other and for further purposes that he would there disclose. Then these lines:

"I must apologize for seeming mysterious, but things being as they are with the media, I am compelled to caution. Hopefully what I say now will soothe your curiosity. I can imagine the several thoughts that may have come into your mind on reading this. Allow me to suggest that they all likely have some basis in fact. I look forward to seeing you again..."

The thoughts that came into Jill's mind were not several, but many and various. Firstly, she recalled William's eyes drifting on occasion to her breasts as she lay in her hospital bed. Her face having been bandaged, he may have felt embarrassed to look at her directly; but she could not discount the fact that he had chosen her breasts for an alternative. Given the anti-royal sentiment that now flourished in the country, a sentiment that her advent on the public stage had to some degree assuaged, might it be the case that the Windsor's doddering political sensibilities had been engaged and that they saw her in an opportunity to make a popular marriage for their randy prince, giving the proles a further rosy myth to cherish. Once safely and suitably married to England's New Rose, William would then be able—as had his father before him—to pursue more diverse pleasures without drawing unfavorable notice. This snowy getaway, then, was a test of her suitability. And if that were not the case, if his purpose was nothing more than a bout of Oedipally-inflected mattress-thumping (Jill had the impression that he was in every way a mummy's boy and that her status as an older woman and New Rose were significant attractors), it nevertheless suited her purpose, a purpose that crystallized as she read the note and was embedded in a flash of venomous satisfaction, an appreciation of glorious success after a myriad failures. Such emotional lightnings were, her therapist advised, typical of head trauma victims and, though she did not completely accept his explanation, she was accustomed to dealing with them as such. Whatever its cause, she was influenced by the force of her emotion to respond favorably to the invitation and, intending to do so, reached for her note pad.

Paul Osteen harrumphed. "Excuse me, Ma'am. We would prefer that you write your reply on the note itself."

We, thought Jill. So we are "we," are we? And we want no evidence.

"Of course," she said.

Discarding a number of potential responses as too florid, too eager, too formal, too something, she wrote a single word, yes, by this conveying a decisive nature and a minimal measure of mystery to match the prince's own. Osteen replaced the note in its envelope and indicated that "we" would be in touch.

Once he had gone, Jill felt much as she might after having consumed too heavy a lunch, afflicted by a sluggishness that, in this instance, was characterized by an unsettling sensation. It was as if her mind were being idly stirred, as if her skull were a fish tank in which an eel was lazily circulating, its passage causing normally unseen bits to float up from the bottom. Finally, she thought with amusement. A prince. This snatch of self-conversation roused a not-so-violent and thus more articulated incidence of the venom she had experienced on reading the note. Discomforted, she got up from her chair, hoping that an hour or two spent shopping would revitalize her. She did need, after all, need some alpine gear. And, indeed, as she put on her coat, collected her purse and strode toward the lift, her mind cleared; but it was not altogether clear. She jabbed the lobby button, jabbing it many times over and with unnecessary vigor. Disassociate thoughts clamored to be recognized. She sought to ignore them, but a handful of the more vicious stuck in her head. So Prince Willy wanted a fuck, did he? Well, she'd give him one to remember. She'd been saving it up for years. Years of howling, solitary midnights. Damn it! Where was the lift? She jabbed the button again and again, until her finger grew sore. Pale custard people with flimsy little souls. Victims begging for a fatal bite. Out of the fire, into the flame. England might be safe from storms, yet not from her.

THE MUD FORK COTTONMOUTH EXPEDITION

ERIC M. WITCHEY

I headed over to Steve Carson's house looking for someone to go hunt snakes with. Steve was better for baseball and swimming and war, but in a pinch he'd do for snake hunting. Really, the best kid in the neighborhood for snakes was Jon-Jon. He had the ear and the eye for it, and he knew how to sit still—really still like a rock, like a rock that was there in the grass so long that all the mice and frogs and spiders and snakes around us would come up to him and sniff him or climb under his shoe to hide.

Of course, he was a littlest kid. He was seven, and I was eleven. I wasn't a big kid, but I wasn't a littlest kid. Steve was ten. Besides, Jon-Jon was across town at day camp.

So, I headed for Steve's, and he was gone too. Mrs. Carson was there, and she knew I still remembered that she had my favorite tree killed to build their house. I don't think she ever liked me any more than I liked her. But maybe on that day she felt really sorry for me because she came to the door and found me playing a jumping game in her carport by myself.

I tossed a pebble up to the ceiling of the car port and then tried to see how many times I could jump up and down before the pebble hit the ground.

"Alex?" she asked through the screen door.

I knew she wasn't just asking if it was me. "Seven," I said. "If I jump really low, I can get my feet off the ground seven times before the stone comes down."

"Oh," she said. She let her head sort of turn to the side like she was a crow looking at a pull-tab from a beer can. Her cigarette smoked between her fingers, and she had a white handkerchief thing over the curlers in her bleached hair. "Steve isn't here."

I jumped up on the concrete step beneath her screen door.

She stepped back.

"Where'd he go?" I asked.

"His father took him to the wrecking yard."

"To work?"

"If you really must know, to find a clutch for the station wagon. I'll tell him you were here."

I knew I was supposed to leave. She turned away, and she closed the vinyl-sided inside door. The black, metal eagle seemed to stare at me for a minute. Finally, I winked at it, jumped back down to the concrete, and resumed my game. I figured if I could do eight, I'd be ready to introduce the game to some of the big kids. Especially to my brother, Wayph. He needed a game he would lose at, and I had the advantage in my new game, *Stone Jump*. I was shorter. I was quicker. I might even be able to bet one of the bigger kids and win a chance to count in one of the big ball games. Steve's brother, Gordon, didn't hate me. Neither did Dave Lobby or Jimmy Lutz. Mostly, they just didn't care one way or the other as long as I wasn't on their team. If I was, then they made sure I didn't count.

I'd show 'em, I figured, but I never did get my jumps up to eight. Almost. Real close, but somehow that pebble always hit the concrete before I got back down from my eighth jump.

"What in Sam Hill's name are you doing, Gitter?" That's what some of the big kids called me, Gitter. Wayph said it was because all I was good for was gitting stuff, but I liked it. Dave Lobby gave me that name. He saw me climbing a tree to get his kite, and he said I was a Go Gitter, and it stuck, and I was proud of it.

I jumped up onto the concrete step again. Gordon was there. He was nearly a third taller than me, and he had muscles. When we played ball, he was one of only three kids who could hit the ball out over centerfield, clear the bulk oil tanks, clear the pump house, and hit the truck lot on the other side. Sometimes, his balls would bounce all the way down Wilson Ave. before somebody could run 'em down and field 'em.

"Got a new game," I said.

"Yeah. So, you looking for Steve?"

"Yeah. Wanted him to go hunt snakes. I was going up the tracks to the swamp and maybe up around the banks of the reservoir."

"Garter snakes, then?"

"Yeah! You hunt snakes?" I was amazed. It had never occurred to me that any of the big kids ever hunted snakes. I suppose it should have. They had all lived there longer than me. They were born first. Still, some stuff just didn't seem to make sense, and big kids hunting snakes was one of them.

He laughed and opened the screen door. I stepped back and let him out on the car port. He didn't say anything at all, but he walked to the back of the car port where they had big double storage doors. The doors had padlocks on 'em, and when he took a key out of his pocket, I kinda stared in awe. I knew Steve didn't have a key. When Gordon opened the doors and pulled out a moped, I almost choked. I'd never seen it before. Steve never talked about it.

"That yours?"

"The moped?"

"Uh huh."

"Yeah." He horsed the front wheel out far enough so he could roll it out. It was red and chrome, and it sure looked like it worked. He kicked down a kickstand and leaned it upright, then he went back into the storage shed.

While I was looking over the moped, he was rummaging in the shed. There was some gas on the carburetor, and it wasn't all gritty like old gas. The tires were hard with pressure. The peddles had some wear on them, but they weren't broken.

"It looks like it works," I said.

"It does," he said. "Let's go."

I stood up and looked at him. He had a linen bag and a snake hook. Not an old bent putter or a bad curtain rod, but an honest-to-God snake hook. He got on the moped, handed me the bag and the hook, and said, "Get on."

"Me? You? Hunting snakes? With that? On this?"

"Jesus," he said. "Get on."

I suddenly knew what it was like to be Jon-Jon going snake hunting with me. I decided right there to shut up and get on.

We headed out Mickey Road, which was to hell and gone farther than I was supposed to go. It was past the swamp and the reservoir, and I had no idea where we were going, except that it was sort of toward one of Wayph's buddy's houses out in the sticks.

He stopped us in the road shoulder gravel before the Mickey Road bridge over the Mud Fork River. The river was maybe twenty yards across, and it wasn't really much of a river at all. Dad said they called it a river because rivers had to be navigable, and this one had been when the biggest boat in the area was a flat-bottomed canal boat.

Gordon flipped the fuel lever, turned off the moped, and put the keys in his pocket.

I looked around for the field grass we'd normally hunt snakes in. Downstream, toward the reservoir, all I could see was scrub willow and blackberry canes. Upstream, toward the farmlands, the banks were high, slick mud with large cottonwood trees and some pasture access. Nothing that looked like the dry grass and cattails the big garters liked. "Where do we go?" I asked.

"You've never been here before?"

"Well, yeah," I lied. "Hunting frogs."

He nodded and took the hook from me. "Upstream," he said.

"For frogs?"

"Water moccasins," he said.

"There's no water moccasins in Ohio," I said. I did know a bit about my snakes, and I knew that ten thousand years before, the glaciers that cut out the great lakes had scraped away all the poisonous snakes. Except the Massassauga rattlers that lived in the muck near Willard, but there weren't any moccasins, not in all of Ohio. At least I was pretty sure there weren't.

"Are," he said. "And I'm going to show you where they are."

If Gordon said there were, then I was ready to believe it. "I didn't bring a snake bite kit," I said, as if I owned one.

"Don't get bit," he said. He pulled a little black pack out from under the seat of the moped. It unrolled like one of Dad's woood-working tool sets. Inside, there were tools and some cigarettes. "Want one?" he asked.

"Nah," I said. I tried to make it sound like I might have said yes, but he laughed anyway.

He flipped the lid on his Zippo lighter and lit up. "Keeps the mosquitoes away."

"Yeah," I said. "So, these water moccasins. How do you catch 'em?"

"Different ways," he said. He followed a gravel trail behind the bridge abutment guardrail, past the concrete footings, and down under the steel span that held up the pavement. On the broken concrete below the bridge, he picked his way down to the water's edge and walked right into the river up to his knees.

"Come on," he said.

I was still picking my way across the broken concrete. "I'm coming," but at the water, I hesitated.

"Afraid of the leeches?" he asked. "Smoke in the blood keeps 'em off."

He grinned around the edges of his Marlboro. "Bullshit," I said.

"So, what's keeping you? It's easiest to walk in the water."

What was keeping me was the realization that came with the moment of truth when I was about to put my brand new Converse tennis shoes into the water of the Mud Fork, water I shouldn't have been anywhere near, shoes that were supposed to keep me through the coming school year, with a guy who was smoking, and we'd got there on a moped, and I didn't have permission for any of this, and if the leeches did get me or if I drowned or if I even fell and got cut, all hell would break loose and I'd be grounded for fucking ever!

Gordon didn't care. He was a big kid. He didn't have to ask. He could smoke. He had keys to the storage and a moped. He turned away from me and waded upstream in the brown water.

I stepped in, and the water was up to my waist. My feet sank into the muck on the bottom. Pockets of iridescent oil rose to the surface of the water and trailed away from my legs.

After I was committed, I figured I could only be grounded once, and wouldn't Wayph be deep-pissed when he found out what I'd done to get grounded. I was pretty damn sure he'd never been snake hunting on the Mud Fork, and I was totally sure he'd never been on Gordon's moped, because if he had I'd have heard all about it. So, for an couple of hours, I was one happy kid. I got soaked. I got muddy. I caught a couple of frogs. We got one snapping turtle, but it was just a little one that Gordon saw sunning itself long before it saw us. Confused the hell out of it when

Gordon came at it from the water. He actually caught it in mid air when it slipped off the lip of the high, mud bank. I asked him how it got up there to begin with, and he told me snapping turtles could fly if they needed to. They preferred swimming, but in a pinch, they could fly.

"Bullshit."

He laughed.

I liked that I was making him laugh. We were buddies. Me and Gordon, mopedding around, hunting snakes, smoking, catching turtles and shit. It was sweet.

It was real sweet, until we found a water moccasin.

We had come to a place where Gordon said the river got too deep to wade. We climbed the mud bank, using muskrat holes for steps and him reaching down to pull me up onto the grass bank. A creek came into the Mud Fork there, and the water was dark green. It cut a line out into the brown water of the Mud Fork, and the two streams kinda wandered along downstream mixing up until all you could see was the brown of the Mud Fork again cause it took over all the green of the creek.

"Steiner's Creek," Gordon said. "We need to walk up to the bridge to cross."

"Yeah," I said. "Can I carry the hook for a while?"

He handed it to me.

I was sooo cool, and I was wishing somebody would come along at the bridge and see me being so cool with Gordon.

We cut through some trees and crossed through a rusty barbwire fence. Then we came to a gravel road, but the bridge was maybe half a football field from where we came out.

Wet, muddy, tired, and happy as a frog in a muck pool, I followed Gordon.

He hopped up on the low, concrete side-wall of the bridge. Steiner's creek was small—like in places maybe we could have jumped across.

Gordon froze. He did the still-like-a-rock thing like nobody I'd ever seen. He did it better'n me and better'n Jon-Jon. He was a statue on that bridge abutment. He was stone and steel, and he'd been there for a thousand million years.

"What is it?" I whispered. He was looking down into the green, farm runoff under the bridge.

"Moccasins," he whispered.

"Here." I hunkered down and came along the middle of the road so I wouldn't spook 'em. I held up the stick for him.

He didn't take it. His hands were out like he wanted it, or like he was keeping his balance, but he didn't take the stick.

"Shit," he said.

I crept closer. Sure as hell, there were big, fat, black snakes with white lips laying in the sun on the sloped mud banks. Three of 'em. One was maybe the size of a big garter. One was easy five feet, and it was four inches through the middle if it was one.

"Water moccasins," I said. "Big ones," I said. "Cool. What do we do?"

Gordon stepped back into the road, away from the abutment and the snakes. "Come on, Gitter," he said.

I followed his lead and backed away carefully. I handed him the hook. This time he took it.

"You gonna sneak up on 'em?"

"We'll go see if we can find bigger ones on the main Mud Fork," he said.

"These are the first ones we've seen all day."

"So, there'll be more," he said.

"Let's get one of these so we can at least say we got one. If we get a bigger one, we can keep it too."

He stood there a second—all wet, muddy muscles and tall and a little pale. "Yeah," he said. "Okay."

"Okay! What do I do?"

"Yeah. Okay," he said again. "Okay. This is what you do. You sneak back up on the abutment and watch them. I'll take the hook down and sneak up on them. I'll pin the big one. We'll let the other ones go in the water."

"And what do I do?"

"Once I pin him, you come down with the bag. You hold it open wide while I get a grip on his head. Then we slip him in the bag and head on to the main stream for some really big ones."

I swear, I was shaking. Wayph was gonna pee. My Dad would ground me forever, but I'd be a fucking legend! "Cool," I said. I tried to sound like a big kid. Like I *was* cool. Like I knew this was the way to catch a moccasin.

I did my part. I stood on the abutment. I was a fucking rock. I was soo a fucking rock. I locked my eyes on the big one.

Gordon snuck around the side. He made a lot of noise, but the snakes just stood still. I figured Gordon knew they didn't hear so well, that they felt things in their bellies and tasted the air with their tongues. Noise wasn't such a big deal, but bumping the ground and thumping was.

He pushed through the last grass and brush and stood within reach of the snakes. The small ones moved like slithering, black lightning. They were just gone into the murky green pool under the bridge.

The big one held his place. Gordon looked confused. He stepped forward and slapped the hook down, flat into the mud. He missed. The big-ass moccasin moved. It hit the water too. Gordon slapped the hook after it two more times, but it was too late. The snakes were all in the water.

"Shit," he said. He looked up at me and shrugged. "Close," he said. "Almost."

I didn't know what to say. I'd have had 'em. I knew I would have. I'd have been quieter going in, lower, and I'd sure as hell have pinned the big one from that close.

Gordon came back up onto the bridge. "There'll be more on the main stream," he said.

I was still staring at the water. "They might not have gone far."

"They're on their way to Willard by now."

A black head came up from the green murk. "Look!" I pointed. Another appeared.

"So?"

"So, maybe you can hook one from the bank and pull him out?"

"Fuck you," he said.

The big head came up. The big, black head. I looked at it. I wanted it. I was in the air and then in the water. My hand was on the black body, and I knew I was in deep shit and maybe even dead, but I was in and had no choice. I pulled the snake backward against the current of the stream, trying to figure out how to get a grip on its head.

"You fucking idiot! Gitter! Get out of there!"

I pulled that snake backward and around in a circle. I spun in the green water. I looked frantically for the other snakes. I looked for a way out onto the bank. I looked for a way to pin that damn head.

A rock rolled under my foot. I went down. Under the green, still gripping my catch, I scrambled for footing and thrashed back up into the air. The snake came up out of the water into the air, and its head was flat, and its mouth was open, and it was pink.

I stood dead still. That big, black snake was trying to bite me with all its reptile heart, and I just stood there with it hanging from mid belly from my hand. I stood and stared into its big, pink, fangless mouth.

It got me. It rolled back on itself and laid teeth into my forearm. Teeth snagged in my arm, I grabbed it behind the head. I was too excited to feel any pain. The snake let go. Blood flowed freely, mixing with algae water and dripping off my arm. "I got it!" I screamed. "I got it!"

"You dumb shit, Gitter!"

"Get the bag!"

"You stupid son of a bitch!"

I scrambled out. I had to climb up the bank and back up to the road.

"We gotta get you to a hospital," Gordon said.

"Open the bag!"

"Dump the snake. We need to get the hell out of here before you die."

"Bag!" I held the snake behind the head. With my other hand, I took the bag from Gordon. When the snake was bagged, I tied it off. Then I screamed and whooped for a while.

He jumped up and down trying to get a grip on me. "Come on," he said. "Come on, dammit!"

Finally, I stopped my jumping and whooping. I looked at his ashen face. I saw his shaking hands. He was scared. Really scared. Seeing him so scared made me doubt what I thought I knew. I wiped the blood off my arm. A horseshoe shape of needle pricks. It was like a garter snake bite, only a lot bigger.

"No fangs," I said. "They aren't moccasins. They're water snakes." I showed him the bite. "No fangs. Pink mouths. Not white."

"Bullshit," he said.

"No bullshit," I said.

"You're fucked up," he said. "You jumped off that bridge into them snakes."

"I got him," I said.

"You got him. And he's one big son of a bitch."

We stood there grinning at each other for a while. Finally, we walked the gravel road back to Mickey and the moped. Gordon dropped me off at my house. Dad was there trimming bushes. Wayph was there too. Gordon walked up into the yard with me.

"Gordon!" Wayph called. "Can I have a ride?"

Dad wasn't interested in the moped at all. He saw the bag. He saw the mud, the shoes, the blood. He didn't even ask. He put down his hedge trimmers and walked across the lawn to meet us.

"I took him snake hunting," Gordon said.

Dad looked at Gordon.

"Out the Mud Fork past Mickey," Gordon said, like it was just a fact, like it was something him and me did every day. "We did pretty good. Want to see?"

"Cool bike," Wayph said. He was looking the moped over.

Dad nodded. He folded his arms.

"Show him, Gitter," Gordon said.

I dumped the bag. Dad stepped back. His arms came unfolded all on their own.

Gordon handed me the hook. I pinned the snake, caught it behind the head, and picked it up, body draped over one hand, head in the other.

"Jesus!" It was Wayph. His blue eyes were wide, and he was looking at me and my bloody arm instead of the snake.

"Looks like it was some kind of wrestling match," Dad said.

"You should have seen it," Gordon said. "Gitter here is absolutely fearless. He jumped off Steiner's bridge, hit the water, and wrestled the snake in. I never saw anything like it."

"Bad bite?" Dad asked.

"Nah," I said. "It bled clean." I'd heard that on TV somewhere. It made Dad smile and laugh.

Gordon laughed too. He turned to head for his moped. "Wanna play some ball tomorrow, Gitter?"

But I was pretty sure I was gonna be hunting garters with Jon-Jon instead.

"You're on my team."

"Jesus," Wayph said. "That's huge."

WHEN THEY CAME

DON WEBB

He wanted her the minute he saw her.

The party was ending early, as all parties did in those days when the griffin infestation was at its worst. They flew more frequently at night, preying on hapless pedestrians and smaller cars, usually imports.

She was tall and muscular, skin a light bronze that demanded the attention of a tongue and soft brush. Her eyes were a rare brown amber that made him think of the gem called tiger's eye, and her hair was a light brown kissed by flame. Her dress was long and tight and semitransparent.

He did not know how he could have missed her all afternoon. The house the party was held in was not large, it did not boast of secret rooms or shadowy nooks that could have held so rare a beauty as she.

He sprinted across the room hoping at least to learn her name, but the cry of a griffin flying overhead put everyone into running panic. He tripped and his hosts helped him up and to the shelter, a legacy from the Cold War.

She did not go to the shelter, and he began his quest wondering if she had been a victim to the griffins.

He did not know anyone who had actually died of griffin attack, death and his social circle were unacquainted, but he had no doubt of their vicious nature. It was made graphically clear on the evening news.

He asked after her of course. No one seemed to know quite who he had meant. Maybe it was that Janet something-or-other, who had taught school in China, maybe it was Karen the sculptor, or Dan's friend what-was-her-name.

So the first few days he had a checklist to go on. These were nice women, Karen even suitable for bedding, but never even under the caresses of her strong cool hands did he cease thinking of her.

He did not do well at the office, but he had done well for the past ten quarters so no one commented on his unfocused state.

He wanted her so bad, it was as though she was sex itself.

There was much fear in those days, because of the griffins. I remembered when they first came, flying out of the night--raiding Fort Knox and jewelry stores for gold to build their nests. I remembered them preening their wings while they perched on the great buildings of the city, sharpening their talons against the sidewalks, carrying off children and the homeless.

I knew their coming meant one thing. I would never go hungry again.

I had been a cab driver. Most people don't remember this, but at one time having a Ph.D. in folklorist studies didn't mean you had it made.

Those of us without books on microwave poodles and baby trains, and especially those of us without tenure, were often marginally employed.

I was watching a griffin with scarlet wings and a black coat from behind the bullet proof glass of my high rise office while he droned on and on about the woman.

"The point being," I said, "Mr. Gordon, is that you want me to tell you if this woman you saw is some kind of supernatural figure."

"Yes, I mean no one seems to have seen her other than me and I've heard that there are other creatures coming into the world, not just the griffins," he said.

"There have been sightings, nothing confirmed, of course, of fairies, of mermaids, of sylphs and undines and gnomes. There was a giant photographed in Canada last month, and I have heard on good authority that kobolds and blue caps are in disused mines in Germany. But I doubt that your woman was one of these. Men have fallen hard for women long before the coming of this Age."

"I would do anything, give anything to meet her."

"How much," I asked, "is anything?"

He named a figure that would have bought a new cab outright.

"I believe I will help you, Mr. Gordon," I said. "The woman you seek is named Tania Owlright. I had to do some consulting for her earlier this year."

"What kind of consulting?'

"That is something I would rather not talk about. You may leave your check with my secretary."

"That's it?"

"That's it. You hardly expect me to hold her leg for you while you try the glass slipper on, do you?"

I saw the griffin take flight on its scarlet wings, I could almost hear the great pumping of its pinions. I wondered if I had said too much. It is difficult to know their code. In a few weeks I would hear it all from Tania anyway.

It cost a good deal of money even after Dr. Biscayne' said to find Tania, but Anthony Gordon found her. She lived alone in the Palisades of New Jersey. She had an unimportant job for the state, that required hours and hours of on-line research. Her hobbies included parachuting, cave diving, and rock climbing. She had been to the party at Bob and Cheryl's because a friend of a friend had invited her to come.

Arranging a chance meeting with her was hard. Outside of her work and adventure hobbies, she rarely went anywhere save for the library.

Tony made it his business to haunt the town library.

It took weeks, but he met his quarry.

There she sat in a short black skirt and pearl embroidered black blouse. Her legs slightly parted, a pen held to her mouth while she read Mary Denning's Donna Young: A Work in Regress. Tony knew then the gods were on his side, because he had written a paper on that book in his senior year at Columbia.

He moved to sit beside her, which wasn't too conspicuous in the crowded library. When she put the book down, he pounced.

"That's one of my favorites. I wrote a paper in school on how Denning creates the illusion of the book being shorter each time you read it."

"Oh," said Tania in one of those breathless bedroom voices that all men were born to hear. "How does she do it?"

"Well, I sort of gave a line of bullshit, I didn't really know, I just wanted to read the book and I hadn't much time that semester."

"Well, a line of bullshit is a good thing if it gets you what you want."

She smiled, and Tony knew at once that he was out of his league and that he would get lucky tonight.

Over dessert he asked the question everyone asks, "So what do you think the griffins want?"

"They're predators, humans are prey, what more is thereto know?"

"Well where do they come from? Why are they here?"

"Presumptuous questions from a deer to a lion. Do human beings know where they come from, do we know why we're here?"

Later still he traced the pattern of scars over her breasts that a rock climbing accident gave her, then caressed the breasts which were small and hard like pears. Her nipples were dark amber and tasted of some subtle perfume. She was wild, thrashing and raking with her nails, screaming and begging for more, then gently reviving him with lips the gods would have died for.

They made love five times, but she would not let him spend the night.

As he left her lonely cabin, he thought he heard the sound of wings.

She came to see me some weeks later.

"I know that you want to know what has happened between me and Tony."

"I just want to know if you've told him."

"Not yet."

"Are you going to keep seeing him?"

She paused, and then said, "Why do you care?"

"I am at the beginning of a myth, I want to see something when it happens instead of collecting tales from other sources."

"Yes, I am going to keep seeing him. Yes, I'm going to tell him."

"Then I don't need to know more. I have some photos of nightmares on the Russian steppes. Would you like to see them? They're much more dangerous than griffins."

I wrote a book about the griffins shortly after their arrival. It was in the early days, when some authorities were denying their existence altogether. The CIA seized copies of it, I thought you might like to read part of it.

"Theories abound as to the origin of the griffins. Some blame the overuse of the electromagnetic spectrum--too many cell-phones and hand-held faxes. Others suggest that they are a manifestation of some collective sin of mankind suddenly appearing when some critical mass of sin was achieved. Others still hold that they are space aliens arriving in invisible saucers for sinister reasons. I will tell you why they are here.

"They are here because we want them to be here. We want to see them copulate in midair, because we long for the wing-haunted night of the witches' sabbat. We want to see them tear into the flesh of our neighbors, for over-breeding and contempt have run the veneer of civilization too thin. We want to hear the cry of the eagle and hear the slashing talons of the lion. They are here so we can put those fallout shelters to work, to know what it means to hide and huddle when we want to play at that—or to risk all when we want to gather flowers Persephone-like in the spring. What has happened since they are among us? Violent crime is gone, wars are ending. Have we done the logical or sensible thing, like to try to hunt them down? Why has no politician run on a campaign of eliminating the griffins? Do we even limit our outdoor activities during the day? We may hide from them at nigh--but has there ever been a night attack that has been documented? I have seen griffins sleeping at night in Central Park.

"We invited them here. They are the only things that make our lives worth living. It is the only form of the divine we can trust, it is the only form of the beast we can fear. If you doubt that the griffins, which will be the first wave of the divine invasion, aren't here as our guests, try the following. Stand by your window. Picture a griffin in your mind, its strong lion body with black or green or golden fur, and its great eagle wings of white or scarlet or indigo. Picture it sailing high above your city, riding the thermals with a body so large that even you know it defies the laws of aerodynamics. Picture it swooping suddenly, suddenly down toward you.

"Now see how you feel? We would have to invent the griffins if we had not already done so."

From *Our Griffins, Our Selves* by Thomas Biscayne

Some copies leaked into the world, and it is on that book I made my fortune. But I've learned my lessons and I'll not speak so frankly again.

They were dining at a sidewalk cafe. A simple meal, wine and bread and cheese. All Tony could think of was how much he wanted to eat her after the meal, to suck at her sweet juices, to sink his teeth into her thighs, to please and hurt and please her till she screamed. Every inch of his skin tingled, every finger ached to just brush against the thin fabric of the tight white dress she was wearing.

She was chewing her food slowly to torment him, drinking her wine with painstaking care. Speaking of nothing. It was a ploy to get him so hot that he would carry her away from the cafe and take her on the grass of a nearby park.

She had been talking about skydiving for several minutes. He had been trying hard to follow, but lust was singing in his ears. Now! He wanted her now! To push into her softness, her hot wetness.

There was a muffled scream some hundreds of feet above, and a splash of red liquid hit her white dress at the crotch.

A griffin was flying overhead in the crisp blue air of fall. In its beak it carried a white dog, or perhaps a baby.

She seemed embarrassed, and ran off for the subway station.

Later she wouldn't talk to him, or return his calls.

On the night of the first full moon in November, he decided to go out to her cabin in the Palisades and force her to see him. He didn't know what line he had crossed, all he knew was that he had been blissfully happy filled with that mad fire that begins as lust and in the very fortunate few winds up as love.

He wanted to smell her. He needed to smell her hair just once again. He needed to touch her hand, even if that was all she would let him touch. He wanted to see the perfect skin of her back, the small place at the base of her neck where she loved to be bitten. She was the only thing he saw, the charts and graphs at work disappeared, TV disappeared, he could not read, nor sleep nor eat but ache with wanting her.

Surely that want would open any door, surely so much need would do the magic that would undo whatever stood between them.

He came upon them making love in the snow behind her cabin.

The griffin was huge, its plumage and fur black by moonlight. She had to wrap her legs around the body so that it could thrust its massive black member into her. She had to grab the thick feather-covered neck.

The griffin stood on its back paws, it wings beating the air, driving snow in a silvery blast behind it. One of its forepaws held her head. The other slashed at the air.

At times the griffin's excitement would cause them to leave the ground rising three or four feet in the air — and then outward over the cliff, over the deadly moonlit water below. It would cry like an eagle, and she would scream like a woman. But sometimes their cries blended into one ecstatic scream that was surely the scream of the gods.

When the griffin was done with her, it flung her into the snow. She was bleeding from small cuts, and her vagina actually steamed into the cold air.

He stood still for a long time, wondering if she were dead, or merely spent, his own lust vanished as well as most of his understanding of how the world worked.

She moaned and stirred. He went over to her.

She opened one eye and looked at him.

"So," she said, "you've seen. You know."

"I've seen, " he said, "but I don't know. What have I seen? What do I know?"

"You have a rival."

"Have I always had a rival?"

"Always. It's what half of me has always wanted, to fuck death and danger. It's in the skydiving, it's in the cave diving, and it's in the poems I write then burn. You've always had a rival. If I could fly off with him, and be as he is I would do so in a minute."

"So what's his name?"

"Look this isn't some nice humanized 'Beauty and the Beast' thing. I don't know his name. I don't talk with him. He isn't some wise protector. If he ever got hungry during one of our sessions, my neck would be gone."

"So I guess there isn't any talking you out of it."

"I guess not. I like you, look I may even love you, but this is what I am. I was this way the first day one of them flew over the city and its shadow flew across me like an embrace."

113

"So what does this mean for us?"

"What do you want it to mean?"

Tony said, "I need to think about this."

It was later, much later when the city was in its Christmas rush and everything was covered in green and redder gold and silver that he called her up, and they began seeing each other again.

They were not the only couples working such things through. It's hard and amazing and different. They will be a chapter in my next book though.

It will probably get banned too.

Over Alsace

Forrest Aguirre

Helmuth Bruderbund breathed fast and hard, wiping away the hot oil spattering up from the engine of his Fokker Albatross. The plane lurched beneath him, a bullet-ridden derelict, adrift on the ether, tugged down by gravity's tide. Flaming paper shreds and molten lead shards bounced off his flying goggles, coat and helmet as he disengaged and abandoned the doomed craft for free fall. The weight of the parachute pack spun him around backwards, forcing thoughts percolating through his head as he tumbled toward France below, consciousness fading.

She was beautiful, a blonde vision in blue dress. A glowing aura scintillated from her skin as light flooded the stage. Words slid forth from her platinum pure throat, her silver tongue, a sounding from that small misty tavern then echoing across all Alsace:

"Quelque chose de toi flotte dans l'air,
Qui me pénètre la mémoire."

A flash of stage light—no—the Sun, and the mist was gone. The Fokker vomited smoke below him as it headed for the fields below. France. Debussy's France. And Helmuth Bruderbund was about to become a prisoner of war, a shame to his country, to his compatriots at the War Academy.

"Shame!" His mother.

"But Mother, I love her."

"She is French!"

"I will marry her," defiant, like a good Prussian.

"I will not have you marry some French singing whore you picked up in a Gasthaus. Your father turns in his grave at the mere suggestion. Your inheritance is at stake, impudent young man . . ."

"Shame!" Cassandre.

"I have my family name to consider—a reputation."

"But I love you!"

"No, it must not be. I was foolish to think . . ."

"You are foolish! A curse on your noble family name."

Cassandre leaves. She will not return. Her voice haunts him, ever haunts him.

"Et mon âme, trahie er délaissée,
Est encor tout entière à toi."

The pull was sudden, painful. A jolt to the jaw and jerk to the arm and Helmuth knew the shoulder was dislocated. It burned in the back as the wind whipped his face cold, biting his skin. The sound of flapping silk reassured—the parachute had worked, he would live. A prisoner. But alive, at least. Or perhaps Cassandre lived in that village below or just down the road. Yes, she would forgive him, shelter him, harbor him from the enemy. All would be well.

"A curse . . ."

The sun glinted off a white-robed form in the clouds, a winged being, an angel—Cassandre, his love. No, another memory—Cassandre had committed suicide a week after her departure from Germany.

A blunderbuss shivered as Baelphoegele, the destroying angel—Cassandre—

Shrack

Shrack

Shracked

the ramrod down the weapon's chrome throat. It tried in vain to regurgitate

beryl,

onyx,

ruby,

gold:

The Grapeshot of Mammon;

then awaited the leveling of the weapon, the trigger pull, the shattering echo that heralds the final departure of its victim into the world of the dead.

In the distance, propellers sliced into the world's skin, wings plowed a field, flames consumed the earth-bound aircraft. Helmuth continued to fall.

Baelphoegele's—Cassandre's—smile disappeared behind a puff of smoke as the thunderstick responded in discharge to celestial command, a crusader-king's ransom of flechette finding its mark on The Fatherland's Iron Cross.

"*Gott**"

"*Ô bruit doux de la pluie*
Par terre et sur let toits!
Pour un cœur qui s' ennuie
Ô le bruit de la pluie!"

STATE CHANGE

KEN LIU

Every night, before going to bed, Rina checked the refrigerators.

There were two in the kitchen, on separate circuits, one with a fancy ice dispenser on the door. There was one in the living room holding up the TV, and one in the bedroom doubling as a nightstand. A small cubical unit meant for college dorm rooms was in the hallway, and a cooler that Rina refilled with fresh ice every night was in the bathroom, under the sink.

Rina opened the door of each refrigerator and looked in. Most of the refrigerators were empty most of the time. This didn't bother Rina. She wasn't interested in filling them. The checks were a matter of life and death. It was about the preservation of her soul.

What she was interested in were the freezer compartments. She liked to hold each door open for a few seconds, let the cold mist of condensation dissipate, and feel the chill on her fingers, breasts, face. She closed the door when the motor kicked in.

By the time she was done with all of the refrigerators, the apartment was filled with the bass chorus of all of the motors, a low, confident hum that to Rina was the sound of safety.

In her bedroom, Rina got into bed and pulled the covers over her. She had hung some pictures of glaciers and icebergs on the walls, and she looked at them as pictures of old friends. There was also a framed picture on the refrigerator by her bed, this one of Amy, her roommate in college. They had lost touch over the years, but Rina kept her picture there anyway.

Rina opened the refrigerator next to her bed. She stared into the glass dish that held her ice cube. Every time she looked, it seemed to get smaller.

Rina closed the refrigerator and picked up the book lying on top of it.

Edna St. Vincent Millay: A Portrait in Letters by Friends, Foes, and Lovers —

New York, January 23, 1921

My Dearest Viv —

Finally got up the courage to go see Vincent at her hotel today. She told me she wasn't in love with me any more. I cried. She became angry and told me that if I couldn't keep myself under control then I might as well leave. I asked her to make me some tea.

It's that boy she's been seen with. I knew that. Still, it was terrible to hear it from her own lips. The little savage.

She smoked two cigarettes and offered me the box. I couldn't stand the bitterness so I stopped after one. Afterwards she gave me her lipstick so I could fix my lips, as if nothing had happened, as if we were still in our room at Vassar.

"Write a poem for me," I said. She owed me at least that.

She looked as if she wanted to argue, but stopped herself. She took out her candle, put it in that candleholder I made for her and lit it at both ends. When she lit her soul like that she was at her most beautiful. Her face glowed. Her pale skin was lit from within like a Chinese paper lantern about to burst into flame. She paced around the room as if she would tear down the walls. I drew up my feet on the bed, and wrapped her scarlet shawl around me, staying out of her way.

Then she sat down at her desk and wrote out her poem. As soon as it was done she blew out her candle, stingy with what remained of it. The smell of hot wax made me all teary-eyed again. She made out a clean copy for herself and gave the original to me.

"I _did_ love you, Elaine," she said. "Now be a good girl and leave me alone."

This is how her poem starts:

What lips my lips have kissed, and where, and why,
I have forgotten, and what arms have lain
Under my head till morning, but the rain
Is full of ghosts tonight, that tap and sigh —

Viv, for a moment I wanted to take her candle and break it in half, to throw the pieces into the fireplace and melt her soul into nothing. I wanted to see her writhing at my feet, begging me to let her live.

But all I did was to throw that poem in her face, and I left.

I've been wandering around the streets of New York all day. I can't keep her savage beauty out of my mind. I wish my soul was heavier, more solid, something that could weigh itself down. I wish my soul wasn't this feather, this ugly wisp of goose down in my pocket, lifted up and buffeted about by the wind around her flame. I feel like a moth.

Your Elaine

Rina put the book down.

To be able to set your soul afire, she thought, *to be able to draw men and women to you at your will, to be brilliant, fearless of consequences, what would she not give to live a life like that?*

Millay chose to light her candle at both ends, and lived an incandescent life. When her candle ran out, she died sick, addicted, and much too young. But each day of her life she could decide, "Am I going to be brilliant today?"

Rina imagined her ice cube in the dark, cold cocoon of the freezer. *Stay calm,* she thought. *Block it out. This is your life. This bit of almost-death.*

Rina turned out the light.

When Rina's soul finally materialized, the nurse in charge of watching the afterbirth almost missed it. All of a sudden, there, in the stainless steel pan, was an ice cube, the sort you would find clinking around in glasses at cocktail parties. A pool of water was already forming around it. The edges of the ice cube were becoming rounded, indistinct.

An emergency refrigeration unit was rushed in, and the ice cube was packed away.

"I'm sorry," the doctor said to Rina's mother, who looked into the serene face of her baby daughter. No matter how careful they were, how long could they keep the ice cube from melting? It wasn't as if they could just keep it in a freezer somewhere and forget about it. The soul had to be pretty close to the body; otherwise the body would die.

Nobody in the room said anything. The air around the baby was awkward, still, silent. Words froze in their throats.

Rina worked in a large building downtown, next to the piers and docked yachts she had never been on. On each floor, there were offices with windows around the sides, the ones overlooking the harbor being bigger and better furnished than the others.

In the middle of the floor were the cubicles, one of which was Rina's. Next to her were two printers. The hum of the printers was a bit like the hum of refrigerators. Lots of people passed by her cubicle on the way to pick up their printouts. Sometimes they stopped, thinking they would say hello to the quiet girl sitting there, with her pale skin and ice-blond hair, and always a sweater around her shoulders. Nobody knew what color her eyes were because she did not look up from her desk.

But there was a chill in the air around her, a fragile silence that did not want to be broken. Even though they saw her every day, most people did not know Rina's name. After a while, it became too embarrassing to ask. While the chattering life of the office ebbed and flowed around her, people left her alone.

Under Rina's desk was a small freezer that the firm had installed just for her. Each morning Rina would rush into her cubicle, unzip her insulated lunch bag, and from her thermos stuffed with ice cubes, she would carefully pull out the sandwich bag holding her one special ice cube and put it into the freezer. She would sigh, and sit in her chair, and wait for her heart to slow down.

The job of the people in the smaller offices away from the harbor was to look up, on their computers, the answers to questions asked by people in the offices facing the harbor. Rina's job was to take those answers and use the right fonts to squeeze them into the right places on the right pieces of paper to be sent back to the people in the harbor offices. Sometimes the people in the smaller offices were too busy and they would dictate their answers onto cassette tapes. Rina would then type up the answers.

Rina ate her lunch at her cubicle. Even though one could go some distance away from one's soul for short periods of time without getting sick, Rina liked to be as close to the freezer as possible. When she had to be away sometimes to deliver an envelope to some office on another floor, she had visions of sudden power failures. Out of breath, she would then hurry through the halls to get back to the safety of her freezer.

Rina tried not to think that life was unfair to her. Had she been born before the invention of Frigidaire she never would have survived. She didn't want to be ungrateful. But sometimes it was difficult.

After work, instead of going dancing with the other girls or getting ready for a date, she spent her nights at home, reading biographies to lose herself in other lives.

Morning Walks with T. S. Eliot: A Memoir—

Between 1958 and 1963, Eliot was a member of the Commission for the Revised Psalter of the Book of Common Prayer. He was rather frail by this time, and avoided tapping into his tin of coffee altogether.

One exception was when the Commission came to revise Psalm 23. Four centuries earlier, Bishop Coversdale had been rather free with his translation from the Hebrew. The correct English rendition for the central metaphor in the Psalm, the Commission agreed, was "the valley of deep darkness."

At the meeting, for the first time in months, Eliot brewed a cup of his coffee. The rich, dark aroma was unforgettable to me.

Eliot took a sip of his coffee, and then, in that same mesmerizing voice he used to read *The Wasteland*, he recited the traditional version that had infused itself into the blood of every Englishman: "Though I walk through the valley of the shadow of death, I shall fear no evil."

The vote was unanimous to keep Coversdale's version, embellished though it might have been.

I think it always surprised people how deep was Eliot's devotion to tradition, to the Anglican Church, and also how thoroughly his soul had been imbibed by the English.

I believe that was the last time Eliot tasted his soul, and often since then I have wished that I could again smell that aroma: bitter, burnt, and restrained. It was not only the spirit of a true Englishman, but also that of the genius of poetry.

To measure out a life with coffee spoons, Rina thought, *must have seemed dreadful sometimes. Perhaps that was why Eliot had no sense of humor.*

But a soul in a coffee tin was also lovely in its own way. It enlivened the air around him, made everyone who heard his voice alert, awake, open and receptive to the mysteries of his difficult, dense verse. Eliot could not have written, and the world would have understood, *Four Quartets* without the scent of Eliot's soul, the edge it gave to every word, the sharp tang of having drunk something deeply significant.

I would love to have the mermaids sing to me, Rina thought. *Was that what Eliot dreamed of after drinking his coffee before sleep?*

Instead of mermaids, she dreamt of glaciers that night. Miles and miles of ice that would take a hundred years to melt. Though there was no life in sight, Rina smiled in her sleep. It was her life.

On the first day the new man showed up at work, Rina could tell that he was not going to be in his office for long.

His shirt was a few years out of style, and he did not take care to polish his shoes that morning. He was not very tall, and his chin was not very sharp. His office was down the hall from Rina's cubicle, and it was small, with only one window facing the building next to this one. The nametag outside the office said *Jimmy Kesnow*. By all signs he should have been just another one of the anonymous, ambitious, disappointed young men passing through the building every day.

But Jimmy was the most comfortable person Rina had ever seen. Wherever he was, he acted like he belonged. He was not loud and he did not talk fast, but conversations and crowds opened up places for him. He would say only a few words, but people would laugh and afterwards feel a little wittier themselves. He would smile at people, and they would feel happier, more handsome, more beautiful. He popped in and out of his office all morning, managing to look purposeful and relaxed enough to stop and chat at the same time. Offices remained open after he had left, and their occupants felt no desire to close the doors.

Rina saw that the girl in the cubicle next to hers primped herself when she heard Jimmy's voice coming down the hall.

It seemed difficult to even remember what life in the office was like before Jimmy.

Rina knew that young men like that did not stay in small offices with only one window facing an alley for very long. They moved into offices facing the harbor, or maybe on the next floor. Rina imagined that his soul was probably a silver spoon, effortlessly dazzling and desirable.

The Trial of Joan of Arc —

"At night the soldiers and Joan slept together on the ground. When Joan took off her armor we could see her breasts, which were beautiful. And yet never once did she awake in me carnal desires.

"Joan would become angry when the soldiers swore in her presence or spoke of the pleasures of the flesh. She always chased away the women who followed soldiers with her sword unless a soldier promised to marry such a woman.

"Joan's purity came from her soul, which she always carried on her body whether she was riding into battle or getting ready to sleep for the night. This was a beech branch. Not far from Douremy, her home village, there was an old beech tree called the Ladies' Tree by a spring. Her soul came from that tree, for the branch gave off a smell that those who knew Joan in her childhood swore was the same smell given off by the spring by the Ladies' Tree.

"Whoever came into Joan's presence with a sinful thought would instantly have that flame extinguished by the influence of her soul. Thus she remained pure, as I do swear to tell the truth, even though she would sometimes be naked as the rest of the soldiers."

"Hey," Jimmy said. "What's your name?"

"Joan," Rina said. She blushed, and put her book down. "Rina, I meant." Instead of looking at him she looked down at the half-eaten salad on her desk. She wandered if there was anything at the corners of her mouth. She thought about wiping her mouth with the napkin but decided that would draw too much attention.

"You know, I've been asking around the office all morning, and no one could tell me your name."

Even though Rina already knew this was true, she felt a little sad, as if she had disappointed him. She shrugged.

"But now I know something no one else here knows," Jimmy said, and sounded as if she had told him a wonderful secret.

Did they finally turn down the air conditioning? Rina thought. *It didn't feel as cold as it usually did.* She thought about taking off her sweater.

"Hey Jimmy," the girl in the cubicle next to Rina's called out. "Come over here. Let me show you those pictures I was telling you about."

"See you later," Jimmy said, and smiled at her. She knew because she was looking up, looking into his face, which she realized could be handsome.

Legends of the Romans —

Cicero was born with a pebble. Therefore, no one expected him to amount to much.

Cicero practiced public speaking with the pebble in his mouth. Sometimes he almost choked on it. He learned to use simple words and direct sentences. He learned to push his voice past the pebble in his mouth, to articulate, to speak clearly even when his tongue betrayed him.

He became the greatest orator of his age.

"You read a lot," Jimmy said.

Rina nodded. Then she smiled at him.

"I've never seen eyes with your shade of blue," Jimmy said, looking directly into her eyes. "It's like the sea, but through a layer of ice." He said this casually, as if he was talking about a vacation he had taken, a movie he had seen. This was why Rina knew he was being sincere, and she felt as if she had given him another secret, one she didn't even know she had.

Neither of them said anything. This would usually be awkward. But Jimmy simply leaned against the wall of the cubicle, admiring the stack of books on Rina's desk. He settled into the silence, relaxed into it. And so Rina felt content to let the silence go on.

"Oh, Catullus," Jimmy said. He picked up one of the books. "Which poem is your favorite?"

Rina pondered this. It seemed too bold to say that it was "Let us live, my Lesbia, and let us love." It seemed too coy to say that it was "You ask me how many kisses."

She agonized over the answer.

He waited, not hurrying her.

She couldn't decide. She began to say something, anything, but nothing came out. A pebble was in her throat, an ice-cold pebble. She was angry with herself. She must have looked like such an idiot to him.

"Sorry," Jimmy said. "Steve is waving at me to come to his office. I'll catch up with you later."

Amy was Rina's roommate in college. She was the only person Rina ever pitied. Amy's soul was a pack of cigarettes.

But Amy did not act like she wanted to be pitied. By the time Rina met her, Amy had less than half a pack left.

"What happened to the rest of them?" Rina was horrified. She could not imagine herself being so careless with her life.

Amy wanted Rina to go out with her at nights, to dance, to drink, and to meet boys. Rina kept on saying no.

"Do it for me," Amy said. "You feel sorry for me, right? Well, I'm asking you to come with me, just once."

Amy took Rina to a bar. Rina hugged her thermos to her the whole way. Amy pried it out of her hand, dropped Rina's ice cube into a shot glass, and told the bartender to keep it chilled in the freezer.

Boys came up to try to pick them up. Rina ignored them. She was terrified. She wouldn't take her eyes off the freezer.

"Try to act like you are having fun, will you?" Amy said.

The next time a boy came up to them, Amy took out one of her cigarettes.

"You see this?" she said to the boy. Her eyes flashing in the glow from the neon lights behind the bar. "I'm going to start smoking it right now. If you can get my friend here to laugh before I finish it, I will go home with you tonight."

"How about both of you come home with me tonight?"

"Sure," Amy said. "Why not? You better get cracking though." She flicked her lighter and took a long drag on her cigarette. She threw her head back and blew the smoke high into the air.

"This is what I live for," Amy whispered to Rina, her pupils unfocused, wild. "All life is an experiment." Smoke drifted from her nostrils and made Rina cough.

Rina stared at Amy. Then she turned around to face the boy. She felt a little lightheaded. The crooked nose on the boy's face seemed funny and sad at the same time.

Amy's soul was infectious.

"I'm jealous," Amy said to Rina the next morning. "You have a very sexy laugh." Rina smiled when she heard that.

Rina found the shot glass with her ice cube in the boy's freezer. She took the shot glass home with her.

Still, that was the last time Rina agreed to go with Amy.

They lost touch after college. When Rina thought about Amy, she wished that her pack of cigarettes would magically refill itself.

Rina had been paying attention to the flow of paper out of the printers next to her. She knew that Jimmy was going to move to an office upstairs soon. She didn't have a lot of time.

She went shopping over the weekend. She made her choices carefully. Her color was ice blue. She had her nails done, to go with her eyes.

Rina decided on Wednesday. People tended to have more to talk about at the beginning of the week and the end of the week, either about what they had done over the weekend or what they were about to do the next weekend. There was not so much to talk about on Wednesdays.

Rina brought her shot glass with her, for good luck, and because the glass was easy to chill.

She made her move after lunch. There was still a lot of work in the afternoon, and the gossip tended to die down then.

She opened the freezer door, took out the chilled shot glass and the sandwich bag with her ice cube. She took the ice cube out of the bag and put it into the shot glass. Condensation immediately formed on the outside of the glass.

She took off her sweater, picked up the glass in her hand and began to walk around the office.

She walked wherever there were groups of people—in the hallways, by the printers, next to the coffee machines. As she approached, people felt a sudden chill in the air, and there would be a lull in the conversation. Witticisms sounded flat and stupid. Arguments died. Suddenly everyone would remember how much work he still had to do and make up some excuse to get away. Office doors closed as she passed them.

She walked around until the halls were quiet, and the only office with its door open was Jimmy's.

She looked down into the glass. There was a small pool of water at the bottom of the glass; soon the ice cube would be floating.

She still had time, if she hurried.

Kiss me, before I disappear.

She put the shot glass down outside the door to Jimmy's office. *I am not Joan of Arc.*

She walked into Jimmy's office and closed the door behind her.

"Hello," she said. Now that she was alone with him, she didn't know what else to do.

"Hey," he said. "It's so quiet around here today. What's going on?"

"*Si tecum attuleris bonam atque magnam cenam, non sine candida puella,*" she said. "If you bring with you a good meal and lots of it, and not without a pretty girl. That's the one. That's my favorite poem."

She felt shy, but warm. There was no weight on her tongue, no pebble in her throat. Her soul was outside that door, but she was not anxious. She was not counting down the seconds. The shot glass with her life in it was in another time, another place.

"*Et uino et sale et omnibus cachinnis,*" he finished for her. "And wine and salt and all the laughter."

She saw that there was a saltshaker on his desk. Salt made the blandest food palatable. Salt was like wit and laughter in conversation. Salt made the plain extraordinary. Salt made the simple beautiful. Salt was his soul.

And salt made it harder to freeze.

She laughed.

She unbuttoned her blouse. He began to get up, to stop her. She shook her head and smiled at him.

I have no candle to burn at both ends. I won't measure my life with coffee spoons. I have no spring water to quiet desire because I have left behind my frozen bit of almost-death. What I have is my life.

"All life is an experiment," she said.

She shook off her blouse and stepped out of her skirt. He could now see what she had bought over the weekend.

Ice blue was her color.

She remembered laughing, and she remembered him laughing back. She worked hard to memorize every touch, every quickened breath. What she didn't want to remember was the time.

The noise of the people outside the door gradually rose and then gradually settled down. They lingered in his office.

What lips my lips have kissed, she thought, and realized that it was again completely quiet outside the office. Sunlight in the room was taking on a red tinge.

She got up, stepping away from his grasp, and put on her blouse, stepped into her skirt. She opened the door to his office and picked up the shot glass.

She looked, and looked frantically, for a sliver of ice. Even the tiniest crystal would suffice. She would keep it frozen and eke out the rest of her life on the memory of this one day, this one day when she was alive.

But there was only water in the glass, clear, pure water.

She waited for her heart to stop beating. She waited for her lungs to stop breathing. She walked back into his office so that she could die looking into his eyes.

It would be hard to freeze salty water.

She felt warm, inviting, open. Something flowed into the coldest, quietest, and emptiest corners of her heart and filled her ears with the roar of waves. She thought she had so much to say to him that she would never have time to read again.

Rina,

I hope you are well. It has been a long time since we last saw each other.

I would imagine the immediate question on your mind is how many cigarettes I have left. Well, the good news is that I have quit smoking. The bad news is that my last cigarette was finished six months ago.

But as you can see, I am still alive.

Souls are tricky things, Rina, and I thought I had it all figured out. All my life I thought my fate was to be reckless, to gamble with each moment of my life. I thought that was what I was meant to do. The only moments when I felt alive were those times when I lit up a bit of my soul, daring for something extraordinary to happen before the flame and ashes touched my fingers. I would be alert during those times, sensitive to every vibration in my ears, every bit of color in my eyes. My life was a clock running down. The months between my cigarettes were just dress rehearsals for the real performance, and I was engaged for twenty showings.

I was down to my last cigarette, and I was terrified. I had planned for some big final splash, to go out with a bang. But when it came time to smoke that last cigarette, I lost my courage. When you realize you are going to die after you have finished that last breath, suddenly your hands start to shake, and you cannot hold a match steady or flick a lighter with your thumb.

I got drunk at a beach party, passed out. Someone needed a nicotine fix, pawed through my purse and found my last cigarette. By the time I woke up the empty box was on the sand next to me, and a little crab had crawled into it and made it its home.

Like I said, I didn't die.

All my life I thought my soul was in those cigarettes, and I never even thought about the box. I never paid any attention to that paper shell of quiet, that enclosed bit of emptiness.

An empty box is a home for lost spiders you want to carry outside. It holds loose change, buttons that have fallen off, needles and thread. It works tolerably well for lipstick, eye pencil, and a bit of blush. It is open to whatever you'd like to put in it.

And that is how I feel: open, careless, adaptable. Yes, life is now truly just an experiment. What can I do next? Anything.

But to get here, I first had to smoke my cigarettes.

What happened to me was a state change. When my soul turned from a box of cigarettes to a box, I grew up.

I thought of writing to you because you remind me of myself. You thought you understood your soul, and you thought you knew how you needed to live your life. I thought you were wrong then, but I didn't have the right answer myself.

But now I do. I think you are ready for a state change.

Your friend always, Amy

HIGH RISE HIGH

KIT REED

The situation at the school is about like you'd expect: total anarchy, bikers roaring through the halls pillaging and laying waste; big guys hanging screaming frosh out of windows by their feet, shut up or I let go; bathroom floods and flaming mattresses, minor explosions and who knows how many teacher hostages; this is worse than Attica and the monster prom that puts the arm in Armageddon is Saturday night. The theme is Tinsel Dreams; expect wild carnage fueled by kid gangs sallying forth to trash your neighborhood and bring back anything they want. Who knows how they got out of the citadel? Who can say exactly how they get back in?

An interesting thing has happened. Nobody's cell phone works inside the walls. Worse. The land lines have been cut so you can't phone in.

Then there is the problem with the baby. See, this Bruce Brill, he tries to get down with the kids, you know, call me Bruce, but the kids call him the Motivator? He's always, like, "Come on, if you want to, you can get a C," big mistake trying that on Johnny Slater: "Why are you holding back like this? You could go to MIT!" Well, that and his stupid play. OK, this is what you get for pissing Johnny off. He and his gang have snatched your pregnant wife, they broke into your house while you were scrubbing your hands in front of English class, we'll Macbeth *you*. Johnny is holding pregnant Jane in the woodworking shop while his seven best buds rig the table saw to rip her fuckin in half. Boy, you should hear her scream. Listen, when Mr. McShy the band teacher begged them to let her go the seven of them did, yes they *did* smash sensitive Eddie McShy's Stradivarius over his sensitive head; while he weeps and the pregnant lady screams for help,

Johnny uses the splinters to pick his front teeth.

It's Teach, this eager jerk Bruce Brill, that alerted us in the city. "I tried to tell you but you wouldn't listen." Look up from supper and Teach is on your screen sobbing for Global TV. "Now it's too late."

Hunkered down in his office with a handful of survivors, deposed principal Irving Wardlaw shakes his fist at the TV. Frankly, the riot broke out because Bruce tried to make Johnny play a fairy in his "Midsummer Night's Dream." Fucking Shakespeare, what do you expect?

"It's a jungle in there!" Bruce's eyes are wet with disappointment. "I had such hopes."

Yeah right, Wardlaw growls, observing on the Watchman in his still-smoking office. *You shoulda had a gun.*

Then Bruce completely loses it. "My wife is trapped! My baby's coming even as we speak!" And because Teach made it to the Global studios before the kids or the Mayor's men could bring him down the whole world is watching, so instead of saying "We'll look into it" and back-burnering like he does everything else, the Mayor will have to act.

In any other city conquest and recovery would be a snap. SWAT teams on the roof of the school, they could rappel from there no problem, and end the siege; paratroopers could knife in through the skylight, shattering the stained glass with spiked jackboots to break up the Tinsel Prom; the Feds could plant explosives or the governor could call out the National Guard to crack skulls and restore order, but not here. We are ahead of the wave, second to none in doing what we have to do to keep our sanity.

High Rise High is a fortress unto itself.

Listen, these walls are slicker than glass. No pikes and crampons here! We're talking a hundred stories built on bedrock, nobody tunnels out and no mole gets in. The vertical face is tougher to storm than Masada or the Haunted Mesa, when your enemies can't get a toehold you are proof against siege. The first ten floors are windowless, girdled by coiled razor wire bolted tight to the glossy molybdenum face.

What were they thinking when they built HRH? Keeping you out? No. Keeping your kids *in.*

Listen, you wanted it this way. The teen population is out of control, you said, and believe me, you came begging. You showed us your lip that he split when you wouldn't give him the car and the bruises she left in the fight and you whined, "Our kids won't *do* like they should," when you meant, they won't do like we say. Fine, we said. Let's put them all in a good, safe place, with their dope and their dirty underwear and loud rock music, and let's make the walls thick enough so their speakers won't bother us and while we're at it let's make sure they can't get out. We aren't doing anything, we just want our children in some nice, secure environment where they can be happy, i.e. so if they smoke, drink, pop or snort and exchange STDs and flaunt their tongue studs and anarchic tattoos, we won't have to see.

Ergo: High Rise High.

The ten stories with the no windows? Security! Perfect, until you need to get in. The power source is self-contained on One. Nine floors are thickly packed with hydroponics and walk-in freezers and stacks of freeze-dried TV dinners and canned foods, so you can forget about starving them out. Living quarters from Eleven on up to the fortieth floor, where you get the RV and rock climbing areas, the rollerblade floor, swimming pool and football field floors, dirt bike mountains, graffiti heaven and the skateboard park floor, a bunch of you-name-it floors and above that on the top five stories, HRH 1Z to HRH 5, the school. External faculty elevators that shoot up at tremendous speeds and bypass the kids' dorms without opening so no craven grownup can infiltrate, as in, sneak into your private place, and, like, read your diary, try to break all your bad habits or smell your underwear, in other situations unscrupulous 'rents have been known to creep into your room in spite of the sign that says *Keep Out* and pounce on you like *that*.

Privacy. That's how we baited the trap.

Assurances. How else do you think we got the kids to bite? They filed into the entrance we sealed behind them like so many dumb animals, crazy to get inside where we couldn't watch what they were doing, probably so they could get high or abuse themselves and each other, or worse.

So. Basically, every teen troublemaker in the greater metropolitan area is socked inside our citadel, free to riot at their round-the-clock raves, plus — surprise! — spill out and sack your neighborhoods and then go home to the highrise and pop, snort or drink themselves senseless while you quake in your quiet, childless, orderly houses and your adults-only condos, and there isn't a law enforcement agency in the greater U.S. that can touch them because nobody can figure out how to get inside, even though from the beginning it was clear that the very worst kids had found a way out. Nobody cared much until the riot started and this Bruce went on TV. "My unborn baby! My wife!"

It seemed like a good idea at the time.

Remember, you mandated this when you voted for High Rise High.

Cheer up. All the best heads in law enforcement are huddling on this problem, they brainstorm around the clock but so far nobody's figured out how to broach the walls so that whichever local or national forces can carry out whatever threats and let us decent, God-fearing grownups restore order so we can get some sleep.

Bruce the idealist has been dragged into The Big Meeting by the Democratic candidate. The Republican mayor wants to stonewall the jerk, but remember Global; they are being watched. Municipal switchboards are flooded; the city server is clogged with gigabytes of protest mails. Crowds are gathering in front of the Mayor's residence and City Hall. The president reaches the unlisted red phone. Mayor Patton has caller ID so he has to pick up. "Yes sir." Our nation's leader cracks the whip. "Global laughing stock." The mayor's teeth clench. "I'll end it, yes. No matter what it takes."

At High Rise High, a bloodstained note hurtles into the crowd, tied to a rock. MY STRADIVARIUS!

The crowd's rumble rises to a roar. "You've got to get them out!"

Heads of State send emissaries to plead with us. *End this terrible siege.*

In the nation's capitol, a prayer vigil begins on the mall.

Because the world is watching, the mayor has to name a blue ribbon task force to investigate. That poor pregnant woman. The Stradivarius! We have no choice.

"It's clear there's a way in," Agent Betsy says at the Big Meeting. "Otherwise, how do they get out?"

The mayor doesn't like this woman much, but single-handed, she quelled the riot at Attica, so he has hopes. Five feet tall and less than a hundred pounds and she terrifies him. He says as smoothly as he can manage, "Good point."

She bites the words off and spits them at him like nails. "Don't. You. Condescend to me."

"Go ahead," he snarls. "You have four days."

The governor makes a better show of it. "May God go with you. You have the thanks of a grateful nation."

Agent Betsy snaps, "Not yet."

Daunted, he turns to his aide. "Take it away, Harry. Help make this thing work."

The governor's aide assesses the woman operative. Plain, with her straight brown hair and no makeup and the standard issue Navy blue suit. Tough, Harry Klein thinks, and fit. Very fit. Her eyes crackle and his catch fire. "What are you going to do?"

"I'm going under cover."

"You?"

Agent Betsy sweeps her hair back into a Scrunchy and pops a wad of gum. "Think I can pass?"

Harry grins. She looks about twelve. "The place is a fortress. You'll never make it past the ground floor."

"You think." Although Agent Betsy carries herself as though she thinks this is going to be easy, it takes all her strength and intelligence to keep her voice from trembling. "I'll need two police matrons and a Juvenile Services van." Her glare is so sharp that it makes even Harry tremble. She hands him a piece of paper: a list. He smiles. In that moment they are bonded. "Get me this stuff. I'm going in."

Specially uniformed for the mission she knows would make her father proud of her if he had lived, Agent Betsy has turned over her ID; she is holding out her wrists for the matrons to put on the cuffs when the mayor comes to wish her well. Using a fake hug to cover his real intentions, he grates into her ear, "Saturday. You have until Saturday to fix this. Then we nuke the place."

Inside the school, things aren't going so well. Before he disappeared, Ace Freewalter the custodian stopped the flooding but there's swash in the halls and smoke from hidden fires curls up from the air conditioning ducts. Although there are random shots and they hear the occasional scream, the survivors in Wardlaw's office can't guess how many colleagues are being held hostage in the gym. Some teachers bailed before the insurrection and the concomitant elevator shutdown, as in, after the riot boiled out of the auditorium and overflowed the halls and the cops were notified, the kids blew up the faculty elevator shafts which, as far as the embattled parents in the city know, are the only way in.

While countless hostages huddle in the gym, the escapees are holed up in here, and Ace? Did the bikers bring him down or is he lying dead at the bottom of the incinerator chute just when they need his military expertise? Who knows what happened to him? Safe, for now: Principal Irving Wardlaw, Harvard PhD who regrets the day he ever agreed to take this job, never mind the hazardous duty pay, the Hyundai and the perks. Plump, stately French teacher Beverly Flan— still single, and at her age. To her left is Marva Liu, the beautiful Asiamerican swimming coach. At the window stands the gym teacher Bill Dykstra, a gentleman of color who also taught woodworking until Johnny and his droogs commandeered his immaculate shop and trashed the place. Broken by shock, Edward McShy, who escaped the shop after Johnny's guys smashed his Stradivarius, hunches in a corner where he gibbers and sobs.

"McShy, stop that!"

"I can't!"

Wardlaw sighs heavily. The school he worked so hard to build is a shambles. The shame! He'll never get another job. "What are we going to do?"

At the window Dykstra says, "Come here."

"Paratroopers?"

"Not exactly."

"Helicopter?"

"In your dreams."

"Swat team? What?"

Dykstra is not looking up; he's looking down. He points. "Special delivery. Get a load."

At this height it's hard to make out what's going on, but Dykstra has liberated the custodian's binoculars from the utility closet. Before he burned out in the Gulf War, Ace Freewalter the don't-call-me-a-janitor was a Green Beret. Wardlaw grabs the glasses and takes a squint. There is a disturbance in the street below. Crowds scatter as a van painted Juvenile Detention Center blue noses in to the razor wire and stops. Two matrons step down, straight-arming a struggling teenager who slashes at their shins with chunky alligator boots. They undo the handcuffs, drop the teen on the sidewalk and get in the van and leave. Wardlaw says, "What?"

"Looks like a new student to me. Unless it's a diversionary tactic. They open the doors for this kid and Commandos rush in."

"Then we're saved," Beverly Flan flutes with a hopeful smile.

Coach grins. "Not so's you'd notice."

The principal sighs. "The entrance is sealed, we saw it on TV. Dykstra, what's going on?"

"Too soon to tell."

Nothing happens for a very long time. Night falls. Arc lights bathe the main entrance. The Detention Center dropoff sits on the sidewalk, hugging her knees. They see her on TV. She's a girl with silver wire woven into green corn rows and studs everywhere and the greatest of all possible tattoos. The girl shakes her fist at the Fox Nightly News camera, but it isn't us she is talking to. She is talking to *them*. Your children! She says, "Let me the fuck in."

The remaining staff clusters around Principal Wardlaw's Watchman, which doesn't show them much. Later they take turns watching while the others sleep. Near dawn, Dykstra sees it. The razor wire at ground floor level is stirring. A door opens where even the principal didn't know there was a door.

Dykstra says in a low voice, "They're coming out."

"No, somebody's taking her in."

"Give me those." Beverly Flan looks. "It's Johnny Slater!"

"How do you know?"

"I know Johnny when I see him. Why, I had him in French!"

The group in the office roars, "Get the bastard!"

Edward McShy cries, "My Stradivarius!"

The crowd below begins to part like grain when the rats run through it. They see it on TV. Snipers' bullets strike sparks on the razor wire.

Marva Liu says, "If Johnny's down there, maybe we can sneak over to the shop and rescue poor Bruce's wife!"

Dykstra reaches for her hand. "That's not a job for civilians, dear."

Dear. For the moment, Marva is glad they're under siege. Later, she thinks joyfully, something will come of this. "Oh, Bill."

Below, men in helmets like mushrooms break cover and swarm the entrance steps. Wardlaw's breath explodes into words. "Thank God, Marines!"

But Johnny and his gang yank the girl inside and before the first wave of jarheads can reach the pediment an explosion seals the door.

The new kid is squirming in Johnny Slater's grasp. Johnny is tall, stringy and good-looking with the blond Mohawk and piercing green eyes. *Cute.* The girl snarls, "What took you, meathead?"

She doesn't look so bad herself: DayGlo green hair, skinny pants and a skimpy, spangled top. He is leading her through a maze of generators and steam pipes to the hidden elevator, the one you in the city don't know about. There's a lot you don't know. These two, alone! It is love at first sight. "We had to be sure. The name is Johnny, you skank."

Agent Betsy thinks for a moment. "I'm Trinket." Johnny slips a silver Scrunchy on her wrist: invitation to the Tinsel Prom. Her voice ripples with surprise. *Yo, Trinket.* "I am!"

They go up a dozen floors. The doors open on a cluttered kid room, the kind we all wanted back then: Indian mirrorwork pillows, Astroturf and Furbys, posters and plastic shit from record stores, eight generations of Playstation, windup toys and model rockets and action figures, you name it, fox fur with the head and dangling feet and the chattering vinyl skull with skeleton attached, ripped off from the bio lab. Trinket lets her voice go soft with wonder. "Is this your *place*?"

Deep in the school sub basement where you can't go, Lance Corporal Ace Freewalter USA (retired) considers his options. He outran the bike gang on HRH3, but he barely escaped the motorized razor scooters on HRH2; the enemy took out after him with blowtorches, intent on burning him alive. Trained in survival tactics, Ace has gone to ground where even the toughest kids don't have the guts to follow. He is holed up behind the generator on HRH1Z, where he keeps his war diary. Iraq was Kissinger's fault. This defeat is his. Opening a metal chest he keeps concealed here, Ace studies his arsenal. Tactical weapons. Smart bombs. You name it. Scowling, he blackens his face. The HRH shutdown is his fault. With gritted teeth, he ties a black band around his head, tucking in the ends with a determined glare. It's up

---

to him to win the building back.

"Hakuna Matata." The mayor has been awake for 48 hours now and is getting a little schizzy. "Sorry. Good evening. I am taking this opportunity to let you know that the situation at High Rise High is under control and we will make every effort to keep it contained. We have armed guards securing the perimeter and, rest assured, the neighborhood raids have ceased."

Unfortunately the live feed suggests otherwise, but His Honor can't know what the networks have chosen to put on our screens. There are flameouts in the Greenmont and Springdale areas, explosions in Parkhurst, and person or persons unknown have brought down a police helicopter in the park.

"We will not rest until the faculty and Mrs. Um. Bruce's wife and unborn baby are safe." He rests his knuckles on his desk and leans into the camera. "And we will search and destroy if we have to, to rescue the innocent. We will get them out at all costs."

Mayor Patton looks deep into the camera, trying to lock eyes with us. "We have made these young savages an extraordinary offer. A chance to release the hostages and walk free. And we are prepared to back it up with cash. If the students of High Rise High don't settle this peacefully and give themselves up we will be forced to invade, and if the invasion fails..."

Rage opens its red jaws and without meaning to, the mayor accidentally tips his hand. He snarls, "Well, we will take drastic steps to stem this human plague."

Somewhere in the city, a thousand mothers groan, but the mayor is too mad at you to hear.

"Explosives. ICBMS. We're prepared to take a few prisoners and kill a lot more but..." He is speaking for us, remember, the exhausted parents of these terrible kids, but *in extremis* as he is, Mayor Patton forgets who he's talking to. "If that doesn't work we'll blow the building and everybody in it straight to hell."

Mayor Patton, the city's mothers are listening. "My baby!" a woman in the Hill District shouts and women everywhere take up the cry. Pressed though they were by their children's demands and glad as they were to get rid of them, the mayor's threats bite deep. They remind these women what they used to do.

"Billy, please don't hurt Billy," someone sobs, and a block away another mother cries, "Nobody touches Maryann!" The voices spill out of open windows and fill the streets. "Not Lizzy." "Not my Dave!" The chorus overflows your buildings, it swells until the vibration drowns out thought. *"Don't you dare touch our children!"* You fobbed your teenaged children off on the city but they are still yours, and you are resolute.

In a barren, freshly-scoured apartment in the projects, one woman in particular hears. "You better not lay a hand on my kid!" Rolling up her sleeves, she looks around her tiny apartment for weapons. She's a decent woman. Except for a steak knife and sewing shears, there is nothing at hand. Never mind. She picks up her mobile phone and grabs her late husband's safari jacket. Unarmed, Marybeth Slater will take on anybody and everything that threatens her son. "I'm getting Johnny out. If I have to, I'll kill."

The studio switchboard lights up like a fireworks finale. The women get an open mike. "Patton you bastard. Murderer!"

"Ladies and gentlemen, I'm sorry for any confusion. When I say blow them up it isn't an exact meaning." Caught in the act, Mayor Patton is getting shrill. "It's just a matter of speaking." His press officer mutters into his ear: too late. He screeches, "It's a metaphor!"

Agent Betsy looks up from the locket Johnny just gave her. "I guess you're not having school in here any more."

"Not so's you'd notice."

"What, um." She has to make it sound like kid conversation instead of a leading question. "What do you guys want?"

"What do you mean what do we want?"

"I mean, do you have, um, like, demands?"

The answer is too complicated for Johnny Slater to come up with, at least right now. "Everything not sucking, that's all."

"Everything always sucks, it's no big," Trinket says. *Come on, Johnny, give me something I can work with.* Entrance and escape routes, weak spots, ways to get him to back down, Agent Betsy is thinking, but she is also thinking, *he really is cute.* Trinket rubs against him, but only a little bit, "I mean, do you guys want to get out of this stupid place or what?"

He explodes. "I just want them to leave us alone, that's all."

"It looks to me like that, you got."

"This isn't alone, this is..." He lifts Bruce Brill's stupid Titania wig that started the whole thing. It looks like a microwaved rat. Words pop out of him like exploding shells. "This asshole Teach tried to put me in a *play*."

"And you snatched his wife for that?"

"Nobody makes a pussy out of J. Slater." He gestures at the crates that line the room where they are standing. "Look what I got."

What has he got? What doesn't he have. Cases of assault weapons, gravity knives and mounded six-packs of mace, a crate filled with Gulf War era grenades. Anthrax pellets, for all she knows. Agent Betsy gulps. "What's the plan?"

He picks up a grenade. "What makes you think there's a plan?"

She knows enough to shrug. "Beats the shit out of me."

He drops it into the crate. It lands with a clank. "You're the new kid and you think I'm gonna tell you the plan? I love ya baby, but, sheesh!"

This isn't a job for psychology, she realizes, looking into the open crate. Shit she knew that. Shit this kid is dangerous. The mayor has given her until Saturday to get results; it'll take that long to worm her way into Johnny Slater's head.

"Yo Trinket," he says, and the look he gives her slides between love and hate. Worse. He sees the break in concentration as the agent glances over her shoulder to see who he's talking to, the second it takes her to find and replace *Betsy* with her new name. In a flash he clenches his elbow around her neck. "Come with me."

How did our children get this way? When did they start to fight us over every little thing, and what makes them so judgmental? What turned them mean? They started out little and cute and now they scare the shit out of us.

When something like this comes up everybody has excuses, and with or without one, we scramble for an explanation. Better that than admitting there are things about us that nobody can explain.

Bad parenting, you say, some of you, and the finger you are pointing is never at yourself.

You say, *You didn't listen to them, you always gave them what they wanted/always said no.*

You say, *You neglected/overprotected them.*

Another theory? *You gave them everything they wanted but you couldn't give them love* or, *You gave them what they wanted when discipline is what they need.* Or: *You gave them too much/you didn't give them enough.*

Television, you say. *It's what you get when kids watch too much TV.*

Poverty, you say, *That's the root cause. They're angry because they grew up poor,* except you know as well as we do that these aren't only ghetto kids rampaging, they are people like us. They come out of upmarket apartments, lots of them, some from posh brownstones and more from shiny tract houses or treelined neighborhoods in the 'burbs, so what's going on here isn't only a function of poverty, although which of us is to say what makes a family poor?

It is, however, a function of rage. Why else would they do everything and hurt everybody and trash the place?

Bad companions, you say, *bad influence. H/she never would have gotten into this all by h/erself, it's all this hanging out with the wrong kind of kids* — you think this, every one of you even though, hey, *somebody's* kid's gotta be wrong or they'd all be perfect, right? You think, if only we save our nice, nice children from all that bad company and talk sense to them!

Do any of you remember what it's like to be sixteen?

Race, you say, or *religious discrimination,* but if you look at the mix in HRH you will find it is a perfect mix, kids seething like roaches in the same melting pot.

Oh, oh! If only I hadn't refused her the car/made fun of the crush/made rules/made him wear that purple shirt!

When kids go bad, it's never what you think.

What did she do wrong? What changed? Grimly, Johnny frogmarches Agent Betsy to the elevator and with his arm still locked around her neck, drags her inside. They shoot up, up and up into the ruined school. When she can speak she asks, "Where are we going?"

"I'm done showing you around." The door opens on HRH1 and he forces her into the hall.

"You didn't show me shit." She wants to try, *why don't you show me that you like me* but she is strangling as he drags her along. "Where are we really going?"

"Check on things."

"So. What. Are we going to the prom together or not?"

Johnny laughs and tightens his grip. "You're my number one woman, right?"

"Then. Agh." She chokes out the words. "Why are you hurting me?"

Johnny unlocks his arm and turns. He lifts her off her feet by the tightly braided green pony tail, sets her down and gives her a kiss. "It's just the way I am."

In Wardlaw's office, Beverly Flan whimpers, "We're running out of food."

Coach Dykstra says, "The situation is desperate. We have to get a message out."

Wardlaw pounds on his dead Totalphone and skates his muted cellphone across his desk and into the trash. "How?"

"I have an idea." Patting her gray satin front, Beverly Flan smiles brightly. Wardlaw hates Beverly Flan. "We can open a window and drop a note!"

Wardlaw says through his teeth, "You know as well as I do that these windows can't open. At this altitude the wind would create a vacuum and suck us all to hell."

Huddled in his corner, Edward McShy is shaken by a coughing fit. Remember that note he attached to a rock that almost brained a rubbernecker? MY STRADIVARIUS. What window did he open that he shouldn't have opened, to drop it out, and if that window is still open, what will happen if some kid crashes his way into the music closet, which has formed its own airlock, breaking the seal?

And in the governor's office, with nothing on TV but reruns of the Bruce Brill interview and the mayor's speech, Harry Klein paces and frets. On the surveillance monitor, the silhouette of High Rise High looms, huge in the encroaching dawn. The woman he thinks he loves is under cover somewhere in there, and he's afraid she is in danger. Is she OK? She promised to let him know. The city's phones are dead and the police scanner gives back only background racket, nightmare static from beyond the pale. Betsy has to get in touch, but how? She swore she'd find a way to let Harry know she was all right. He saw her go in, all right, but nothing has come out.

Amazing what happens when systems break down, Trinket thinks as her new boyfriend rushes her along. Order in institutions is always delicately balanced, a masterpiece of tension. Amazing, how long so few could control so many particles. A thousand kids kept at bay for all these months by a hundred teachers at most, few of them particularly physically strong and even fewer armed. Teachers plus the custodian who, the folder they gave her at the briefing told her, had been a Green Beret. Everything running smoothly until...

Brill, she thinks. That idiot Bruce Brill.

Now the adults are absent or neutralized in a holding pen, and order has gone out the window. The place is falling apart. The school isn't exactly a charnel house but by this time it's pretty much a mess. Instead of going back to their dorms after the riot, the kids seem to want to hang together. It's either a gut fear of being alone or herd instinct or maybe it's a victory thing. Nerved up and chattering, they've holed up in various classrooms to extend the experience, jittering teenagers on a perpetual roll. Maybe they think if they go home to bed, the adults will swarm them and take over while they sleep. They've dragged mattresses into the school precincts and set up little camps in labs and classrooms— bikers here, ravers there, the tightly knit Geeks and Monsters here in the computer lab on HRH2, wrapped up in a multi-level chess game in which the National Honor Society kids have just checkmated the Science Club in six dimensions, happy and peaceable because they've played for two days straight undisturbed by the need to change classes or leave here to go to Study Hall. *Kids*, Betsy wants to yell, although she's strangling and can't yell anything, *put your eggheads together and come up with a plan to save the school.*

Johnny drags her along past kid fundamentalists ranting in the nondenominational chapel and hard core druggies zoning in the cafeteria on HRH 3 and there is, of course, the Rifle Club holding the hostages at their encampment in the gym on 4. Agent Betsy notes that the HRH gangs have divided according to every possible line a group could draw between itself and another group: racial lines, gender lines, politics; they have divided according to everything from sexual orientation to religion: Muslim Alliance, Baptist Youth, Murray Atheists, Holy Rollers, Bayit, Rosicrucians, to say nothing of the Republican Youth, young Democrats, Conservative Fucks; you name it, a splinter group is here. Oh yes, and the school chapter of A.A., which is meeting over coffee in the abandoned teachers' lounge. Meanwhile the real drinkers have taken over the school library; as Johnny steers her past, kid drunks reel out to High Five him, giggling and happily plotzed.

"These are my people," he says into her ear.

She does not say, *You'd be better off at MIT.*

"And this is my place."

What Agent Betsy doesn't know, rolling down the hall with the school's number one tough guy, is that if Johnny Slater tried to raise an army now, it wouldn't necessarily be *his* army. The kids of HRH would tear each other to pieces trying to decide who ought to be in charge.

Outside the gym, the silence is impressive. Inside, the hostages — half the faculty — are bedded down on exercise mats while the Rifle Club patrols with M20s and with fatigues tucked into tightly laced boots. There's blood on the floor in a couple of places — that'll teach you to argue with us. Solid as a truck, fat, blue-eyed Chunk MacKenzie goes from mat to mat with a flashlight, turning over huddled teachers with a heavily shod toe. He is looking for the light of his life. She's a tad too old for him but he is meant to be with the only woman whose heft matches his — big as a tub but beautifully dressed with pretty blonde permanent hair and what a pretty face — his love the one and only French teacher, Ms. Beverly Flan. His heart is breaking. Where is she? Around him, other guys and girls in the Rifle Club are getting off their rocks getting even with the teachers who humiliated them in math or told them to shut up or just plain gave them a D, but Chunk's head is on a different track. Enough hitting and kicking for him, enough pushing teachers to their knees and making them beg. His heart is in the high place. *We can be together when this is over*, he tells himself, unless he is trying to tell Beverly.

Everybody has a dream, and this is Chunk's. *I'll save her and she'll forget I'm too young and start talking to me in French. I'll save her and she'll thank me, you'll see.*

As they reach the end of the fourth floor hall Johnny relaxes his grip slightly, letting Trinket slide down a bit; they're going along like sweethearts now, cute couple walking close. "We took this place down in fifteen minutes," he says. "The school is ours."

Words fail her. "Kewl."

Overhead there is ominous thudding and rumbling: the Decorations Committee hanging pink balloons and mylar streamers from the rafters under the skylight, decorating the Olympic sized indoor track with Styrofoam snowmen and silver KMart Christmas trees for the Tinsel Prom.

They reach the machine shop. Johnny's guys have given up on the table saw and instead are flipping cigarette butts at the Teach's gravely pregnant wife, who turns her head with a cold glare. Even though her eyes are swollen from hours of crying so quietly that nobody will know, when Mrs. Brill sees Johnny coming in with Agent Betsy, she understands. Kids are only kids, but women know. They exchange looks. Agent Betsy's hair is crazy green and she's dressed like a kid; she carries herself like a kid, but women know what's up before men have a clue. Jane Brill's eyes kindle at the sight of her, but Johnny's watching so the pregnant woman quenches them fast. A lesser person would beg for her life but Jane is a lot smarter than her husband the bright-eyed Teach. "Oh," she says with absolutely no inflection. Not surprised. Not scared. Not anything, just observing, the way you'd say, *It's raining.* "You're back."

"Look what I got," Johnny says, putting Agent Betsy in front of him like a prize he won at the carnival. God, is he trying to impress her? The woman is tied to a chair! "This my girlfriend Trinket, Mrs. Teach. In case you thought..."

It seems wise to act impressed. Agent Betsy says, "Is that your *hostage*?"

"Hell no. Better. This is my ticket to ride."

Quick as *that*— maybe two quickly for a guy's girlfriend, Trinket asks, "Ride where?"

When you're seventeen sometimes your body takes you places your mind isn't ready to be. Johnny gives her a look of naked doubt, but covers quickly. "Like I'd tell you."

In the chair, Jane Brill sits without moving. Agent Betsy notes that her ankles have begun to swell. Sometimes women can communicate without words. Trinket lowers her voice. "Has this lady, like, been to the bathroom?"

"Who gives a shit?"

"She's no good to you if she croaks." She hisses like something out of a scary movie. "Did you ever hear of *toxemia*?"

"Oh," Johnny says. Smart, remember; in his time this kid has read everything.

"See how her ankles are puffing up?"

"Oh, shit."

"You better let her go before she pops."

Seven louts in black Spandex and Army surplus boots converge, all cartridge belts and jangling chains. "Did we win yet?" "What took you?" "What did we get from them?" "You were going to bring pizza." The biggest, the one with Sidekick written all over him, gives Johnny a bearish nudge. "Where's the beer?"

"Fuck off, Dolph," he says. "I'm bringing Trinket for the girls to take care of while I'm busy." He means: *surveill*. He know the word but he knows not to say it. "But first. Trinket, these are the guys. Guys, Trinket."

The gratifying rumble tells Trinket she is looking good.

"So, the Slaterettes are holed up... where?"

"Music room, what's left of it. Susie's putting up a tent."

Dolph mutters, "You're taking your chick to the *girls*?"

Johnny grins. "You got a problem with that?"

"You know how they are with new kids," Dolph says.

Trinket gives him a sharp look. "I can take care of myself."

He bends over Trinket with an amiable leer. "Just watch the fuck out for Mad Maggie."

Then Johnny says something that absolutely terrifies her. "Fuck that shit, she's mine. Mag knows I saw her first."

Think fast, Trinket. "Like, you don't want me to take Mrs. Teach here to the bathroom? If she pops on you, you're screwed."

Jane Brill says, "Especially if I pop right here."

Trinket bores in. "You want dead baby all over the place?"

"Shut up."

Jane's voice is shaking but she says, "Think of the mess."

Ever the cop, Trinket clinches it. "By me, that makes it Murder One."

Jane says, "And they still fry killers in America."

"I said, shut up." Johnny plasters duct tape over Jane Brill's mouth. Then he takes out his knife. Cool as she is, the teacher's wife shrinks as the point touches her front. In a swift gesture, he cuts the tape that keeps her in her chair. "Go with them, Dolph."

Dolph does. About the conversation between these women: there will be no conversation. Dolph lounges while Betsy helps the teacher's wife stagger to the bathroom; he props the stall door open as she sits and without Trinket there to drop one strap of her tank top, creating a distraction, Johnny's sidekick would have watched the pregnant lady peeing like a customer ogling a pole dancer in a topless bar. What he won't see, no matter how carefully he watches, is the look of complicity, or that Trinket has slipped a razor blade into Jane Brill's palm.

Deep in the bowels of the school's heating system, Ace Freewalter has belted on the necessary equipment and snaked into a ventilating duct. Juvenile perps and Saddam wannabes, watch out. The Ace is on the move.

Days pass faster than they should. The prom is almost here! Adults in the city outside are in a righteous frenzy. No school has ever capped its prom with a human sacrifice, but there's always a first.

The time whips by like nothing for the waiting city because we are more excited than we are scared— what a show!— and even faster for the excited kids, who are definitely on a roll, trying on outfits and dragging a lifetime supply of glits and Mylar and phosphorescent tubes up to the fifth floor, burning their favorites on CDs for the prom DJ and rehearsing some live music of their own; Johnny has the idea that they should dress Principal Wardlaw up as a Christmas tree and make him sing the kickoff number at the Tinsel Prom.

For the adults trapped inside High Rise High, chomping on graham crackers and Pepperidge Farms goldfish in Irving Wardlaw's office or tossing on filthy wrestling mats in the gym while they wait to be rescued, however, the days and nights seem interminable.

Trinket, however, is like a cat jittering on a fence. Time is whipping by too fast, in terms of Agent Betsy's mission. In the last four days she's tried a lot of things and accomplished zip. She had hoped to undermine the revolution or at the very least open the main doors downstairs for the SWAT team by this time, but when you're in a building this size everything takes longer than you think. Plus she's heavily surveilled. For Agent Betsy, the clock is ticking and time is running out.

And Trinket? This is taking *forever*. She can hardly wait for the prom! When he isn't with her, Johnny turns her over to the Slaterettes. She was worried about it going in, like this Mad Mag kid would mess her up, but it's cool. This Mad Maggie everybody's so afraid of turned out to be a fat, soft bully with a big voice. When Mag came down on this kid Evie for no reason, Trinket used her police training to deck the two-hundred pound bitch and all the other Slaterettes clapped. Now she and Evie are best friends. Agent Betsy's expertise has made Trinket something of a hero. To say nothing of her wardrobe sense. With Evie riding post, Trinket and the Slaterettes have raided closets on the dormitory floors for everything from dental mirrors to wing nuts and jewelry and hubcaps to pin onto costumes from the aborted Shakespeare thing. With Trinket as personal shopper, the Slaterettes scored big. Now they're in the music room working on their Look.

"Don't have much time," Trinket says, suddenly confused. She looks up from the black gauze shift she is decorating, surprised. "It's tomorrow night."

Oh, man. Remember the mayor's secret ultimatum? Agent Betsy has forgotten a lot of the things she had in mind but she hasn't forgotten the threat the mayor made right before he patted her on the butt and sent her in on this secret mission. If she can't bring the revolution down by the time they crown the prom queen, he's going to send in planes to nuke the place.

But tonight is the pep rally, and for a kid in high school, first things come first. It's cool. After all, it's a big world in here, and she still has twenty-four hours.

They like me, Trinket thinks, doing makeup for the pep rally. Makeup: after her drab girlhood as a police officer's orphan child, after rigorous police training to make up for it, hanging out with kids doing makeup is a trip.

And Johnny, she thinks, even though she should not be thinking it, not with Harry Klein parting the razor wire down below and running his laser knife around a sealed opening that you don't know about, not with Harry letting himself into the bottom of the exhaust shaft where he labors upward in spite of fumes and grit-filled smoke. She definitely should not be thinking, *and Johnny*, not with Harry tightening the crampons to climb a hundred stories straight up if he has to, just to get to her, but Agent Betsy is giddy with success and for a dead cop's daughter who's having her first real *girlhood*, this is distracting. If Trinket had a diary, her kid life in HRH has left her in such a state that she'd write, *Dear Diary*, she thinks because she never had a diary, but instead of writing it down or speaking aloud she burns the words into the air: *They really like me. And Johnny. Johnny likes me.*

In the streets of the city in crisis, mothers are on the march. They don't know the mayor set the clock ticking, but they do know he has made threats. They think as one: *Not my kid.*

Imagine being in a mothers' march. Someone like you! Time's gone by but you are still a mother and it twists in your gut like a knife. *My baby, my kid*!

Your kids got too big for the nest, you thought, when they went off to school it was a relief. Then why do you find yourselves wandering into their empty rooms on bright autumn afternoons, remembering how cute they were when they were little and (yes, Marie!) satisfied with a little toy, and now they are at risk so never mind what they do to you for breaking into their special place, you are out to bring them back. You don't want them at home, really, but you do want them at home sort of, they used to be so *cute*, and you are determined to get them out of that school because no matter what he did to you, you love him, and you love her no matter what she said during the fight because whether or not you intended it, once you have become a mother you are a mother all your life; you have, etched into your consciousness, the legend of the mother's heart. One more time: the thief cuts out his mother's heart for a profit, he's running to the highest bidder to collect the cash when he trips and falls in the dirt and drops the heart and the heart cries out, *are you hurt*?

Mothers, do not hope to get into the building. Do not expect to change the outcome, you are only a mother and mothers can't. Just go to the place and do what you always do. Coursing through the streets, you are joined by others occupying the same head, house cleaners and brain surgeons alike: intent not so much on their occupations or accomplishments or dreams or even maternal duties as on their job description, which is both name and self- fulfilling prophecy. There are thousands of you now.

In the refurbished auditorium, Johnny and Trinket are onstage for the pep rally, him in a red shirt with gazillion safety pins and slashes, her looking cool in a shift she made out of a rug she found.

"This is it, guys," Johnny says but even he must notice that nobody's listening. They are distracted by the threats in the sky outside—warnings from the mayor etched in the clouds in phosphorescent pink smoke. GIVE UP. The ultimatum hinted at. TOMORROW BY MIDNIGHT. The antique plane doing the writing has just put the final flourish on: OR ELSE.

There is, furthermore, the mysterious clanking coming from somewhere deep in the building, as though somebody's running a fork lift into the trash chute which, incidentally, is pretty much jammed right now since this Ace Freewalter guy, you know, the supe, disappeared without starting the incinerator and kids are throwing things in at such a rate that the stink is piling up. Still, these are his people and Johnny Slater is on a roll.

By this time he's forgotten how this thing got started; he's forgotten the promises he made to get his people going and he's almost forgotten the Teach's pregnant wife who is by this time sitting in her chair in the shop with a pool of water at her feet— don't ask. What he's thinking about now as he looks out over the assembly is that this is going to be the bitchinest prom ever, he's here with an extremely sweet new woman, even though she still hasn't let him fuck her it's close, and nobody is never, ever gonna make him put on a stupid wig. He raises his hand for silence, which, forget it.

"Guys."

Wait. No great moment gets launched without a slogan, but the uprising at High Rise High was spontaneous, no big moment he can point to, no main reason, just a thousand kids exploding all at once. Now Johnny's people are milling and jabbering and he has to come up with some slogan or he'll blow this deal. "Guys," he says, but it's getting so loud in here that nobody hears.

In the back of the auditorium kids have started throwing ninja blades at the velvet curtains onstage and one of them zips close, maybe too close to Johnny's head. "Guys."

Funny, it's Mayor Patton that gets their attention. Amazing, his geeks have patched a remote into the school's PA system and his voice is booming from every speaker. GIVE UP OR WE NUKE YOU TO SAVE THE INSTALLATION. They think it's a bluff so only Agent Betsy knows it is true. The Mayor booms on, silencing the rally. HAVE YOU CHILDREN EVER HEARD OF NERVE GAS?

All it takes to move mountains is a really good threat. Kids start bumming right and left. Five minutes of this and they'll be storming the secret staircase, swarming out like rats.

"Babe," Johnny whispers into Trinket's DayGlo hair. "It's you and me to the end."

It's odd, what happens to Agent Betsy then. *He loves me. Johnny loves me.*

On the other hand, you can find ways to turn a really good threat, to make people mobilize. At Johnny Slater's side, his girl Trinket starts shaking like a rocket at liftoff. Her thought balloon has a light bulb in it. She pulls a stick of something out of her front and with a wild grin, she lights it off. Johnny flinches but it isn't dynamite Trinket holds over head like the Statue of Liberty's torch; it's a flare. "That's just shit!" she cries, and in the front row Dolf mutters to the guys, "What did she just say?" and Fred yells, "I think she said *what the shit!*" This rocks so strong that every kid in the place takes it up, and as it passes through the room Agent Betsy's angry outcry morphs into the kickass slogan to end all slogans. Pretty soon the place is rocking with it: "What the shit. What the shit!"

Crouched in the school ventilator system, Ace Freewalter rocks and nods in time to the chant. He is considering his options. With the stuff he's packing, he could blow every kid in the auditorium to smithereens, but you don't get the Congressional Medal for nuking a batch of high school kids when your mission is to bring them in under guard with a white flag to seal the surrender. He could use a Smart Bomb to take out the leader and his girlfriend but like any good soldier Ace knows every group like this has its unsuspected secret agent and he's pretty sure he knows who the city's agent is. All he needs to do, then, is separate this green-haired girl in the ruggy-looking shift from the boyfriend and give her the grip. He needs to get with this woman agent and figure out the best way to liberate this place. He and the agent will exchange passwords and together they'll figure out how to save the day and do it without harming the hair on a single kid.

Onstage with Johnny, cute, popular little Trinket is so caught up in the moment that she forgets who she used to be. The crowd roars and that stringy, unhappy, capable person whose dad died in the line of duty which is why she's such a good cop fades away. She fingers the silver Scrunchy Johnny put on her wrist excitedly because she's about to get everything she wants! In her life outside HRH, Betsy Gallagher went to her high school junior prom alone and her senior prom with a blind date who threw up on her feet, and no matter how smart a woman is, or how accomplished, no matter how smart *you* are, hurts incurred in high school never go away; they just go on hurting. Well, life's unexpectedly turned around for her. Trinket is going to the Tinsel Prom at HRH with the hottest boy in the entire school. It's soon! Overhead, the decorating committee thuds back and forth in a crepe paper and Mylar-fueled frenzy. Only one day left to get ready for the prom.

It is a long night, broken only by the mysterious architectural clanks and thuds characteristic of any building under siege. Unless something else is going on.

In the plaza outside HRH the mothers have merged into a solid, slow-moving wedge, pushing into the wall of Marine guards in front of the sealed front door. One has made it to the steps and is hammering angrily, in hopes that she's front and center on the school's surveillance cameras which have, incidentally, gone dead. She shouts in a voice big enough to crack stone, "Rafe Michaels, you come the hell out or I'm coming in."

The mothers won't know that this is like trying to storm a pyramid and if they did know it wouldn't stop them; mothers— even very small ones— have been known to occupy entire cities through sheer force of will. In the ranks, some of you are preparing your speeches. Threats: "Come out or *else*." Expressions of rage: "You'd talk to your *mother* like that?" Invitations to shame: "I'm glad Grandma Jo didn't live to see this." Some of you prepare to make promises— cars, trips to Cambodia, you name it—and some of you have come armed with the most powerful weapon of all. "I've got brownies, the kind with Heath bar chunks," or the simpler, more powerful, "I baked."

Under orders to protect the perimeter at all costs, the Marines shift and try to close ranks but nobody gets in the way of women once they mobilize and nothing stops mothers on the move. They aren't as strong as the troops and they're relatively slow, but together they can move anything. They come down on the regiment with the force of an avalanche. In minutes the first of them are at the razor wire, watching mutely as some of their number move in with blowtorches, working until the wire at the base falls away from the walls, at least as far up as the tallest of them can reach.

Now it is morning. Everybody's on edge because they were too excited to sleep much. That funny thing where time flies at the same time that it doesn't move an inch. Kids have started wrangling out of sheer tension. Factions have formed and even more are forming.

It is axiomatic that every revolution spawns a counter-revolution, and Chunk Mackenzie didn't give up after Johnny's gang flattened him. If he can crack the captive teachers out, he will be a hero to the woman he loves. Looking for his true love, he found the pocket of holdouts in the principal's office. Now he's come back with his gang because he's convinced his love is inside. Ms. Flan, I mean Beverly, is waiting for him with, like they say in the romance paperbacks he secretly reads, with open arms. His Beverly isn't in the gym and she didn't evacuate with the fifty who got away, so she's gotta be in there. Listen, when Chunk breaks in and rescues her, she'll forget about him being a dull normal and fall in love with him for true.

It's either ESP or behind the door Beverly really is whispering, "Chunk, watch out!"

Then Principal Wardlaw sends Coach Dykstra out with an offer of amnesty. Armed with Marva Liu's can of mace, to keep himself from falling into enemy hands, he holds it up. Chunk leaps for it like a dolphin surfacing in a tank. He knows the handwriting! The principal told her what words to put, but the flowery writing is all Beverly Flan. He recognizes it from his last French paper. *Not quite C work, Charles but for you, this is merveilleuse.* He reads aloud:

Let us out and you'll all walk free. Plus expense-paid shopping sprees at the Brookdale Mall for all.

"Go forth," Chunk mutters, "and tell the people." Climbing on a chair he yells, "Let them go and we walk free." He repeats because nobody seems to care: Chunk, who turns out to be the real idealist. Again, louder. "Let them go and we walk free!"

But a girl named Patsy looked on his paper before he got on the chair and she picks up on the real issue. "Listen," she shrieks, "It says let'em go and it's the mall for all!"

Boy, does this brings them running! "The Mall for All."

Pretty soon the halls of HRH (well, the classroom floors, at least) are rattling with colliding slogans. Alerted by the racket, Johnny's people come down in waves, roaring:

"What the shit,"

while Chunk's buds from the wrestling team try to push them back, yelling, "WALK FREE, TURN OUR TEACHERS LOOSE,"

intercut with the airheads who picked up on the mall part of the message only and are screaming, "The Mall for all."

while in the library, the forgotten vestiges of the National Honor Society, the chess club and the choir sit among the comatose drinkers, singing so dolefully that you can't hear them, "Let my people go."

At the moment, the mall crowd is prevailing. For kids interned in this high-ticket institution packed with everything they thought they wanted, the call to the mall tugs with a powerful force. It isn't *stuff* they're interested in, the city baited this place with more stuff they can use, clothes, computer games, cell phones, roller blades, you name it — it's the chance to walk free — well not free exactly, but in the place where everybody, like, you know, hangs out?

Where they just might accidentally bump into whoever or whatever it is that will end the boredom and do the magic that changes their life.

See, this is the thing. Our lives don't hang on what happens. Not back then, not now. It doesn't how many defeats we suffer or how bad it hurts, the thing that keeps us going is: what *might* happen. Here's what's important to us. It was important back then when we were in high school and it is important now.

Possibilities.

The skirmish outside Principal Wardlaw's office is short and ugly. It ends with Dolph, Fred and the rest of Johnny's gang on top, and what they are on top of? Dolph is standing at the peak of the mound Chunk Mackenzie's gasping body makes with eight guys bearing down on him—yes, Johnny led the charge, he shoulder-checked Chunk and tipped him. Then Dolph and the others pushed him down. Inside, perhaps aware that this cavalry charge led by her dumbest student was a product of true love, Ms. Flan pats her lavender satin bosom and sighs. "That boy who took the note? I think I *know* that boy."

The clanking sound traveling up from the ground floor is nothing to worry about, it's just a pale reflection of the anger and frustration driving Harry Klein. The exhaust tube turned out to be a dead end for him, the sides were too slippery to climb and he was driven back by the fumes. Back at ground level after hours of effort, he used the climber's pick he boosted from his boss's mountaineering pack to hack his way out of the tube. Frustrated at every turn, he bashed the hell out of the clogged incinerator chute because the more he needs to find Betsy, the more frustrations the building hands out. Avenue after avenue turned out to be closed to him: faculty elevator shafts imploded, freight elevator disabled for good and all. In the end Harry threaded the maze of generators on the ground floor, intent on locating the emergency staircase he knew had to be in place somewhere. Before he worked on the governor's first campaign and was rewarded with a staff position, Harry was an architect, and he knows the state board would never approve a building that didn't come up to code.

Working with only the light from a pencil flash, he walked the walls until he found the secret staircase: the emergency exit, which is his emergency entrance, had been sheetrocked and painted over. In seconds, he pried off the sheetrock and then, using safe cracking tools that happens to be his own from high school, he opens it. The stairs! By his reckoning, to get to HS1X, he will have to go up almost a hundred flights. What remains of the night before the prom will spin out unbroken for Harry Klein. Gnawing on a Power Bar, Agent Betsy's partner and, he hopes, upcoming life-partner, takes a deep breath and begins his climb.

All this coming and going, Doc Glazer thinks crossly, removing the sheetrock some fool just dropped on the skylight to his place. It might look like a dumpster to you, but by God it is his home. All this coming and going has turned it into a hellhole. *When am I, a simple hermit, going to get any peace?* When Doc could no longer shave his age and get away with it, hard-hearted Irving Wardlaw let the old English teacher go. The fool hired Bruce Brill, but survival is triumph; witness Doc. As it turns out, younger does not always mean better. Young Brill's stupidity started this whole riot thing, which serves Irv Wardlaw right.

And Doc is here to tell you that being let go doesn't mean you have to let go. When Howard Glazer cleaned out his desk after the farewell party last year and took the faculty elevator down for the last time, he contrived to ride down alone, which means that somewhere en route Doc managed to stop the nonstop elevator and climb on top of one of his less important cartons to get himself and the things he cared about out of the ceiling hatch. He pried open the doors on a storage floor and put his stuff through the opening, one box at a time. It took him six weeks to work himself and his stuff down to One which was important because Doc spied for long enough to find out that kids came and went down here, and then he spied long enough to learn where the kids' secret exit is located, because he likes to go out for an evening walk, although he's so jealous of his spot on the ground floor that he never leaves the grounds. In the months since, he's turned this dumpster into a showplace, raiding the upper floors as needed for supplies.

Now there are so many people milling in the plaza outside that he can't slip out for his constitutional. He misses the fresh air. Worse, the combination of the mothers' thumping on the facade and the mayor's amplified SURRENDER message is so loud that he can't sleep and the mothers rock the building just enough so he can't rest, either. Worst of all, the ground floor is full of rabble: that pesky custodian, who tramped around all week collecting things instead of setting the incinerator on autostoke, which means the chute is jammed and the whole place is beginning to smell.

Doc can't be sure but he thinks there's a mother loose in here somewhere, and now this.

Sighing, he does what any good scholar does when presented with a problem. As he's alone here, he can't call a committee meeting about it, so Howard Glazer does the next best thing. He pulls out the books he has on riots and begins. When in doubt, he always says, research.

In the woodworking shop, Jane Brill is damn glad she isn't really in labor. She used the razor blade Agent Betsy gave her to slit the gallon water bottle by her chair so she could scare the crap out of Dolph and the rest of Johnny's gang by screeching, "My water broke!" You bet it cleared the room. The seven of them streamed out the door with their funky hair on end, and it won't matter what this Johnny says to them, no way are they coming back. For the first time, she's alone in the shop. Working quickly, she uses Agent Betsy's razor blade to free her other hand and with enormous difficulty, because she's in the ninth month and rather close to the end, does the necessary contortions so she can saw through the duct tape securing her feet.

Where the hell is Bruce, now that she needs him? What was he thinking when he tried to turn this kid Johnny into a surrogate son? This seventeen-year-old is plenty smart, witness his diatribe when they broke into her house, she particularly admired his choice of the words "assaholic pedant," and the imitation of Bruce in high mentor mode was dead on. Hell, he's probably smart enough to run this place, which means the last thing Johnny Slater wants to do is sit down and learn a thousand new words for the SATs, a test about memory tricks and test-taking skills, not smarts. But that isn't really what pissed him off. What pissed him off was Bruce running at him with the Titania wig and one of his gushy speeches about how in Shakespeare's day, all the girl parts went to the smartest and best looking young men. What probably toppled the kid was the smarmy smile Bruce gets whenever he talks about "the bard." Jane knows kids have an astoundingly low threshold when it comes to sentimental crap.

So yeah, when you come right down to it this whole mess in High Rise High is Bruce's fault.

It's the kind of thing that makes you wonder whether you want your baby, which Bruce is trying to name Hamnet— whether you want your baby growing up under the influence of a chuckleheaded jerk. Oh yes she is angry, and she isn't just mad at Johnny or Dolf or Fred and the others who brought her here and taped her to the chair with only the briefest of pit stops and few chances to lie down. She is stark boiling pissed off at idealistic, boyish and well meaning but careless, blundering Bruce.

It's a good thing she can't hear the gloppy things he's saying about her on Global TV right now.

Instead she's busy standing up, a project that takes more time than it ought to, and stretching her aching muscles one by one. When she finishes with the case of Devil Dogs Johnny's gang brought upstairs to pass the time in here, she's going to chug the quart of GatorAde they left behind and stretch out somewhere. She needs time for the blood to make its way back to her head so she can come up with a plan.

How odd. It's the morning of prom day and Trinket and Johnny are having a fight. Maybe it's excitement, maybe it's the mayor's ultimatum and the fact that time is getting short. They've been at it for so long that she forgets what started it; the kid part of her thinks something she said made Johnny jealous, in spite of the arrested development she's old enough that clearly, even in the most constricted life, he can't be her first. The mature Agent Betsy is reflecting on the causes of arrested development and the fact that when you let two children, even two children who love each other very much, play together long enough, they get tired and start to fight.

"Go to hell," she says.

"No," he says, "you go to hell and while you're at it lose the hair, it looks like shit."

She ought to find the way down the stairs/chute/elevator, however the kids get out, and exit the building and let what happens happen, it would serve him right. At the same time she can't write Johnny off, she thinks, regarding him from a great emotional distance while Trinket rips off the tinsel Scrunchy and, weeping, says, "Fine, and you can damn well find a new bug to take to the damn prom."

When she settles this riot thing and the attack squad comes in, she'll do everything she possibly can to cut a nice deal for the kid, but by hell she came in here to settle this riot thing and she is going to end it no matter what. On second thought, maybe she should throw a rope over the rafters in the indoor track and watch Johnny and all his sadistic buddies swing. OK he just grabbed her by the green pony tail and threw her in a corner, yelling, "Fine, I will."

She shouts, "So much for you, asshole," but she is thinking: *now I'll never get to wear my dress.*

"Asshole your own asshole," he barks and stamps out of the music room which is empty just now because the girls are in the teachers' bathroom, trying on dress after dress. The Trinket part of her is sobbing angrily, but in there so deep that he can't guess, Agent Betsy is thinking: *Fine*.

Perhaps you have forgotten about the mayor. Fair enough, it's not like he's doing anything to end the occupation here.

He's busy polishing his image as he prepares to give his primetime Prom Night ultimatum for international Webcast as well as worldwide TV satellite relay so that even the most private geeks happily mousing in the school's ruined computer labs will have to acknowledge that something's going on, never mind that the server is down and every kid who tries to connect is pounding on a blank screen. If you must know, Mayor Timothy a.k.a. Timid Tim Patton is grooming himself for a run for the Senate enroute to the White House, and this is his first big step on the long road to DC.

Up Harry climbs, exhausted by now but driven by the need to resolve the situation— not so he will be a hero, but because he hates any kind of waste and millions of dollars and hundreds of kids are being wasted here. That and he's afraid Agent Betsy is in danger. Four days and not a sign! Of course he's been climbing the gigantic baffle the stairwell makes and therefore out of radio contact with the gov for the last twenty-four hours, and since he's the governor's man, his is the only information Harry trusts. He has to emerge into the school proper before he can run a sound test and there, he has to be careful because if they spot him, the kids will know at once that his fingernail-sized radio is government issue. Better keep it silenced, he thinks, and hope Betsy's faring forward and together they can put the lid on this riot at the Tinsel Prom. He has a few tactical weapons in his pack; he also has a plan.

In fact, he has a costume.

Once he reaches HRH1 he intends to put on his disguise and do his best to blend in with the panting rowdies and their ditsy girlfriends heading for the prom. Although he's too far north of thirty to make it stick Harry has studied the language, so that's not a problem, and he's devised the perfect costume, which he did by picking up on the Tinsel theme, which is, basically, silver everything. To make things simple, Harry decided to stay with the clothes he has on — plaid shirt, jeans, hiking boots, hell, he'll pass — and concentrate on the mask. For his arrival at the prom, he has chosen an antique. It is riding on his hip right now: a C3PO mask that's so old it has turned silver, remember *Star Wars*? You may not, but rest easy, Harry Klein does. He's in touch with the *zeitgeist*. He knows kids, and he knows what they like.

Now, why this prom is so important. The prom is important because no matter where you started out in life or how far you've come since the big night, if you spent four years in an American public high school, you are formed by the way it came down at your prom. Nobody ever gets over it, and one way or another, you will try to get it back — or compensate for how bad it was for the rest of your life. You think you're a grownup, you think you're fine, but it doesn't matter what you've done to yourself between your prom night and now, any more than it matters what you have accomplished; you can lose the weight/tighten the abs and build the pecs/fix the hair/get the lift/have electrolysis/make the fortune, but in the beginning there was that problem with the prom and no matter how fast you've run, we know, and we know you know, that you are the same person.

Even if it was good your prom wasn't good enough. They never are. Even if you go with the hottest kid in the school, even if your hair is perfect, it's built in. It's supposed to be the happiest night of your life, which means no prom can be as good as you want. *All that*, you think, *and this is all I get?*

More likely, it was bad.

Either way, look back and be humbled by the prom you didn't make, the date you didn't get, the chance you missed because you went with the wrong person, or the existential question: why, when you went with the right person and everything went right, you came home feeling so empty and flat.

Mind you, this is not necessarily a bad thing. For the rest of our lives, people like us jump higher, try harder.

Well, Agent Betsy isn't going to get it back. Instead, she thinks, dressing for the prom again and getting ready to go without a date — again — if she can't get it back, she thinks...

She will get even.

In the best stories about high school, it all comes down at the prom.

In that ideal world we invent when we make stories, the prison riot and siege at High Rise High would end in the only possible way: at the prom.

It would end in the indoor track a.k.a. ballroom with all the kid factions and sympathizers present and the key outsiders— the mayor's agent and the governor's agent and the Gulf War vet and the pregnant woman and poor little McShy of the busted Stradavarius working their way through the littered halls or up through the bowels of the school for a gorgeous conflation, and at the height of the excitement— probably when Johnny crowns the wrong girl prom queen (*my man and my best friend*: the rat went with Evie!), when Johnny puts the Mylar crown on Evie Jones, the five valiant outsiders would burst into the ballroom followed by a thousand seething moms led by upstairs by a cranky Doc Slater, and said mothers would shame their kids into submission while the mayor and the governor come in through the shattered skylight to declare amnesty and pin hastily engraved medals on Agent Betsy and Harry Klein who would, OK, who would kiss, take *that* Johnny Slater, while Jan Brill fingered Johnny as her kidnapper and the tardy SWAT team read him his rights and dragged him away.

But remember, even when it goes well your high school prom is never what you thought it was going to be, so don't be surprised.

This one isn't either.

Every high school prom is a symphony of near misses. Maybe it's only the difference between the dress you thought you bought and the way it really looks on you, or the hopes you had for the peach tuxedo you rented with matching shirt and cummerbund, which looked pretty stupid when the cops were taking your particulars after you lost control and crunched it nose and front wheels halfway up the Whites' humongous forsythia; or your near miss may be something bigger, but only slightly bigger because these things never get as big as our hopes. The way proms like this one end is less likely to be a function of old scores settled and dramatic deflowerings and true love and moonbeams and wrongs righted than it is simple fatigue: the relieved sigh as you finally drop her off at her house (she was cute, but she was shrill) or take off your shoes (it was like kissing a cardboard Tom Cruise cutout on a lobby card), which have begun to bite; we all have dreams about the big moments in our lives but trust me, they are only expectations. When it comes right down to it, most things in life as we know it aren't resolved in fireworks or car crashes or explosions, instead they happen simply or accidentally or capriciously; they are settled out of fatigue or ennui or sheer boredom, so the real outcome, the true and final outcome of the stand at High Rise High?

1. The Federal Government was fully aware of the mayor's threats and dispatched local police to arrest him as his unilaterally set deadline neared. There is a full investigation being made of the city's nuclear arsenal, which turns out to be fuller than any state or federal authorities imagined. The mayor himself has been interned and certain irregularities in the matter of the building of High Rise High are under investigation.

2. The prom went just fine, or about the way proms usually do, in spite of the no adult faculty around to supervise. Remember, the riots began a week ago and nobody's slept in a real bed since so everybody arrived excited, but staggering with exhaustion. Eventually everybody at the prom just got tired of dancing and getting high and they straggled home to bed to crash or to the quiet park floor in the building to sleep on the artificial beach, or they drifted back into the corners they'd staked out in the library and the computer lab, in the sentimental wish to spend one last night in the camps they had set up at the beginning of the high school revolution, when they had such hopes. Right now not one of the kids who rioted and took over HRH could tell you what they'd hoped to gain.

3. Emerging in the last minutes of the dance, i.e. at the moment when Dolph, designated stand-in for Principal Wardlaw, was crowning Johnny Slater prom king, Jan Brill slipped out from behind the bandstand and made a terrified Chunk Mackenzie show her to the single functioning elevator. Stampeding him with a touch of the end- stage breathing she'd learned at LaMaze, you know, the kind you're supposed use when you bear down at the end? she pressed the button and rode down alone, and...

4. at the bottom the mothers milling on the ground floor parted like the Red Sea—she's a mother, like *us*—so Doctor Howard Glazer, HRH (retired), could lead the nice lady to the kids' secret exit (it was behind the incinerator!), open the hatch and usher her outside, so that from the front

you saw double doors in the foundation opening and a small, angry, very pregnant woman marching out, spreading her arms to the fresh air. If you were glued to your television or your computer screen like the rest of us you may have seen the Marine lieutenant in charge mutter into the little woman's ear and if you did, you saw her bark a response that made him flinch. Our microphones didn't pick up what either said but apparently the lieutenant offered to take her to her husband, he was worried about her, and that's what set her off.

"Aha," the mayor said from the police van, where the Chief was keeping track on his Watchman while he dealt with the city's most important prisoner. "I was right. They're giving in!"

"Bullshit," the kids would have said, if any of the kids had been awake to see it. They'd partied till they puked and then some, "We're going the hell to bed."

They were bored of the riot anyway.

Which means that in the principal's office, Irving Wardlaw wakes up to daylight and the awareness that the riot is over. The prom is over. The music's stopped and with it, the relentless thump of the bass speakers that vibrated on every floor. So has the thud of a thousand teenagers jumping up and down. The smell of weed has dissipated and the laughter's died. They are gone. The first to wake, he studies his embattled colleagues. The sleeping McShy's fingers are moving on his bony chest as though he's still playing his ruined violin, while Beverly Flan sleeps with her fat mouth pursed in the face she makes when she tries to teach freshmen how to pronounce le. Smiling, Dykstra and Marva Liu sleep in each other's arms. It's Sunday morning, which means they have the day off. He needs to decide whether to keep the staff in the office here, along with the teacher hostages sleeping in the gym, so he'll have a skeleton staff in place when classes start on Monday morning, or whether to cancel graduation so he can give them next week off to recover and the rest of the summer off. Maybe the latter, he thinks, looking at the broken glass in his office door with a sigh. It's going to take at least that long to get this place cleaned up. But then. He feels that little ripple of excitement that comes every time he thinks the word *September*. Then we'll have our second wind by the time school starts in the fall.

Fall, he thinks. Definitely time for a fresh start.

Meanwhile Klein and Agent Betsy have found each other. It happened early in the prom, he came busting out of the woodwork in his C3PO mask and they knew each other at once, which means they were dancing close by the time Johnny gave Evie the tinsel crown which nonetheless snagged what was left of Trinket's girly heart. But it felt so good, slow-dancing with Harry, that Betsy hardly minded. She thinks. She and Harry danced straight through until daylight filtered through the shattered glass overhead and then fell down on a pile of coats. After the weeklong siege, they are too tired to do anything but talk.

He says, "This was supposed to be our big moment."

"Yeah, I guess it was." Looking around at the littered ballroom, the debris of a thousand high school kids' hopes, she says quietly, "Is it always like this?"

"What do you mean?"

"You know, no denouement and no real resolution, no clinch and no ticker tape parade."

"Probably. But you're wrong about the clinch."

"So there's that," Betsy says, beginning to smile.

"Yes," he says, tightening his arm around her wiry little back. Even though there is only one prom, there is always a next time. "There is."

In the tinsel archway looking back, Johnny tightens his hold on Evie's hand until she squeaks. In this light Trinket looks like, she looks like a... She doesn't, but now that he knows Trinket is really Agent Betsy, who is thirty-five years old, he can write the thought that will make sense of this. *What, me care about that old hag?*

Oddly, the mothers in the building do not leave the building, even though the matter of the riot is settled and by Presidential order, the mayor's threat is no longer a threat. They're bopping around among the crates and blocks of heavy equipment on the ground floor because like it or not, this thing has brought home the fact that they still care. They miss their kids, they really do; they miss these near-adults their babies and they miss having them at home but now that push comes to shove they are conflicted and confused. Homesick for the way things used to be and fully aware that once puberty hits, nothing is ever the same, they can't decide whether they should stay and see their sons and daughters, at least to find out how they are doing, or whether they should avoid the aggravation (what if h/she wants to come home?/ what if h/she doesn't want to come home even if I beg?) and go.

Meanwhile, in the military it is axiomatic that there's always one in every organization that doesn't get the word. Ace Mackenzie hunkers down in the ventilator system directly over the girls' locker room. Eventually the revolution is going to boil in here and he can swing down and take control of the sub-group that brings down the leaders of this fucking riot and when he does that he's going to take out all the troublemakers and bring this place to order, and when he does...

He doesn't know, but he can think about it. Right now he has nothing but time.

THE STORYTELLER'S STORY

GAVIN J. GRANT

"It blooms once in every man's life," he said, and we settled down to listen. "And some say twice in a woman's." We laughed.

"It blooms on a different day for different people and for no two people in the same place. I think I know where to look for mine is, and I have an idea that the day is in June."

It was March, the snow was packed into ice, and June seemed impossibly far away.

"I think," he said, changing the subject, "next year I'll be visiting you in summer."

"Why?" I asked.

"Because next year I'll come by train," he said.

"No!" said my father, going from sleepy to fully awake. "No," he said, delighted, "really?"

"Perhaps," said the storyteller. "It's only a hundred miles or so from here now. This is a busy town, it seems like a good match."

My mother nodded to me and I jumped up and stirred the bean soup. The train. It was a gigantic thought, too big for me. I put bowls and spoons on the table, refilled everyone's mugs with dad's beer. For once Alder stirred his lazy self and got the bread. Mother served dinner and the storyteller told us that year's story:

Anna Maria, resting from the dance, blinked when this man, this stranger, a little older than either of you, but many years younger than me, asked her to marry him. She had been courted for four years by another

169

man and this young man had danced with her twice this night, asked her if she would like a drink, and when she took the beer stein, he'd dropped to one knee and asked her to marry him.

She knew the language of courtship, she thought she knew the language of love, but she did not know the language this man spoke.

"Pardon me, sir," she said, as polite as a maiden must be, "but I do not know you."

The young man was serious, and, still on one knee. "You will come to know me," he said, "and if you do not love me now, it will come soon enough."

She threw her head back, but found she couldn't laugh. She tried to shrug his hand away, but he held on. It was quiet around them and she realized others had heard his proposal.

"No!" she cried. "No!"

"Anna Marie," he said, and she looked into his dark green eyes. . .like the forest, and deep within them a light, a cottage with a light in the window, the dried, shrunken head of a pig above the door, the smell of the tanning skins never far away. She blinked and he laughed.

"That's not us," he said.

She was curious and once again she leant forward to look into his eyes. They were green the color of a fir tree against the frozen snow of deep winter. There was a light in his eyes, a light that glinted off something lying in the snow. A knife, handle half-buried, blood dried black on the blade.

"No," he said. "Neither is that me. Let those stories go."

She looked one last time, and she was down on her knees although she didn't know it. Green, green eyes the color of grass late in a wet spring. There was a darkness: he stood beside a well hauling on a rope and she knew he was hauling up a wooden bucket. She could hear screams but when he drew the bucket up, inside was a boy, three or four years old, trying to hold onto the sides and clap his hands at the same time.

"Again," called the child, and the dark-haired man pretended to let the rope go. The child screamed, the man turned to her as she looked down from the sky and said, "Anna Maria?"

Later, when I was walking the last miles toward the Red Cliffs, I thought he'd been talking about a flower after all. Listening to him then, fourteen years old, I thought I was smart because I *knew* he hadn't been talking about a flower.

The train tracks had passed to the south and already something was draining from our town. And here I was, wandering in the wilderness looking for a flower. And if he was right, that for everyone there's some special flower, some special something, and I was looking for his flower, not my own, what was I doing?

I had been looking for complications but perhaps he was as simple as a man looking for a flower. I must have been simple then, too, thinking there was more to it. Does that mean I'm simple now compared to what I will be when in the future I look back to today?

My favorite story, the one that made me walk out here, is one he told when I was eleven. A story of a boy something like me:

"No," the woman said. The farmer's youngest son had just stepped forward, rag paper sheets he'd made himself in hand, words on his lips. He hadn't said a thing.

He stopped and the next boy in line made to step forward, "No," she said, again. The second boy faltered, stopped, stepped back. And the boy next to him, a boy he knew, Bruce, jumped forward, hands empty, before she could speak. Bruce closed his eyes and began shouting his poem. The first boy was still one step forward, alone, a step away from the line of boys that he'd come in with.

He took another step forward. He felt rather than saw the man sitting next to the woman acknowledge his step. He took another step. Nothing his parents had ever told him about Factory Day had ever included this. He wanted his chance to read his epic, and then he would be taken to the city where he would get to work in the fantasy factory. He'd known from an early age that he belonged there. He'd made up stories about it, imagined it, even used his precious paper (the scraps, if truth be told) to draw the factory the way he imagined it.

Bruce's shouting ran down, and the woman looked up from the book—which book? The boy had only ever seen two books, and this wasn't either. She shook her head. Oddly enough, the first boy felt sorry for Bruce. Epic poetry—all those swords and windmills and men who are wolves or horses—hadn't won a place in the factory in longer than he could remember.

He looked along the line of children. He'd come twenty-two miles with his parents. They had taken the omnibus, left the farm in his older brothers' hands. He worried about that. Would they feed his stinky, noisy chickens? They never did when he was there. And what about all these other boys here—had they come as far as him? All of them knew that most would not be taken.

Another boy was reciting. He was tall for his age, with hair the color of an ash tree. Not blond, but silver, or gray. How strange. The first boy shook his head. He had begun to wonder if he might get another chance to read. If standing out front might be the act that got him noticed. Or, if that didn't work, if he could slip his story into the woman's luggage for her to read later, and come back for him.

"Guard," the woman said, with a nod that might have been a tic. At the door there was a straightening of an already ramrod straight figure.

"Escort this one out."

The farmer's boy pursed his lips, he hadn't thought the ashtree-boy had been that bad. But the woman didn't mean him. Without seeming to contemplate the possibility that he would fight back, the guard picked the stocky body of the farmer's youngest boy up, carried him to the door, dropped him onto his feet, and shoved him outside.

"Wait," he said to the door. "Wait. . ." He had so many questions: What had she seen that stopped her from even allowing him to read? If not this, then what?

It was a long ride back to the farm. He never found out who went to the factory.

I never wanted to work in a factory, not the way my father's cousin did from the first time he saw the place. Of course, right up until this moment I still don't know *what I want to do* or for that matter *what I'm going to be.* I could fish for bricks, I could be the man who drew horses on horseshit, or maybe something as simple as the town drunk. I was good at drinking; I had yet to try the first two.

"Can you write?" the storyteller had asked me one year. I'd been embarrassed but I'd never done anything about it. I can imagine him telling me a story in which someone would say "Don't live your life in fear." Little good it did me.

So now I'm trying to find the flower. If I can do that, and maybe even if I can't, I'll try to find the storyteller's home to see what happened to him.

I had nightmares for years afterwards about the story he told when I was eight. I don't remember all of it, but there were parts I could never forget. It wasn't like his other stories and it was about him. It went something like this:

Once, not so long ago, and not as far from here as you might wish, I stole a soul bag.

I'd been to that place as often as I've been here, but I'd never seen *anything* like that bag before.

The outskirts of town were quiet so I walked in to the market at the long-broken Fountain Circle. As I approached, I realized two things: nearly all the townspeople were there, and I was a week earlier than usual.

An old woman, Maggie, whom I knew from years past, was speaking to the crowd. She was old, still straight-backed, gray haired, apple-cheeked, but in the green direction instead of red. She was holding something on a string, swinging it in a strange rhythm. In the past I'd known and liked her well enough so I edged forward into the crowd. I kept looking to see anyone else I knew, but they were watching Maggie, not me.

The thing on the string was a shriveled and raw-looking bag. It was the size of a child's fist, and, looking at it, I felt the hungry emptiness of my stomach turn to sour acid.

Maggie spoke louder and I couldn't understand her. I knew this place, knew the language. It is fair to say I know at least as many languages as the years I have been alive. But of what she said I could only catch glimpses and flashes.

The people called back to her and she called again and although I didn't know the language, I recognized the building rhythms, and I wanted to escape the crowd, but they were closing up, holding me within them.

I thought I might be in trouble. I've sat late at night in the bars of the larger towns and swapped stories like this with other wanderers. This mob, if they noticed me, might tear me apart, and afterward no one would be able to say who had started it, done it, ended it. I concentrated on what they said, mouthed along with the chants. Raised my fist when they sang. Watched the small dark bag swinging on a multicolored rope I thought must be made from hair.

I'd arrived in late afternoon and now the sun began to set, but no one made a move to leave for food or light. The crowd pressed still closer in. I found it hard to breathe.

Maggie closed her eyes; she held the bag at her side. The crowd grew quiet and I could feel everyone watching it.

She said something and those at the front fell to their knees. A young man, a boy really, was pushed forward. He shivered but didn't fall back.

Maggie touched the boy's forehead and he fell to the ground. She bent and I couldn't see what was happening. The crowd held its breath, everyone staring, people pushing up over one another to see. I thought I knew what was happening.

Maggie, and then two men at the front of the crowd, stood. The men went forward and helped the boy to his feet.

Now a young girl was pushed to her feet, pushed forward, her forehead received the touch, she fell to the ground. On it went, all the children old enough to have hair on scrote or breasts appearing, and my curiosity grew. What was being done here?

The hours passed. I crept forward, got close to the front. Another boy was pushed forward, touched, fell.

Maggie grabbed his trousers, pulled them down. A bit more gently she took his shrinking cock and balls in one hand. With the other she took the bag and placed it over his genitals. I was truly confused. She murmured more words in this language I could not understand and the boy's body jerked in her arms. When she lifted the bag from him his cock was still hard and there was blood mixed with the cum at the tip.

The boy was carried away and a girl took his place. Maggie stripped the girl's trousers off and with one hand opened the girl's small vagina and put the bag into or onto it. I couldn't watch, didn't want to see that binding jerk.

I lied when I said I stole the bag. I wanted to. I thought I could stop whatever was happening. I thought whatever was happening needed to be stopped. I thought I was the one who should decide what should happen.

You never know what's going on, no matter what you think. I'd been visiting that town for twenty years. How could I have known what was going on? I still don't really know what it was, nor whether it was even bad. Were people being hurt? I don't know. No one stopped me leaving, nor tried to explain; which was enough to stop me from returning.

The night he told that story I went to sleep with my tiny cock cradled in my hands. I still sleep that way and more than one woman has woken me with her laughter when she sees me sleeping. I've told some of them the story, but it never seems to frighten them. I'm sure there's something missing from the story, something that I've forgotten, that would make it more frightening. But the memory of him telling the story is so old and worn, retreaded and reused so many times, I can't tell what I've added on, and what I've left out.

The man never told the same story twice and I would never have asked him to tell that story again, but the next year Alder — knowing how many times I'd cried myself asleep or woken in terror — asked him.

"I have principles," the man said. "You never ask me to eat last year's dinner and I never expect you to listen to last year's story."

If I did not love him before, I loved him then. Then, before Alder could get annoyed, he told us why he passed through our small town every year:

Long ago, before I came to this country, I happened to stop at a famous convent high in the Mountains of the Sky. The abbess was kind enough to take me in and it was not too long until we learned enough of one another's languages to enjoy speaking to each other.

She told me that their convent was dedicated to cultivating all kinds of flowers. They traded for all their worldly needs in nasturtiums, daisies, and violets.

The sisters — and apparently the men that lived with them — believed that somewhere in the world there is one flower that blooms especially for each person.

I spent a dozen years — or was it three or four times that? I couldn't say. Time passes differently in those mountains — studying everything in their great flower library.

Eventually I decided I might have an idea where a certain man born on a certain day in a certain country might look to find a certain flower that might bloom only for him. I supposed it might be an early summer flower, something unobtrusive—like a peony—something that might survive without the care of a gardener.

I met the abbess in the garden of late spring vegetables and asked her to consider my finding. By then we were great friends and my appreciation for her wisdom only grew—still grows—as the years passed.

"I have a supposition," I said, nervous that I was overstating my case.

She nodded and said, "Tell me now, but I cannot comment until I have reflected upon what you say."

"It is really nothing more than an educated guess. I think that my flower is not native to this country." She did not stop me, nor say anything.

I laid out my conjecture for her: this flower, this place, this time of year. I hesitated to add the color I thought most likely, but could not resist.

She asked me to come back in a week so that she could consider what I had said. Nothing was done quickly in the mountains. We were too near the sky. During the week we avoided talking about my flower, and in the time I did not spend tending the garden, I thought about my leaving the convent.

When the week had passed, the abbess met me in the convent's highest garden, a tiny square on the roof of the bell tower where the sisters planted only the hardiest flowers. She gave me a small packet and said I was not to open it until I had reached this country. I was, unimaginably, speechless. Was this all there was after my years of work, my studies?

One of the sisters appeared with everything I had, already folded neatly in my pack. The abbess kissed my cheek and said I should visit again if I had the chance, then she led me down through the convent. We walked through the indoor gardens and then out through the scrub mazes, the herb gardens, the grass gardens, the secret path through the impassable hedge, by the immense compost heap, scrambled over the rock garden, past the butterfly clock (I would not miss it: for two years my task had been to move the appropriate blooms into place), and out to the path, down the mountain, to the outside world.

I'm sure you're wondering what was in the packet. During the long journey to your country, I thought it must be the seeds to the flower that I had been looking for. Then I decided that was too simple, but I could not work out what, then, it could be.

When my ship docked, I made my way through the port and out into the country. I was happy to be on land again. I am not a good sailor, and the new and yet familiar smells of the country were a relief after the salt sea. I took out the packet and opened it. Inside was a note from the abbess in a language I did not read. It was your language, which, of course, I did not yet speak.

If you are curious about the note, these are the exact words, and then I must go to sleep: 'Some of what you have said today is true,' it said. 'Some of it is not. Good luck.'

We were walking out of the village. I was almost a teenager. I should be able to remember what age I was, but I don't. I wasn't a child, not a boy or a man, just in between everything. I spent my days wanting—but not knowing what it was I wanted. He asked me about my life. I couldn't put into words what I wanted to, so I was dramatic and told him I was trapped.

He laughed, of course, and told me a story that I got to keep all to myself:

Once some years ago a man was walking through mountains similar to those far to the north that you can see on a clear day. It was late autumn and since it was a beautiful day he took a turn by the White River where he usually went straight.

He followed a rough path beside the river as the land rose, until the river was just a stream. He jumped the stream and kept climbing, head down, puffing away. He didn't see the badger until almost too late.

Have you ever met a hungry badger? This man had hunted badger with dogs. He knew badgers have great, strong claws but he also knew they never win. The dogs usually ate them, although he had tried badger meat himself. Tough meat; good if long-simmered and stewed.

The badger charged and he fell back down the hill, rolling over and over, trying to stop himself and still see where the badger was. He didn't fall down the path he had walked up. When he stopped rolling, and after he'd rested, he gathered up his belongings—his pack was lighter now, but he could not tell what was missing. When he stood, he saw lights a little ways down the hill. It was getting dark, and, being curious, a little tired, and maybe thirsty, and thinking that there might be a comfy bed where he'd anticipated sleeping in the rough, he started making his way toward them.

What he saw. . .years later, when I met him, it still kept him awake at night. Someone told a story there, wrapped it up tightly, and trapped those people in it.

You've heard of wizards and witches and curses and words that have more power when spoken a certain way. There was something of that here. A curse or a binding.

You're a modern man and you might not believe this. You're lucky: a curse might slide by you, a binding not set. But there are places where there are words that, if you say them wrongly, they'll cut your tongue out for speaking. Of course, if you get them right, you can do what you want to whomever heard you. But make a mistake and if they leave you alive, they'll cut words into your face for all the world to see. Then you must live in your village as an outcast, unloved and unwanted, but certain to be hunted down and killed if you try and leave. Words have power and words give power and some use them to take power over others.

When the man walked down to this village he did not see anything wrong. He was off-balance, bruised, missing his dignity and a few other things, but it's only luck that he walked away again.

He waved down to the people he could see, when he thought they might see him. No one returned his wave, but he was on a dark hill, wearing dark clothes, so he wasn't surprised.

Then, well, he'd have liked to pick something out and say he saw *this* or *that* and knew something was wrong, but he couldn't. But there was a moment when he knew and he found himself stopping. He didn't know why.

Think about it. Think about it for years, and listen to yourself when you talk, and don't fill in what wasn't there.

He watched the village. It was autumn, night was falling, and he was getting cold. He was just wondering why he shouldn't head down to what looked like a nice-enough place when he realized these people weren't dressed for the weather.

He stood watching. The village was smaller than your village, but there were a fair number of people around. He was beginning to see what was wrong, but he didn't yet know for certain. Three men were walking toward him, as if they were heading out of the village and up the hill. But when they reached the end of the village, they stopped. They must have been forty yards from him, but still they never spoke nor waved. They stood still, the way three men together never stand still, then they turned and walked back into the village.

That's when he realized that when he'd first seen the village those three men had seemed to be walking ahead of him into it.

They were trapped. He watched them all night and they kept repeating the same actions over and over. Occasionally someone would fall over, asleep. Those that could, ate, but they were repeating themselves every couple of hours and he could tell that some of the bundles on the ground were those who had starved to death.

He had never heard anyone mention that village. He didn't know when they were cursed, when they were trapped in their cul-de-sac of time.

What would have happened if he had come by in spring? Perhaps he would have stayed on the path and not met the badger, he wouldn't have taken a tumble, he wouldn't have been trapped there for the rest of my days!

Now, away home! I'll see you on the way back. And don't trip over your big ears on the way. Adios!

Later I thought he was a wise man. He'd given up years of his life looking for a flower that might not exist, that might not be where he was looking, that might not bloom on the day he came. How had he decided on the Red Cliffs? Why June?

But what else should he do? Should he have farmed like my family? Gone to the factories in the new cities like all my mother's brothers? What should a man do with his life?

I would never get to ask him any of these questions, but on the way to the cliff I held imaginary conversations with him on how to live. And he smiled at me, told me to live my own life, no matter how tempting it might be to slip into his.

There were stories he told that only I heard and stories I overheard when I listened at the door when I should have been out working, or in bed, asleep. Stories where woman's fingers turned to music, where a man's heart might be kept in a box hidden in the chimney, where bears mined gold and spun it into honey. These stories were forbidden and incomprehensible. I loved them best of all.

"Once upon a time," he would say, and I wanted to tear the ears of my head and hide them in his pockets so that I would hear every story he ever told.

"Once upon a time," I whispered to myself when Alder was sleeping, "a young boy with no ears and the biggest smile anyone had ever seen lived in a village halfway between the seas." But my stories were nothing like his: I got lost in the middles and forgot where I started and always gave up long before the end.

The year before last he never finished his story because my mother fell asleep and he didn't want to wake her. I wanted to hear the end because I'm a younger brother. He just shushed me and said, next year. And of course I should have expected that this year he would not come.

This is his last story:

Tony, the unluckiest man I've ever heard of lived with his family in a far away forest. He was the second of three brothers. He was the one with the sheep missing to the wolves; the bad luck; the broken tongue; the fallen arches; the house in the shade of the tall, tall trees where nothing would grow.

Tony was a superstitious, scared, and suspicious man. Growing up, he had read too many stories and he suspected he was only in this world to make up the numbers: he was the middle brother, the one skipped over in all the tales of the handsome oldest and smart youngest brothers. He saw himself in the stories: fat, greasy; slow-witted, mean. His job was to hinder his elder brother and poke fun — or worse — at his younger brother.

One day, Tony surprised everyone by running away. He left a note for his long-suffering wife:

"I am following the footprints of the wolves out of this damned forest where the only women I meet are old witches, the only water is a poisoned stream, where I am old before my time and my younger brother comes by twice a year to see if I am dead at last, so that he can quest, or marry, or fall down a well and become king of some strange and wondrous land or whatever his glorious fate is to be."

Of his journey, I know nothing. Whether Tony met three beggars or whether he found a golden key, I don't know. But he made it to a city, not one you will ever know, and settled into the life of a young wastrel about town.

Tony was determined to rewrite his story so he changed it every time he found a new place to live. He soon owed rent at three hostels. The city made him sly of hand, quick of thought, and quick off the mark. His tongue was silvering up nicely, his boots were soft, soft calfskin, he considered his leaving the forest the best idea he had ever had, until he saw a wolfprint outside the bar he fell out of at closing time.

The wolves, you see, were all Tony's family had given him. It was an inheritance: something like a game, although he had never known the rules. His father had told him that *his* father had been a furrier, and, looking at his father's eyebrows, he had wondered how close his father was to the wolves. His family still trapped wolves and he had grown up sleeping under wolf skins — more in winter, less in summer — and selling and trading what was left over.

While his brothers had been doing whatever eldest and youngest brothers do, Tony had followed wolf tracks — when he left for the city it was wolf tracks that led him to freedom.

He put his hand in the mud beside a wolf print. Not sober, no longer drunk, he made his way to first one hostel, then another, until he found the one he was staying in.

Tony had found work as an unskilled warehouseman. The day after finding the wolf track he was surprised to find that the old woman who ran his favorite lunch stand had slipped an extra pork dumpling into his paper bag. He thanked her, but he didn't have enough time to talk, so as usual he ate as he walked back to the warehouse.

He went home after work and spent most of the evening watching the road in front of the house. The hostel was on a busy street and it wasn't until long after midnight that it grew quiet.

When he left for work in the morning he found wolfprints in front of the hostel.

At lunch the old woman gave him two extra dumplings.

He came home and spent the evening watching the road.

The wolfprints were there the next morning, although he thought he had watched all night.

That day he told the foreman he had to take lunch early and went to the lunch stand. The old woman, wrapped in scarves, was still setting up her stand.

"Excuse me," he said.

"I'm not open 'til eleven," she said.

"But." He didn't know what to say. "Every day you've given me an extra dumpling."

She stopped cutting cabbage and turned to him with her cleaver still in her hand.

"So," she said, and he saw it wasn't the same woman. "My sister's been feeding you up, has she? Come to pay me back, have you?" she asked, and laughed at him.

"Here," she said, reaching under the stand. "I won't have the dumplings ready in time for you to get back to work. Take my sandwich and I'll make myself some dumplings later."

He protested, but she began to chop cabbage again, and eventually he made his way back to the warehouse.

When he got home after work his landlord and two large men, cudgels in hand, were waiting for him.

"Tony, I don't want you to rush to judgment," said his landlord, "about what, if anything, the presence of my friends might indicate. I'm sure it's of no matter that in two days it will be a month since you moved here—and I have still to see a penny of rent."

One of the large men pushed open the door to his room and everyone could see that Tony had not yet unpacked his bags.

"Yes," the landlord said. "Let's talk."

After a short talk that left everyone satisfied, the landlord and his friends showed themselves out. The landlord was richer, Tony was three month's rent poorer, and the two large men had had a relaxing fifteen minute discussion of the view from Tony's window.

The storyteller stopped, and, pointing to my sleeping mother, motioned us to be quiet. "I'm sorry," he said, "I'll finish it in the morning."

No one moved or said anything until he rose. I led him to his bed and father woke mother and we all went to our beds.
In the morning he left even before my father woke.

Once his story went like this:

"Touch it."
"No."

And that was it.

Last year he did not come. Day-to-day his non-appearance was normal. He shouldn't have appeared while I was putting the seed potatoes in pots. Neither should he be there when I moved them outside. His arrival was later than that. Nearer high summer, when it was almost too hot to do anything. Not that that ever stopped us.
Autumn came and even Alder noticed.
"Where's that boring old prick storyteller?" he asked—not our parents, but me. He was old enough that they might decide it was easier to throw him out than put up with him. When he remembered this, not often enough, I thought, his tread got quieter. He'd even begun to help out around the house, something he'd rarely done before. If I wasn't sure he completely lacked any imagination, I'd have thought he'd realized his princess was never going to come. He'd have to marry, work, raise children, and die, all probably within this village. The girls he still tormented might not look too kindly on him in the future.
The thought of him trying to look after himself was enough to make me laugh. I couldn't get the look of guilt off my face in time, so it earned me a thumping. But it still made me laugh.

There was no sign that anyone had ever visited or lived at the Red Cliffs. The cliffs looked raw. I lay down on the edge and watched the waves far below. Hours later I came out of my trance and walked along the cliff top until it sloped down to the ocean, pitched my tent and slept.

The next morning, woken by gulls, I retraced my steps, past the point where I had first come to the cliffs, and went on until I came to a chasm cut by a river I had heard roaring for a mile before I had come to it.

These were the Red Cliffs I had heard the storyteller talk about all my life. I knew I would find him here, yet there was nothing; no sign of him. The bushes were scraggy and scratched me, the rocky ground was nearly bare, and there were no flowers in sight.

I stayed there for three more days. I ate my dried food and worried about running out. On the last day I walked along the cliff top again. At one point I leant over and scratched my name on the soft rock face. Then I packed up my small campsite and began the walk home.

I thought I might look for an old woman who might be a wolf or whose wise words might help me to understand the missing parts of the stories I had heard all these years.

Had the storyteller really been looking for a flower or was that just another story? If so, why? Or should it be why not? I could not tell.

Three days of walking took me to the first village on the way back to my home town and my parent's house.

"You're back," said a girl carrying a basket of clothes. "We didn't expect you until next year."

"Ah," I said, "Thanks. I thought that's how it might end."

MEMREE

JENN REESE

The birds stood thick together on the roof of Vee's house, like a carpet of mold on a piece of old, dark bread. Vee died this morning, but the white truck still hadn't come. The birds, they stood watch. Never singing, barely moving. Only their feathers ruffling in the dull shimmer of summer heat.

The dogs came, too. All shapes and sizes, some with collars but most without. The demons loved it when a Dead Girl died. They laughed and lolled their tongues and rolled in shit in the streets.

I sat on Vee's front stoop, listening to the sobs coming from inside the house and throwing stones at the dogs as they laughed. Vee's mother cried a lot. I cried, too, but not as much. Then again, it wasn't my fault that Vee was a Dead Girl.

The white truck rolled up in front of the house around dinner. No sirens. No need. The dogs scattered in front of the wheels then went off to cause mischief someplace else. They liked to trip old ladies in the street and gnaw on the bums under the bridge. They spread evil thoughts to the boys and the men and carried guns in their teeth like their bitches carried pups.

Demons, every last one.

I followed the men inside, quiet. What was I? Just a kid to them, another thing to ignore or else carry away in a big, black Ziploc. They didn't smile or even talk much to Vee's mom. They moved her aside like they were moving a plant and took Vee from the blood-soaked mattress.

Earlier, in the morning, I found Vee just like that on the bed. Laid out on the sheets with a bloody aura, all spreading from the place between her legs.

Dead Girls, they don't survive the change. The blood starts to come, and soon it doesn't stop. Not until it sucks all the fire out of a girl. Vee had a lot of fire, judging from the amount of blood. More than I ever seen.

I wish I was one of them.

They started to zip Vee up in her body bag. I ran over, threw myself on her stiff body all angled wrong. My hand slipped between the edges of the zipper and I dropped a little scrap of paper on Vee's body before they pulled me off.

We stood in our circle in the dark parking lot—just eight Dead Girls and me—and talked about Vee. The birds came and joined us, another circle of small shapes just beyond ours. The Dead Girls heard them talking, offering their memories of Vee to our small fire. I heard nothing, not even from the halfway damned pigeons with the loud, ugly warbles.

"Vee clarifies," Keisha said.

"Vee is a blend of mangoes and kiwi," I added.

"Repeat Vee as necessary," said Trude.

Tomorrow we'll take our labels—shampoo and conditioner, mostly, but some gels and mousses—and stick them all over town. Vee's been collecting them her whole life since she was seven, and the shoebox is full. We'll cut out the letter Vee from our stacks of magazines and newspapers, and we'll spread the word of Vee all-City.

Vee had long hair as shiny as Keisha's bike and as twisted as barbed wire. Everything got stuck in that mass. My bubblegum, Trude's fingers, feathers. Vee loved it.

"Vee was not tested on animals."

My momma died two months ago, which is okay. She didn't take the orange pills when she was pregnant with me, and that's okay, too, I guess. I'd rather be a Dead Girl than what I am, just a girl. But it's better than being a boy, or a dog, and the Dead Girls treat me like one of them, as much as they can, anyway. They call me Memree, and I do what I can to live up to it. Someone should remember the Dead Girls, and not just from the messages they leave on benches and posters and lampposts.

I spend a lot of time thinking about my message. I'm not obsessed about my hair like Vee was, or cats, like Noshi. I guess I just want my message to be bigger somehow. Maybe people will see my words on the bus, or walking along the street at night, or behind a brick building. Maybe they'll read my words and, for a minute, stop and think. Maybe they'll wonder who I was.

But it's stupid to think about it. I'm not a Dead Girl and I don't know when I'm going to die.

We split up, each with our bag of words and our gummy, white glue in bottles and cans and whatever we could find. I took my normal path up the hill, left at the 7-11, and straight for five blocks till the high school. Above me, big ugly sneakers dangled in pairs from almost every electrical wire. Wards to keep away the birds and their sharp eyes. Stupid, smelly boy-shoes. The Dead Girls don't like going here, don't like the silence of no birds, but it's no trouble for me.

It was early, the sun still sitting lazy near the earth. When I got near the high school, I heard the smack of a ball on the black tar and I walked to the back in order to watch.

A girl was shooting hoops alone, just her and some dirty brown ball and a set of matching sweats. I stood by the chain fence and pulled some scraps from my bag. Keeping one eye on her, I glued a decent-sized "V" to the fence post, and stuck "for damaged hair" right after it. I put the extra scraps back in my pocket and saw her looking at me, that smudged ball wedged under her too-long arm.

"Come here," she called. I stared. She looked tall as my dad, her hair pulled into some great puff of a ponytail behind her head.

"Come here, girl."

I smoothed the words of Vee's message until a little white ring of extra glue surrounded it. The others would come soon, in their cars and on their bikes, with their books and music and bright skirts and glittering teeth. They chittered like birds across the pavement, hopping from one cluster to the next, until that distant bell rang, and the school sucked them all inside.

She went back to her shooting and bouncing. I found the latch in the fence and stepped in, my shoes scuffling in the dirt and the dying grass. Inside. I looked back through the fence and the whole world was criss-crossed with metal links like a patchwork quilt my momma used to have, of browns and blues and cars and signs.

"Here," the girl said, holding out that ball on one huge hand towards me. "Take it."

I put my glue down on the grass next to the black tar ground and took the ball in both hands. It was nubbly and still smooth, wet where her hand had held it.

"Shoot it," she said.

Broken chains dangled from the hoop in another criss-cross of metal. The wood board behind it looked battered and yellowed, with one great chunk ripped from the top right corner like some demon-dog as big as a bus had gnawed on it.

I threw the ball. It didn't even make it halfway up to that hoop or those hanging chains. It just thudded on the earth beyond and rolled to a stop. She jogged after it and picked it up.

"What's your name?" she said, walking back.

"Memree."

"Well, Memree, you got to aim a little higher than that this time, all right?"

I nodded and took the ball from her again. This time I threw it as high as I could. It tapped the rim of the hoop, tickled the chains, and plopped back down near my feet. I scrambled to pick it up before it rolled off the black.

"See? Much better, Memree. Try again."

But I didn't. I stared at her with her long stick arms and long stick legs, with her braces and her ponytail and her breasts. I put the ball back on the ground and it rolled to the side. I grabbed my jar of glue and ran back to the fence and the latch and the outside.

I heard the smack of the ball against the black tar and the jingle of it hitting the chains. "Yes!" she laughed, but not like a boy or a dog, and the smacking started again.

I walked around the whole school with my scraps, and then to the deli and the liquor store. Trashcans covered in old messages guarded the door: "Noshi loves the taste of tuna." "Look for Jill in hardcover by Christmas." "Anita gets your clothes extra white." Vee felt right at home with the other Dead Girls, her message wavy and wet from the fresh glue.

We huddled in the tight space behind Trude's garage. Trude's parents weren't home. They weren't ever home. But if they weren't off doing their drugs, Trude wouldn't be a Dead Girl, and we figured it was a good trade.

The circle formed. Keisha snapped a match to life and threw it in the trashcan between us all. Wood and paper cracked and hissed and the flames climbed high. The fire danced in Keisha's black eyes, and off her fat lip and the healing cut across her ear.

"Heat for our bodies," she said.

"Heat for our hearts," the rest of us said back.

Keisha held up a magazine picture of a woman crying. "This is justice," she said, and she threw the picture into the fire. The edges curled and twisted as it danced, turning black the whole time.

We took turns offering our hopes to the fire. Marina threw in a feather for freedom and a new bike, Trude had been saving a book she found for smarts. The fire took them all. On my turn, I threw in half a pencil I found near the high school on my way home, but I don't know why. "For... memory," I said, and the Dead Girls answered, "Amen."

Then I took my place in the center of the circle, next to the wild fire and the heat. I closed my eyes and started with Leeza, some short freckled little thing who died last year. She never said no to an apple, she got bit once by the little brown piece-of-shit dog her parents kept. Some of the Dead Girls remembered Leeza, and they added their stories to the fire, offering up their laughter and their sadness.

My job is easy right now, since I haven't been with the Dead Girls so long, and not that many of them have died. But after a while, I'll be the only one who remembers, the only one who can tell the new Dead Girls what came before them. How much Vee loved her damn shiny hair, and how Anita washed her clothes every night in a basin of cold, soapy water while her mamma yelled at her to get inside.

I looked around the circle and stopped at Keisha, with her lumpy chest and scarred face. The birds talked to her more than anyone now, and I knew it would be days or weeks but not months before we walked our paths and plastered the city with little strips of paper and her name. She led the Dead Girls better than anyone, and I didn't know who had the voice and the heart to lead us after the fire fled her body.

I've been losing fire, just a little at a time, but I haven't told anyone. I can't tell my dad, even if he was home, and mamma's gone forever. I don't want to tell the Dead Girls. It's not a big deal, at least not yet.

I went to the high school a week later but the girl wasn't there. Just some demon of a dog sniffing around and pissing on everything, and a couple of his boys leaning against the wall and smoking their thin cigarettes. When the dog saw me, he grinned and all of his teeth glared white as glue.

I waited anyway, just outside the fence, and eventually the demon and his pups got bored and moved off, probably to the liquor store. She arrived not long after.

"Hey, Memree, how's it going?"

One of her long arms swung as she walked, the other held tight to her basketball. She tossed the ball onto the black ground and ran after it, her hair bobbing. Her hand reached it and she shoved at the earth, hard, dribbling towards the chain hoop.

"You coming in, or what?" she called.

I opened the fence door, shut it behind me to keep out the dogs, and scuffled to the court, kicking up dry earth as I went. She passed me the ball and I trapped it against my chest, between the new flesh starting to press out, to make breasts. I stared at the dangling chains and threw the ball high. It bounced off the chewed up backboard and fell at her feet.

"Good shot, girl, you're getting better every time."

She offered me the ball again but I shook my head and sank to my knees just off the black ground, watching. She ran around, all muscle and grace, and tossed that dirty ball of hers against the wood and into the hoop, jangling those chains.

She grinned at me a few times, called my name and told me about the shots she was throwing, all the while drops of sweat formed and dripped and fell from her face.

Someday.

I took the message box out of my bedroom that night. I took the little lines of words and colors and faces and I dumped them in the trash under the sink. I'm not "the perfect getaway" or "the number one cure for headaches." I don't know what I am. And soon, not in days or in weeks, I won't belong with the Dead Girls and they won't belong with me. And the sad thing is, they'll be none of them that even remember.

THE EYE

ELIOT FINTUSHEL

I fit anywhere. Out the keyhole of a cedar chest I see Frank and Emma hump. Framed by a death's head, they knot the percale. They huff and thrash. All the bedding ends on the floor. The lamp is upturned and the bulb smashes. After her come cry he's still thrusting. She claws and squeezes. Pretty soon he throws his *sforzando* into her—but they keep at it. Why?

A month later they're quits, my boss and his wifey, ex-wifey, sweet-boned but wrinkly, crab on a poking stick. I start to see Frank trolling for a new lover after hours at places like Solomon Gamorra's, my Sophie's haunt: coffee and.

Short folk know everything—if it takes a cedar chest. It's the wormwood in our mothers' milk. Dwarfs don't come from dwarfs and live; either mom or pop is big-boned. We're the spoiled hope. What did Sophie admire in that? Something. She took me on as a mascot, though I'm ugly as sin.

"Hey Big Head!"

"Hey Tits!"

"C'mon sit down with us, Herbie."

"Sure thing." I pulled up a chair. She was sitting with two other foxes. Three girls in their mid-twenties, all legs and breasts and gift-wrapped bellies, looking to see who was looking: tablefuls of rubbernecking stallions, icy punk ethos and *café au lait*, white noise rolling off studded tongues.

"This is how you castle, Soph." Across the table from Sophie her two friends rubbed tattoos and played the black pieces. One, an anorexic with fudge-bar eyebrows, kept brushing rook pawns to the floor with a cuff of her faux leopard-skin coat. The other, rainbow-haired, tongued from the inside a diamond stud below her lips — bobber on a trout stream. She wore a black jumpsuit and looked deathly serious. Sizing up pawn structure. Unraveling the mysteries of queenside castling. They nodded to me, pretending not to be interested in my proportions, but I know everything.

"Nettie, Louisa, this is Herbie, the love of my life." *Luff uf my life,* actually, and *Herfie:* Sophie's speech defect. Features sharp as a scalpel, rose petal cheeks, and under the stitches of her fine black brow, eyes of azure blue. Skin tight to the bone, both on her face, small and cat-like, and on the rest of her. Her neat breasts impaled you — if you happened to be partial to neat breasts.

Azure blue. Through a ceiling fan fixed to the bare joists overhead, light strobed, enhancing her twinkle. I almost failed to notice the blemish. Was that a spot of makeup half-hidden behind one earlobe? She spied me lingering on it: "It's a scratch, Herbie. Pin of an earring. Back off."

"You caught me."

"You're not in a cedar chest, you know."

I blushed. I'd told her about the adventure with Frank — a gambit to get to know her. I'd been at a table near Sophie's one time and cracked wise on the old man for her benefit. She acted horrified at first but then laughed. I reeled her in. Frank never saw me: I have that talent. Sophie and I became pals.

You think I'm disloyal? Wise up.

"Pleased to meet you, Herbie." Nettie, the leopard skin girl, was over me now. (First they stare, then look away, then act bored. I'm used to it.) She picked up a fallen bishop.

Rainbow screwed it into the middle of its square, the way some do. "You go now, Sophie." Then to me: "Yeah, *enchanté.*"

Sophie nudged a pawn, discovering mate.

"You hustler."

Sophie just smiled. "I'm a quick study, girls."

I didn't want to laugh too hard before I was better acquainted with Nettie and Louisa — short people need all the friends we can get — so I turned away. And saw Frank. He was peeling a Cremora at the condiments station five or six tables distant. Under the drapery of a middle-aged face, eyes as clear as a dry martini. He wore a turtleneck and blue jeans, Andy Warhol style. Nothing worked. He was thickening, let's face it, and balding. Nice glasses, but glasses—bifocals in fact. Guccis, it's true. Don't tuck your shirt in Frank: hide that midriff. But what to do about the crows' feet and a hairline galloping into the sunset?

"Isn't that the one—"

"Yes, Sophie," I said.

"Wave him over."

"You're not going to—"

"I'll be good. C'mon, short stuff, do it."

His lucky day. "Hey, Frank!"

"Herbie!" Nasal voice—commanding but unaesthetic. He took in my table mates. He spilled some coffee, mopped it up, spilled some more, left it, oh fuck it, and started toward us.

Nettie iced over. "Who's the ancient?"

Louisa was still burning over the hustle. "I want a rematch. You said you were a beginner. I wasn't really trying." Rainbow coif and a chessic ego. Ya gotta love it. She withdrew into herself—and damn the squeeze—so that by the time Frank cleared his throat she was too deep to even have to look up. Zenned to the cuticles, she set up the chess pieces—bishops and knights the wrong way, I noticed. Nettie sorted through the toolbox she called a purse.

"Herbie, I didn't know you spent so much time at Solomon Gamorra's."

Sophie fielded it. "Herfie? He's nefer anywhere else."

"*Sprechen zie Deutch?*"

Give me credit: I kept a straight face.

"No," she said, "my uppers are hafing a luf affair with the inside uf my lower lif. Did you know that . . . " Picture me lipsynching the following with my Sophie. " . . . the inside uf the lower lif is the most sensuous part uf the human anatomy?" She caught me at it. I smiled. Frank was in the dark.

"I'm sorry. I thought . . . I mean . . . Isn't this a great place? Hey, are you and Herbie friends? Herbie and I work together." Charitably put. I love the way people brag about knowing me—once they get over avoiding me like the goddam plague. "Herbie, you've been keeping secrets from me."

"You don't know the half of it," I said, and Sophie burst out laughing.

"I'm sorry, Frank. This is Sophie. And these are the other two Fates, Spindle and Snip."

Louisa managed, "Very funny." Nettie raked through vice grips and box end wrenches.

"I'm Frank."

"I gathered."

Pause. He looked like a fellow trying to see the duck, the rabbit, the duck. How was he doing? Couldn't tell. Me, I know fishermen. Sophie was letting out line.

He tried: "Say, haven't we . . . ?"

"No."

"Sorry."

"'Sokay. Lots of men think they know me from somewhere—have you ever been married?"

He paused. "Yes."

"Maybe I remind you of an old wife, hm?"

Frank's face went limp for a moment, then dimpled into a smile. He saw the duck, I guess. He laughed a little harder than was appropriate. "May I join you?"

She shrugged. "No room."

"Yeah, well, nice to meet you."

Sophie reached her hand across the table to squeeze Frank's. "Nice to meet you, Frank." Oh, the jingle of her bangles. Oh, the rearing of her tits.

He nodded. Continental. Then he left, turned back, left, looked at me, and left. Grinning the whole time. I shot a couple of question marks at Sophie, but she shrugged them off.

Louisa screwed her king in. "Play. I'm going to even the score, bitch."

"Even?" My chance to shine. "As of now it's zero all."

"What do you mean?" Sophie pinched her lips—a sunburst of fine wrinkles. "I mopped the floor with them."

"No you didn't, Soph. That game was a nullity. Look at the board. Black square in the lower right. It's supposed to be white. You played with the board cockeyed."

I could tell that Louisa was starting to like me. "I thought something was funny." She swiped the board clean, turned it ninety degrees, and started to set up pieces again. "My queen was on the right color, but left and right were mixed up."

"On the nose." I smiled at my Sophie. What was it to her, anyway? She'd never lose.

That night, a phone call. I was, I don't know, lying in my shoebox reading matchbook covers by the light of a wristwatch display.

"Herbie? Frank." Snuffling—a nose-spray addict. You'd think big money would exempt a fellow from indignities like that. "That girl this afternoon, um, Sophie, do you have her phone number?"

"Isn't she kind of young for you?"

"Or tall for you?"

"Hey!"

"They have a procedure to lengthen the bones, you know. I'm serious. I know a doctor in Beverly Hills."

"They always did. The rack."

"How about the number, Herbie? I won't call her right away, okay? I'll wait till she's a little older."

"She might have a different number by then."

"I'll chance it. So?"

"She wasn't exactly giving you a green light, boss, no offence. Anyway, you can do better. What gives?"

"Chemistry, that's all."

"You can get all the chemistry you want, big man: just flash your wallet."

"Herbie."

"I get it. You're looking for an ingenue. Something sweet. Not a professional woman. Not rich like yourself—a diamond in the rough—and not too cunning, not a gold digger."

"Cut two words and you can run that in the Post Standard personals."

"You want me to?"

"Just give me the damn number, Herbie—what is it with you, anyway?" It always comes to this: when they can't win, they counsel. "Why can't you be straight for half a minute? Might do you some good."

"All you big stiffs, you just make me laugh, boss. You think your altitude makes you my mummies and daddies."

"Yeah, and that's exactly how you treat us, isn't it? Filial piety—you're lousy with it."

"Believe me, you don't want me to treat you like I treated my daddy and mummy, Frank-o."

"What did you do, gnaw off their ankles?"

"Worse. I watched them."

It was a quiet night in the city. Car alarms, wheel well rumble and perforated mufflers, the white noise of air conditioner hum, canned laughter leaking from an Argus of teevees. A dog barked. A kid cried and cried and cried. The dog barked again.

The phone was making my ear sweat.

"I ought to fire you, honest to God," Frank said.

I said, "You love me too much."

"The number."

"How lonely can you be, Frank?" Nasty business, separation — and his son, just out of high school, taking the mother's side, one hears. That's got to weigh on a man. Well, get used to it, is my philosophy. God hates a whiner.

"Damn fucking lonely, Herbie."

"I'm not a pimp."

"I'm not a John."

I shrugged. I shared. I went back to my matchbook. But he didn't call her. Not that night. Not the next or the next either. Sophie would have told me. And the night after that, Frank left town for a month.

I'm a head hunter. Well, officially, Frank's the head hunter. I'm just an operative; in spyspräche, he *runs* me. I run. I make nice with corporate secretaries to procure information on disgruntlable executives for Frank's boys to shmooze and sweeten. I'm murder on the telephone. I could talk to J. Edgar for five minutes collect and find out which side he hangs on.

I have my ways.

But where the hell was Frank? I'd never seen such a firewall of malarkey and misdirection. My sucker lists were issued. My paychecks came on time. My lowdowns I slipped into the Genesee Street drop box, but whither thence? Come home, big man. All is forgiven. Uncle Herbie aches to debrief.

Meanwhile, sure enough, Sophie's number changed.

"Boyfriend," Louisa told me.

I hadn't seen Sophie for two weeks. I ran into Louisa right in front of my apartment building. She had a temp job registering new voters. Don't waste your time on me, I told her. I'm not new anything.

"He's a hunk. Older guy. Thirties."

"Poor Frank," I said.

"Who's Frank?" She looked away. "You mean the bald guy? He came onto me once. Yes, me. No, thank you, I told him. I mean, he was nice, he was okay, he wasn't trying to buy me or anything, but no thank you. I'm not into old. I'm into young. Unless they're cute, like you."

"What are you hiding?"

"Nothing."

"Come clean, Louisa."

She tousled my hair, and I could have killed her on the spot, but I purred instead. She liked that. I told her about Frank's phone call. We had a little laugh, and she let me buy her a Cinnabun and coffee.

"She cheats. That's Sophie. You saw how she cheated me at that chess game. She cheats at everything. Lies about everything. Her and the inside of her lower *lif.*" Suddenly in her eyes: the whirligig, the siren. She pulled herself over. "Sophie's okay, though. She's okay."

"How long have you known her?"

"A month—she has a kid, by the way."

"No—Sophie?"

"Yes, Sophie—shh." She tugged her spine straight—runway stuff. She smiled a chilly little smile and tilted her a chin a bit. Barely moving her lips: "I like this guy. Don't look, though. He works at the store across from here. He let me register him. I think he was already registered though. Don't look. I think he likes me. Is he looking at me?"

"You said not to look."

"So look now, you little shit."

"He's staring at you, Louisa. Don't turn your head. Jesus, the guy is stricken." I couldn't tell who she was talking about.

"I knew it. Is he gone?"

"Yes."

"I knew it. I'm going to go buy something over there."

"You were joking about Sophie having a kid, right?"

"No. I'm not a liar, Herbie, not like her. How long you known her?"

"Not as long as you. But more deeply."

"She picks him up somewhere, takes him somewhere, something, every day practically. Listen—when you hang out, you see the bumps in a person's schedule. Or things fall out of their purse."

"Good old gravity—what are you waiting for me to say?"

"Huh? Nothing. I think I saw his picture once, actually. The kid's. He's a teenager."

"That's not possible."

"She must have had him when she was, like, three or something. I don't know." Chin to clavicle: "I'm lousy at this. I'm not supposed to tell you any of this."

"Lousy at what?"

Inspired: "I bet you Sophie is fishing for some guy to pick up the tab, you know what I mean?"

"Junior's tab?"

"Yeah—he was actually staring, huh?"

"Glued."

She primped. "I have assets."

Sometimes it's hard to distinguish between calculation and distraction, but dwarfs know everything. The *emes*? Louisa was playing with a black square in her lower right corner.

I found Sophie's lover and therefore Sophie. For Frank, of course, out of friendship. Coffee and a cinnamon roll are often good for a street address. The stud had digs in a swank uptown apartment building. The patisserie across the street made a convenient observation post. Coffee: tolerable. Croissants: not half bad. The stools along the window counter were insultingly low for a gent of my particular stature, but that meant I could see without being seen. Worth an indignity, yes? Tricks of the trade.

At eight forty-five in the morning, with hair unkempt and the beefy look of dawn, she flew out, alone, in a gauzy thing. Nobody wakes up beautiful.

I dashed out. "Tits!"

She blanched. I crossed. Too late to ignore me. "Herfie, what are you doing this end uf town?"

"Is he home?"

"Who?"

"Your new boyfriend, sweetie. And hey, what's wrong with your cheek? Looks blue. He hitting you?"

"There's nothing wrong with my cheek — did you follow me?"

"He's not home, is he? Take me up. I want to see your place."

"What the hell are you doing here? What do you want, anyway?"

"I want to see your abode. I miss you. Okay?"

"I'm busy. I have to catch a bus." She maneuvered past me to the curb and looked down the street the way they do. It's not fair to use the superior length of your legs to maneuver past a small person.

But I have moves of my own. I ducked between two passersby and appeared at her side. "Picking up your kid?"

"My kid?"

"Hey, Soph, this is Herfie you're talking to. I know everything, remember? Does he know you have a kid?"

"Stay out of it, will you? What do you want?"

"You don't want him to know, do you? Hey, you're right not to. I bet it would scare him off. Guys with bachelor pads don't like to be encumbered."

She cocked. She craned. She pretended to look for the bus, but she was, as we all know, under the bus at this point, wheel wells, oil pan, muffler. I floored it. "Don't worry. I know everything; however, I am hermetically sealed. No leaks. Nada. I mean, for people such as yourself, who are nice to me. You'd be surprised how rare that is for a shrimp like me. It gets so I can't stand how people treat me sometimes. I'm afraid I get very mean about it, too. I'm a vengeful little guy."

"Dammit, what do you want?"

"I just want to take a peek at your love nest, sweetie. No big deal. In and out. Humor a poor little person."

"It's not a love nest. It's just an apartment."

"In and out."

Her breath sounded like an iron on damp cotton. It was not good for a person's complexion, the thing she was doing with her face. She pivoted toward her lover's building, expecting me to follow.

Which I did. Up the lift. Down the hall. Very very nice. Sunken living room. Zinc bar. Jacuzzi. Circular bed. Walk-in closets.

"Collect the munchkin, Soph. I'll just stick around awhile, okay? I got some time to burn."

"Dammit, this isn't my place. I shouldn't even have let you in here."

"I'll wash all my glasses and put away the gin."

I could see that twitch in the arms that presages violence. A fellow of my altitude has to watch for signs like that. Next to the prospect of an easy victory, moral training's worth crap.

"What *are* you?"

"Oh, c'mon, Soph. Be a pal. I'm just a little working stiff, yes? I want to be Queen for a Day, like you. Come on. I won't make a mess, and if he gets back early, hey, you know how good I am at hiding. Under his nut cup I go. Or twixt the bristles of the gentleman's toothbrush. Come on."

"Make sure the lock clicks when you leave." She slammed the door. The lock clicked.

I pondered. In haggling, if the guy says yes too fast, you know you've underpriced yourself. You want to see a little pain. I had not seen enough pain in Sophie. Hm.

But hot damn.

I stripped. I opened all the windows. I turned on the TV, stereo, radio, Jacuzzi jets, and all the hot and cold water taps, plus the garbage disposal and the can opener and the kitchen timer and the fan and the heat and the air conditioning and the Cuisinart and the desktop and the laptop, and I danced. Danced. I clogged a few turns around the coffee table. I pulled some pretty fair cartwheels. I climbed up a barstool and sprang onto the pale blue bar for a jig that would have made old Ozymandias hoot. I can touch my elbow with the same-arm pinky and my head sideways to my shin. I can balance a swizzle stick on the flat between my eyes and make my bowed legs fly. You ain't seen nothing till you've seen me caper.

When I was tired and sweaty and had emptied my bottle, I stopped. I woke up on the bar a couple hours later, sick as a dog but satisfied. I commenced to clean the place up. I throbbed and wobbled, but mastered the job. I always do. I shut all and cleaned all and vomited nicely. I cleaned that, and I was done.

I disabled the hinge on the closet door; if you set the door open and jimmy the top pin, it won't close without a lot of scrape and clatter. Who'd bother? Call the super, and he'll fix it in the morning, yes? Then I grabbed me a paw full of a fine dinner jacket that was hanging up at the front, and so climbed button to button to the shelf above. Oh, what a sweet package am I! I wouldn't trade one of me for two of you and all the tea in China.

In the dark with the shoe boxes and the hats, I had a fine clear view of that circular bed. I wrapped myself up in a fringed silk scarf and once more fell asleep.

I woke thinking of dry rot, then seeing it. I didn't know that I saw it, at first. Just: dry rot. You're all dry rot. That's how it is. You wake dry rot, and then there's a you and seeing it. It comes in stages. That's the truth. Read Proust. A patch of plaster missing between the laths, hidden, like me, in the closet dark, opened into dry rot. A tickle of light revealed it and might reveal me as well, I calculated, so I jockeyed a couple of boxes and a bunch of shoe rags to hide me better.

Dry rot in such palatial digs. Belie me.

I saw lights flash on, silvering the windows—a couple dancing on black air—then flash off. A woman: "Don't. Leave it dark." *Leef*, actually.

He's got her in the doorway: bones thrum on the casement. A long sigh. The light flashes on again. Laughter. "I didn't mean to," he says. Then off.

"Mm. Good. Good. You feel good."

"Do I? Do you really like how I feel?" he says.

"Mm. Your skin is so nice. So smooth. I love your thick black hair. I love to rake my fingers through your thick black hair." *Luf*, actually. "I love my belly on your brrr-awny belly. Take me."

He trips over something. Had I missed a tumbler? "Damn. Sorry. Shit."

She giggles. "Get up. Come on. It doesn't matter."

"Sorry."

More stumbling, her laughter, his curses. How long can he have lived here? Bet he doesn't know about the dry rot. Maybe I'll leave him an anonymous note. What does he pay, I wonder? Then candlelight, not without a burnt thumb. Wax puddles on an end table.

It's Frank. It's not Frank. It's Frank. That's how it is: thinking and seeing are the same when the light is dim. This guy is an Adonis, or it's a trick of the dark: it's Frank minus the curling and the slow descent, the two marriages, the carnivorous career, the dry rot behind the laths.

God bless me, in my dotage I'll have no stature to lose.

I remember Frank and Emma wrestling. The smell of cedar and the death's head frame of the keyhole. "I left the Kodox mailing at home," the boss had said. "Go fetch." I fetched. I stayed. I burrowed. Anyone who gives me a key deserves what he gets, say I. The way they grappled put me in mind of Sidney Greenstreet whittling lead off the Maltese Falcon. It made a little fellow laugh to see them whittle each other for a gone jewel.

Not so these two. They stand apart for the pleasure of it. They do each other a slow strip tease. They unbutton, unzip, peel off, pull down. They are like children showing off birthday boodle: these breasts, this belly, these pecs, this pecker. Celebrate each with a kiss.

You think I'm jealous. I'm not. I'm nobody. I'm the dark of the window. I'm dry rot. I'm the sigh. I'm the slow caress. I'm him. I'm her. Who is there to be jealous? I'm the electricity between their skins. Have I not the gift of rapture?

She thwarts a love bite. "What? What were you looking at? What?"

"Nothing."

"What?"

"Nothing. Okay, tell me what's wrong with your cheek."

"Oh, for Christ's sake."

"You asked. I'm sorry."

"Why do you have to spoil it?"

"I'm sorry — tell me."

"Now of all times."

"You asked. What's going on?"

"The skin's too tight, that's all. It happens. You have to make a big deal out of everything. He can fix it."

"You can practically see bone."

"He'll fix it."

"Like he fixed your mouth."

"Shit." She storms out of the room, slams the door. The candle gutters. He stands there paralyzed, while his shadow dances like a dwarf on a zinc bar.

He slumps back onto the bed, which puckers around him as if it were a mud pool. Ah, a waterbed. Nice, very nice. He stares at the ceiling — wait. I crane my neck, such as it is: there is a mirror mounted up there. The pervert. Adam, he lies naked before himself and me. If I should call to him now, would he cover himself and blame her? Or am I miscast as God? Am I the snake?

He caresses his skin: silk, GQ, is the feeling; won't the girls love it. But he pouts. "Stupid bitch. I'm the one who should be angry. Damn angry. Why do I always give in to you, anyway? Because I love you? That's it. But, God, you can be such a bitch. I'm mad as hell. Oh, maybe not at you. Maybe not at you. Maybe not. Maybe I'm mad at that butcher." Strokes his belly. "Did all right by me, though, in the end. Pretty good. Pretty damn good, in the end." He starts, looks toward the door. No, she's not coming in again, just harrowing the cabinets, fixing herself a Bloody Mary, let's guess—and cyanide for him.

Hey, what's that, Adonis? Damn me if I don't spy a scar across his gaster nasty enough to be seen even at double distance via the mirror on the ceiling. What the hell?

"I just get younger and younger, don't I?" He throws off a few lines of *Danny Boy* in a silken tenor. He blows himself a kiss. He fills his lungs and lets his ribs settle: the bathtub draining, the bather dreaming.

Loudly: "Come back. I'm horny."

"Go pick up some chick in a coffeehouse, why don't you?" They burst out laughing. I hear her sputter in the next room—"It isn't funny."—while he pounds the quilt and snorts.

"Come on. Come to papa. Let me kiss your numb lips."

"It's not funny."

À la Lugosi: "I vant to fondle your laser-perfect skin."

"The scratch under my ear will distract you."

"Oh, stop it. I'm sorry. Come to me,"—still gazing at himself. Small children do this. It's obnoxious in grownups. I'm sure I've never done it—quite the opposite.

"I wish I could haf seen your scalp when Dr. Saffron blew up the balloon inside it."

"Shut up."

She peeks in at the door. "Were you completely doped up, or were you able to watch when he stretched it and sectioned it and sewed it together? Gussets and darts, like a tailored shirt. Then the hair transplants, right?"

"I don't want you to talk about it. You're spoiling the whole thing."

She throws the door open, steps in, and slams it behind her. "You listen, Mr. Tummy Tuck, Mr. Fountain of Youth, I did all this for you."

"For me! Hah! For me, she says." He crawls, naked, to the rim of the bed, on all fours, like a pointer dog. He talks to her from there. "Let's drop this, Emma. I don't care. God, you're beautiful. You're beautiful, and I want you."

"I'm not Emma. I'm Sophie."

"Emma, Sophie, who cares? C'mere."

"Sophie. I care."

"You're you. You're beautiful now. C'mere."

"I never wanted to do my thighs. It was for you. You didn't love Emma. Emma wasn't beautiful."

"Sophie, Emma, what's the difference? You're you. You're you. You're more you than ever. Emma wasn't more you. Emma was gravity and friction and bad genes."

"Jack is disgusted by the whole thing, you know. He doesn't even want to see me anymore."

"He'll get over it."

"He could be in Princeton. He's going to move to Alaska with that hideous girlfriend of his."

"Don't believe it. It's just a phase. C'mere, Em-, Sophie."

"What we've done is selfish, perverted. We're too old for this."

"No, damn it, that's just the point. We're too young. We're too young to be old. Don't you see?"

"You sound like one of Saffron's ads," she says, but she lets him take her hand. He sits her down on the edge of the bed. She rests limply in his arms. Now she can say anything. That's the way it is. Everybody wants to be a child, to be held, to be allowed to say anything at all and be forgiven. She will let herself say anything at all now—I know that look and that languid inflexion:

"What if you hadn't found me?"

"The whole idea was to find you, dear. You wanted to fall in love again, didn't you? And we did, Sophie. We fell in love again. I found you."

"At Solomon Gamorra's."

"With Herbie."

"Yes, with Herbie—he's here, isn't he?"

I stop breathing.

"Of course he is."

"Louisa?"

"Yes. Through Louisa."

"Hi, Herbie."

I lie still.

"Frank, don't."

"Bodies like these have to be seen. What fun is it otherwise? Otherwise they're not quite real, are they? Hi, Herbie."

"Stop it."

"He doesn't matter. He's nothing but an eye, Sophie."

"Tell me I'm beautiful."

Thus easily the matter of me is settled. I'm an eye, is all. They're off to another topic. I'm still not breathing.

"You're beautiful, Sophie."

"You were shy, Frank."

"I was shy the first time too, remember, with Emma?"

"Yes, I remember. Of course I remember. You're just shy, Frank. You're the shy sort. You should be more confident."

"I was so old."

She strokes his lips with two fingers. One finger is affection. Two fingers is ownership. "That's all over, isn't it?"

"I felt so pathetic, a pathetic old man in those goddam coffeehouses among all the children, looking for you."

"You're young now. Forget it. Kiss me, Frank."

Watch them wrestle.

She pulls away. "Don't you feel sorry for the poor little schmuck?"

"Sorry for him? We should charge him money."

She laughs. "I suppose."

Shouting: "This one's for you, little guy."

"You're terrible."

It's perfectly possible to cry without making a sound. You just have to exercise a little self-control.

After, they go somewhere fancy to eat. I should break everything and steal what I don't break. I should piss all over the round bed. I should lie in wait to kill them.

THE TRAIN THERE'S NO GETTING OFF

BRUCE HOLLAND ROGERS
RAY VUKCEVICH
HOLLY ARROW

1. Daddy

Peg said to me, "You're sure you want to come? They don't always know until the blood tests come back." But I wanted to take the day off. This was an occasion. Besides, it was a beautiful day. There wasn't a cloud in the sky. We took a streetcar, then walked two blocks. In the trees over Chester Avenue, squirrels frolicked and robins chirped. I saw people walking jolly dogs. Sunlight glinted on the windshields of parked cars. I held Peg's hand.

The nurse called Peg's name and took her to see the doctor. When Peg reappeared, she had a smile for me. "They'll call when they get the lab report. But the doctor says she can already tell. I am. You're going to be a daddy."

I smiled. I kissed her. As we walked hand in hand to the streetcar stop, I noticed again that there wasn't a cloud in the sky, and I remembered that sunlight can give you cancer. I wished for an umbrella. The trees over Chester Avenue were full of squirrels and robins. The fleas on squirrels can transmit plague. Birds made me think of West Nile virus. And all these dogs... Any one of them can bite, can carry rabies. As we crossed the street, I glared at the drivers. Sharp chrome. Glass. Peg said, "You're hurting my hand." I said I was sorry, and I lessened my grip. But not much.

2. Maybe the Moon

Whatever it's like for you, it must be very different for Mary who tells you she feels like a cow and you tell her she's nothing like a cow and she tells you to stop telling her how she feels and slams the bathroom door behind herself and you can hear her making throwing up sounds but you can't tell if they're real and you realize they might not be because she's gotten so weird lately with her big baby belly and her flying saucer hat in honor of the father who she says is only you in a strictly biological sense. The saucer is all about something spiritual something from the stars or maybe the moon or one of the planets would you stop cross-examining me? Shut up and go away. Where are you? Say something. So you say something but maybe you haven't spoken with enough volume to be understood because she bangs out of the bathroom shouting that's the last straw! Do you hear me? The very last straw! You look around wildly and spot her flying saucer hat on the bed and you pick it up and put it on your own head and smile and her face falls and she bursts into tears and runs into your arms and you go down with her onto the bed and hold and rock her and the baby kicks hello hello is there anyone out there?

3. Goddess

By the time Yvonne was seven months pregnant, she had given up on finding her big break, at least for now. She went to the party in Soho anyway. She hadn't been there for fifteen minutes when Arturo Antonioni crossed the room in long strides, looked her slowly up and down, and proclaimed, "A goddess." A week later, he came—in person—to her first shoot with Cesco, arriving as Yvonne modeled a black and white strapless Antonioni evening gown. A maternity gown.

The photographer's studio lights were hot. Yvonne's back ached. Her feet were sore. But with Antonioni in the room, she had no trouble smiling for the camera. "My dear," Antonioni said, "you are a goddess. An absolute goddess. After I met you, I said to Cesco, Where was this goddess keeping herself? Tell her, Cesco."

"Yes," the photographer said. He reeled off three more exposures. "That's what you said. Yvonne, head up a little more, darling. Perfect."

"You inspire me," Antonioni said. "Such ideas I have. We're going to use you a lot, right until they wheel you into the delivery room!"

Yvonne figured she had it made. She did three more shoots for Antonioni. He came to every one of them.

Later, however, it seemed that she wasn't a goddess after all. She delivered her baby, a beautiful boy, and set out at once to recover her shape.

When she wasn't nursing, she was exercising. Once Yvonne and her agent agreed that she was ready, Yvonne went to one of Antonioni's parties. She found him talking to another model, one of the long-time goddesses. Yvonne stood at the periphery, waiting to be noticed. He ignored her. Finally, Yvonne's agent came over, touched Antonioni's elbow, and said, "Arturo, you remember my client...."

Antonioni's gaze flicked from the agent to Yvonne. Then he resumed his conversation with the other model. End of story.

Yvonne's agent did her best, but two months of work for Antonioni somehow wasn't enough to interest any other designers. Yvonne could have returned to posing for small catalogues or department store flyers. But she didn't. She quit modeling. Eventually, she found a job as a sales clerk in a downtown boutique.

In time, she got pregnant again.

She was about six months along when Antonioni and his entourage happened to come into the store, fingering the goods and ignoring the sales staff. She thought until that moment that she had recovered from her disappointment. Seeing Antonioni, however, made her feel the ice of rejection all over again. She stayed away from him and hoped that he and his people would leave.

But then Antonioni saw her. He crossed the room in long strides, stopped before her, and peered over his sunglasses. He looked her up and down. He said, "Ah, a goddess. Where has this goddess been all my life?"

4. Some Things

Two things. First, his unborn daughter, Abby, was made of glass, and second, she might not be alone in there. Knowing when she had company was a skill that would serve him well. Someday he'd be able to just look at her bedroom door and know if some boy had climbed up the trellis.

When she finally did burst upon the scene, she'd look so cute in her little tie-dyed dresses and high-top sneakers or her denim overalls with a orange bear on the front and a pot of honey and the US flag on the butt pockets, and he'd be able to see right into her head, so he'd always know what she was thinking, but when she bumped into things, pieces would break off of her, and if she banged hard enough into something, she'd shatter.

He must warn her not to do that!

He put his ear to Mary's big belly to have a word with his daughter. Mary gave him a harrumph but didn't stop turning the pages of her magazine.

Listening carefully and looking with his eyes closed, he confirmed his supposition about Abby's invisible twin. It was like a ghost that quickly slipped out of sight as soon as he arrived.

"What was that?" he asked.

"What are you talking about, Daddy?" Abby asked.

"Hey, don't play dumb with me," he said. "What are you hiding behind your back?"

"Nothing."

"Come on. I can see right through you," he said. "What is that?"

Mary brought her magazine down on his head several times like she was shaking seeds in a grain basket. "What are you saying down there?"

"My father told me that back when I was born," he said, "they didn't allow fathers to attend the birth, so he spent the time pacing the waiting room and sneaking secret sips of scotch from a silver flask."

"Why am I not surprised?"

"There are 238 things to know about being a girl," he said to Abby.

"Lovely," Mary said.

"Only 238?" Abby asked.

"So, while I'm not sure, I think my first memory of him must be a red face looming in out of a cloud of alcohol fumes."

"Not to mention his stinking cigars," said Mary who always made the old man go outside to smoke when he came over for dinner which was not so often since he was always traveling on undisclosed business. His son wanted to make a career of undisclosed business, too, so it was lucky Mary brought home a regular check from the Fire Department.

"Yes, but you have to know all 238," he told Abby. "But believe me, that's child's play compared to what you need to know to be the girl's father."

"I think there would be a lot more things to know about being a girl," Abby said, "than there would be to know about being a father if I were the one imagining this conversation and you were made of glass and hiding something behind your. . . . oh, forget it."

"The first thing to know is how you must be very very careful not to bang into things," he said looking off to one side so she wouldn't notice he was scooting around to the side so he could get a better look at what she was hiding, because he now realized that even if you could see right through your daughter, the view was wildly distorted.

"So, that's your big advice?" Mary asked. "Don't bump into stuff?"

As he moved, the creature behind Abby moved, too, so he could never get a good look at it which was why, he supposed, he thought of it as her "invisible" twin. He realized he would name it and learn of its nature some time in the future.

"That," he said, "and always be aware of where your bottom is in time and space."

"Daddy!"

"What a totally sexist thing to say," Mary said. "You wouldn't be talking about bottoms and bumping into things if she were a boy."

"Yes," he said, "But knowing what's important is one of those billions and billions of things you need to know if you're the father of a glass girl with an invisible twin," he said.

"Well, at least you don't smoke cigars," Mary said.

5. What Shall We Name the Baby?

On the one hand, they could name her Molly. Mary wanted to name her Molly. On the other hand, they could name her Abby which was, in fact, her real name. If they named her Molly, his daughter Abby would never be born. He needed to make Mary understand that.

"It's just too too perfect," Mary said. "Molly Williams was the first for sure woman firefighter in America."

"Oh?"

"Maybe the world!"

"Maybe the universe," he said.

"Listen to this," Mary said, "she was held as a slave by some guy with the Oceanus Engine Company number eleven in New York City!"

"Wouldn't you know it?" he said.

"You got that right," Mary said. "Nothing much has changed. Oh, and in the blizzard of 1818, Molly pulled a pumper all by herself through some really deep snow!"

"Amazing," he said.

"While wearing a 'calico dress and checked apron!'"

"Boy oh boy," he said.

"So, we should name the baby after her."

They had moved the computer out of the office, which was to be first the nursery and then Abby's bedroom. There had been no place to put it but on the coffee table in the living room. He was always telling Mary to watch out for the wires. Now he was sitting on the edge of the couch hunched over the keyboard trying to get Google to cough up some ammunition for his side of the argument. Mary was on his right with a stack of books between them. Not that this really was an argument. But sooner or later it would become an argument, and he was doing his preemptive best to make sure Abby (and not some other little girl) emerged from the rubble.

"Aren't there any famous firefighters named Abby?" he asked.

He could feel her eyes on him. He didn't look up from the computer screen. After a moment, she said, "Well, the first woman to actually be paid as a firefighter was named Sandra Forcier, and it looks like the first woman to make a career out of was named Judith Livers."

"Sandra and Judith," he said.

"Do you like those?"

"I don't think so," he said.

"Molly is better," she said.

If Molly won, she might follow her mother into the Fire Department. The two of them would work together, Mary in her yellow hat and long heavy coat and boots and axe, and little waist-high Molly in her calico dress and checked apron. What the heck was calico, anyway? Like the cat? And what color were the checks? Okay, make the checks red and green and check Google again for the calico. Ah ha! He should have known. Calico was a freaking ghost town in California. It was also some kind of ghostly white cotton cloth. Mary and Molly would be out to all hours of the night with the sirens screaming and the burning beams falling and the ladders swaying and the people jumping and the water spraying. Wasn't it bad enough one of them was so often in danger? Did she really need a pint-sized sidekick? Molly wouldn't be wearing shoes, and her little feet would be sooty. Mary would make a sweeping "this way!" gesture without looking back, and Molly would stop slapping out small flames with her little shovel.

She'd put down her sand bucket so she could drag the big hose up behind her mother.

"And what about the snow?"

"What snow?" asked Mary who would trigger the nozzle, and the water would shoot out, and Molly would be hanging on to the hose behind her mother, and everything would be so hot and noisy and broken. There would be puppies yelping for help from the lower stories, and Molly would have to let go of the hose and run across broken glass to rescue them.

"And what about the broken glass?"

"What broken glass?"

Abby, on the other hand, could stay home and learn to play the cello.

"Hey!" Mary said.

"What?" He glanced over to see her grinning and holding up one of the baby name books.

"Molly means, among other things, 'the perfect one!'"

Oh, great. Not only would his daughter be a firefighting superhero, she'd also be perfect. They'd be sitting around the dinner table and he'd grab the wrong fork or do something unusual with his napkin and she'd make a sound of absolute astonishment at his ignorance and uncouthness. Daddy! No, she'd probably call him Father. She'd be a cheerleader and an honor student, and later she'd study economics in college and marry some bozo in a three-piece suit. There would be three little unsmiling grandchildren in matching outfits. Everyone would be so polite.

"Don't you think being perfect will make her a little hard to live with?" he asked. "What does Abby mean?"

"She'll be perfect to me no matter what," Mary said. "Hang on a moment. Oh, here it is. Actually, Abby doesn't mean anything."

"That can't be right."

"That's what it says," Mary said. "Abby is just from Abigail. It's like a nickname or something."

"Nonsense," he said, "I've known women named Abby."

"Anyone in particular?"

"Yes!" he said because his search had just that moment turned up something good. "I'm thinking of that famous abolitionist and feminist Abby Kelley Foster!"

The web page didn't say if Abby Kelley Foster had played the cello, but she must have played something. Everyone played something in those days. Maybe the clavichord. The clavichord would be okay.

Mary scooted over to him and put her hand on his shoulder. "Tell me why it is so important to you that we name her Abby."

He took a moment to put his thoughts in order, and then he said, "I already know who she is, see. She's Abby. Someday she'll play the cello. If we name her Molly, she'll be somebody else." He scooted close to Mary and put his arm around her shoulders. "One day I'll look at our daughter, and I won't recognize her. I'll say to her, 'Who are you, young lady?' And she'll say, 'It's me, Daddy.' And I'll say, 'Abby?' And she'll say, 'No.'"

Mary studied his face for a moment. Then she said, "You do know Molly is a form of Mary, don't you?"

"No," he said. "I didn't know that. But it does make a big difference. This means we can name her after you without causing huge confusion. I am really conflicted."

"I didn't give you all the information," Mary said. "Abby might be short for Abigail, but Abigail means 'My Father rejoices.'"

"Of course it does," he said.

"So could it be Abigail instead of just Abby?" Mary asked.

"Let me check." He closed his eyes and pictured her there with her cello. Yes. In fact, when she played in Carnegie Hall, she might want to use Abigail instead of Abby. "Yes, Abigail would be fine."

"Then we must use both names," Mary said. "Molly Abigail."

"Abigail Molly," he said.

She would be a cello player who sometimes helped her mother fight fires.

"They'll call her Molly," Mary said.

"They'll call her Abby," he said.

6. Surprise Guests

Kevin said for the third time, "You're pregnant?"

"I wish you could see your face," Dawn told him.

"Well," he said. He looked at her face, and couldn't help thinking that she no longer looked like a woman young enough to be pregnant. She was attractive, still trim. She played tennis and swam. But the lines around her brown eyes had been deepening for years.

"You're not happy?"

"It's just that I was starting to think that we'd have the house to ourselves soon." He did a quick calculation. The fourth set of college tuition bills would start after he was retired. Maybe he'd delay retirement? No. Better move some savings back into the stock market.

"Somebody new," Dawn said. She took his hand and pressed it against her belly.

"I'll be damned." He managed a smile. Then he said, "The doctor is sure?"

"He's sure." She laughed. "He said, 'There's a lot of this going around lately.'"

"But at..." He had almost said at your age. "At our age?"

"It's funny," she said. "Vicki is pregnant, too." Vicki was Dawn's tennis partner. Kevin worked with her husband.

"Wait," Kevin said. "Ralph had a vasectomy."

"Sometimes it doesn't work. And Rhonda across the street told me that she's pregnant."

Rhonda, still in her twenties, wasn't a surprise, but he said, "It's an epidemic."

Holding her belly, Dawn said, "Who's coming to see us, I wonder?"

She had always talked that way, as if babies were surprise guests. When pregnant, Dawn speculated. Melissa, their first, did everything late. She took forever to start kicking in the womb. She threatened to be a breach birth, not turning head-down until long past her due date. Dawn said, "I think she's shy."

Dawn had to be induced for Melissa's birth, and then Melissa had indeed come into the world like a shy person entering a party where she knows no one. As a baby, she startled easily. The smallest surprise — Kevin's laughter, a red hat, or the cat jumping onto a chair across the room — could make her cry. Melissa was twenty now, studying literature in college, but there was still that delicacy about her, that wide-eyed look, alert to danger.

That night's local news ended with a feature about a midwife in Florida who was claiming that there was an epidemic of pregnancies. It was the last story of the evening, and the co-anchors made a joke about unforseen effects of Florida orange juice.

Kevin said, "You don't suppose." But Dawn was reading. She hadn't paid attention.

The next afternoon, Kevin's sister called him at work. After a decade of seeing reproductive specialists, she finally had great news. Kevin congratulated her a bit numbly, hung up the phone, and called his broker. "Majid," he said, "I'm looking for some pure plays in babies. Baby food. Day care."

"You're the third client to ask," Majid said. "What do you know?"

The third? So it was too late to get in. He needed to think ahead. "Scratch that. Get me into cotton futures."

"How much? Which contract?"

"Just get me out of bonds and into cotton."

"Everything?"

"Everything."

Kevin had a meeting with the assembly line supervisor that he couldn't put off, so he called home. Hedda, his second daughter, answered. Perfect.

Hedda was efficient. When Dawn was pregnant with her, Hedda had started to kick right on time, energetically, as if she needed more room. Dawn's contractions started early, and after the first few she gripped Kevin's arm and said, "Let's go. This one knows what she wants, and she's in a hurry." They arrived in the delivery room just ahead of the doctor, and doctor was barely in time to catch Hedda.

Baby Hedda entered the world as the party's guest of honor. When she cried, it was a command. If Dawn or Kevin guessed wrong about what she needed, she was furious, but her rages dissolved the moment she had what she wanted. At four, she would announce what clothes she was wearing for the day, and if Dawn insisted on a different outfit, Hedda threw a fit. It was easier to just let her choose.

Now she was in high school, the leader of a crowd of girls. They shopped wherever she shopped, listened to whatever music Hedda liked. At sixteen, she already had college planned down to her wardrobe.

"Sweetheart," Kevin said, "I need a favor."

"I'm kinda busy," Hedda told him. He heard the voice of a girl pop singer in the background.

"There's a hundred dollars in it for you."

"What do you need?"

"Take the van to Wal-Mart," Kevin said, "and buy disposable diapers.

Fill the van."

"What! Why?"

"If you can, make two trips. Take your brother along to help carry."

"What am I using for money?"

"Put it on your card. I'll pay you back."

"Two trips, two hundred dollars."

"Fill the van both times, floor to ceiling, and it's a deal."

"Deal."

"Drive care—"

She had hung up.

After he had wrapped up the unavoidable meeting, Kevin left work and tried to fill the trunk and passenger seats of his car with diapers. He had to make four stops. Each time, he bought the last of what was on the shelf, and he still didn't fill the car.

He arrived home to find that Hedda's luck was better. She and Charles—in his hockey jersey—were stacking diapers in the garage like bales of hay in a barn. "Three full loads," she said. "Okay?"

"Brilliant."

"For three hundred."

"No argument."

"Score!"

Charles said, "Do I get three hundred bucks?"

"You...," Kevin said, "...get...something even better."

"What?"

"I don't know. We'll figure it out. Let's surprise your mom and have dinner started before she gets here."

Kevin had the news on while he boiled spaghetti. The spate of pregnancies was a national story now, and was treated as real news. He stirred marinara sauce with elan. He was, after all, a man with a gold mine in his garage. Disposable diapers would be scarce from now on. Soon they'd be getting expensive.

Now he needed to think two steps ahead of everyone else. What next?

Later, his mood was more somber. At dinner, Hedda had asked Dawn if she was pregnant. This wasn't the way that Dawn had wanted to break the news to the kids, but the diapers invited the question. So Dawn was mad at him. Worse, the late news had shifted the story. It wasn't just the unusual number of pregnancies making news, but who the expectant mothers were, from girls as young as eleven to women on the cusp of menopause.

The phone rang. It was Melissa calling from college. "Oh, Daddy," she said. "I don't know how this could have happened." Then she was crying. Between sobs, she asked to speak to her mother.

Virgins were pregnant. Lesbians who had never been with a man were pregnant. In seven or eight months, it seemed that every fertile woman in the world would be giving birth. Radio talk shows buzzed. Was this a divine sign? An alien invasion? When Kevin went on a fruitless hunt for more diapers, he saw the tabloid covers illustrated with the bat-babies or space-babies or devil-babies that the headlines said were waiting to be born.

Dawn took Hedda, sweet sixteen Hedda, to see the doctor. The test results made Hedda mad. "This is going to really mess things up," she said. "I had plans!"

Kevin read the news magazines. Religious leaders had scoured their holy texts and now announced that these babies wold be the generation of Kali Yaga, when the host of the living outnumber the dead. They were souls of the Redeemed, come to make the New Jerusalem, or they were the legions of Armageddon, to be born without souls. Theologians argued. Where did it say that the Messiah would be just one person? Couldn't the Madhi arrive as an entire generation? How could anyone be sure that there weren't this many Bodhisattvas?

He read the newspapers. Hormones in meat production couldn't explain this. Vegetarian women were pregnant, too.

Walkie talkies.

Demand for abortions soared. Courts from Bangkok to Des Moines battled over the rights of pre-teens whose parents didn't want them to be mothers. Genetic studies of aborted fetuses turned up nothing strange. Screening out the mother's DNA didn't reveal a common father.

Cotton futures went through the roof.

On the news there was a story about husbands who wanted nothing to do with these babies. They had filed a class action lawsuit against their wives.

"I do wonder," Kevin told Dawn. "I mean, I'm just wondering. Is this kid mine?"

"Don't get any crazy ideas," she said.

"Are you kidding? In the face of what's happening, I can't have crazy ideas?"

"Settle down. I'm your wife, it's your baby."

Dawn brought Melissa home from college. "This will be an adventure," Kevin heard her telling the girls. "We'll take care of each other. Don't worry."

All the rest of the world was worrying. Parliaments debated. Dictators ordered abortions, or forbade them. Worried couples divorced or married. The World Health Organization asked the U.N. to declare a global emergency. How could enough birthing facilities be set up in time? Ministers of agriculture called on baby food companies to ramp up production. Menopausal women were drafted into the midwife service.

Kevin bought extra locks for the garage. He took Charles to hockey practice and noticed a foul mood among the hockey moms and dads. He wondered if the girl at the concession counter had had an abortion.

Dawn wouldn't discuss the possibility for Melissa or Hedda. "We're talking about babies," she said. "Would you stop worrying? Find a project."

He had let himself be distracted from the walkie talkie plan, but it wasn't too late. Wholesale warehouses weren't limiting the supplies. He could still buy the radios in bulk, at a discount. Charles, riding along in the van to pick up the merchandise, said, "I don't get it."

"What happens when lots of moms need rides at the same time?" Kevin asked him. "What do they do?"

Charles shrugged. "Call somebody."

"Land lines will jam. Cell phones won't be able to handle the volume, either." He winked at his son.

Charles grinned. "I get it!" Then he added, "We should get batteries, too."

Kevin looked at him. "I hadn't thought of that." Smart kid. "I've been thinking. We'll want to be getting out of the house next winter."

"We will?"

"Trust me. What do you say to Avalanche season tickets?"

Charles whooped. "Yes!"

Dawn didn't need a project to keep her busy. She was studying her pregnancy. She thought she might have a boy. Charles had kicked in brief bursts like this. A rough-and-tumble boy like Charles, perhaps.

She went out for a walk every morning with Melissa and Hedda. She made sure the girls were eating right.

Melissa's baby was kicking now, too. And Hedda's. One morning at breakfast, all three of them said, "Oh!" at the same time, then looked at one another, amazed.

Dawn woke Kevin in the middle of the night. She took his hand and put it on her belly. "Feel that?"

He had felt a baby moving inside her before. This was no different.

"Don't you love a mystery?" she said. "Who is this baby going to be?"

And Kevin thought, Who indeed?

7. Man to Man

Name: Clint Stewart Neelen

Blood type: B

Age: Sixteen

Favorite food: A huge greasy hero sandwich featuring pastrami, baloney, and sauerkraut known locally as "The Eliminator."

Favorite drink: Hot Chocolate

Special Talents and Abilities: Clint is never without his Universal Tool which he once used to amaze his mother by fixing the toaster. He might also be able to control giant robots using only his mutant mental powers.

Hobbies: Radio-controlled airplanes, war movies, auto mechanics.

Ambition: Clint wants to someday overpower an enemy machine gun nest by charging in headlong screaming words no one will let him say out loud these days. He also wants to grow a beard and smoke cigars. He is thinking about becoming an aeronautical engineer.

As he sat down on the hard plastic seat toward the back of the bus, Clint thrust his hands in his front pockets. His left hand closed around the pack of cigarettes, still unopened. He did a quick scan of the passengers. Three matron types, with shopping bags, two women with briefcases, and the usual collection of old geezers. No one from school. No one his age. Typical.

Two geezers sitting a couple rows back from Clint were talking about Back in the Days When. "I remember how hard it was to keep boys and girls apart," one of them was saying. "Now it takes work to get them together. They're just not red-blooded like we were."

"It's different," said his companion. His nose was big and red. "It sure is different."

"Everything's been too easy for these kids. No sense of responsibility."

"Hell, if they won't do their duty, I'd be happy to have a go!" the red-nose man said, a little too loudly, and sniggered. The women turned and glared at him.

Clint slouched down a little further in his seat.

Above the windows, the bus was lined with public service ads depicting young men and women in suggestive poses. Between the ads, the geezers, and the contraband in his pocket, Clint was feeling guilty. He was a good kid, did his duty at least as much as the next guy. But at the moment, he wasn't going to see his girlfriend. He was on his way to Jim Marken's house to work on a Mustang they were rebuilding together. And to smoke his first cigarette, if he and Jim could slip off into the woods for a bit.

"How about this young fellah?" one of the geezers was saying, and Clint felt his face get hot. "Hey, son," the old man said. "Yeah, I'm talking to you. Who else?"

Clint turned to face them.

"You got a girlfriend?"

"Of course." Everybody at school had a girlfriend.

"Well? Get her pregnant yet?"

As if it were that easy. As if you could just look at a girl in the right way and make her pregnant. As if having sex with her just a few times would reliably do the trick.

The bus was still blocks short of Clint's stop, but he pulled on the cord that would signal the driver. "Up yours," he mumbled, and turned to face front again.

"What?" said the old man. "What did you say?"

Clint got up and stood by the exit doors.

"Coffee," said the other old man. "Drink plenty of coffee."

There was a coffee urn at the back of every classroom at the high school. For the boys only. Caffeine increased sperm motility, but it decreased fertility for girls. When Dick Tolufsen got caught sneaking a cup of coffee to a girl in his class, they were both suspended for a week.

The bus stopped, and Clint stepped down.

"He's probably sneaking hot chocolate," the first old guy said. "And cigarettes! You wouldn't believe the nerve of these kids."

"Like I said," the second geezer said, quieter this time. "They should let us have a go."

Name: James Kevin Marken

Blood type: O

Age: Sixteen

Favorite food: Pepperoni Pizza and shredded beef tacos

Favorite drink: Hot Chocolate

Special Talents and Abilities: Jim is a master of the Kama Sutra positions known as the "Black Bee" and "Feeding the Peacock." He can also make realistic farting sounds using only his fist and underarm.

Hobbies: The poetry of Gerard Manley Hopkins, bungie jumping, skate boarding, and auto mechanics.

Ambition: Jim wants to be captivated by a beautiful woman, maybe Lana, maybe not, and be dragged under the surface of her blue, gray, green, brown eyes, and be so profoundly in love that sweet poems leap from deep within him whenever he opens his mouth, but he sometimes thinks such a woman might be easier to find if he first runs off to Africa and becomes a famous hunter and guide.

The Mustang was parked on the street. That's what Clint thought for one heart-stopping moment as he approached Jim's house. Their hobby, their pastime that had nothing to do with girls, was there where everyone could see it, with the hood up. Of course, it couldn't be the Mustang. No way.

But it was. There was Jim, wearing jeans and a t-shirt, leaning over the engine block.

Clint hurried. Jim looked up from the plug wire he was wiggling. He took the cigarette out of his mouth. "Hey."

Clint froze in shock. A cigarette? On the street? But all he said was, "Hey."

"These wires are crap. I know it's not the plugs."

"Yeah," Clint said. The plugs were new.

"Want a cigarette?" Jim asked him, and then grinned. "Or did you bring your own?"

Clint looked up and down the street. The yards were empty. He didn't see anyone peering out from their living room windows. Still... "Is this a good idea?"

"Screw 'em," Jim said. "I don't care what they think anymore. Nosy bitches."

Clint laughed, but it wasn't an easy laugh. He felt in his pocket for the cigarettes. If a police cruiser did turn the corner, where could he put them? He pulled the pack part way out of his pocket.

"Give 'em here," Jim said.

Clint hesitated. The pack hadn't been easy to get. "Why?"

Jim smiled around the cigarette, then coughed and waved the smoke out of his eyes. "Because I'm superman. They can't touch me. The cops show up here, I'll say, 'Yes, ma'am, I am smoking a cigarette. And as long as I continue to perform, who gives a rat's ass?" He took the cigarettes from Clint and rolled them into the sleeve of his t-shirt. Now that looked cool.

"As long as you continue to...."

"Lana's pregnant, you shit-for-brains. I'm golden."

Clint felt the ground tilt. "Oh."

Jim picked up a plug wrench. In a lowered voice, he said, "But it's not going to turn out like it usually does. I'm not going to college."

Clint just looked at him. He and Jim had been friends since they were little kids. They had built forts together in the woods, made and demolished model airplanes, lurked in neighborhood back yards after dark like suburban ninjas, and quizzed each other about the make and model of cars they saw on the street.

"I love her," Jim said. "I'm not going to let them take her away from me."

"Like you have a lot of choice."

"Mexico." Jim pointed the wrench at the engine. "This baby will get us to Mexico."

It took longer for that to sink in than the idea that Lana was pregnant.

"Are you nuts?" Clint said. "You think you can just drive a pregnant girl out of the country?"

"Lower your voice."

"How does doing your duty in prison sound? You like that better than college? What would you do for work? You don't even speak Spanish. Have you asked Lana what she thinks about this?"

"I have to work out some details."

"She won't go for it. Not Lana. She's way too practical."

"I want to be with Lana. I'm not going to just walk away from her."

"Walk away, hell! She's got a future now! This is everything she wants!"

"I think I know my girlfriend better than you do."

"I..." Clint met Jim's gaze, then looked away from him. "I just know that if Julie were pregnant..."

"Well, Julie's not Lana, is she?"

Still staring at the engine, Clint said, "When is she due?"

"I don't know."

Clint looked him in the eye again. "You didn't ask her?"

Jim shrugged. "You're going to keep working on the car with me, right? I need to get it running smooth."

Taking a deep breath, Clint considered his friend. One way or another, they were going to be apart soon. Forever, probably. With Jim would go the car and everything it stood for. "Yeah," he said. "We'll keep working on it together."

Name: Lana Maria Fuentes

Blood type: A

Age: Seventeen

Favorite food: Chocolate cake

Favorite drink: Coffee

Special Talents and Abilities: Lana has the ability to accurately calculate the odds of any given event without having to do the boring mathematics. Also dogs do what she says.

Hobbies: Knowing and telling people interesting facts like the way it's super important that you know your blood's Rh factor when you're pregnant. You could be negative and the baby might get the father's Rh positive blood and your negative blood could attack the baby's blood and maybe kill it and the only thing they could do about the problem is drain out all the baby's blood and put in new positive blood like the Mom's. So everyone should know about their Rh factor, don't you think?

Ambition: After college, Lana wants to capitalize on her position as an exiled elfin princess with powers over animals to become a world renowned dog trainer with her own shop where you'll also be able to get your dog washed and combed. She visualizes the shop as having posters of cute cartoon animals doing adorable and funny things on the walls and special enclosures for the dogs that will be more like little doggy apartments than cages.

Clint's mother had already heard the news from Jim's mom. Clint hadn't even closed the door behind him before she was saying, "So when to I get to brag about my son? And don't roll your eyes."

He stared at her, deadpan. He shut the door hard.

"Julie's been calling you," his mother continued, undiminished. "Now that Lana's going to college of course Julie can't help being just a little bit jealous. But the two of you could be headed for college, too. If you'd just apply yourself, make a steady effort with Julie instead of wasting time with that car every afternoon..."

"Should I point out that working on the car didn't keep Jim from knocking up Lana? Or would you eventually figure that out on your own?"

"Now don't start."

Clint put up his hands. "What did I start? I'm barely home, and you're all over me about Julie! You're as bad as her mother. 'Why don't you two take a study break and go have sex in Julie's room. I'll bake cookies.'"

"Well, honey, you should be enjoying it."

"Mom..."

"You do enjoy it don't you?"

He rolled his eyes.

"Answer the question."

"No! I mean, yes! None of your business!"

"If you're going to get anywhere in life, you're going to have to get into college."

"It's not the only way to get into college, Mom. I could pay for college."

"Yeah." She folded her arms. "And what exactly would you use for money?"

"I'd work my way through." He headed for the kitchen. "I'd take out loans..."

"That you'd be paying back for the rest of your life," his mother said, following him. "Do you have any idea what college costs?"

Clint opened the refrigerator. He took out a gallon jug of milk, uncapped it, and took three long swallows. For once, his mother didn't yell at him for it. He put the jug back and started to take out mayonnaise, bread, salami, and cheese.

His mother said, "I am making dinner, you know."

"Just a snack. I'm starved."

She gave him that look, as if she hadn't ever been a teenager herself.

He slapped together the sandwich so that he could get to his room and be alone. But then the phone rang.

"Oh, hello, Julie," his mother said. "We were just talking about you. How's school?"

"I'll take it in my room."

"Hang on, Julie. Clint is right here." She handed him the receiver.

He sighed. He took a bite of his sandwich and, mouth full, spoke into the phone. "Hey, babe."

Julie's voice said, "Are you coming over tonight?"

"We haven't had dinner yet."

His mother said, "You can eat over there," at the same time that Julie said, "My mom's just setting the table. We'll set a place for you."

"I don't know, babe."

"What's wrong?"

"I don't know."

"I got something new at Victoria's Secret. You'll like it."

Clint smiled. "Is it black?"

"Red."

Clint's mother raised her voice to say, "He'll be happy to join you for dinner!" Then to Clint, she said, "Go! Go!"

Clint said, "I bet it's great."

"We need to spend more time together," Julie said. "Or we'll get reassigned."

"I like you," Clint said. "And I like red. You know I do. It's just, I don't know."

"What!" said his mother. "What are you saying to that poor girl!"

He couldn't say what he wanted to. He couldn't say, Jim and I have been friends for a long time, and now we're going to be separated, one way or another. He couldn't say, I just want to stay in my room tonight and watch old war movies and think. Not with his mother standing right there. And he'd have a good time with Julie. He always did. "I'll be over in fifteen minutes," he said.

When he hung up, his mother said, "Take your toothbrush."

The phone rang again almost immediately. This time, Clint answered it. It was the Verification Board. Could he come in tomorrow morning for a cheek swab?

"Shit," Clint said. He'd forgotten about this. Lana had given them his name.

"Excuse me?" said the woman with the VB.

"I'll be there," he said, and hung up.

"Who was that?" said his mother. "Was that Julie again?"

"I'm going," he told her.

Name: Julie Samantha Banks

Blood type: AB

Age: Sixteen

Favorite food: Lemon chicken and pork fried rice

Favorite drink: Coffee

Special Talents and Abilities: Julie can make knots just by thinking really hard about the things she wants to tie up.

Hobbies: Julie likes to knit without using her special powers. There is just something magical, she says, about a sweater made without using magic, if you see what I mean. She also collects contemporary art marbles and enjoys Greco-Roman wrestling while wearing outrageously sexy outfits.

Ambition: Julie wants to develop and trademark a magical knitted nightie which she will sell to Victoria's Secret and make a million dollars. It will be known as the "Julie." Guys will say things like, "Honey, why don't you slip into your Julie while I pour the wine and put on some romantic music."

The time alone in his room had to wait a few days. Clint worked on the Mustang with Jim the next two afternoons. He ate over at Julie's house and spent the night two nights in a row. But Friday afternoon, he told Jim he didn't feel like working on the car. He went straight home from school. He checked the answering machine. No calls yet.

In truth, working on the car was exactly what he wanted to be doing, today and for a long time to come. He wanted both of them to have packs of cigarettes rolled up in their t-shirt sleeves, like men. He wanted to talk about cars the way men did in old movies, call them she.

There was more to it than that, the thing that he wanted. There was more to it than what you could figure out by watching movies or talking to the geezers who had been alive when the movies were made. Between the geezers and now, there was a gap that the virus had left behind.

The phone rang. Clint answered. A woman said, "I'd like to speak to Mr. Clint Stewart Neelen."

And he knew. They wouldn't be calling him today if it wasn't him. For the sorry-not-this-time calls they waited another day. "Clint Neelen. That's me."

"Date of birth..." She read his birth date.

Again, he said, "That's me."

"This is the Verification Board. I'm calling in regards to the case file for Lana Fuentes. DNA confirms parentage. Congratulations, son. You're a man now."

"Am I." That was what it took, officially. Get a girl pregnant, and you were legally an adult male, eligible for all the rights and privileges pertaining thereunto. Blah blah blah.

"You'll be contacted by the College Board shortly about career plans. As I'm sure you know, males don't always get their first choice. But you're in. All you'll have to do to stay in is keep getting girls pregnant."

"Great. Does Lana know that I'm the father?"

"She's been informed, yes."

"I'm not her boyfriend. My best friend is."

The briefest pause. "And you're not sure how he'll take it."

"He didn't know. With me and her, it was just the one time."

"My," said the VB woman. "You are a lucky young man."

"She just wanted to...improve her odds. He didn't know."

"I see. I'll put you through to Counseling and Reconciliation Services. Please hold."

But Clint hung up. Counseling and Reconciliation Services would be some middle-aged woman who would set up some kind of structured meeting between Clint and Jim. Everything would be safe and reasonable and motherly. Blah blah blah.

Clint would go to Jim's house. They'd take a walk in the woods. Maybe they'd smoke cigarettes. And Clint would tell him. No escape to Mexico, not that Lana would have ever agreed with that scheme. No college for Jim, either. Not yet, anyway. He'd have to stay in high school and keep trying. They'd give him someone else to try with. Maybe Julie.

Jim might punch him.

That would be all right.

They'd work it out, man to man.

Quiz:

A young woman with type A blood and a guy with type B blood can have babies with which blood type?

A. Type A

B. Type B

C. Type AB

D. Type O

E. All of the above

F. None of the above

8. Failure

Today, at last, Mary was a real firefighter. Training complete, probationary period over, she'd be home any minute from her first day on the job. They had partied after her graduation, but today another celebration was in order. She might not expect this one.

He had considered a main course of fish. Perhaps poached Dover sole and fresh asparagus and tiny boiled red potatoes. Not quite right. Well, fowl then—a nice duck with plum sauce and wild rice and artichoke hearts?

No.

The occasion called for something with big bones. Something colorful and messy and loud. Something they could get all over the place. They might not toss the bones over their shoulders for the dogs, there were no dogs, but they could still lick grease from their lips and fingers and shoot one another steamy looks across the dinner table.

Fried chicken, then.

Or rack of lamb.

No and no again.

He settled on barbequed spare ribs and mashed potatoes and broccoli. He selected a good red wine—a local vintage that would say, yes, they were finally settled in this new place and situation, and yes, Mary, was a real firefighter. She was, in fact, the only woman firefighter in town. She had to work hard so they wouldn't turn her into some kind of spokesperson. She would not be a token. She wanted to swing an axe and kick down doors and run into burning buildings to save people.

Why couldn't she want to be an accountant?

Why couldn't she long to add up long columns of numbers? He could pick her up at the office at the end of the day. He'd come in, and she'd be bent over her work—many sharpened pencils in a jar by her coffee mug which would have a slogan something like Things Always Add Up.

But if he had married an accountant, he wouldn't have married Mary, and that was unthinkable, so he'd be happy for her. Happy happy happy. She'd finally get to use her axe and hose and ladder. They'd let her ding the bell and maybe steer the rear end of the big engine as it screamed around corners. She'd get to scratch the Dalmatian behind the ears.

If he tried to turn her into an accountant, the real Mary would have to be someone else if she was anyone at all. She might just disappear in a cloud of smoke. He liked her just the way she was, but he worried about her all the time.

Tonight there would be candles everywhere, and Mary would go from room to room blowing them out in a symbolic affirmation of her new status as Firefighter. She'd blow the candles out here and she'd blow them out there, and they'd eat the ribs and throw the bones to the imaginary dogs who would not be Dalmatians because you shouldn't bring that much of your work home with you but you could bring your yellow helmet home if you promised to wear it and nothing else when you blew the last candles out in the bedroom.

The candles were his way of saying, "I knew you could do it!"

He set the table and checked on the ribs sizzling in the oven. He opened the wine and looked at his watch. He got the broccoli ready to go into the hot water. Then with nothing left to do, he counted down the minutes until he judged the moment was just right and went into the bedroom to start lighting the candles.

It hadn't been easy to find things to hold up all the candles. He'd had to make do with empty bottles and saucers and tin cans. There was a candle on each of the bedside tables. On the left, there was a pewter horse with candle growing out its head. This had been a wedding gift from his father. Mary had hidden the ugly thing in a box, but he had found it. On the right, her side, there was the silver candlestick he had bought her in Mexico. Originally there had been two of them, but the other one had been lost in one of their moves. He lighted the candles by the bed and then two more on the dresser and moved on to the other rooms.

In the second bedroom which was his office, he lighted a single candle in an empty Baby Clams can. They wouldn't be in here much, just a quick in and out as she blew out the candle.

He wondered if the heat or smoke or whatever would hurt the computer but decided he couldn't worry about it.

The living room and the dining room had to be just right. When she came in, it should be like coming into a church. Well, maybe not a church, they would not be doing things you should do in a church, but some setting where there were lots of candles! Hundreds of flickering flames. Okay, a few dozen anyway. But artfully placed! He had spent a lot of time moving his odd collection of candleholders around to achieve pleasing arrangements. Little groups of three and six. On the coffee table. Atop the bookshelves where they could not singe the books. Candles all around the fish tank. The fish didn't seem to mind. In fact, they seemed hypnotized by the flames.

Almost done.

He heard a noise like someone hitting the wall with a sock full of sand and then a hissing and soft crackling. The ribs? The water in the broccoli pot? He looked at his watch again. She should be there any minute now. The air was slightly smoky. Yes, there was her key in the door.

"Honey, I'm home," she called—their little joke, but this time he really did have some splaining to do because just as she came in, the smoke detector went off.

Mary rushed by him into the bedroom.

"Get the extinguisher!" she yelled.

What extinguisher?

He ran into the kitchen and got down on his knees and pulled stuff out from under the sink thinking that if he had a fire extinguisher, that was where he would certainly have kept it. Maybe he had bought one and forgotten. Mary seemed to think they had one. But if she had bought one, where would she put it? No, she wouldn't have bought one. She left the household details to him.

There was no extinguisher beneath the sink. He jumped up and opened and closed cupboards and pulled out drawers, but he knew he would not find what didn't exist.

He spotted the pot of boiling water that he had planned on dropping the broccoli into. He snatched it off the stove and dumped the hot water in the sink and filled it again from the faucet. That was a stupid waste of time, he realized. The boiling water would have worked just as well, but he was making this up as he went along.

He hurried back to the bedroom trying not to spill too much of the water and found her slapping at flames licking up the side of a lampshade. She looked sharply in his direction, and he could see the desperation on her face. He could tell what was going on in her mind as clearly as if she were speaking to him. This couldn't be happening. Not today of all days. If the guys had to come and put out a fire in her apartment on her very first day on the job, she would simply die of embarrassment.

They would have to leave town.

They'd probably have to change their names.

Wear brown paper bags over their heads.

Hell, she might lose her job and be forced to become an accountant.

"There is no extinguisher," he said.

"Give me what you've got," she said. She would be hoping he had not brought a pot of cooked spaghetti. Or maybe she would be thinking nothing of the sort. He handed the pot across to her. She threw the water on the flames, and a moment later the fire was out.

They stood looking at one another over the bed.

"Nice job!" he said.

She wouldn't eat dinner until he read the pamphlet on home fire safety.

"I can't believe you carry these around with you," he said.

"Lucky I do!" she said. "Just read it."

He sat down on the couch and pretended to read while she went around blowing out the rest of the candles. A question came to his mind. He could ask it. He could say, hey, how come a hotshot firefighter lives in a place where she doesn't even know there is no stinking fire extinguisher anyway? Shouldn't she have noticed that fact? But he was not out to make points. And it was his fault. It probably said as much somewhere in the pamphlet. He kept his questions to himself.

"What's the deal with all the candles anyway?"

"It's symbolic," he said. "It's all about how I knew you could do get through your training and pass all your tests. And today's your first day on the job, and I just wanted you to know."

She made one more sweep through the apartment to make sure she hadn't missed any of his candles, and then she sat down on the couch beside him. He turned a page in the pamphlet. She kissed him on the cheek.

"It was a sweet thought," she said.

They threw no bones, but dinner was a big success. The ribs were spicy, juicy and very messy. The broccoli was perfectly crisp. If there was one thing he knew how to do, it was cook broccoli. The smoke had cleared from the apartment, and it was hard to tell anything had ever been burning. He'd ruined food that left more odors than this. He wondered if they should call someone about the accident. Was there a report to file? He didn't mention it. She would know. There was no damage to the apartment itself aside from some discoloration on the ceiling in the bedroom. He would paint over that tomorrow, and everything would be as good as new.

"Have some more wine," he said.

"Okay," she said.

He got up and came around her chair and leaned in and kissed her neck as he filled her glass again.

The celebration he had planned for her could have been an incredible disaster.

But all's well that end's well.

After they made love, he discovered the condom had failed. He hadn't noticed at the time, and he didn't think Mary had noticed either. She hadn't said anything about it, and now as he dropped the dripping prophylactic into the bowl and flushed the toilet, he knew he was not going to say anything about it either. That was a decision he made without really making it. He did not weigh the pros and cons. He just went into the bedroom and crawled back in bed with her. This was her big day.

"Thank you for tonight," she muttered.

He made a sound of contentment and kissed her and pulled her in close to sleep.

He had almost burned the house down.

But she had put it out.

Maybe this new thing he was so carefully not thinking about would not be a disaster. After all, what were the odds?

9. Hibernation

Tory changed out of the flimsy examination gown and sat down to wait for the doctor. She looked at the walls. She had been in lots of examination rooms lately, but this one was different. Dr. Blumen's walls were hung with framed photographs of animals: A dolphin nudging her calf to the surface for its first breath. A calico cat nursing kittens. A bear asleep on a bed of leaves. A mare dropping her foal. A sort of feel good alternative to the usual clinical decor of anatomy diagrams and plastic models of body parts. This one was teenage-girl cute. Not Tory's style. But in her current state of mind, preferable to poster-sized illustrations of arthritis or ectopic pregnancy.

Not a model skull in sight here. Good. Nine months ago she had seen enough plastic skulls to last a lifetime. Doctors at the hospital had used them to illustrate Ramsey's injuries and explain why her husband's brain was dead. Here, the shelves were covered with animal figurines. Nursing pigs. Puppies. Terminally cute.

Dr. Blumen rapped twice on the door and came in. He sat across from

Tory, opened her chart, and stroked his white beard.

"If I didn't know better," Tory said, "I'd think this was a veterinarian's office."

Blumen smiled a bit absently, still reading.

"If I were trying to conceive, and couldn't," Tory went on, "then I would just love all these baby animals."

Blumen looked up from the chart to meet her gaze. "And if you weren't trying to conceive, but had?"

"Even better."

"Your uterus is enlarged. I've reviewed your blood work. Then there's the ultrasound. The evidence all says that you're pregnant."

"Yeah, the evidence keeps saying that. And I keep telling doctors that I can't be."

He held her gaze and said nothing. His eyes were dark and warm.

"Look," Tory told him. "I'm not lying. I've got no reason to lie. I haven't been with anyone since my husband died. Unless they changed the rules, you can't catch pregnancy like a cold. This is an adorable little ovarian cancer pretending to be a baby."

"Okay." Blumen got up, came to sit beside her, and showed her the chart. High levels of hCG. Normal levels of lysoPC. Results of the pelvic exam. He explained the expected ranges, the meanings of these numbers. Then he showed her the sonogram. "Some uncommon tumors can mimic pregnancy, but not to this degree," he concluded.

"Great. My cancer is unusually talented. I'm thrilled."

"I don't see cancer."

"The other doctors didn't believe me, either."

"I haven't said I don't believe you. I'm giving you the truth as I see it. You're giving me your truth. In between, there's a mystery."

That stopped her. Then she said, "I get it. A mystery. As in, How crazy is she? Why is she in denial? Or—"

"No," he said. He stood up, leaned against the examination table, and folded his arms. "I don't think you're crazy. You do have an advanced case of sarcasm, though, and I suspect it's a chronic condition."

She laughed. "That was good," she said. "It's been a while since I laughed in a doctor's office."

"Have you ever had memory lapses? Periods of time you couldn't account for?"

"No. Not even time for a quickie."

"You were hospitalized for severe depression."

"So what? I was grieving."

"Depression can interfere with memory."

"I was messed up, but not like that. Sex I would remember. Even if it was bad. I remember plenty of bad sex from before I was married."

"What were you doing three, four months ago?"

"I had gotten out of the hospital. I was getting my life together. Alone."

"There are drugs that affect memory, particularly in combination with alcohol. If someone slipped Rohypnol into a drink..."

"What part of alone is unclear? I wasn't socializing. I wasn't dating. I haven't had the urge. You think I want to have cancer?"

"Do you?"

"Oh, now that is bullshit!"

"Let's see." He opened her chart and paged back. "Involuntary admission. Depression. Malnutrition." He looked up. "You had stopped eating."

She looked away. "I lost everything when he died."

He paused. "Not eating is one way of expressing that you have nothing left to live for."

She looked back at him. "I wasn't expressing anything. I wasn't trying to kill myself. I was just out of it."

"Back to the mystery," Blumen said. "I know you are pregnant. For the sake of your baby, you need to know it, too."

"It's impossible!"

"When was your last menstrual period before your husband died?"

She felt cold.

He said, "Help me out here."

"Six weeks."

"Were you eating normally then?"

"Yes."

"Exercising excessively, enough to stop menses?"

"No."

"So you had missed a period. You thought you were pregnant."

"I thought I might be."

"When you were admitted to the hospital for malnutrition, you weren't menstruating."

"Jeez. They write everything down."

"What do you know about reproduction in bears?"

"Nothing." Tory laughed. "Hey, maybe you're the one who is crazy."

"Maybe." He motioned for her to stand. "Come over here and have a look at something." Above the shelf of animal figurines, it was the bear picture that he wanted her to see. He pointed. "Great photograph, even though it's dark. See what's happening there?"

The part of the picture he indicated was mostly shadow.

"She's giving birth during her hibernation," Dr. Blumen said. "Female bears are impregnated in the spring. But the fertilized egg doesn't grow. It floats in the uterine cavity until the late fall. If conditions are right, if the bear has put on enough winter fat, then the egg implants and develops. Until then, the bear is in a state of suspended pregnancy."

"Brilliant. Except I'm not a bear." She noticed that one of the figurines in front of her was a mother bear and two cubs. She picked it up. "It can't happen to people, what happens to bears."

"I'd certainly be surprised to see it. Who ever heard of a woman suspending her pregnancy because she was too sad to have a baby?"

"It's nonsense." Her fingers closed around the bear and cubs.

"Yes," he agreed.

"Impossible," she said. Pregnant with Ramsey's child? "Totally impossible." She was squeezing the figurine as if it were a treasure that someone might try to take from her.

"If you want another doctor's opinion, I understand. In the meantime, however, I want to see you for prenatal care." He wrote out a prescription and gave it to her. "Take your vitamins."

"It's absurd," she said. "Ridiculous." She took the prescription and stuffed it in her purse.

He walked out to reception with her to make her next appointment. "You don't really believe it, do you?" Tory said. "Telling me about bears is just a way to make sure I'll come back." She looked at the bears in her hand, then at Dr. Blumen. He smiled.

"I'll see you in a month," he said. He held out his hand for the figurine.

"Yes you will." Tory grinned and put the bears in her purse. "We'll be back."

10. Championship Season

Tammy found Sharon sitting alone at the far end of the field. "Hey, girlfriend." Their husbands had been picked in the same draft, three years ago.

"Hey." Sharon patted the empty bleacher space beside her. Tammy sat. Far across the field, her husband and the other linebackers did tip drills with the defensive backs. Sharon's husband, a tight end, practiced with the receivers, sprinting to catch footballs that shot out of a machine.

"I've heard the news," Tammy said. "Congratulations. Us, too."

"Congratulations!" Sharon hugged her. "When are you due?"

"January. You?"

"February."

"That's perfect. That's after the Superbowl."

Sharon grimaced. "Yeah."

"Jeremy's happy?"

"He's happy. I guess." Sharon took a deep breath.

"I know." In the distance, her husband batted a ball into the air. "I don't mind the away games so much. But right now, he's not home when he's home. I keep telling myself that it's training camp."

"And it will get better once the season starts? You've been married to a ball player how long?"

"But he's a good man."

"Mine, too. During the season, though, it's one more trip to the training room, just another hour with the play book."

"That's what got them here. Being competitive."

"Uh-huh."

Number eighty, the expensive rookie, turned half a step late. The ball popped off his shoulder pads, high into the air. Jeremy backpedaled, caught the ball, and waved it in the rookie's face.

Sharon said, "Was Antwaan a big baby? Big birthweight?"

"I don't know. He's big now."

"About the same as Jeremy, right? Jeremy's 238."

"A little more. Why?"

At first, Sharon just smiled.

In the nutrition store, bagging the supplements, the clerk said, "Hey, aren't you Antwaan Ekkes? Can I tell the manager you came in? That you buy your supplements from us?"

"You can tell him," Antwaan said. "But these aren't for me."

At home, he found Tammy on the sofa reading.

"Babe, I got you something." He knelt and started to put plastic bottles on the coffee table. B Complex. D and E. Lecithin. Soluble Calcium. Ester C.

There were a dozen more still in the bag when Tammy said, "You trying to choke me with pills?"

"You've got to take care of your nutrition."

"I have vitamins already. What I need is real food."

He stood up. "What do you want?"

"There are pork chops I was going to fry. And mustard greens."

He walked into the kitchen. When he came back, he wore an apron. "What else? If I bake a custard, will you have some?"

"I haven't seen you in an apron since before we were married." She smiled.

"After lunch," Antwaan said, "we're going for a walk."

"What about your run?"

"I'll run later. You need exercise."

For the Miami game, Tammy reserved two seats on the aisle, close to the bathrooms. Sharon arrived in a maternity dress in team colors.

Tammy said, "You're looking good."

"It's all the care and attention I'm getting at home."

Tammy smiled. "Can't be any better than at our house. You're a genius."

Sharon said, "You work with what you've got."

After the first playoff game, players lingered in the Jacuzzis, trying to soak out their bruises. One of the linemen grunted as he got out of the water. "Well," he said, "that's one down."

"I hope we get Seattle," said a receiver. "I feast on that secondary."

Jeremy Laws said, "I don't care who we get. They're going down."

"That's for sure," said someone else.

"No shit."

"Going down."

Water bubbled. A trainer came in and picked up towels.

"Just so you know, Laws," said Antwaan Ekkes, "my wife is big as a house."

"Yeah? Well Sharon is huge. I think she's got an elephant in there."

"Tammy packs in ice cream a quart at a time."

"That's nothing—"

The rookie receiver said, "What are you guys talking about?"

"You haven't heard?" the trainer said. "Those two have a thousand bucks riding on whose baby weighs more at birth." He tossed the towels into a bin.

An inside linebacker said, "I've seen your skinny wife, Laws. You're going down."

"No way," said a safety. "He's having a girl. Girls weigh more."

"Bullshit they do."

The rookie said, "Is it too late to get in on this?"

11. I See You

He goes a very small distance into the future, not far enough to see his heart breaking and not far enough to see himself get over whatever it was that broke his heart in the first place, the organ in question like a soup can she puts back up on the fence so she can take another shot at it, not far enough for the doctors and the police, too many counselors, late night walks in and out of rooms and up and down stairs, the clocks always saying she's late, she's so late and it's dark, not so far as to hear himself say that when she turned 18, she was supposed to move away and never call them, boo hoo, we'll be so lonely in this big empty house, Abby, what will we do, shall we get a motor home, no make it a boat, and we'll sail off to the Greek Islands at last, no not that far, just a little way into the future, beyond the baffling birth and the first few sleepless weeks in which he will come to realize his daughter will one day be Queen of the Galaxy and will rule wisely and firmly but fairly, nevertheless still making many mistakes the guilt over which will drive her home to the cottage in the woods to cry on Daddy's shoulder who will tell her she is so pretty and wonderful and she'll go back and solve the too-many-rockets-between-here-and-Mars problem with a sweep of her hand just like that and everyone will go oooh and aahh, but that's too far, too, he goes only maybe six months, no nine months into the future, yes she's big and her eyes are bright and she makes many interesting sounds, and he can see she's already got a philosophy, but not so far into the future that she's running all over the place banging her head against sharp corners and putting stuff up her nose and eating bugs, nine months then, and he's just stepped out of the shower and Mommy hands her over while she herself gets into her firefighter's uniform and Abby snuggles against his chest and he breathes in the cosmic baby smell of her hair. This is the moment. Never mind the cough later, the neighbor kid's kiss, the cops, the dance where she doesn't get to dance, strange new drugs, her angst over the shape of her nose, tell me you didn't get your tongue pierced, shut up, what do you mean not your tongue, don't tell me, and cars, good god don't even talk about teaching her to drive. She puts both her little hands on his chest and pushes away and gives him a big smile. Peek-a-boo. She's about to tell him something. What will she say? Yes, just this far and not a second more.

12. What to Expect

Experiences in the first month vary. You may feel fatigued, nauseous, bloated. Your breasts may feel tender. You may crave certain foods, but food aversions are just as common.

In the second month you may feel dizzy, irritable. You may experience mood swings. By the third month, your appetite will probably increase. Veins thicken in your abdomen and legs.

In the fourth month, any nausea you felt may decrease. Or increase. Or you may feel nauseous for the first time. Your ankles and feet may swell. Experiences vary. You may have trouble concentrating.

By the fifth month, you will likely feel the fetus moving. Leg cramps are not unusual in the sixth or seventh month, and you may have difficulty sleeping. Braxton Hicks contractions begin. You may dream of the baby. You may feel giddy. You may feel like crying. You may cry.

In the ninth month, contractions may wake you.

In the eleventh month, your sleep will almost certainly be disrupted. You may experience mood swings, nipple soreness, pain.

In the thirtieth month, arguing and tantrums are common. You may feel tired, irritable, irrational.

In the 200th month, sleep disruptions often return. You may lie awake waiting for the phone to ring. If you sleep, the phone may wake you. You may imagine that you hear a key in the door. Anxiety is common. You may experience mood swings. You may dream of your baby. Experiences vary.

13. What I Don't Say to Her

You're doing great, I say. I say nothing about my sudden realization that the past is an illusion and that anything at all might happen next. Expecting anything is foolish. The idea that millions of people have done this very thing before is baloney. Push, I tell her, because that's what they told me to say. I am so afraid, but she must be afraid, too, and if I say I'm afraid, she might become more afraid. I don't tell her that this moment is all there is, that we are brand new and clueless, and just as the birth occurs, a simultaneous monkey might spring from the head of a moose, who can say? And our lovely new daughter, little Abby, the apple of her father's eye, might get a lifelong furry companion, not exactly a brother and not exactly an imaginary playmate, and maybe we'll call him Sparky. Abby and Sparky. Look at them. They go everywhere together. Breathe, I tell her. Whosss whosss whosss, I demonstrate. It is an incantation to disguise the fact that we know nothing. This is supposed to be such a joyous experience, but it looks like an injury to me. These people in white should be fixing it instead of smiling and joking like they've seen it all before. They've seen nothing. Do something, you people, make it stop, help her. Everything, I tell her, is going to be okay.

BABY LOVE

MICHAEL BISHOP

At thirty-seven, Briggs Captor became the sole guardian of his infant daughter, Adelaide. This transformation occurred when the right front tire of his wife Irene's sedan shredded on I-85, near Atlanta, and an eighteen-wheeler ploughed into her automobile as she limped across four lanes of traffic toward an off-ramp bracketed by violets. But in her padded seat, Adelaide — or Addie, as Briggs called her — flew out the flapping rear door into a mattress of violets, surviving her expulsion like an astronaut splashing down in a space capsule. A piece of metal pierced her earlobe, daubing it and her jaw with ruby flecks — but she otherwise escaped injury, and Briggs Captor, miles away, unknowingly entered the country of single fatherhood.

Irene's mangled sedan burst into flames. A week later, a socially inept friend sent Briggs a video of the car burning on the interstate, and he watched it over and over, haggard in his fixity of purpose, until Ted Chutney, a neighbor, popped the video out and disposed of it. But the image of that car fire stayed in Briggs's brain, a pyre of such iconic loss that it occasionally manifested for him on drives along backcountry blacktop roads: a soul-searing mirage.

Briggs retired from his job as a calamity analyst to take care of Addie. (Few people had grasped what he did, even when he explained it as "performing autopsies on stillborn construction projects.") He did not *need* to work. He had solid equities, Irene's will kicked in, and he had long wanted to part from his business associate, a workaholic lawyer.

Soon, everyone in Chinaberry knew about Addie and her bereaved daddy. In huaraches, khaki shorts, and a Georgia Bulldog jersey, Briggs pushed Addie about town in a stroller. Folks hailed him. They chucked Addie's chin. They invited him to dinner, offered to babysit, and lauded him for his devotion.

Briggs asked, "May I call you when she poops?"

Addie's melon head and fawn-eyed face tickled him. She looked at once like a photograph of chanteuse Edith Piaf and a portrait of that exemplar of imperial neotony, Napoleon Bonaparte. Her large head had caused Irene to labor for nineteen hours before letting her doctor do a C-section. Then Addie had emerged "timely ripped," as Irene later put it, a purple and yellow nematode.

Now, Briggs spooned vegetables into Addie from fist-sized jars. He haggled at yard sales for wooden puzzles, snap-crotch jumpers, and rubber dolls. He clutched her to his chest as Jay Leno lulled them to sleep every night. In her crib or his bed, Addie sprawled like empire. Briggs did not care. He slept soundly, exiling to his id every nightmare that had burnt him since that pyre on I-85.

Part of Briggs thrilled to Chinaberry's acclaim. *"What a guy." "You don't see many single men caring for a baby." "Never thought he had it in him."* But another part cringed, for what really fired him like new sparkplugs, was Addie—cooing, crotchety, or grinning like an idiot savant. He loved her fiercely, as in his courting days he had loved the recently immolated Irene Forest.

Some evenings Briggs carried Addie to The Inlet, a bar on the highway, where he held her on his lap, nursed a beer, and shot the breeze with Walleye Prine. In its neon-lit haze, he schmoozed with grease monkeys, potheads, and GBI drug agents in laughably oldfangled hippie disguises.

"This is no place for a kid," Walleye said.

"It's hardly a place for a grownup." When Briggs pulled on his beer, Addie reached for the bottle.

Another patron said, "Give her a sip, Briggs."

"Not on your life. You don't give an infant booze."

Leigh-Anne Cowper sauntered over in a gust of schnapps and formaldehyde and leaned into Briggs. Walleye called her Morticia (but not to her face) because she worked in a funeral home and had a clear whiff of carnality or mortality about her. Divorced, childless, and fast approaching forty, she swung her peroxided hair and her comely body like a teenager.

"If it's Addie's health you're fretting over," Leigh-Anne said, "look." She waved her hand. Smoke eddied in blue volutes.

"God, you're right." Briggs paid for his beer.

"Bring her to my place. I don't smoke."

"Well, that's a sacrifice," Walleye said. "If I worked where you do, I'd carry a pine torch."

Briggs left before a gender-blind slugfest ensued.

In his two-story house, where he now felt like a BB in a rain barrel, Briggs carried Addie upstairs.

Recently she had begun to talk. "Bey-bey," she said, straining in Briggs's arms. *"Bey-BEY!"*

In the sewing room, he carried her over to a glass-faced cabinet in which Irene had displayed her own and her late mother's dolls: Madame Alexanders, Barbies, Dutch and Finnish models, threadbare Raggedy Anns. Addie pointed to a doll no bigger than a beanbag, dressed in dotted gingham. He gave it to her, and she clasped it in an elbow crook. Addie often held it as she dozed on his belly, the gray-blue television screen their nightlight.

During the day, Briggs made Addie chuckle by lifting the doll and crooning, *"Bey-bey, Bey-Baaay, Bey-BAAAY!"* Often she giggled until she choked, crazy for his Little Richard impersonation.

Her adulation intoxicated him. Despite his croaky voice, he tried other songs: "Light My Fire," "Baby Love," "The Star-Spangled Banner," a pseudo-cockney number that his father, a Vietnam veteran, trotted out when he wanted to embarrass Briggs's mother:

I came to town to see
That old tattooed lydy.
Tattooed from head to knee,
She was a sight to see.

The song listed the lady's tattoos topographically, from the Royal Flying Corps on her jaw to the Union Jack on her back to the gods of wine that wreathed her spine to the fleet of battleships circumnavigating her hips. It concluded, never soon enough for Mrs. Captor,

And over her left kidney
Was a bird's-eye view of Sidney,
But what I liked best
Was upon her chest
My little home in Waikiki.

Singing, Briggs scrunched his face up like Popeye's and protracted *Waikiki*'s last two syllables. Addie watched as if committing each line to memory.

A few months after Irene's death, after she began to say *light* and *dog* and *Barney*, Addie coined a name for Briggs: *Baba*. He had hoped that she might call him *Daddy* or *Papa*, but once she hit upon Baba, she never abandoned it.

In Russian the word meant *Grandma* and in English *rum cake*, but Addie applied it to Briggs. If he praised her—"You look cute in that jumper, kiddo"—she always said, "Tank you, Baba," and he genuflected before her in his heart.

Dirty diapers Briggs changed easily. Viruses, infected ears, bellyaches, and colic took more out of him. If her nose ran, Addie wiped mucus over her face and up into her hair. Briggs yelled, "Jesus, do you want to make *me* sick too?" Whereupon Addie said, "Baba mad," and Briggs repented.

"Baba's not mad, punkin, Baba's scared."

A few months on, Briggs's best friend Craig Gale e-mailed news that he and his German fiancée planned to marry that June in Heidelberg. Briggs told Ted Chutney, and one day, near the frozen-food case in the local grocery, Leigh-Anne Cowper marched up and asked if he intended to take Addie to the wedding.

"Of course."

"By yourself? With no help?"

"I've got no help to speak of here." Briggs cocked his head. "Does Addie look puny or neglected to you?"

"I could go as a sort of nanny."

Briggs said, "I can't afford—"

"I'd pay my own way. I'd like to see Europe and help with the rug rat."

Briggs gazed at the cartons of microwave-ready pizzas and TV dinners.

"Strictly business," Leigh-Anne said. "No hanky-panky. I get my own room wherever we go."

So Briggs agreed. "Just keep it quiet. Or Walleye and Ted will splash it around like yard-sale paint."

In her seat in the shopping cart, Addie stuck her arms straight up. "Leah go too," she said.

They flew Lufthansa, the German airline, in a Boeing jet packed with passengers, including a golden retriever puppy. Addie, facing backward in her padded seat, eyed the puppy warily. Leigh-Anne sat apart from them, as if traveling alone.

"Puppy get me," Addie said.

"No," Briggs said. "He looks about as fierce as cotton candy."

"It's weird how your kid has to sit facing us," the man next to Briggs said. "She stares at us, we stare at her."

"It's a safety regulation."

"As if sitting backward would help her if we drop into the Atlantic."

"Who knows? Addie was riding in this seat when an eighteen-wheeler wiped out my wife. Irene was crushed like a bug, but the kid survived."

The other man shut up.

Every time Briggs told this story, it stopped conversation dead.

They landed in Frankfurt, rented a blue Renault, and drove to Heidelberg, where they found Craig and his fiancée Gisela Riess talking to Mrs. Riess in Gisela's sixth-floor apartment on Bergheimerstrasse.

None of them knew what to make of Leigh-Anne, who had changed from jeans into a gold-lamé gown and glossy black heels. The wedding was a week away. Because they still had arrangements to make, Craig told Briggs to follow his ideal itinerary—to travel in Belgium and France before returning to Heidelberg. Meanwhile, Gisela and her mother passed Addie back and forth like a rare cantaloupe.

"You must *leave* this one with us," Gisela said.

"Oh no," Briggs said. "This one's my life."

Leigh-Anne framed a brittle smile.

They spent the night in separate rooms and departed the following morning for Trier, reputedly the oldest city in Germany, the site of historic Roman landmarks. In the Renault, passing fields of sunflowers, Briggs asked Leigh-Anne why she had donned her showy wedding outfit.

"I wanted to impress them."

"Really? They probably thought you were a sex-channel porn queen pretending to respectability."

Leigh-Anne mulled this silently.

In her car seat, Addie threw a handful of Cheerios and squirmed like a torture victim. "Out," she wailed. "Addie get out." They had hardly driven an hour, but she sounded oppressed and miserable.

"Calm her down," Briggs said. "Earn your keep."

"I've paid my way. Calm her down yourself." But Leigh-Anne rummaged up a pacifier—in German, her *Schnulli*—and slipped it into Addie's mouth. She also handed the kid her doll and stroked her hair until she drifted off to sleep.

"Thanks," Briggs said.

"Up yours," Leigh-Anne said.

In Trier they ate at the Roemergrill on Simeonstrasse, stared over the city from the top of the lofty Roman gate, and walked like penitents the aisles of the cathedral. Addie, wearing a floppy lavender hat, jogged in Briggs's backpack. Leigh-Anne's face looked less horsy than usual. She smelled not of formaldehyde, but of a sweet amalgam of apple juice, White Shoulders, and sweat.

A day later, in Brussels, they realized that they had only travelers' checks and deutsche marks, no Belgian francs. They had arrived in the city with no prior familiarity and evaporating reservoirs of patience. Brussels spread to the horizons, traffic bleated, and the people—especially in the Asian barrios, before Briggs asked for help—seemed to regard them with indifference if not outright loathing.

When they failed to locate the train station (so they could change their travelers' checks), Briggs wheeled the Renault through defiles clogged with taxis, pushcarts, and canvas-draped trucks. He refused to ask for directions again, so they recursively doubled back or idled in infuriating jams.

"Briggs, we need to feed Addie. You're getting us nowhere."

He zipped through a turnabout on a wide boulevard and hit the brakes before a big beige building with overflowing trashcans along its sidewalk.

They hiked across four lanes of traffic to a music store. The sun dangled like an evil gong. The clerk spoke broken English and pointed them down a street that Briggs feared would end at a Turkish enclave that they had already visited.

Ahead, behind barricades shingled with handbills and trimmed with plump graffiti, lay the Brussels train station. Briggs seized Leigh-Anne's arm and led her by a dingy reflecting pool into the station's fluorescent-lit maw. At a booth near the food court he traded for Belgium francs. Leigh-Anne, who had left her passport in the car, asked him for a small loan.

"Never mind," Briggs said. "Sit over there and feed Addie" — he nodded at some metal tables — "and I'll fetch us something." In the air conditioning, he could feel his mood modulating, softening. The court sold pizza, hamburgers, fried fish, and Chinese food, but he headed for a stand offering pita sandwiches.

Nearby, a squat professorial-looking man in a tweed jacket buttonholed Leigh-Anne and tickled Addie. His crimson mouth framed an O. His eyebrows danced. His brown umbrella waggled behind him, a lewd appendage.

A harmless coot, Briggs decided, ordering sandwiches and lemonades. Then, with a cardboard food caddy, he approached the dining area.

As if from nowhere, the old man manifested before him in a boxer's pose. His umbrella clattered to the floor like a musket. "*Ha!*"

Briggs said, "*Ha!* yourself."

"You're an American?"

"Yes," Briggs said. "We're from Georgia."

"Ah. Georgia." The old man jabbed, but stopped his fist just shy of Briggs's belt buckle. He probably thought he was being funny.

"Atlanta hosted the 'ninety-six Olympics," Briggs said.

"Pickup trucks, black people, Johnny Reb." The old man feinted at him. "I know America. I taught in *Chicago.*"

"You're a professor?"

"A professor and a boxer. If my students got unruly, I knocked them out."

Briggs's stomach flopped. "Then you probably liked the Olympic boxing."

"Pfaugh. Black brawlers, only black brawlers. I prefer the gymnastics of the women — the naked half-moons of their asses."

"Have a nice day somewhere else." Briggs tried to sidestep the old man, who turned with him, chin pointed and fists cocked — a threat more of embarrassment than of physical injury.

"I *loved* Chicago," the old man said. "I loved the *whores* in my classes." The old man thrust his crotch forward. "The ones who got good grades I screwed. If *they* wanted A's, they screwed *me*."

Briggs edged behind a column, but the old man leapt into his path again. "Fuck Georgia!" he cried demonically. "Fuck Atlanta!"

"Leave off, old man." Briggs set the food tray on a table and pivoted. "You really don't want to mess with me today."

The old man scurried aside, picked up his umbrella, and twirled it in Briggs's face. "I'll call the police."

"*You'll* call the police?"

"Give me your baby. I'll show her how really smart girls make good grades." His umbrella went transparent. Beyond its fabric, a brown galaxy bloomed within the station, light-shot architectures.

Outraged, Briggs stalked the old man, visible now through the fabric as a frail hobgoblin.

Leigh-Anne, with Addie in her arms, caught the old man's elbow. "Go away now. Before something bad happens." She let go of him and held her palm up to Briggs as plea or warning.

"Fuck Georgia," the old man said. "Fuck *you*." He collapsed the umbrella and marched out of the station, a boxer taking a unanimous decision. Briggs stared after him incredulously.

Leigh-Anne said, "He's sick, like the schizos in downtown Atlanta."

She led him to their table. They sampled their pita sandwiches, travesties of pineapple, meat gobs, and sauce. Leigh-Anne threw hers away. Briggs chewed his unhappily.

Addie said, "Sing Baba's Song."

Briggs did not feel like singing. Addie leaned toward him from Leigh-Anne's arms and pinched his cheeks between her hands: "Sing Baba's Song." He tried "Light My Fire," "Baby Love," and "The Star-Spangled

Banner." Addie frowned and repeated, "Sing Baba's Song." At last he sang "That Old Tattooed Lydy," and Addie listened as if to the world's most soothing lullaby.

"That's terrible," Leigh-Anne said. "Really terrible." Briggs shrugged. Leigh-Anne laughed. They all laughed.

They left Brussels and drove to Bruges to see Michelangelo's *Mary and Child* in one of its churches. They arrived during a soccer tournament and retreated to Oostkamp, where they took cheap rooms at the Het Shaack Hotel. Leigh-Anne wanted to return to Bruges for the Michelangelo and to spend the next night there. Most of the soccer fans would have left by then. The day after, they could drive to Paris.

"Paris?" Briggs said. "Total pandemonium all over again."

"You can't visit Europe without seeing Paris."

"Listen, the French dislike Americans. If you don't know the language, they *despise* you." At a buffet-style restaurant in Strasbourg several years ago, the staff had stood by as Irene and he tried to determine which line to enter, where to get utensils, and whom to pay. He could not imagine Americas treating foreign visitors that way.

"You must mean *rich* foreigners," Leigh-Anne said. "We treat *poor* foreigners as badly as anyone."

Two days later, Briggs, Leigh-Anne, and Addie schussed down Highway A-1 through a cobwebby rain. Under charcoal skies, the fields shimmered green. Although Briggs had never visited this part of France before, it felt almost friendly; however, fear of a replay of their traffic disaster in Brussels made him uneasy.

"We should park in Chantilly and ride the train into Paris," Leigh-Anne said, poring over a map. "That way, no big-city traffic."

Briggs said, "Can you even *do* that?"

"This is Europe. People ride trains. Let's stop in Chantilly and see."

They stopped. A young woman in the visitor's center told Briggs that Leigh-Anne's plan made perfect sense. She made reservations for them at a hotel on the Rue de St. Denis that a British couple in Bruges had suggested as cheap and clean. They bought a full-day parking permit and parked in front of the train depot. In the incessant gauzy rain, they consolidated items for one night into three small bags and stepped inside to buy round-trip suburban-line tickets and metro-access passes.

Then they gawked in alarm at the changing overhead rail schedule. To whom did they give their tickets? Where did they board? Once in Paris, how did they travel to the Chatelet de las Halles exit? In her backpack, Addie twisted Briggs's ears as if trying to tune in a radio station, then slammed her body backward so that he almost toppled.

"*Addie!*" Briggs caught himself.

A handsome Latino man stepped up and took Addie's hand. "What a charming child." He kissed her fingers. "May I assist you?"

The man hailed from Uruguay, but taught classical guitar in Paris. He told them that they must notch their tickets or risk expulsion from the train and possibly even arrest. He led them onto the platform and into a double-decker passenger car.

In thirty minutes this car pulled into the Gare du Nord in Paris. Just as Briggs sensed the onset of a new panic attack, the man reappeared and led them through a crush of commuters to the train to the Chatelet de las Halles station. Then he vanished again, and Addie's face shone in the car's window glass when the rocketing tunnel wall turned it into a haunted mirror.

It was an easy walk — the rain had ceased — to the Rue de St. Denis and their hotel. As they hiked, Briggs told Leigh-Anne that they owed their good fortune, the intercession of the Uruguayan man, all to Addie. She had *bewitched* him.

"Addie's pure gold," Leigh-Anne said, "but *she* didn't figure out using Chantilly as a steppingstone to Paris."

At the Hotel de la Vallée, a walkup to a series of close-packed rooms, they found that the Egyptian desk clerk had let one of their rooms to another guest. Briggs protested that they had reservations. The clerk shrugged.

"I'm sorry. Another person has already paid."

Briggs and Leigh-Anne conferred. They could share a room for one night. The issue of observing middle-class proprieties seemed moot in Paris, even if they intended to observe them.

They had expected a tiny room, but this one stunned them. It reminded Briggs of a walk-in closet. The door abutted the thin bed, which abutted the wall. The room had a sink, a dowel for hang-ups, a bidet, and a third-story window. At this window he gazed down on a sex shop, the words

BOTIQUE EROTIQUE ablaze in neon. A thuggish-looking crowd loitered on the wet cobbles.

"We're in a red-light district," Briggs said, laughing. "I can tell Ted that in Paris I slept with two beautiful females at once."

They ate at a nondescript Italian restaurant on the Rue de Rivoli. Rain had begun to fall again, gently. Still afoot, they went in search of the Louvre. On a concrete island at a red light, a laughing young woman, a real fashion-model type, approached Addie in her backpack and rubbed noses with her.

"Forgive me," she said in English, looking up. "I could *not* resist."

Waiting for the light, they talked. The woman, learning that they were going to the Louvre, said, "Then you must turn and go the *other* way." They thanked her and, marching off, arrived in time not only to enter the museum through the glass pyramid but also to visit two of its four wings before its closing. Briggs took pictures of Leigh-Anne holding Addie in front of *The Raft of the Medusa,* the *Mona Lisa,* and the *Venus de Milo.* Then uniformed guards ushered everyone out.

Walking in the rain across the courtyard, Briggs said, "Addie saved us again. If that pretty French gal hadn't seen her and set us straight, we'd have never made it to the museum tonight."

At their hotel, a toilet perched halfway up the staircase between their floor and the next. It reminded Briggs of airline toilets, except that it had no sink and he could see out its tiny portal to an old brick apartment building.

When he returned to their room, Leigh-Anne wore a flannel nightgown and Addie lay on the bed totally zonked.

"You take the outside," Leigh-Anne said. "We'll let Addie have the wall."

They killed the light and lay down, Briggs in his burgundy boxers. He had no fear of lying next to Leigh-Anne. He had matured *beyond* sex. Once down, though, her *nearness* had surprising power, and he faced away.

"You're a lucky man, Briggs." Her whisper warmed the back of his neck.

"Because Irene died in a car crash?"

Leigh-Anne squeezed his collarbone, but did not speak.

"Tell me *how* I'm lucky."

"You fathered a sweet kid. You have no money worries. Ninety-nine percent of the world's people would trade places with you."

"You think?"

"Sure. Give Bill Gates five minutes to think about it and even he might make the switch."

"Because I'm lying next to *you*?"

"I don't think that much of myself. And —"

"And what?"

"I can't have children, Briggs. Not after a quack in Atlanta helped me *not* have one." She touched him between his shoulder blades. "We could make love." One hand crept over his flank and found what it sought.

Briggs slid off the bed and stalked to the window over the BOTIQUE EROTIQUE. "Suppose Addie woke and saw us, like dogs in rut?"

"It happens, Briggs—not everybody owns a Victorian house with five bedrooms and only two occupants."

"Well, it *shouldn't*. It would terrify her. She'd probably think we were trying to devour each other."

"Addie's asleep, and you've *got* more horns on you than a cattle ranch."

"Knock it off—*Morticia*."

Leigh-Anne climbed out of bed, gathered up her slippers and her carryall, and let herself into the hall. Briggs had no time to stop her.

Addie sprawled like empire. Light snores issued from her gullet, like faraway harmonica notes.

Briggs ventured out, leaving the door ajar, and looked up and down the stairwell. Leigh-Anne sat above him on the step outside the toilet. Even from the landing he could see the blood in her eyes.

"What're you doing, Leigh-Anne?"

"In two minutes I'll step into this toilet and dress. Then I'm leaving."

"Where will you go? It's almost midnight."

"I don't know. Barcelona, maybe, or Prague—pick a city."

"The rest of your stuff's up in Chantilly. You may need it." When she declined to respond, Briggs said, "Leigh-Anne—"

Her eyes winked copper. "Get back to Addie. She could wake up any minute, Baba." She entered the toilet, whose OCCUPIED sign flashed on.

In the morning, Addie said, "Where Leah go?"

Briggs had shaved and pulled together their belongings. He turned and looked at her. "On an adventure. From now on, kiddo, it's just you and me."

Carrying Addie and two bags, Briggs checked out, walked down the steps, and surveyed the street for Leigh-Anne—futilely.

At the Chatelet station, he bought a carnet, a packet of ten metro tickets, and rode with Addie to the *Charles de Gaulle* exit, where he climbed aboveground to see the *Arc d'Triomphe*. There, amid pigeons and pavement, loomed the Arch—a big neoclassical deal. You could hike down into a tunnel, walk beneath the traffic circle, and pay to climb to the top, but Briggs, lacking the heart, asked Addie if they could skip it.

Absolutely, she said. *For God's sake, Baba, please yourself.*

Saving back one ticket, Briggs gave his leftover subway tickets to a stranger and hauled Addie to the subway for their return trip to the *Gare du Nord*, where they ordered a chicken-salad sandwich on a gallery overlooking a dozen or more suburban train bays. Twenty minutes later, they boarded the train to Chantilly and sat in the upper level of a nonsmoking car.

A young man in a tattered grey jersey stopped in the aisle and mounted a stirring appeal in French on behalf of the poor. A well-dressed Parisian who had been conversing with them in English pretended not to understand, but Addie put her palm on Briggs's cheek and said, *Give him fifty francs, Baba.* Briggs obeyed, and their stingy seatmate fell silent the rest of the way to Chantilly.

They retrieved the Renault, and Briggs snugged Addie into her car seat. After a stop for gasoline, they drove to Soissons, from Soissons to Reims, and so on eastward on autobahn-like surfaces toward Strasbourg. An hour passed, and then two, and then three, and still they bore on toward that city, which an Englishman at a rest stop told them was rife with Arab-immigrant crime.

Helplessly facing backward, Addie said, *What will Craig and Gisela say when we get back to Heidelberg without Leigh-Anne?*

"I don't know," Briggs said.

Evening neared, but the light hung on like an amorous hand. Addie fussed. He dropped her special doll in her lap. He sang to her. He coasted off the highway into a rest area with dog-walking areas and fast-food facilities. He changed her diaper and let her totter about a windy meadow as if its gravity had properties alien to her. He found her *Schnulli*. Despite her protests, he strapped her back into her seat. She keened around the pacifier like a heartbroken ghost.

"Addie, hush!"

Trying to regain the autobahn, Briggs swerved to the shoulder when a truck cab pulling two canvas-sided trailers whooshed past with an air-horn blast. Addie screamed, and Briggs pummeled the wheel, outraged by her terror.

Back on the highway, they rode another hour, exited into Strasbourg, and parked on a split boulevard. After a long search, carrying Addie every step, Briggs found a fifth-floor room in the Vendome Hotel, across the plaza from the railway station. The woman at the desk spoke bantering English, as often to Addie as to him, clearly anxious that they find a place to lay their heads. He asked where he could park, and the woman suggested the underground garage on the remodeled street out front.

"Don't leave your car aboveground," she said. "There have been burnings."

Briggs paid with a credit card and hauled Addie outside to drive the Renault into the subterranean car park. This floodlit cavern swallowed them hungrily. Its yellow-grey light drifted like smoke, and smelled faintly of char.

Get me out of this plastic animal trap, Addie said.

Briggs undid the clasps and pulled her out. She kissed him under the eye. The grotto's urinous light thickened. After a dozen steps, Briggs halted and gazed about like a robot. An engine growled to life somewhere, and Briggs set Addie down. She seized his pant leg. Tires squealed at a far exit, and faded stridulously away. Briggs walked Addie to a concrete niche where patrons paid for their parking. Here he groaned and sat down on the curb. Addie eased down beside him. He laid his hand on her nape but then, as if someone had thrown a switch, altogether ceased to move.

"Baba," Addie said. "Get up, Baba." She peered up at his profile. "Baba, get up." She climbed into his lap and laid her head against his chest.

Footsteps approached — many footsteps, as if a small hostile army were coming through the garage toward them.

"Sing," Addie said. "Sing Baba's Song." She made him close his fingers around her doll. "Sing, Baba."

And Briggs, in his frailest voice, mechanically obeyed.

Psyche and Eros

Diana Sherman

She listens as her sisters tell her that her husband is a monster. They are sitting in a courtyard with grey-veined marble, ringed by pomegranate, orange, and peach. The leaves are full and green, and the blossoms are just opening. The scent of orange is strongest. She braids those ivory blossoms into her long black hair and listens to the sound of waves far below.

"His eyes!" One of her sisters cries, and Psyche shivers. She imagines them blood dark, wine dark.

"Wings," cries the other, "Black as night!"

Oh, yes, wings. She knows the feel of those wings, her hands wrapped around that soft place where feather becomes skin. She holds tight as his body blends into her own and her nails draw blood. She knows how his body shivers when her fingers touch lightly over those sensitive wings. Oh, yes.

She knows he is a monster, knows that her father sold her to him. She shakes her head and smiles, knowing that her sisters do not, will not, understand.

"Have you seen him?" One of them demands. "Do you know what he looks like?"

And the question startles her. She knows, of course she knows! She lies beside him each night, running her hands over the mysteries of his body. She knows his skin, his sweat, his taste, his blood. He is her beast. Of course she knows! And yet… she has never seen him.

Her sisters leave, satisfied. They have seen her complacency slip, they have seen that small flame of uncertainty light in her eyes. Her marriage will never be the same. Now they can go home to their human husbands who have no command over the winds, no palace with invisible servants, no magic at all, and they can be happy again.

She lies in the darkness, trembling. This is not unusual. She waits for her lover, her husband, the beast she shares her bed with. There is no light—heavy curtains cover the arched windows. She cannot see the room he built for her with its ivory and gold, its arches and columns, but she can feel it sheltering her. She waits eagerly.

Wind brushes across her bare breasts and she can see stars for a moment before the curtains close again. His weight settles beside her and his breath is hot against her cheek. She shapes her hand around the flesh and bone rim of his wing, runs her hand along the length of it. He pulls her close, his wings closing around her, as his hands mold her. She knows it would take only a moment's carelessness for him to break her, snap fragile bone and skin, and her breath rushes at the thought. But he is careful. There will be bruises, there will be pain, but there will be pleasure, too. Her hands curve at the base of his wings and her teeth find the soft skin running from neck to shoulder. His blood fills her mouth with the taste of copper. For now, she forgets her uncertainty, forgets her sisters' questions.

He sleeps beside her, now, and while her body is sated, her mind echoes with questions. What does he look like, her beast? He hides himself from her, leaving her alone before daybreak each morning, coming only at night. His words soothe her, make her forget that she has never seen him. She wants to tell him that he can show himself to her, she isn't afraid, or rather, she does not mind the fear. But he will say no. She knows him well enough by now. He will say no.

It is easy, oh so easy, to find the lamp she has placed beneath her bed, to light the oil, to turn, to look. And she sees him for the first time. He is pink and gold and pale. Soft skin shines in the lamp light, golden curls tumble around her face. His pretty face with its full lips, delicate flush of pink, long golden lashes, skin so smooth it has never seen a razor (she knows the feel of that skin). His wings are white. She is sure that his eyes must be blue, like a summer sky.

This is her beast? She feels as if she is looking in a mirror, save for he is golden where she is dark, and his wings... She is betrayed. All that she loved, all that she thought she knew, was never there. And he let her believe, let her trust. This boy is no monster, no violent power barely sheathed. He is merely clumsy and overeager with youth. He is not her beast, and she is angry.

She knows there is nothing she can do. She is married to a god—she knows who he is, now. She should put out the lamp, climb into bed, and pretend he is still her beast. But she is angry and she is who she is, she is Psyche, and she will act. She drips the hot oil on that soft skin, drop by burning drop.

He cries out and opens his eyes—blood dark, wine dark eyes—and the room fills with his power. She falls back from him, overwhelmed, and the lamp trembles in her hand. She sees her reflection in his eyes, sees her anger, her despair, and knows that he is seeing the same. He lets out a sound like gulls crying. Before he can see her anger turn to wonder he spreads his wings, those strong wings that have cradled her, and takes flight.

He's gone. Leaving behind the empty bed and his foolish bride, or at least, so she thinks now. The scent of him is still strong. She kneels, breathing it in, and closes her eyes. He won't return. Blood dark, wine dark. She will never forget his eyes and she knows now that she must find him. She must regain her husband, her monster, no matter how long or how impossible a task it might be. And she understands for the first time that love is not a gentle blue-eyed boy, he is a beast and he has ridden her well.

HART AND BOOT

TIM PRATT

The man's head and torso emerged from a hole in the ground, just a few feet from the rock where Pearl Hart sat smoking her last cigarette. His appearance surprised her, and she cussed him at some length. The man stared at her during the outpouring of profanity, his mild face smeared with dirt, his body still half-submerged. Pearl stopped cussing and squinted at him in the fading sunlight. He didn't have on a shirt, and Pearl, being Pearl, wondered immediately if he was wearing pants.

"Who the hell are you?" she demanded. She'd been sitting for hours here on the outskirts of a Kansas mining town, waiting for dark, so she could find a bar and a man to buy her drinks. She was in a foul mood lately, as her plans for a life of riotous adventure had thus far come to nothing. She'd fled a teenage marriage in Canada after seeing a Wild West show, complete with savage Indians and lady sharpshooters, and come west to seek her fortune among such fierce characters. Her career as an outlaw was not going well so far. The problem, of course, was men. The problem was *always* men, and the fact that she enjoyed many male qualities didn't change that fact. Seeing a man now, uninvited and interrupting her brooding, made her angry enough to spit in a sidewinder's eye. "What're you doing in the ground?"

"I'm not sure," the man said.

Pearl couldn't place his accent. New England, maybe? "What the hell's that mean? How'd you end up in a damn hole without knowing how you got there?"

He considered that for a moment, then said "You swear a lot, for a woman."

Pearl dropped the remains of her cigarette to the ground. "I swear a lot for anybody. Are you a miner or something?" She couldn't think of any other reason a man would be underground, popping up like a prairie dog — and even that didn't make much sense, not when you thought past the surface.

"A miner?" He chewed his lip. "Could be."

"You have any money?" Pearl said. She didn't have any more bullets, but she could hit him on the head with her gun, if he had something worth stealing.

"I don't think so."

She sighed. "Get out of that hole. I'm getting a crick in my neck, looking down at you."

He climbed out and stood before her, covered in dirt from head to toe, naked except for a pair of better-than-average boots. Hardly standard uniform for a miner, but she didn't get flustered. She'd seen her share of naked men during her eighteen years on earth, and she had to admit he was one of the nicest she'd seen, dirt and all, with those broad shoulders. Back in Canada (after seeing the Wild West show, but before deciding to leave her husband) she'd had several dreams about a tall, faceless man coming toward her bed, naked except for cowboy boots.

Apart from the dirt, and the lack of a bed, and her not being asleep and all, this was just like the dream.

She finally looked at his face. He seemed uncomfortable, like a man afraid of making a fool of himself, half-afraid he already has. "Nice boots," she said. "What'd you say your name was?"

"Uh." He looked down at his feet, then back at her face. "Boot?"

"I'll just call you John," she said. This could work out. A handsome man, big enough to look threatening, and clearly addle-brained. Just what she needed. "John Boot. I'm Pearl Hart." She stood and extended her hand. After a moment's hesitation, he shook. Soft hands, like a baby's. No way he was a miner. That was all right. Whatever he was, he'd have a new trade soon enough. He'd be a stagecoach robber, just like in the Wild West show.

"Not on my account, honey," she said, dropping a hand below his waist and smiling when he gasped, "but we ought to find you some clothes. If I lured a fella about your size out behind a bar, you think you could hit him on the head hard enough to knock him out?"

"I suppose so, Pearl," he said, as her experienced hand moved up and down on him. "I'll do whatever you want, as long as you keep doing that."

Hart and Boot robbed their way west. Pearl had tried to hold up a stagecoach once on her own, without success. She'd stepped into the road, gun in hand, and shouted for the driver to stop. He slowed down, peered at her from his high seat, and burst out laughing. He snapped the reins and the horses nearly ran Pearl down, forcing her out of the road. A woman poked her head out the window as the stage passed, her face doughy, her mouth gaping. Pearl shot at her, irritated. The recoil stung her hand, and she missed by a mile.

Clearly, she was not a natural lady sharpshooter. She needed a man, the right *kind* of man, one who could be tough and do the necessary, but *also* do as he was told, a man for the look of the thing, so people would take her seriously, and it would be best if he was a man she liked to fuck. She didn't believe such a man existed, except in her dreams.

Until she met John Boot.

They had a simple, and, to Pearl's mind, amusing method of robbing coaches. Pearl would stand weeping and wailing in the road wearing a tore-up dirty dress. There wasn't a stagecoach driver in the West who'd drive past a woman in need, and when they stopped, John Boot would emerge from cover, guns in hand. Pearl would pull her own weapons, and they'd relieve the coach of baggage, money, and mail. John Boot was always very polite, but what with Pearl's cussing, the bewildered victims seldom noticed.

Despite her insistence that John Boot always pull out, Pearl got pregnant once during those wild months. She didn't even realize she'd caught pregnant until the miscarriage. After she'd passed it all she just kicked dirt over the mess, glad to have avoided motherhood. John Boot wept when he found out about it, though, and Pearl, disturbed, left him to his tears. John Boot had depths she didn't care to explore. He mostly did whatever she told him, and didn't argue back, which was all she wanted, but it was hard to think of him in terms of his simple usefulness when he cried.

One night after Pearl came back from pissing behind a rock she found

John Boot staring up at the stars. Pearl sat with him, drunk a touch on whiskey, feeling good. She liked the stars, the big Western sky, the first man in her life who wasn't more trouble than he was worth.

"We have to stop robbing coaches," Boot said.

This display of personal opinion irritated Pearl. "Why's that?"

"They're on to us anyway," he said, not looking at her. "There's not a coach left that'll stop for a woman in distress anymore."

"Hasn't failed us yet."

"Next time." He paused. "I know. They'll come in shooting, next time."

Pearl considered. John Boot didn't talk much. Most men talked all the time and didn't know shit. Maybe with John Boot the reverse was true. "Damn," she said at last. "Well, it couldn't last forever. But we don't have to *stop*, just change our style."

After that they robbed coaches in the traditional manner, stepping from cover with guns drawn. That worked pretty well.

One night in Arizona, Pearl had trouble sleeping. Seemed like every way she rolled a rock stuck in her back or side, and the coyotes kept howling, and the big moon made everything too bright. She figured a good roll with John Boot might tire her out, so she went to wake him up. No man liked getting roused in the middle of the night, but when they got sex in return, they kept their complaints to a minimum.

Pearl didn't believe in ghosts, but when she saw John Boot lying on his bedroll, she thought he'd died and become one. He held his familiar shape, but she could see the ground right through him, as if he were made of smoke and starlight.

Pearl didn't faint away. She said "John Boot, stop this goddamn nonsense *now*!"

His solidity returned as he opened his eyes. "Pearl," he said blearily. "What— "

"You're going like a ghost on me John Boot, and I don't appreciate it."

His eyes took on a familiar pained, guarded look—the expression of a dog being scolded for reasons far beyond its comprehension. "Sorry, Pearl," he said, which was about the only consistently safe response in their conversations.

"I *need* you," she said.

"And I need you, Pearl." He sat up. "More than you know. Sometimes, when you aren't paying attention to me, or you're not nearby, I get so tired, and everything gets dim, kind of smoky..." He shook his head. "I don't understand it. It's like I'm not even strong enough to be real on my own. I want to stay for you, I think I have to, but I get so damn *tired*."

John Boot almost never cussed. Pearl took his hand. "Don't you dare go away from me, John Boot."

"Do you love me, Pearl?" he asked, looking at her hand in his.

Most men, she'd have said yes just to keep them quiet. But after these past months, she owed John Boot more than that. "I don't know that I love you, but I wouldn't want you gone."

He nodded. "How long do you intend to live like this?"

"As long as it's fun," she said.

"When it stops being fun, Pearl... will you let me go? Let me be tired, and just... see what happens to me then?"

Pearl sighed. "Help me get these clothes off, John Boot. We'll figure this out later. All this talking makes me want to do something else."

He smiled, and a little of the sadness and weariness receded from his eyes.

The next day a posse caught up with them, and once Pearl and John Boot were relieved of their weapons it became clear that they were being charged with stagecoach robberies and murders. Someone was killing lone travelers in the area, and Hart and Boot were convenient to take the blame for that, though they had nothing to do with it. Pearl declared their innocence of all crimes, but she'd taken a pearl-handled gun in the last robbery, a distinctive weapon, and when the posse found that, it settled all questions in their minds.

Pearl and John Boot never robbed another coach, and neither did anyone else. Stagecoaches and stagecoach robbers, like lady outlaws and wild Indians, were dying breeds. Hart and Boot were the last of their kind.

The lovers were taken to Pima County jail in Florence, Arizona, a depressingly dusty place with no accommodations for women. For propriety's sake the authorities decided to leave John Boot in Florence and take Pearl to a county jail in Tucson. She argued against that course with a blue streak of profanity, but they took her away all the same, and Pearl was separated from John Boot for the first time since he'd crawled out of the ground in Kansas.

Pearl sat in her cell, looking at the rough wooden partition that divided the "women's quarters" from the other half of the cell. She was wishing for a cigarette and thinking about John Boot. What if he just went to smoke and starlight again, and disappeared?

She wanted him with her, wanted him fiercely, and around midnight a knife point poked through the thin wooden partition. Pearl watched with interest as the knife made a ragged circular opening, and a familiar head poked through.

"John Boot," she said, not without admiration. "How'd you get out? And how'd you get here all the way from Florence?"

"I'm not sure," he said. "You wanted me, and I came... but it made me awfully tired. Can we go?"

Pearl crawled through the hole. The adjoining cell was unoccupied, the door unlocked, and they walked out together as if they had every right in the world to leave. *We can be caught but we can't be kept*, she thought, elated, as they stepped into the starry night.

They stole horses and rode farther southwest, because they hadn't been that way yet.

A week later they blundered into a posse in New Mexico. The men were looking for cattle rustlers, but they settled for Hart and Boot. Pearl offered the men sexual favors in exchange for freedom, and called them every nasty name she could think of when they refused. John Boot just stood unresisting, as if the strength had been sapped out of him, as if he'd seen all this coming and knew how it would end.

The lovers were taken back to Florence (Pearl was beginning to hate that place), where they were put on trial immediately. The officers didn't want to keep them overnight and give them a chance to escape again.

The judge, a bald man with pince-nez glasses, sentenced John Boot to thirty years in the Arizona Territorial Penitentiary, a place famed for its snakepit of a dungeon, tiny cells, and ruthless guards. John Boot listened to the sentence with his usual calm, nodding to show he understood.

Then the judge looked at Pearl and frowned, clearly undecided about how to deal with her.

I'm young, she thought, *and a woman, so he thinks I got railroaded into this, that I'm John Boot's bedwarmer, a little girl led astray.*

Pearl couldn't abide that. "What the hell are you waiting for, you silly old bastard?" she asked.

John Boot winced. The judge reddened, then said "I sentence you to five years in the same place!" He banged his gavel, and Pearl blew him a kiss.

She'd never been to prison before. She figured she wouldn't like it, but she didn't expect to be there for very long.

She was right on the first count, but sadly wrong on the second.

Pearl and John Boot weren't separated during the long ride through the desert, and Pearl vented her fury at him as they bounced along in the back of the wagon, under armed guard. "Thirty years he gave you, and me five. They think five years will knock the piss and wildcat out of me?"

"How do you stay so energetic all the time?" John Boot asked. "You've got enough strength of will for any two people. I'm surprised fire and lightning don't come shooting out your ears sometimes!"

Pearl rode silently for a long time, thinking on that. "You reckon that's how you came to be?" she asked, looking down at her knees. "Some of that fire and lightning I've got too much of spilled out, and made you?"

They'd never really talked about this before, about where John Boot came from, where he might someday return, and Pearl looked up in irritation when he didn't reply.

He was sleeping, head leaning back against the side of the cart.

Pearl sighed. At least she couldn't see the boards through his head this time. He hadn't gone to smoke and starlight. She let him be.

Pearl and John Boot climbed out of the wagon and stood in the rocky prison yard. The landscape outside was ugly, just flat desert and the dark water of the Colorado river, but the prison impressed her. Pearl had never seen a building so big. It seemed more a natural part of the landscape than something man-made. Like a palace for a scorpion queen.

"Put out that cigarette," the warden snapped. His wife stared at Pearl sternly. The warden looked tough, Pearl thought, and his stringy wife in her colorless dress looked even tougher.

Pearl flashed a smile. She took a last drag off her cigarette and flicked it away.

John Boot looked from Pearl to the warden to the warden's wife like a man watching a snake stalking a rat.

"Welcome to the Arizona Territorial Penitentiary," the warden said.

His boots aren't nearly as nice as John's, Pearl thought.

"I hear you two are escape artists," the warden said. "Well, you can forget about that nonsense here." He began to pace, hands knotted behind him. "Back the way you came there's fifty miles of desert crawling with scorpions, snakes, and Indians. The Indians get a reward for bringing back escapees, fifty dollars a head, and we don't care how banged up the prisoners get on the way. They'd love to catch a woman out there, Hart. We'd get you back, but you wouldn't be the same, and I truly don't want that to happen to you, no matter how bad you are."

"I bet I could teach them Indians a few things," Pearl said.

The warden paused in his pacing, then resumed. "Keep your tongue in your mouth, girl. Besides the desert, there's two branches of the Colorado river bordering this prison, moving fast enough that you can't swim across. Then there's the charming town of Yuma." He pointed west. "You try to go that way, and the folks in town will shoot you. They're not real friendly." He turned smartly on his bootheel and paced the other way. "That's not real important, though, because you won't get outside. The cells are carved into solid granite, so you can't cut your way out with a pocketknife." He pointed to a tower at one corner of the wall. "That's a Gatling gun on a turret up there—it can sweep the whole yard. There was an attempted prison break not long ago, and my *wife* manned the gun. Cut those convicts down."

"Ladylike," Pearl said. "Mighty Christian, too."

The wife stiffened and crossed her arms.

"I'm not happy about having you here, Hart," the warden said, putting his face close to hers, exhaling meat-and-tobacco-laden breath. "I had to tear out six bunks to make a ladies-only cell for you, and we had to hire a seamstress to make a special uniform."

"Shit, you dumb bastard," she said. "I'll sleep anywhere, and I'd just as soon go naked as wear whatever burlap sack you've got for me."

John Boot groaned.

"We're gonna clean that backtalk out of you, Hart," the warden said. He turned to the guards. "Get this man to his cell," he said, pointing at John

Boot. "My wife and I will escort Miss Hart to her quarters."

The guards led John Boot away. The warden later wrote that he looked distinctly relieved to be leaving his lover.

Pearl went with the warden and his wife through an archway into a cramped corridor. Iron bars filled every opening, and the low ceiling made her want to duck, even though her head cleared it by a good margin. The hall smelled like sweat and urine.

"Did you enjoy shooting those boys, Mrs. Warden? Feeling that big gun jump and buck in your hands?"

"That's enough, Hart," the warden said. "Get in." He pointed to an open cell door. Pearl could see the boltholes on the wall where the bunks had been removed. A curtain hung from the ceiling, blocking the open-pit latrine from view. She'd expected open-faced cells, like at the county jail, but these cells had real doors.

"Cozy," Pearl said, and sauntered in. Men hollered unintelligibly down the corridor.

"We're going to make every effort to guard your modesty," the warden said. "You'll never be alone with a man. My wife or a female attendant will accompany me and the guards if we ever need to see you privately."

"Doesn't sound like much fun," Pearl said. "Maybe just one man alone with me every couple days? You could hold a lottery, maybe." She showed her teeth.

The warden shut the door without a word.

Pearl sat on the bunk for a while, thinking. The cell was tiny, with a narrow window set high in one rock wall. She'd roast all day and freeze all night, she knew. John Boot had better get her out soon.

She got bored, and after a while she went to the door, looking out the iron grille set in the wood. "Hey boys!" she yelled. "I'm your new neighbor, Pearl!" Hoots and whistles came down the hall. "I bet you get lonely in here! How'd you like to pass some time with me?" She went on to talk as dirty as she knew how, which was considerable. She wondered if John Boot was in earshot. He liked it when she talked like this, though he always blushed.

The men howled like coyotes, and the guards came shouting. Pearl sat down on the bunk again. She'd wait until the men quieted down, then start yelling again. That should get under the warden's skin, and pass the time until John Boot came to set her free.

Pearl woke when John Boot touched her shoulder. She sat up, brushing her hair away from her face. John Boot looked tense and dusty.

"Are we on our way, then?" Pearl asked.

He shook his head, sitting down beside her. "I don't think I can get us out, Pearl."

"What do you mean? You got into my cell, so you can get us out."

"I can get myself out, sure." He laughed forlornly. "Walls don't take much notice of me, sometimes. But you're different. Back in Tucson I had to cut you an opening." He thumped his fist on the granite wall. "I can't do that here."

"You could steal keys," Pearl said, thinking furiously. "Take a guard prisoner, and..." She trailed off. There was the Gatling gun to think of, and fifty miles of desert, if they somehow did make it out. "What are we going to do?"

"You've only got five years," he said, "and you being a woman, if you behaved yourself—"

"No! They ain't winning. Or if they do win, I'll make them miserable, so they can't enjoy it. You keep looking, John Boot. Every place has holes. You find one we can slip out of, hear?"

"I'll try Pearl, but..." He shook his head. "Don't expect too much."

"Long as you're here," Pearl said, unbuttoning her shirt.

"No," he said. "It's tiring, Pearl, going in and out like this. It's not hard to get dim, but it's hard to come *back*. Look at me." He held up his hand. It shook like a coach bouncing down a bumpy road.

"You're about as much good as bloomers in a whorehouse, John Boot," she said. "Go on back to bed, then." She watched him, curious to see how he moved in and out of impossible places.

He stood, then cleared his throat. "I don't think I can go with you watching me. I always feel more... all together... when you're paying close attention to me."

Pearl turned away. "I thought only ladies were supposed to be modest." She listened closely, but heard nothing except the distant coughs and moans of the other prisoners. She turned, and John Boot was gone, passed through her cell walls like a ghost.

Hell, she thought, *now I'm up, I won't be able to fall back asleep.* She took a deep breath, then loosed a stream of curses at the top of her lungs. The prisoners down the hall shouted back, angrily, and soon cacophony filled the granite depths of the prison.

After listening to that for a while, Pearl slept like a babe.

Pearl gave up on John Boot after about a month, but she didn't figure out a better idea for two years. The boredom nearly crushed her, sometimes, but the time passed. She got to see John Boot a lot, at least—he came to her almost every night, and seemed weaker every time.

"The warden was in here the other day," she said one night. John Boot sat against the wall, tired after his latest half-hearted search for an escape route. "Telling me what a model prisoner you are, how you never spit on the guards at bed check or raise a fuss in the middle of the night. They said you're practically rehabilitated, and that you'd want me to behave myself." She punched her thin mattress. "They still think I'm a helpless innocent, led astray by *your* wicked ways, even though I've done my damndest to show them otherwise. Stupid bastards."

John Boot nodded. He'd heard all this before.

Pearl, sitting on the edge of her bunk, leaned toward him. "I'm tired of being here, John Boot. Two years, and there's only so much hell I can raise from inside a stone box. We have to leave this place."

"I don't see how — "

"Listen a minute. All my life I've hated being a woman—well, not hated *being* one, but hated the way people treated me, and expected me to act. It's about time I used that against the bastards, don't you think?"

John Boot looked interested now. He hadn't heard this before. "What do you mean?"

She crossed her legs. "I mean it's time for you to leave, John Boot. Go ghost on me, fade away, get as tired as you want. I think if you hadn't been coming to see me every night, you'd have turned to smoke a long time ago."

His face betrayed equal parts confusion and hope. "But why? How will my leaving help?"

She told him what she had in mind.

"That might work," he said. "But if it doesn't..."

"Then I'll figure out something else. Don't waste time, all right? I'm not up for a sentimental goodbye."

He put his hand on her knee. "One last?"

She considered. Why not? "Just be sure to pull out. I don't want to start my free life with a swelled-up belly."

After, he lay against her in the narrow bunk. "I'm a little nervous now," he said. "I'll miss you."

She stretched her arms over her head, comfortable. "I wouldn't think it. You've seemed pretty eager to get away."

"Well... in a way. Don't you ever want to go to sleep, and never have to wake up again?"

"No," she said truthfully. "I'll sleep plenty when I'm dead."

He was quiet for a moment, and then said "I don't think I have a choice. About loving you."

Pearl touched his hair, letting her usual defenses slip a little. "I'll miss you, too, John Boot. You're the only man I could ever stand for more than a night at a time. But it's time I let you go."

"Don't look," he said, getting out of bed.

She closed her eyes.

"Goodbye, Pearl," he said, his voice faint. He went away.

It took two days for anyone to notice that John Boot was gone—he'd been so unassuming that they overlooked his empty cell at the first bed check. When the warden and his wife came to tell Pearl that John Boot had escaped, she made a big show of breaking down and crying, saying "He told me to stay strong, that we'd walk out of here together, that as long as I didn't give in to you he wouldn't leave me!" Weeping with her face in her hands, she could glimpse the warden and his wife through her fingers. They exchanged sympathetic looks—they believed it, the stupid bastards, they still believed that John Boot was the cause of Pearl's bad behavior.

Pearl's behavior changed completely after that. In the following weeks she began wearing a dress, and having polite conversation with the warden's wife, and even started writing poetry, the sappiest, most flowery stuff she could, all about babies and sunlight and flowers. The warden's wife loved it, her tough exterior softening. "Pearl," she said once, "I feel like you and I are much the same, underneath it all." It was all Pearl could do to keep from laughing—talk like this, from the woman who'd once gunned down a yard full of convicts! That was no stranger than a stagecoach robber writing poems, maybe—Black Bart aside, of course—but with Pearl it was an *act*.

She missed John Boot a little, but if his leaving could help get her get out of prison, it was worth it. The warden told Pearl that, with John Boot's influence lifted, she was blossoming into a fine young woman. Two months after John Boot "escaped," the warden and his wife came to visit Pearl again, both of them smiling like cowboys in a whorehouse. "The governor's coming to inspect the prison soon, Pearl," the warden said. "I've talked to him about your case, discussed the possibility of giving you a pardon and an early release... and he wants to meet with you."

"That would be just fine," Pearl said demurely, thinking, *Hot damn! About time!*

The governor came into her cell, middle-aged and serious. He wore a nice gray suit and boots with swirling patterns in the leather. The warden and his wife introduced him to Pearl, then stood off to the side, beaming at their new favorite prisoner. The governor looked at them, raised an eyebrow, and said "Could I have a little time alone with Miss Hart, to discuss her situation?" The warden and his wife practically fell over themselves getting out the door. The governor stood up and closed the cell door. "A little privacy," he said.

"Sir, I'm so glad you decided to meet with me," Pearl began. She'd been practicing this speech for days. It had loads of respect, repentance, and a fair bit about Jesus. If it didn't get her a pardon, nothing would.

"Yes, well," he said, interrupting her. He took a pocket watch from his vest, looked at it, and frowned. Then he looked Pearl up and down, and grunted. "How bad do you want a pardon, girl?"

Pearl kept smiling, though she didn't like that look in his eyes. "Very much, warden, I've learned my lesson, I—"

"Listen, little girl, that's enough talking. I don't care how sorry you are for what you've done. You're in the worst goddamn place in the whole desert, of course you're sorry, even a rattlesnake would repent his sinful ways if he got locked up here. Now I don't have a whole lot of *time*. There's one way for you to get a pardon, and it doesn't have anything to do with talking, if you see what I mean."

Pearl stared at him, her eyes narrowed.

He looked at his watch again. "Look, you can just bend over your bunk there, you don't even need to take off your dress, I'll just lift it up."

"You go to hell, you bastard," Pearl said, crossing her arms. If he tried to touch her, she'd put a hurt on him like he'd never felt before. She almost hoped he did touch her. The warden was just like all the others, like her husband, like all the men before she'd met John Boot. Boot seemed like just about the only good man in the whole world, and she'd pretty much had to make him up out of her own mind, hadn't she?

The governor went white in the face, then red. "You're going to rot here, Miss Hart. You could've given me five minutes of your time, done what you've probably done with hundreds of filthy men, and been free. But instead— "

"I may've done it with filthy men," Pearl said, "but I've never done it yet with a nasty old pig like you."

The governor rapped on the door, and a guard came to let him out. He left without a word. The warden and his wife bustled in soon after and asked how it went. Pearl thought about telling them, but what was the use?

"It went just fine," she said.

That night, for the first time in years, Pearl cried.

Pearl dreamed of lying in her old bedroom in Canada, giving birth. The baby slid out painlessly, crying, and she picked it up, unsure how to hold it, wrinkling her nose in distaste. The baby looked like a miniature version of the governor, with piercing eyes and grim lines around his mouth. The baby's tongue slid out, over its lips, and Pearl hurled the thing away in disgust. It hit the knotty pine wall and bounced. When it landed, its face had changed, and John Boot's eyes regarded her sadly.

Pearl sat up in the dark of her cell, shivering, but not because the dream disturbed her. She shivered with excitement, because she saw a possibility, a chance at a way out.

She lay back down and thought fondly of John Boot, her wonderful John Boot, her lover, her companion, calling to him in her mind.

Nothing happened, except for time passing, and Pearl's frustration rising. Finally she fell asleep again, fists clenched tight enough to leave nail marks in her palms.

"Pearl," John Boot said.

She opened her eyes, sitting up. It was still dark, but Pearl felt like dawn was near. John Boot was on the floor — no, *in* the floor, half in a hole, just like the first time she'd met him. "Am I dreaming?" she asked.

"No, I'm really here. You felt... very angry, Pearl. It pulled me back."

Maybe that's where I went wrong, she thought. *I tried to think sweet thoughts and call him that way, and he didn't feel a thing, but when I got mad, like I was the* first *time, here he comes.* "Pulled you back from where?"

"Someplace where I was sleeping, sort of."

Pearl knelt on the hard granite floor and extended her hand. He took it warily, as if expecting her to try and break his fingers. "I'm not mad at you, John Boot," she said. She wondered about the hole. It would no doubt close up when she wasn't paying attention, as modest in its way as John Boot was himself.

"Then what's wrong?" he asked, letting her help him out of the hole. "Did your plan work, are you getting a pardon?" He sat cross-legged on the floor, naked again, except for his fine boots.

She hesitated. She planned to use John Boot, no two ways about it. Pearl seldom shrank from saying hurtful things, but she hadn't ever hurt John Boot on purpose, and he'd done a lot for her. A little lie to spare his feelings wouldn't do any harm now.

"That's right, I'm getting pardoned," she said. "The governor was very impressed with me. I'm just angry that I have to wait for the order to go through, that I'm stuck here for a few days more... and that I'm going to be alone out there, without you."

He lowered his head. "You want me to come back?"

"I wouldn't ask for that." She put her hand on his bare knee. "But... I want something special to remember you by."

"What?"

"Sleep with me, John Boot. And don't pull out this time. I want to have your baby. We'll do it as many times as we have to, tonight, tomorrow, as long as it takes."

"You mean it, Pearl?" he said, taking her hand. "Really?"

"Yes." She got on the bed. "I want your baby in the worst way."

He came to her.

A little later, lying tight against him in the narrow bed, she said "Let's go again. We've got enough time before bed check."

"We can if you want," he said sleepily. "But we don't have to."

"Why?"

"Because it took."

She pushed herself up on her elbow and looked at him. "What do you mean?"

"The baby. It took. You're kindled." He looked into her eyes. "I can feel it. I felt it the other time, too, when you... lost it. I wish..." He shrugged. "But it's all right now."

"Oh, John Boot. You've made me so happy."

"I should go."

"Wait until dawn? I want to see your face in the morning light one more time."

He held her. When the sun came, he kissed her cheek. "I have to go."

She nodded, then looked away, to give him his privacy.

"No," he said, touching her cheek. "You can look, this time."

She watched. He dissolved like the remnant of a dream, first his warmth fading, then his skin turning to smoke, until finally he disappeared all the way, leaving Pearl with nothing in her arms but emptiness, and a tiny spark of life in her belly.

Pearl waited two months, still behaving herself. Each time she saw the warden she made a point of anxiously asking if he'd heard from the governor. They hadn't, and the warden's wife clucked her tongue and said everything would work out. Pearl had no doubt about that.

After two months, Pearl asked to see a nurse. The woman examined her, and Pearl told her she'd missed two months in a row. The nurse blushed, but didn't ask probing questions. She went to report her findings to the warden.

Pearl's pregnancy created a difficult situation. As far as anyone knew, only one man had been alone with Pearl during her years of incarceration, and that man was the governor. He would say he hadn't slept with Pearl, of course, but she would say otherwise, and publicity like that wouldn't do anybody any good. She knew the governor would take the obvious way out, and avoid the scandal.

She didn't have to wait long.

"In light of your delicate circumstances," the warden said two days later, not meeting her eyes, "the governor has decided to grant you a pardon."

"It's about damn time," Pearl said.

On the day of her release a guard gave her a ride to the nearest train station. Pearl looked at the desert where she'd had her adventures, at the harsh ground that had birthed John Boot. She laced her hands over her belly, content.

There were a lot of reporters at the train station. They'd gotten wind of her plans. Pearl had decided that life as an outlaw was all well and good, but it demanded too much sleeping rough and missing meals. She had a baby to think about, now. Originally she'd planned to get rid of the baby at the earliest opportunity, but she was having second thoughts.

Pearl had a job all lined up as a traveling lecturer. A lady outlaw with risqué stories could really pack a room, and it wouldn't be nearly so strenuous as sharpshooting in a Wild West show. She wasn't much good with a gun anyway.

She waved to the reporters as she boarded the train. They only knew she'd been pardoned, not why. They shouted questions, but she didn't pay much attention. Her mind was on other things.

One question got through to her. "Pearl!" the reporter shouted. "Are you going to meet up with John Boot?"

They still thought she needed a man, after all this time. Would that ever change? "You're a stupid bastard," she replied mildly, and followed the porter to her compartment.

LIFE IN THE MOVIES

MIKAL TRIMM

This is the backdoor to life.

You mess around for a few years, sowing the old wild oats, dreaming the impossible dreams and then watching them fade away like bad film stock as the years go by. Suddenly you're forty, and there's no steady job, no family, no house in the suburbs—just a beat-up Ford Fiesta and a crappy efficiency apartment. No pets allowed, so you don't even have a dog or cat to kick around when you need to vent.

Your last girlfriend, if you could call her that, is now pregnant with another man's child (she made sure to let you know that it couldn't *possibly* be yours), and she still wants to live with you in the closet you call home, because "Jimmy ain't got no place I can stay." Worst part is, you agree, just to keep the silence away. She doesn't even clean up after herself, and there's no sex, uh-uh, you're just *friends* now; so you pick up after her and pretend this is a relationship.

The bar you frequent, well, *frequently*, the place where everybody knows not only your name but your political and religious views, your past history, hell, even the size of your package, thanks to a mouthy drunk—that bar is a place you wouldn't have been seen dead in ten, no, *five* years ago. Now the regulars here know you better than your parents (who you haven't spoken to in five, no, *ten* years, probably.)

There's a Rexall drugstore right around the corner from the crappy, collapsing apartment complex where you live, and whenever you pass by it you ask yourself—*what drugs do they have, non-prescription, that I could swallow enough of and end up taking the dirt nap?* And you almost feel it, you nearly understand the desperation of the hopeless. You don't own a gun, and there's no way you could just open up your veins, but pills might work. Sure, they claim it's a woman's way to end it all, but what do you care? You won't have to listen to anyone's smart-ass comments later, will you?

And you'd do it, maybe you would, if it weren't for that one thing. You know that thing, that *special* thing, that you can do so well...

"C'mon, Henry! We need you!"

Henry Clark rubbed his eyes, pushing himself back into the here-and-now. His latest Amaretto Sour, his drink of choice, was now a watery mess before him. Popping it down in a quick gulp, he sat up from his eternal slouch. "It's always nice to be needed," he muttered. There was a time when he would have signaled for another drink, but he was known here. Marcy already had his next Sour set up, and, as usual, someone had already paid for it. Same-old, same-old...

He knew the scene. Red would be there, since it was Red's voice Henry had responded to, and at least a couple of the regulars—probably Pete and Cutter Bob, since this was a Wednesday—and someone Henry had never seen. Some poor schmuck with a big mouth and a fat wallet, most likely, a visitor to the bar who knew nothing about Henry's 'gift'. *How long did it take them to reel* this *one in*, he thought. The boys tended to work on the newbies, a sort of mental gang-bang. Sooner or later, Henry was pulled into the rape.

Henry turned away from the bar and walked slowly to the 'shady table', as the regulars called it. It huddled under a burned-out neon sign for a beer that was no longer produced. Red spoke up, doing his little song-and-dance for the victim. "Henry," he announced with an obvious wink-and-a-nudge, "this is Oliver."

Henry sat down at the table, a bit clumsy but still in command of his senses. "*Oliver*. Best Picture, 1968. People are still laughing about that one." Oliver blinked, utterly at a loss.

Red laughed, but he shot a warning glance Henry's way. *Don't scare the mark*, it said. Henry nodded slightly, suitably reprimanded. He held out his hand. "Henry Clark, Oliver. Pleashed," he slurred, exaggerating his level of drunkenness to throw Red a bone, "uh, *pleezed* to meet ya." Oliver shook hands hesitantly, like someone expecting a joy-buzzer; Henry could also tell, by the way Oliver fought to focus on the transaction, that the mark was well beyond tipsy and close to falling over.

Cutter Bob played his part. "You're in trouble this time, Henry! Ol' Oliver here, my boy Oliver came up with a tough one. I done told him, ain't no way you gonna get this one, ain't that right, Oliver?" He slapped Oliver on the back, not hard but with enough force to convey a sense of camaraderie. Oliver ate it up, just like he was supposed to. He turned to Bob and gave him this half-assed little drunken grin—*we sure got him now, don't we*, it said. Henry was a master at reading the 'subtle' signals of the well-and-truly soused.

"What's the bet?" Henry tried to look disinterested, but he knew where the money-tree grew. Red smiled and motioned surreptitiously with one hand: *go slow, go slow...*

Oliver straightened up in his chair. "Twenty dollars." He said it like he was passing out free money to the lowly masses.

Cutter Bob spat, disgusted. "Twenty bucks? Damn, Ollie, I thought we was friends! I sit here and tell you everything you need to know to take King Henry here down, and you throw out twenty bucks? I thought you *trusted* me! Down in the foxholes, buddy, remember?"

Henry knew that little ruse. Cutter had been in Vietnam. His big ability, his *gift*, the way Henry saw it, was to buddy up to a complete stranger and, by the end of the night, convince him that, had they been in the 'Nam together, they'd have been blood-brothers, man, attached at the hips, *you could watch my back anytime, buddy, I* trust *you*. The '*semper fi*' was optional.

Cutter threw down two twenties and a ten from his own wallet. "Sound off like you got a pair, son! I'm laying down fifty, I'm so sure you got him!"

Oliver wavered a moment, taking a drink to bolster his buzz. Then he matched the pot. "Right. Fifty bucks. You got it." He flashed a sickly smile Bob's way.

The preliminaries now done with, Henry crossed his arms, looked at Oliver without a hint of emotion, and said, "What you got for me?"

Oliver focused his attention on Henry with a visible effort. "Um. Oh, yeah." He grinned triumphantly. "Orson Welles, *Touch Of Evil*."

Henry shrugged. Not a bad choice, he thought, although it would have been more surprising if the movie hadn't been overhauled and re-released a few years ago. Still, not as obvious as most of the challenges he'd heard lately.

As the small crowd around the table watched in increasing awe, Henry closed his eyes and muttered silently to himself, as if he were going through a script in his head. His shoulders slumped, and his face beaded with sweat. Nothing changed about him physically, but he held himself differently, slumping like a man who was carrying far too much extra weight, his lips puffing out and his cheeks seeming to fill out in the shadows of the bar. When he opened his eyes, they seemed smaller, piggish and cruel.

"Thirty years..." he growled, his voice coming from a well of loathing and viciousness, the voice of a fat, corrupt small-town cop named Hank Quinlan. In Henry's mind, Quinlan's thoughts roiled venomously, *damn wetback, damn dirty Mexican with his little white slut of a wife, thinks he can try to face down Hank Quinlan on my own turf, thinks he's got the huevos to pull something over on me*, and his voice came back, stronger, brutal. "Thirty years of pounding beats and riding cars, thirty years of dirt and crummy pay. For thirty years, I gave my life to this department. And you allow this *foreigner* to accuse me. Answer, answer, why do I have to answer him? No sir!" Henry was on his feet now, his face flushed red, spittle flecking his lips. "I won't take back that badge until the people of this county want me back!" There was no badge on the table, but the others had looked just to make sure, because when Henry was on, he was *on*. Oliver was especially slack-jawed, his eyes open so wide they almost bulged from their sockets. Henry wasn't just doing an Orson Welles impression, he *was* Orson Welles—no, he was Hank Quinlan, all four-hundred pounds of the man, and he was *pissed off*. The atmosphere at the back table seemed hotter, as if the whole group had been transported, for just a small eternity, into the sweltering summer heat of some shabby border town in Texas.

Then Henry sat down, his face relaxing back into its proper form, and it was all over. Henry seemed a bit tired, and his hair hung lankly across his forehead, plastered down with sweat, but he was otherwise unchanged. Emotionless. Bored.

Red scooped the money up from the table; Oliver didn't even notice. Cutter Bob made a show of being upset, can't believe he got that one, who'da thought, but it was all for effect, really. He'd get his money back later, just like always, after he and Red split up Oliver's money. Henry never took any of the money, but he rarely paid for his drinks, either, so it seemed like a fair trade to him.

As Henry turned back to the bar, Red whispered, "Man, you ought to take that act on the road."

Henry sat at his regular stool, trying to keep his hands from shaking with exhaustion. *On the road*, he thought as he ordered another drink, his heart still pounding with Quinlan's rage. *Yeah, right.*

You walk home from the bar because you can't afford a drunk-driving arrest, even though you're not drunk now, not *really*. What the hell, your apartment isn't far from the bar, and it's not a bad night. There's a beer or two in the fridge, if Janice didn't drink them yet; just enough to ease you into the remains of the evening.

You think about the little show you put on back there, remembering the faces of the stunned and amazed, and you still can't believe that they never ask any questions, they never try to figure out how you do it. No curiosity left—maybe the brain cells that demand satisfaction, the ones that wonder how a magician does his tricks, say, are the first ones killed off by alcohol. Or maybe folks still like to have a little mystery in their lives, who knows?

Whatever. You know it's just a parlor trick, really, just a side-effect of your true talent. If you could feel anything right now, it would be the need to laugh at the irony of life. Of course, if you could laugh at life you wouldn't be spending your evenings dragging your liver through Purgatory while playing the performing monkey for a bunch of rednecks.

No laughing for you, pal. No crying, either. What did that one doctor call it when you were a kid? *Flat affect*, that was it. No highs, no lows, just a dull plodding through the middle-ground. Life sentence. Some people take drugs to get where you are naturally, though; you should feel blessed, right?

Hell, at least the drinks are free…

The Narrator's voice faded into the background of Henry's mind when he reached his apartment. The Narrator was always there, spinning a constant voiceover to Henry's poor attempt at a life, trying to make sense of every insignificant detail, trying to find the script that would make everything *fit*. Another side-effect of the talent, and Henry was as accustomed to the Narrator as he was to his ability to mimic any actor he'd ever seen in a movie. The Narrator, on the other hand, served a higher purpose, when the time was right.

The Narrator's voice sounded like Fred MacMurray's in *Double Indemnity*. Henry had no idea why. He was just glad it didn't sound like Peter Lorre's, or Michael J. Pollard's, God forbid.

Henry entered his apartment quietly, expecting to find Janice passed out on the couch, the light from the TV screen flickering aimlessly over her body. The couch was empty.

As was the rest of the apartment. Empty of Janice, and her clothes, and her makeup, and her damned pile of romance paperbacks. Janice had packed up her few meager belongings and deserted him. He could almost see her balancing cardboard packing crates on her distended belly. Maybe the kid kicked every now and then when he got poked in the head by a box corner.

Guess Jimmy finally found a place for her to stay.

Henry knew he should be feeling something at this juncture. Rage? He wondered if that would be an appropriate response. Relief? Longing? Despair? He just didn't know. What do you feel when you lose someone that was once a lover?

Even the Narrator was silent. Waiting for Henry to find the answers.

Janice had left the beer in the fridge, amazingly enough. Henry uncapped a bottle and drained half of it in a gulp. He walked back into the living room, passing the threadbare couch and the cheap 13-inch TV-VCR combo sitting on an orange crate across from it. The far wall of the apartment was lined with bookshelves, each of them overstacked, not with books, but with videos. Hundreds of them, store-bought or bootlegged, many copied from cable channels, AMC and TCM predominantly. At first glance, they seemed utterly without order—alphabetically disarrayed, chronologically challenged. A cryptogram without the right key.

Henry was the key. He ran his fingers along the video boxes as if he were blind and they were encoded in Braille, taking an occasional sip from his beer as a mantra of hope issued silently from his lips. "Show me what to feel," he whispered, "please show me what to feel."

His hand worked as a separate entity, brushing the videos lightly, stopping, moving on. It wavered finally, torn between choices, then plucked a selection from the shelves, satisfied. Henry didn't even look to see if he'd made the right choice. He pulled the movie from its cover and inserted it gently into the VCR; the TV turned itself on automatically.

"Why don't you get a DVD player?" Janice had asked him several times. He tried to get her to watch movies with him, but she rarely agreed, and when she did eventually succumb to boredom and join him, she would gripe and moan about it continuously. *This looks like crap, the sound is fuzzy, who are these people?*

"Just watch the movie." His only comeback. Her voice would finally become nothing more than background noise, and then she'd fall asleep somewhere along the way, and Henry would slide off the couch and let her lie there undisturbed while he mouthed every line of the film to himself, perfectly. He didn't need a DVD—the films were engrained in his memory. They lived in his mind, in full-color and surround sound. He *knew* what everything looked like, sounded like, knew the smells, the tastes, the tactile sensations felt by each character in every movie. It was all part of his gift.

Henry settled himself on the couch as the FBI warnings ran across the television screen. Within seconds, his eyes glazed over; the beer bottle slipped from his fingers, unnoticed. Henry's breathing slowed along with his pulse, nearly stopping; in less than a minute, he reached a state of physical oblivion that even a yogi would envy.

As the grey moors of Yorkshire appeared on the screen, the room darkened; as a disembodied voice described the house, the storm, and a stranger lost in the bleak landscape, the temperature in Henry's apartment fell several degrees. The air turned humid, almost foggy, and the walls faded into some other plane of existence. The scents of Henry's life—the stale smells from the carpet, the subtle undercurrents of body odor and cheap perfume—dwindled and disappeared, replaced by a rich, earthy breath of lush greenery tainted with the subtle miasma of decay. The image on the television wavered, disappeared, and Henry's apartment was gone: he sat at the heart of a dark mansion, filled with shadows and the memory of grandeur.

Time for the Narrator to do his job...

The man bursts into your sanctum, demanding shelter. You would like nothing more than to send him fleeing back into the blackness he came from, but there are Rules that must be obeyed, ridiculous notions of hospitality that must be honored. You can feel that your wife agrees, as well she should. She, too, knows what it is like to be unwanted.

So give him a room for the night. Tell Joseph to take him upstairs, this Mr. Lockwood, and let him sleep in the guest room. Give yourself back to the silence of the Heights.

Then your name is called in the night, your presence *demanded* by the fool upstairs, and he is frightened and as pale as if he'd been touched by Death. "There's someone out there in the storm," he whimpers. "It's a woman. I heard her calling. She said her name! It—Cathy, Cathy, that was it!" And the man keeps talking, sputtering, but you push him from the room, for now you can hear the echo across the moors.

Heathcliff, she calls, and you run to Catherine yet again…

BAGGING THE PEAK

JERRY OLTION

Maggie called it quits at 12,000 feet. The top of the mountain was only a thousand feet higher, but it was up a mile-long slope of boulders the size of cars, and she had already scrambled over enough of those to last a lifetime. Every step felt as if she were bumping into the sky, lifting its entire weight as well as her own. And all for what? "Bagging the peak," Pete called it. Adding another entry to her list of personal accomplishments.

She didn't need that kind of validation to make her feel good about herself. She knew what she was capable of, and she knew what she was willing to do for fun, and climbing another thousand feet wasn't going to change either of those things. It would just make her hurt worse than she already did.

She watched Pete work his way along the ridgeline. Two glacial cirques had eaten their way toward each other from opposite sides of the mountain, leaving a knife-edge of rock that climbers had to balance their way across. It was like walking the top of a wall. A six-foot-wide wall, sure, but the drop on either side was at least five hundred feet. Maggie couldn't see what kept the boulders perched on the edge from tumbling down. The ridgeline dipped in the middle; evidence that they didn't always stay put, but Pete was hopping from one to another as if they were paving stones on a highway, and the rocks were holding fast.

So was Maggie. Coming up here in the first place had been dumb, but going farther would be lunacy. Let Pete bag his peak and join up with her here on the way down. It wasn't like they could miss one another at the neck of the knife-edge.

There was a nice, flat, sun-warmed boulder with a sloping rock wedged against it; a perfect chair for her to sit in and look out over the valley below.

She could see Mistymoon Lake down at the foot of the mountain, small enough to blot out with her outstretched hand. Beyond it, in the U-shaped glacial valley that stretched off to the south, were Marion Lake and Lake Helen, tiny blue jewels amid the gray rock. Down by Lake Helen, there were even trees.

Maggie watched birds circling in the valley below her. Hawks? Eagles? Or vultures? If someone died up here, would anything fly this high to pick their skeletons clean? Not if they had any sense.

Margaret paused at the beginning of the knife-edge and looked into the canyons on either side. Any sensible person would stop here. The peak was a thousand feet higher, but just getting here, to the 12,000-foot level, was accomplishment enough. On the other hand, she wasn't quite dead yet. If she paused for breath every ten steps or so, she could regain enough strength to keep going. Her head ached with the steady pain of oxygen deprivation, but she wasn't dizzy enough to fall off the ridge. Not quite.

She couldn't say why she continued. "Bagging the peak" didn't matter to her. That was Peter's reason. Hers was more personal. She wanted to prove to herself that she could do it. She didn't care if anyone else knew; it was just something she needed to know about herself. Could she climb the tallest peak in the Bighorn Mountains, even if every step was like lifting the weight of the sky and looking at the drop on either side of the ridge made her want to throw up?

Peter was already halfway across. She walked the length of the coffin-shaped boulder she was on, leaped the three-foot gap to the tilted triangle, and let her momentum carry her onward to the mushroom-cap of granite beyond that. Fifteen more feet. That much closer to the top.

The ridge widened out again after a hundred yards or so. No more fear of falling off the edge, but now she had to choose her path. Peter seemed to have an instinctive grasp of the easiest route through the boulders, or maybe it was all easy for him, but he was far enough ahead that she couldn't follow his exact footsteps. She kept finding herself stuck on the wrong side of impossibly long leaps or at the bottom of piles of loose scree that threatened to come down on top of her if she disturbed them. Each time she would have to backtrack and try another route, which only tired her out all the more while Peter's lead grew even longer.

When they had first started out, he had waited for her every few hundred yards, but he always took off again the moment she caught up with him. He had already gotten his rest by then, and he couldn't bear to wait any longer while she rested, too. Now, though, with the peak in sight, he didn't even make a pretense of hiking with her. He would wait for her at the top, maybe, if she didn't dawdle too long on the way.

Screw him, she thought, but then she realized that her camera didn't have a self-timer. If she wanted a picture of herself at the top—and despite her self-assurance that this was just about meeting the personal challenge, she realized she really wanted that photo—then she had to get there while Peter was still there to take it.

Her fingers were starting to hurt from grasping the rough granite. Her throat was dry, but she had already drunk half her water, and this high up there was no run-off to replenish it. The three smallest toes on her left foot were starting to blister, but if she stopped to put Moleskin on them, she probably wouldn't make it to the top before Peter grew bored and came back down. To hell with them, then. Toes could heal. Fingers could heal. And if she sniffed hard, her runny nose would keep her throat from drying out completely.

Gah. The things she did for fun. She could be home reading a book right now—hell, she could be leaning up against a warm rock at their base camp and reading a book right now—but no, she had to climb Cloud Peak.

All Pete said was "You missed a hell of a view," but the look on his face pretty much told Maggie how the rest of the trip was going to go. The view wasn't the issue. Pushing herself until she puked was the issue. Standing up there on the peak beside him so the photo on his web site would not only show how tough he was, but how tough his girlfriend was, too, was the issue. He would no doubt get some mileage out of telling his friends how it was too much for her, but he would've looked better if he could brag about her instead.

She had regained enough strength to second-guess herself. Maybe she could have done it if she had just pushed herself a little harder. Maybe she had given up too soon. She might have gotten her second wind, or third wind, or fifth, if she'd just persevered.

"Storm's coming," Pete said, tilting his head back and sideways to indicate the peak behind him. "We've got to get off this ridge before it hits."

Maggie looked up to see the dark gray underside of the clouds overhead. The afternoon sun was still shining on the flank of the mountain where they stood, but the peak was socked in. "Where did that come from?" she asked. "The wind's coming from the west, and there hasn't been a cloud out there all day."

"It formed right here over our heads," Pete said. "Mountains make their own weather." He walked past her and hopped down to the boulder below. "Come on. It's going to get worse."

A distant rumble of thunder echoed off Black Tooth, the peak a couple miles to the north. Maggie shoved her book in her day pack and slung it over her shoulders. Getting caught up here in a lightning storm would be a lousy way to cap an already lousy day.

Peter was pacing impatiently when Margaret finally reached the summit. "Hurry up," he said. "There's a storm brewing."

"Congratulations...to you...too," she panted, taking the final steps to the flat-topped boulder with the three-foot cairn of loose stones piled atop it.

So this was the peak. Didn't look much different from the rest of the mountain, except there wasn't any more rising up beyond it. The boulders looked the same, and the view was hardly better than it had been from a thousand feet down. She could see farther to the north and the east now, but the valleys and lakes out that way looked pretty much the same as the ones to the south and west.

Then she realized that the mountain ended twenty feet away. It just stopped. She walked closer, feeling the hair standing up on the back of her neck. Her leg muscles wanted to lock up when she got within a few feet of the edge, but she forced herself to take that last step and look down the cliff face.

The knife-edged ridge was nothing compared to this. This cliff was a sheer wall of granite that stretched for a quarter mile straight down to the glacier at its base. There was a lake at the edge of the glacier, its water chalky green instead of the blue of the other lakes farther out.

"Jesus," she whispered, stepping back. A gust of wind could send her right over the edge.

Thunder echoed off Black Tooth to the north. Margaret looked up, seeing the gray clouds overhead for the first time. She'd been concentrating so much on the climb that she hadn't looked at the sky until now.

"We've got to get off this damned peak," Peter said.

"Get our picture first." Margaret backed away from the cliff to stand again by the boulder with the cairn on it. Peter looked up at the clouds, but he set his camera on a rock and rushed over to stand beside her.

"Say 'We bagged it!'" he hollered, raising a fist high.

The camera flashed just as Margaret was raising her arm and saying "Ba—"

"Oh, great," she said. "Take another one."

"No, let's go." He snatched up his camera and started clambering over the rocks, back the way they had come.

Margaret took one last look at the cliff edge, at Black Tooth, at the other peaks that made up the backbone of the Bighorns marching away to the north, burning them into her brain so she could remember them forever, then she turned to follow Peter.

Something buzzed in her left ear. A fly, way up here? She waved her hand at it and felt something crinkly on her shoulder, like cellophane, but when she looked she couldn't see anything there but her own hair. That, she could see just fine, though. It was standing straight out from her head.

"Light—" she said, but the word caught in her throat. "Light...ning!"

She leaped off the rock she was standing on, crouched down beside it while she crab-walked over the edge of the one she had landed on and dropped another two feet into the crevice between it and its neighbor. She looked for Peter, but didn't see him anywhere. Should she get flat, or try to go farther down?

It sounded as if someone was crushing a candy wrapper beside her ears. Her hair felt like it was covered with spider webs. She swept a hand through it, feeling the crackle of static electricity, and she waited for the blue flash of death to strike her down.

Ten seconds passed. Fifteen. Her hair quit crackling. She crept to the edge of the crevice and looked down, but her hair started crackling again so she ducked back, and a second later the world erupted in light and sound.

She actually felt the mountain shake. The boulder she was on ground against the one beside it, and streamers of raw electricity snaked over the surface of the rocks all around her. Her skin felt as if an entire hill of ants were crawling on it.

Instinct took over. She leaped out of the crevice and down the six-foot drop to the boulder below, skipped down its face to rebound with hands and feet off the angled flank of the one below it, and hopped one, two, three over the next three boulders in succession, putting twenty feet of distance and ten of elevation between her and the tallest point in maybe two seconds. She leaped right over Peter, wedged into a crack that wouldn't have held a dog if it wasn't scared to death, and sprinted — sprinted! — another fifty feet over the uneven rockpile, her footing as sure as if she were in a grassy park.

The boulders were bigger here. She got down beside one that didn't stick up quite as far as the rest and waved frantically at Peter, who had pried himself out of the crack and was stumbling down toward her.

His mouth was moving, but she couldn't hear him. The only sound was the ringing in her ears. She couldn't even hear her heart, although it was banging away in her chest like a rock in a blender. Lightning. Jesus. She had nearly been killed. And she wasn't down off this damned pile of rocks yet.

What the hell was she thinking, climbing to the top of a 13,000-foot mountain? She had just wanted to go backpacking, find a nice grassy meadow with a little stream running through it and spend a day or two doing nothing. Risking her life had definitely not been part of the plan.

Peter dropped down beside her. "Are you okay?" he asked, his voice high and thin and squeezed out between panting breaths.

"I need to go to the bathroom."

He laughed. "Me too. Nothing like a near death experience to scare it out of you. But otherwise? You didn't get hit?"

She shook her head. "No, but the storm's not over yet, either. What do you think; should we hunker down here and wait for it to blow over, or should we keep moving?"

He looked up, and she followed his gaze. The clouds were dark and threatening overhead, but they gave way to blue sky just half a mile to the west. It would have been comical how small the storm was and how perfectly centered over their heads it was if it hadn't been trying to kill them.

"I think we should make a break for it," Peter said. "There's no telling if it's going to get any better. It could just build up bigger and bigger all afternoon."

He was probably right. "Okay," she said. "Let's go before I lose my nerve."

"I thought you had to pee."

"I didn't say I had to pee. And it can wait."

She slipped over the edge of the rock they'd been crouching on and started down.

Maggie was feeling miserable by the time they reached their base camp. Not physically; her body actually felt pretty good despite all the exertion. It was the constant second-guessing that was driving her deeper and deeper into depression. She should have gone for the peak. Never mind that it had gotten socked in before they were halfway down the mountain; if she had pushed herself harder she could have kept up with Pete and they both could have made it.

To his credit, he didn't say anything about her failure, but that somehow just made it worse. If he had acted like an ass, then she could have gotten mad at him and felt good about defending herself, but when it was her own voice calling her a quitter, she didn't have much of an argument.

He crawled into the tent and lay on his back, exhausted, but she couldn't allow herself the luxury. She gathered up their empty water bottles and took them over to the stream that ran through the middle of the meadow, where she filled them with the micropore filter pump; then she set to work preparing their dinner. Normally Pete cooked, since he carried the stove, but she could at least do that much extra today. And she could do the dishes afterward. And maybe level the ground under the tent a little better before they settled down for the night. It had been a little bumpy last night.

She looked up at the peak, now shrouded in its namesake clouds. She hadn't made it to the top this time, but someday she would. If she was ever going to live with herself, she was going to have to.

Margaret would have loved to collapse in the tent the moment she got back to camp, but she had one pressing need to take care of first. She hadn't been kidding when she said she had to go to the bathroom. Only trouble was, there were no bathrooms on Cloud Peak, and she hadn't taken toilet paper in the day pack anyway. There weren't any bathrooms in the meadow where they'd camped, either, but there was a copse of trees a couple hundred yards up the valley, and she had a bright red plastic hand-trowel for digging a hole. Oh, the joys of camping.

The mosquitoes were fierce. Insect repellant just made them buzz around before they darted in for the kill. Margaret swatted and squirmed and cursed while she did what she had to do, and in that moment of misery with her pants around her ankles, she realized that this was her last backpacking trip. To hell with this constant endurance test disguised as a vacation. Indoor plumbing and feather beds had been invented for good reason. If she wanted to commune with nature, she could go on a day hike, and if she wanted to climb a mountain, she would do it in a car or on a ski lift. And for damned sure, when it clouded up and lightning started popping around the peaks, she was already going to *be* on low ground.

When she filled in her latrine and started back to camp, she felt much lighter than could be accounted for by simple loss of mass.

Ten months later, Maggie was back in the same meadow. Pete was history, but that was fine with her. He had the totally wrong attitude about personal accomplishments anyway. It wasn't about bagging peaks; it was about the peak experience. Pushing yourself to the limit, and when you found that limit, pushing yourself past it, even if it took more than one try. If she'd learned anything from last year, it was that giving up for good was the only failure.

Ten months later, Margaret was on Po'ipu Beach, lying on her back with her eyes closed while she listened to two college guys a few feet away from her brag to one another about their exploits in voices purposefully loud enough for her to overhear. Normally she would have flirted with them, especially now that Peter had dumped her for a new backpacking companion, but they were talking about the hike up Waimea canyon and the awesome view over the Na Pali coast from the top.

You weenies, she thought. Maybe it was impressive to them, but she knew without bothering to go there that it would be an anticlimax to her. Maybe she would take one of those helicopter sightseeing trips, if she hadn't already maxed out her credit cards, and check it out from the air. Or maybe not. She didn't really care. What did it matter, really? What did anything matter, now that she had bagged Cloud Peak?

The Journal of Philip Schuyler On the Occasion of His Visit to the Island of Manhattan, 1842

Robert Freeman Wexler

Sunday, February 6, 1842 (mid-morning)

I came to this wretched shore willingly. Yet after I disembarked, my first thought was to retrace my way back to the ship, which during the tedious trans-Atlantic crossing had assumed the familiarity of home. How I was soon to wish that such had been my path. But I had accepted a commission. And as the son of a Dutch father and English mother, the history of this settlement called to both sides.

Indeed, my Dutch parentage was the reason for my commission — the man who wrote to me, one Hendrick Stuyvesant, explained that he, and others, were remnants of the city's Dutch founders, and desired a portraitist of the Dutch school. Though the details he presented were few, the monetary offer was quite handsome, an unexpected windfall at a time when such were becoming limited (due to changes in the demand for my style of candlelight painting, and to indiscretions with the wife of a former client, involving her desire for a nude portrait and what arose subsequent to that).

Stuyvesant had given me an address for lodging — the Carlton House Hotel, on Broadway — some distance from the South Street docks. The hansom cab carried me along cobbled streets, past multitudes of wood and brick buildings. I had heard of the jumbled condition of this city, as it raced vainly to catch up with its elder European sisters, and had been warned that neighborhoods of squalor stood side-by-side with those of the upper classes.

Everything in this Manhattan was in motion, everywhere noise and bustle of shopkeepers, drivers. Swine snuffled through garbage in the streets. Ships arrived or departed in a constant flow, to and from every part of the known world.

Others have told me that however obsessed with commerce the inhabitants of Manhattan may seem, they are not devoid of romantic notions, but after my initial impressions I find it no surprise that its citizens need import artists from Europe, for New York had not the atmosphere for creative endeavor.

At the hotel, I supervised the placement of my trunks. Unsure of what I might find here, I had brought my own art supplies, pigment jars wrapped with care to prevent breakage, brushes, canvas, oils, and glazes.

A simple room, with a bed, desk, washstand, bureau. I had been instructed that, upon my arrival, I was to send my employers a message to that effect, but I found myself unwilling. I composed a short note, which I left upon the desk. And I began this journal in a notebook small enough to keep upon my person, secure in an inside pocket of my jacket.

My aim was to add to my account each evening of my stay, the which I did, in the end augmenting and annotating the entries with the reflections of knowledge and events that were to come. But more of those, later.

Outside my windows, Broadway, chief thoroughfare, with a sun warm beyond the season casting a healthy shine upon passing ladies in their colorful silks and satins, parasols held high to block the rays. Vehicles crowded the streets, cabs, coaches of myriad size, many thick and boxy, sturdy enough to traverse the wild country lanes which this city becomes some few miles north.

I decided to venture out to find a barber for I needed a shave. Over the last several days of the voyage on the ever-rolling, never-stable platform of my journey out, I had given up the practice. Though the ship's barber was an experienced hand, I had not the desire to bare my face to his blade until the seas subsided.

After a pleasing shave, and with most of the day yet before me, I set off to explore the surrounding streets. Out there, among the gaily-dressed men and women, I found myself drab indeed, with my scuffed shoes and worn jacket still marked by ocean travel.

I walked the surrounding blocks in fascination, careful to avoid the area known as Five Points, a den of crime and disrepute, I had been told.

East of the dazzle of Broadway I found another large street called Bowery. Here everything was more humble, the houses smaller, the taverns darker, the passersby dressed in a rougher style more to my liking. Passing a one-eared swine, I stepped into a place advertising "Oysters in Every Style."

Sunday, February 6, 1842 (evening)

On my return to the hotel lobby, a man confronted me, a well-dressed, somewhat portly figure with hair fashionably curled over his ears. He introduced himself as Mr. Lilley. Retrieving a watch by means of its massive chain, he glanced at it, then looked to me. "We have not the time for tarrying," he said. "The project at hand requires exacting coordination of schedules and means. Why did you not contact us? No matter. We must depart immediately."

Indicating that I should follow, he strode out of the hotel, returning me to the frenzied avenue. A carriage awaited. The man opened the door and I mounted.

"Colonnade Row," I heard him tell the driver, then he followed me inside, taking the seat opposite. The carriage set off. Once in motion, Mr. Lilley's agitation left him and he became more friendly.

"There is not another city on this earth like New York, nor a land like our United States," Mr. Lilley said. "Your Old World, for all its finery, is passing on." He extended his arms as though embracing the sky, including it in his territorial grasp. "This is the land of dreams. The profits to be made are astounding." He lectured me for some time on the pastime of land speculation, and the risks of boom and bust, of which only men of courage may partake.

The carriage moved jerkily through the streets, stopping here and there as the driver had to find his way around various obstacles, piles of building materials, crowds of workers. A fire brigade stalled our progress. "Fire is our ever-present companion here. Much has been lost, but much gained, as the blazes sweep clean areas for new construction."

As we progressed, the buildings grew fewer, and Mr. Lilley informed me we were nearing the northern edge of the town, reaching quieter neighborhoods of grand residences, constructed far from the bustle of the commercial center. The carriage turned down an alleyway, pulling up behind a block of houses.

"You will have to view the residence from the front another time. This is one of the grandest new row houses in the city. Great columns line the front and the entryways are magnificent. But for now 'tis more expedient to enter from the rear."

"My commission," I said. "The details...."

Mr. Lilley interrupted, telling me that another would be informing me as to the particulars. The carriage stopped and we alighted. Mr. Lilley took me into a parlor, then up a flight of stairs to a sitting room, where another man waited. This man was introduced as Mr. Vanderkemp. He bade me sit, and ordered refreshments from a servant.

"Will Mr. Stuyvesant be joining us?" I asked.

Neither answered for a moment, then Mr. Vanderkemp explained that Stuyvesant was merely a name they used for correspondence, that it represented the interests of their group.

Mr. Lilley and he spoke briefly in voices too low for me to comprehend, then shook hands. While they spoke, I examined my surroundings. The furniture: chairs, settee, was of plain, yet expensive appearance, dark wood with cane bottoms; the carpet: a rich weave, brown and tan of an Oriental design. A doorway framed by ionic columns separated the parlor from a dining room. Several daguerreotypes adorned the walls, portraits of family members. They fascinated me, for I had seen few. The ability to capture likeness was most impressive, but the flatness grew monotonous after extended viewing.

The servant soon returned with a decanter and filled two glasses. Mr. Lilley departed. On leaving, the servant pulled the sliding doors from their recess in the wall and shut them.

"I understand that you would like made plain what your commission entails."

Mr. Vanderkemp spoke in a firm, authoritarian voice, as one accustomed to the giving of orders.

"It is quite simple, as was said in the original letter to you. The aspect of secrecy is merely that the portrait is to be a surprise for a lady's husband. Therefore, we must act while he is away, conducting business in the West Indies and other points.

"You need not know her name, or the name of her husband. The less you know, the easier to keep the secret intact.

"Their residence is nearby. Mr. Lilley will take you in the morning to meet her, and you will begin your work. Supplies, if you need them, can be procured by others. Priming of canvases and other menial tasks can be undertaken for you. It is best that you spend the entirety of you time on the work of the portrait itself."

Some while later, Vanderkemp announced that our meeting was at an end. The butler returned and escorted me outside, where the carriage and Mr. Lilley awaited, and I was anon transported back to my hotel.

Monday, February 7, 1842 (evening)

Mr. Lilley joined me at breakfast, dressed smartly in a smoking jacket of figured velvet, and I went with him in the same carriage (or one similar) to the home of my subject. On the way, I enquired whether Mr. Vanderkemp would be joining us, and Mr. Lilley replied that he had other engagements to attend.

"We are meeting the woman in her own residence, but the actual work of portrait-making will be carried out at Mr. Vanderkemp's. It will be easier to guarantee surprise, should her husband return unexpectedly. And meeting first at her own residence will prevent servant's gossip from touching on the impropriety of her repeated visits to the residence of Mr. Vanderkemp."

I agreed that the plan was a sound one. In our attempt to maintain secrecy, it would prove ill if the husband interpreted the innocent surprise of the portrait as something less honorable.

The carriage drew up to a grand, colonnaded front, and I remarked on the architecture. Mr. Lilley's face fairly glowed with pride as though the design of the structure had been his. "This is what I spoke of last evening. The finest yet, in this city of finery. Designed by the great Alexander Jackson Davis and built by Seth Geer. It is meant to be a New York version of London's Regent's Park. Astor lives here, as do other luminaries. There are nine magnificent residences in all."

We departed the carriage and were met at the door by a butler, who escorted us to an upstairs parlor much like that of Mr. Vanderkemp's. I was, in fact, somewhat confused as to whose house we were in—yesterday at Vanderkemp's, Lilley had praised the magnificent columns, and today as well. Perhaps Vanderkemp lived in another of the nine residences Lilley had mentioned.

The entrance of the lady of the house caused me some surprise, for her skin, though not of the darkest hue, marked her of at least partial connection to a race not commonly found in the houses of the wealthy, save as servant (or slave, in the southern climes of this free land of America). But she wore clothing typical of the comfortable class: silk taffeta dress with embroidered over-sleeves and a pleated bodice. She appeared to be at her ease here.

The lady spoke English with a French accent, a joyous, musical inflection, so unlike the others, whose "Americanisms" had transformed their language into something base. I assumed she came from an island in the Caribbean and was likely an amalgam of races, African and French.

Mere paint would be unable to capture the loveliness of her skin, which had the quality of fine coffee blended with a modicum of cream.

With my having brought a sketchbook, and the lady being eager to begin, we sat in the soft light of her parlor. Thinking her native tongue might set her more at ease, I addressed her in French, and noted a brief look of consternation on the face of Mr. Lilley, as though displeased with his inability to understand our conversation.

I thought little of it at the time. Later events, of course, made the reason apparent.

She proved to be knowledgeable on many topics, literature, politics, history, and we chatted amiably in both French and English while I created a series of sketches, attempting to find the pose that best captured her lovely and regal self. I learned that she had been born into a wealthy family, in one of the few republics wholly governed by those of African descent. Her grandfather had been a Frenchman, an official with the governor's office when the island was under French control. She had met her husband through his business dealings with her family. They had married secretly in her land and lived separately for a year until he arranged for her transportation here.

I expressed admiration for a society which accepted her so readily, but I surmised that this acceptance was more politeness and propriety than actual warmth. Though no one in sound mind could reject such a lovely person. I found myself disappointed when our session drew to a close, even knowing that I could rejoice at the prospect of spending long periods in her company. Because time was of importance, we agreed to meet the following morning at Mr. Vanderkemp's to begin the portrait. I would need take the rest of the day assembling my materials and transporting them to Vanderkemp's house so that all would be ready for the first sitting.

Tuesday, February 8, 1842 (evening)

Today was much colder, and various stoves had been kindled throughout the hotel, casting off an overabundance of heat. I was glad to be spending the day elsewhere.

Again, it was Mr. Lilley who met me at breakfast and accompanied me uptown. At my mention that I would be perfectly able to make way on my own, thereby saving him the trouble, he demurred, saying that it was best for a newcomer to this brusque city to have a guide. The cab drivers could not be trusted, he added, and considered that to be an ending of the idea.

The plunge from the over-warm hotel to the crisp air on the street invigorated me, but I foresaw potential discomfort in this constant fluctuation of surrounding temperature.

Having gone into Mr. Vanderkemp's residence twice now from a back entrance (my first visit and last night, of which I have not written, for there was nothing of note to report), I was surprised when this morning the carriage pulled up to the front, and I saw that Vanderkemp's house indeed shared the same columnar façade as that of my client. In the foyer I was pleased to see a rather charming painting of three children by the acclaimed English-born American artist Thomas Sully, who I had met in England a few years previously, when the city of Philadelphia commissioned him to paint Queen Victoria. And in the dining room an even more pleasing sight awaited me: one of my own paintings, a candle-lit scene of the market of Bruges.

It occurred that Mr. Vanderkemp would be away at his business office downtown during the day, with Mr. Lilley remaining as his representative. We had arrived, of purpose, before the lady in order that I might ready myself and my materials. The previous afternoon (despite Vanderkemp's directive that others would do the work for me), I had prepared a canvas, though for today my plan was to create several studies of gouache on paper in preparation for the actual work. I explained this to Mr. Lilley, whose only comment was to be sure I informed him when ready to begin the actual portrait.

The light of the upstairs parlor well suited my needs, so it was there that I set up my easel and paints. However, I found the heat oppressive and asked if we might open a window for ventilation. Mr. Lilley seemed confused, as though unsure how to carry out my request. He fumbled with the latch for a minute, then raised the pane. Immediately I felt better.

Some short while later, the bell rang below, and Mr. Lilley left to attend to the newcomer, soon returning with a bundle of women's clothing draped over his well-tailored arms. A maid followed, carrying a parcel that contained various accessories of fashion. The lady had not yet herself arrived, having sent ahead several dresses, from which we would make our choices for her costume.

As the maid and Mr. Lilley exited the room, I heard her mutter that she hoped she would not be expected to wait on one of "them." His reply eluded me as they passed down the stairs.

Soon, the lady herself appeared, dispelling a dark current that had swirled around my head after overhearing the maid's remarks. Smiling, I greeted her in French. Her dress was of a similar cut to that of yesterday, though muslin rather than silk, designed more for the everyday wear than for fashion.

The day's work passed well. As an artist's model the lady was quite natural—each turn of her chin or movement of shoulder, the set of her eyes, was a painting unto itself, and I foresaw my only difficulty would be in settling upon only one of this bounty of poses.

At mid-day I indicated that we would pause for refreshment. Mr. Lilley rang for the servant woman, who (however unwillingly) brought us tea, and after we were settled upon it she unwrapped the lady's dresses and hung them over a screen so that we might view them.

Some conversation followed. The lady herself favored a dark red silk, and Mr. Lilley seconded her. I was drawn to a pale blue cotton, the hue of which reminded me of the exquisite paintings of Vermeer, but I found myself won over.

We returned to our work. I had decided to position the lady on a particularly handsome couch ("Duncan Phyfe," Mr. Lilley said with the pride of a man claiming proximity to a pedigree that he might find some of it seeping into him.) The couch, which faced the windows at the front of the house, was well-suited to reclining, having one end open and the other closed, with ample cushion, and I admired the sweeping curve of wood on its back. Finding the columned doorway pleasing, I claimed it as a background and balance, and I also desired to use the red drapes which framed the window on the side wall.

Again, I thought that any position the lady took would have made a magnificent portrait, had I the skill to attain it.

A graceful silver candelabra with three branches stood on the mantle. I transferred it to the low table in front of the sofa and bade Mr. Lilley close the curtains that I might view the lady's pose in candlelight, though the actual work of the painting would take place in daylight, with the shadowy atmosphere and glowing candles imposed upon it in the traditional manner.

After settling on what I felt to be the optimal pose, and, desiring not to over-tax my subject, I called an end to the day. I escorted the lady downstairs to the door and bid her farewell.

Thursday, February 10, 1842 (early morning)

How quaint the last entry looks to me now. Would that I might return to such a calm moment!

Yesterday evening I found myself unable to open my notebook and write of the events of the day; this morning, I resolved to take comfort in the act. In noting my activities, I hoped, by process of expression to reclaim my life and dispel my disgust and dismay at what was presented to me yesterday.

My plan, as I had detailed to Mr. Lilley, was to commit a study in oil as a final preparation for the actual portrait.

On arriving at the house, I began organizing materials as per my habitual way. I found that someone had primed and readied several 34 by 44 inch canvases, which, along with the one I had readied the first day, totaled six. I told Mr. Lilley I had not the need for so many.

"Always set yourself up for eventualities," he said. "Can never possess too much of something. 'Tis our American way." He added that the lady would be appearing somewhat later than usual, in order that I might have more time to prepare, the which I began to do.

At the sound of the bell, Mr. Lilley excused himself.

My spirits had lowered at Mr. Lilley's mention of the lady's later arrival, but the bell raised in me a thrill which I found surprising, for it told of a growing affection for her.

However, Mr. Lilley's return with a bulky parcel, rather than the lady, dispelled my eagerness, though I knew I would see her soon. Without explanation, he placed the parcel in a corner, and I took no further notice of it. I had planned to paint today on board, but there being such an abundance of ready canvas, I raised one to the easel and commenced a layer of imprimatura.

The lady entered, at last, attired in the red dress. On her head she had placed a charming straw bonnet decorated inside the brim with lace and flowers of silk, and over her shoulders was a shawl to cover her flesh left bare by the cut of the dress. I bade her place the bonnet and shawl behind the sofa, out of sight. As she settled into the sofa, I decided I would henceforth call her "Madame Burgundy," for the color of her attire and in honor of her French heritage, which elicited, when I informed her (in French), a lovely, unselfconscious sound of delight.

I cannot put into words how deeply struck I was by the effect of her coffee cream of shoulder against the deep crimson fabric. I only hope my conveyance in paint might express what language cannot.

And time passed in the steady and rewarding exercise of applying paint to canvas, bringing the fine shape and features of Madame Burgundy into appearance before me.

None of what I have expressed here is alarming, is it? A reader might be wondering in what I found this disgust I spoke of, what appalling events silenced my pen for a day.

I saw that I was having difficulty coming to it. But I also wished to set the stage, to reach the events in their proper order. I must take a break here. I had arranged an early breakfast in my room, so that I might eat in peace, without the intrusion of Mr. Lilley, who had begun to haunt my steps and my thoughts, like some avatar of despondency.

Thursday, February 10, 1842 (mid-morning)

Having refreshed myself, I found I must continue, lest I not complete this account before Mr. Lilley's arrival. I dread the work required of me today, but take comfort in knowing I will be in the presence of the dear lady, my subject. I will persevere.

As yesterday afternoon progressed, Madame Burgundy complained of lightheadedness. She had earlier been bled, she revealed, in order to protect against the fevers that often struck the city in the warm seasons, and she regretfully felt the need for further rest before continuing.

She then departed, and I applied myself to the painting. I was unsatisfied with the coloring of the dress, having tried vermillion and carmine without settling on either. I said as much aloud to Mr. Lilley, who sat on a couch to my rear, smoking his pipe and reading the day's news.

"Well then I believe it is time to open this package."

He retrieved the previously-mentioned bundle, which I had long since forgotten, unwrapping the brown paper covering to reveal pint jars: one full, one partially, of a dark crimson liquid.

"Having that pretty red dress made this much easier don't you think?" Mr. Lilley said, to my consternation, for his words confused me.

"It is requested," he said, continuing in a flat tone as though reading from a note of instruction. "Nay, not requested, firmly stated, as a condition of your commission, that you employ this substance in your painting. That this substance" —indicating the jars— "may become fully embodied and incorporated within the painting. Of necessity which will be revealed in more detail anon. Enough for now is that you know of the lady's ancestry, from a land rife with superstition and the use of charms to protect individuals from harm."

I indicated a lack of comprehension, saying that I was fully confident in my ability to choose my own materials and pigments, but Mr. Lilley insisted.

"Must be materials of the subject herself incorporated."

This statement, combined with the depth of color inherent in the liquid, and the lady's comment of her recent medical procedure explained all. It was desired by those who had retained my services that, for this portrait, I was to employ Madame Burgundy's own blood.

A knock falls upon my door. Mr. Lilley, calling on me for today's session, and I must therefore depart. I will return to this account later, after the trials of my day. My only solace is that I will be once again joined by Madame Burgundy.

Thursday, February 10, 1842 (evening)

In the carriage with Mr. Lilley, I spoke but little, while he chattered as unconcernedly as a man on the way to a shooting party at his country estate. He talked of wealth, the wealth of his fair city of New York, the wealth of his young nation, how commerce would bring more and more wealth to these shores until all the world knew their names. His thoughts were not original. They had been spoken throughout the ages, by Greece, Carthage, Rome, Spain, England, even my own Holland, whose commercial enterprise, though corrupt and ill-conceived, founded this city he praises so highly.

I have always been of the opinion that such wealth manifests a corrupting influence, that excessive wealth breeds the insatiable greed for more, which leads nations to aggression over their neighbors. And in this nation, where the barbarity of slavery yet reigns, what would be the moral cost of this gold lust?

Guido Reni of Bologna in the seventeenth century wrote much on the subject of pigments, of color. He described methods for the use of blood, calling for it in combination with a preservative coat of resin, which ensured color retention. The resin must be applied while the blood is still wet, but the two will not mix. The resin sits atop, shielding the blood from the elements, from fading. I thought I had not the proper resin, but on arrival found it provided in abundance.

"The material itself is not yet ready," Mr. Lilly said. "I am told it needs to be distilled and purified. So you are to plan your work accordingly."

With the impending arrival of the lady, I had to compose my mood. I did not wish to appear in any way disturbed, lest my disposition mar our session. My assumption was that the lady did not know of the proposed use of her body's elixir for the portrait, though Mr. Lilley's hint as to its having to do with her ancestry and birthplace spoke otherwise. I found myself not trusting him, or my employers. I had begun to fear some other reason lay behind their demands, something opposed to the lady's continued well-being. I had nothing concrete to support this feeling and would need keep it buried for the present.

And so, with poise and charm that raised my desolate spirits, Madame Burgundy made her appearance, and the morning passed in the joyous interaction of painter and model, painter and paint. I spoke more in French than I had previously, for I wanted to be sure that Mr. Lilley did not understand, and to accustom him to hearing it in a mundane way, so that if something later arose which confirmed my suspicions, I could convey the information to Madame Burgundy without alerting our watcher.

It had been my intent that on concluding the daily sessions with the lady, I would work on the background, but today I was loath to do so. After a half-hearted recreation of the doorway molding, I indicated to Mr. Lilley that I had finished for the day. He seemed displeased with this, but made no protest.

The drapes on the side window of Mr. Vanderkemp's study, the window which would be appearing on the right side of the painting — these drapes were of a red darker than the lady's dress, of a heavy and likely expensive material. I decided that I would not use the blood, as commanded, on the person of Madame Burgundy. If I pursued this course, however, I would need cause the supply in the jar to be diminished. Therefore, I would incorporate it into the drapery.

With Mr. Lilley present more often than not, I would have to take care not to be observed.

Monday, February 14, 1842 (morning)

My last entry was Thursday. I have allowed my account to lapse for a few days, not because of dire circumstances but because the days flowed in a mundane fashion. Friday and Saturday, Madame Burgundy sat for me. I made slight adjustments to her pose, and I began to capture what I felt to be her true character. Enchanted by my sitter and the way the portrait took shape, filling the canvas with her presence, I became lulled, forgetting my previous unease.

We conversed, as usual, in French, and I found her intelligence and charm beyond measure. Being a woman, she was without extensive formal education, but coming from a wealthy family in a realm where the people were industrious in their desire for advancement, she had been well-educated at home, with a tutor in her youth and on her own in later years. She had read much history, literature, and philosophy.

I could easily see how her husband had developed such deep adoration, for I found myself ascending a similar path.

This despite our differences in race. I admired the will of her husband, that he had persevered in bringing his love into a society where such was not looked on with approval.

Yesterday being Sunday, the lady did not sit, though I was nevertheless expected to work. The which I did, taking particular care with the couch, capturing the scrollwork of its arm and the brocade cushions.

In the evening, on my return to the hotel, I was surprised by a chance meeting with a friend, whose presence here has greatly relieved the strain of this commission. As I neared the door to my room, a man called out my name, and I was pleased when the man in question proved to be none other than the illustrious writer Mr. Charles Dickens, who had arrived in New York the previous day and was residing in my hotel.

He and I had become acquainted during a recent stay of mine in London, when I had been called upon to paint portraits of a certain wealthy family, a commission which led to more commissions, causing my residence to extend to a much greater length than first anticipated. It was this extension which enabled me to perfect my grasp of the English language (already having been started on it by my mother), adding it to the French and Italian that accompanied my native Dutch.

Because of the many social calls required of Mr. Dickens, he had procured a private sitting room where he could escape the press of his fame (for he found himself in great demand in all parts of this country, a prospect which daunted him greatly). He took me to this parlor, and a light supper was brought to us.

I sketched the nature of my commission, employing the fabrication my masters had instructed me to use: that I had been brought to New York to paint the children of a man named Bookman (whom I had not even met). Lying to my friend proved to be quite distasteful.

We exchanged our views of America. Mine were, of course, limited to my short time in Manhattan. He described some of what he had seen in Boston and elsewhere.

As Mr. Dickens had an impending social engagement, we cut our visit off at this point, but planned to meet again soon.

Monday, February 14, 1842 (evening)

Madame Burgundy sat for me in the morning as usual. This afternoon, a package was delivered to Mr. Lilley. He opened it. The blood, having been somewhat altered by whatever process had been employed upon it, was now reduced to about three-fourths of a pint jar. Ample, I was sure, for the intended use.

Tuesday, February 15, 1842 (evening)

By Thursday I fear I will no longer need have Madame Burgundy sitting. I will be finished with her. And a few days thereafter will find the portrait complete.

The thought of departing from these shores, from the noise and rot of this frantic and unkempt metropolis filled me with a shining hope. I missed my friends in Amsterdam. I missed my own studio, however drafty it may be in winter. Soon, soon, I will return. Visions of home filled me with a great sense of peace, which I as able to shape into the serene face of my subject.

Thursday, February 18, 1842 (evening)

On this day I bade a heartfelt farewell to Madame Burgundy. Having discovered nothing further about any ill intentions toward her, I had become more at ease, though I carried out my plan of enmeshing the blood with the drapes rather than her dress.

In the evening, I was fortunate in dining with Mr. Dickens, his wife, Catherine, and a man of their recent acquaintance, a Charles Johnson, who was active in the anti-slavery movement.

We settled in a private parlor, served by an attentive waiter whose girth and enthusiasm for the menu indicated his own attraction for dining.

A vast relief flowed through me as I sat among amiable companions, an interlude that removed from my mind the cares and conundrums of my commission. Our group chatted amicably for a time. At some point, the waiter apologized for a delay, saying that if our food didn't come soon, he would "fix matters so that management knew about it."

"Here is something I have noticed in my short stay in America," Mr. Dickens said, after our waiter had departed. "There are few words which perform such various duties as 'fix.' You call upon a gentleman in a country town, and his help informs you that he is 'fixing himself' just now, but will be down directly: by which you are to understand that he is dressing. You inquire, on board a steamboat, of a fellow-passenger, whether breakfast will be ready soon, and he tells you he should think so, for when he was last below, they were 'fixing the tables.' You beg a porter to collect your luggage, and he entreats you not to be uneasy, for he'll 'fix it presently.' If you complain of indisposition, you are advised to have recourse to Doctor So-and-So, who will 'fix you' in no time."

After dinner, I told them of my commission (the truth this time, as I could not continue in the lie), though I made light of the demand for painting in the lady's own blood, attributing it to superstition and hiding my fears.

Mr. Dickens speculated on the identity of my subject, saying that these Yankee traders had amassed great wealth and pretension, and, due to the roughness of their own land, a liking for all things European.

Mr. Johnson, having only recently relocated here from Boston, did not recognize the names I gave, though the social circumstances of the racially-mixed marriage interested him.

"Such a marriage would not go uncommented upon," he said. "And I would be surprised to find it well-accepted."

"There is a wealthy man here who, I'm told, married a former whore," Mr. Dickens said. He had been following the conversation, but due to liberal use of his wine glass, his comments had been few.

"Eliza Jumel," Catherine said.

Mr. Johnson wondered aloud whether Madame Burgundy's husband was at all involved with abolition, and he said he would conduct a few discrete inquiries.

The interest of Mr. Johnson was a fortuitous circumstance, for I had not shaken the sensation that some ill was intended on Madame Burgundy, likely without the knowledge of her absent husband.

Saturday, February 19, 1842 (evening)

There is not a more divine sensation than that which arises upon completion of a work of art.

Sunday, February 20, 1842 (evening)

Today, I find I am no longer free, nor do I see myself soon returning to my home.

It was not until after I finished the portrait that the arcane nature of my commission became apparent.

I journeyed to Vanderkemp's house as usual, in the custody (I use that word drolly though the circumstances report the opposite) of Mr. Lilley.

My intent was to carry out the final glazing of the portrait, for I believed this was all that remained.

I had grown accustomed to the passage along the streets, but when Mr. Lilley's driver made a turn which varied from the norm, I thought nothing of it.

When we stopped before an unfamiliar house, I turned to Mr. Lilley with a question on my lips.

"Mr. Bookman's house," he said. "The gentleman would like to speak to you about painting his children. You will find him most agreeable. He is a collector of antiquities from far-off Greece and Rome and has traveled much in Europe."

I had no intention of executing another portrait in America, but the circumstances dictated that I follow Mr. Lilley into the house, through a foyer decorated with amphora and a marble bust of Roman origin, then up a staircase. In yet another second floor parlor, I found Madame Burgundy's portrait. Mr. Vanderkemp was there, and another who I took to be Bookman, a plump man wearing an ashy coat of an old-fashioned cut.

My assumption was that the pair wished to see the portrait, one to approve, or not, of my endeavor, the other to see if it matched the expectations he held for the likeness of his children. I would have preferred that they had waited until I indicated it was ready for viewing, but as I was used to the thoughtless actions of patrons I made no comment.

Mr. Vanderkemp indicated for me to seat myself, the which I did. Mr. Lilley walked to the portrait and stood in front of it for a time. "This will serve, don't you think?" he finally said.

"Quite a likeness indeed," said the man I assumed to be Bookman. "A fine start to this," he added, and I wondered what he meant.

Turning to me, Mr. Vanderkemp spoke. "There is more to be done here, much more. What you have done is merely the first step. Six in total are required. This one"—as he spoke he pointed at the portrait—"is to hang in the residence of the person you call Madame Burgundy. Five more are required."

"The purpose intended for the others is quite different," Bookman said. Vanderkemp gave him a look which I assumed meant the man should not have spoken.

"The purpose of the other portraits," Vanderkemp said. "Is not your concern. Mr. Beekman here will see to your needs."

"Bookman," the man said. "My grandparents, you see, my grandfather actually...changed from the Dutch way of spelling."

Ignoring him, Vanderkemp informed me that while fulfilling the remainder of the paintings I was to remain here, in the home of Paul Bookman.

I said that I was quite happy with the hotel and the current arrangement, but Vanderkemp said that time was scarce, that it was imperative I finished before a certain date, and proximity to my studio would ensure this.

"This is not part of the commission I accepted," I said. "And I am not inclined toward performing any other actions here. I long for my home in the Netherlands and desire to return."

"Your homecoming must wait," Vanderkemp said. "I consider this to be all-inclusive. By God it must be, for the process to work. It must be your hand that connects all six, as it is the woman's blood that ties them as well. You will receive no payment until the entire group is complete."

I could see that I would not be able to change their views, and I considered walking out that instant, but the prospect of losing my income did not appeal. How I hate to discuss such a gross subject, but the importance of money is unavoidable.

What recourse had I if I left? I was quite familiar, through Mr. Dickens, with the lack of appreciation in this nation for the rights and income of writers, due to an absence of copyright law, which prevented Mr. Dickens and other European writers from earning one cent for their works published in America. I feared that the same would be true of artists, and I had not the funds to retain an attorney to test this supposition. Perhaps through Mr. Dickens, through the hordes of people of import he had met during his stay, I might find more work, more clients, to pay my way while I pursued legal action. I would need find new, less expensive accommodations, for my current patrons were paying for the hotel, and I did not think I could manage the rate on my own.

Oh, but that would mean delaying my return home. And staying here, carrying out this extra commission, caused the same delay.

Bookman and Vanderkemp conferred, their voices too low to pick out any but scattered phrases. "The man from Schoharie" repeated. I found that Mr. Lilley had left the room.

I stood.

Better to delay my return home in circumstances of my own choosing than toil longer in the company of men I dislike and distrust.

Mr. Vanderkemp turned toward me.

"I am not interested in your machinations," I said. "I was hired to paint a portrait, and that is precisely what I have done. Therefore, I shall take my payment and depart this country." I stepped toward the door.

"I will find my own way back to the hotel, if Mr. Lilley's services as coachman are no longer available. Payment can be sent to me there. I am sure you can find another, even here, to fulfill this new contract."

On reaching the door, I found a man blocking it, a wiry man with a cap pulled low over his forehead. Mr. Lilley stood behind him. This newcomer—his very being disturbed me. On his lined, blotchy-red face I saw a callous nature, a disdain for art, for life, for anything but his own advancement.

"Here is the man of whom I spoke," Bookman said.

"Splendid," Vanderkemp said. "Mr. Schuyler, you are to begin immediately." He spoke flatly, commandingly, disregarding my statement of objection, my intention to leave.

Mr. Lilley and the newcomer entered, and I backed away, instinctively, not wanting to be in such proximity with what this person represented.

I found myself once again seated on the couch.

Vanderkemp spoke. "This man must be incorporated. He must appear in the five, in the new paintings. You have left ample room."

The horror of my situation was now made clear—the man, this specimen of the low, was to become a cancer, an eater of beauty.

I was to place him first in the doorway, then, in the succeeding paintings, to move him by degrees closer, closer, closer, to Madame Burgundy until his hands encircled her lovely neck.

Monday, February 21, 1842 (morning)

I awoke on a narrow bed. A small room, a servant's quarters, in the house of this man, Paul Bookman. The door, I knew, was locked.

On awakening I was surprised that I had even slept, for I had sat up late, staring into the dark, my mind disquieted by the day's events.

Yesterday, acquiesced to the inevitability of my having to carry out this addition to my contract, I had bade them empty a room for my use, removing all furniture, carpeting, and ornamentation that I might have nothing to distract me from recreating on canvas the room at Vanderkemp's, and there I began the work of copying Madame Burgundy's portrait five times, beginning with the alla prima and ending....

I did not wish to think forward to that event.

First, I must sketch this newcomer.

I had used two of the original six canvases: one for the study, one for the portrait itself. Another had lately been provided, giving me the five required.

What was the intent of these men? Not the continued health of my friend. I had read various alchemical sources that described the connections between blood and figurative representation, but I was surprised to find such knowledge here. This "man from Schoharie" referred to yesterday, no doubt his involvement was vital.

The reasons were clear why they wished to harm such a harmless being. A marriage of mixed race. Her husband's social position. The social and economic position and continued well-being of the group, these Stuyvesants.

I sketched the garrotter, choosing a doorway to represent the doorway in the painting. I bade him walk across the room, watched the movements of his body, a slight limp in the right leg, the swing of his arms. His facial expression rarely changed, giving me no clue as to what lay beneath the ruddy skin.

A man was sent to bring my belongings from the hotel.

Thinking on the pigments needed to match the garrotter's rutilent face, I concocted a new scheme, one which might not harm him physically, but served as a form of quiet rebellion and revenge on my part, and a further use for some of Madame Burgundy's blood.

I tried not to allow my suspicions to display upon my face or in my actions. I believed my well-being depended on hiding my knowledge, that by affecting ignorance they might relax their guard enough for me to escape and warn Madame Burgundy.

But this morning, I found my resolve, and my health, less assured. When I rose from bed to refresh myself at the washbasin, an all-encompassing dizziness caused me to grip a chair for support.

Returning to the bed, I wrote in my journal, in haste, desiring to update my activities before my jailors came to conduct me to the studio.

Monday, February 21, 1842 (evening)
Flushed and feverish, I paint, for that is what I do.

Wednesday, February 23, 1842 (evening)

The days passed, I painted, my body remained weak. Captivity, I find, is injurious to the health.

I hate this man I am imparting into the presence of the dear lady. Though he might merely have been an actor hired to play the part of garrotter, I knew this was not so. His mood colored his complexion, and his flat way of speaking cast a pall on the room, dampening even Mr. Lilley's usual jocularity. And Mr. Lilley himself, he haunted my every step and brushstroke. He was never far, lounging outside the painting studio, sleeping in the room across from mine. I must take even more care that he does not see my use of the blood for drapery rather than the lady's dress.

These two creatures—I longed to separate myself from them.

After a while, I even ceased to view them as fellow-men, seeing in their eyes the beasts they kept hidden within themselves, beak of vulture, claws of lion, skin of reptile, cold and coarse. Please, let me never see these demons revealed.

Thankfully, I will soon have no further need for this other, this garrotter. Capturing him on canvas has not been difficult, and I hope he will soon depart.

Thursday, February 24, 1842 (evening)

Today my captors allowed me outside for a time, to the garden behind the house. The work has gone well, despite my aversion. These copies will take much less time than the original. I breathed in the free air, still chill but with Spring promising. But what will this Spring send to me?

Friday, February 25, 1842 (evening)

Today, as I sat in the courtyard, a second city, newer yet older, began to emerge, overlapping the garden wall at odd angles, never glimpsed full-on but lingering on the edges of my sight. I practiced catching it, first the edge of a brick arch, the plane of an open door.

Claiming exhaustion, I returned to the privacy of my room, where I sat at the narrow window overlooking the street. Through hours concentrating on keeping my eyes tuned in a leftward pose, I was able to make out across the way a window, a shop window filled with plaster figurines painted in garish reds and greens. A rush of vehicles filled the street, steel carriages, painted in a multitude of colors, chiefly a custard-yellow. What struck me about these carriages—they lacked horses; seemingly self-propelled, by steam engine perhaps, they darted across lanes of traffic, stopping here and there to let off and take in passengers.

My captors appeared not to notice this second city, and I began to hope that it, having manifested to me alone, would provide my means of escape.

I have no further need of the garrotter, yet he remains, having also become Mr. Lilley's partner in attending to my captivity. He brings my meals, but I am loath to ingest any foods his hands have touched.

Saturday, February 26, 1842 (afternoon)

This other city continued to fascinate me, though I was only able to examine it from the garden, the windows of my cell, and those of the room where I work. This morning as I looked out, I saw a man in strange dress—indigo trousers and a thin shirt, of some pliant material, which left his arms bare save for a short sleeve ending inches below the shoulder—and I could have sworn his gaze met mine. He staggered, putting a hand to his head as though taken by a fit. Then—another man passed through him. This second man, by his attire, belonged to the city of my captors. The oddly-clothed man. . .he occupies a space contiguous with my own, yet somehow separate. In another realm of time perhaps. Or perhaps I am mad.

Despite the increasing clarity of this second city, I have not discerned how it might aid me. And I know that this afternoon I will finish the paintings.

Saturday, February 26, 1842 (evening)

They have summoned "the man from Schoharie." Mr. Lilley has taken a train north to bring him hither.

The paintings are complete, save for glazing. Mr. Bookman informed me that the glazing would take place under the supervision of the newcomer, that he would advise me on the materials to be used. Then, they will present Madame Burgundy with her portrait. Then, they will no doubt carry out their schemes.

Sunday, February 27, 1842 (early afternoon)

Early I arose and inspected the paintings. A few details needed attention, but otherwise all were ready. I wished to spend the rest of the morning in the garden, sketching the newly-opened flowers of Spring in an attempt to quiet my apprehension. I had hoped to be allowed this in privacy, but could not escape the company of the garrotter.

Descending the stairs, I saw in the entryway below me Vanderkemp, who had not been in attendance here since the first day. He spoke to someone out of my line of sight. I paused, hoping to catch them unawares.

"Five into one," a stranger's voice said. "That will be how you know. Success, then five into one. Failure, then five remain five."

The garrotter gave a push to the middle of my back, causing me to stumble on the stair. I seized the rail to keep from falling, but my ankle twisted. I looked back at the garrotter, whose face bore no expression, no sign of why he pushed me and he voiced no explanation. Below, Vanderkemp, having heard my approach, moved into another room with the newcomer, who must be this man for whom they have waited.

I limped into the garden and sat on a bench, my desire for sketching banished.

Sunday, February 27, 1842 (evening)

This "man from Schoharie," as they call him (and no name is given me) is not at all what I expected. Looking at his round, bespectacled face, I might guess "manager of a counting house" as an occupation. And his tone is soft, his manner of speaking genteel. Whatever beast might lurk within, it is far better concealed than those of my captors. Under his influence, I find myself doubting my earlier fears.

They had told me at the outset, Mr. Lilley had said, the blood, the preparations, were for enacting a charm of a protective nature. Perhaps I should not have disbelieved them. But this garrotter? His presence pointed toward the opposite of protection. Could he have been called upon merely to play the part? That somehow, his actions against her likeness (actions painted by me), would cause some envelope of safety to surround her?

Surely this man, this kindly uncle from Schoharie would not involve himself in a projection of ill will.

The material he presented me, the which I was to incorporate into the glazing was, he said, a distillate of sap from various plants, medicinal and aromatic.

I glazed the paintings.

Tomorrow, I was to accompany Mr. Lilley and Mr. Bookman to Madame Burgundy to present her portrait.

This would be my first departure from either house or garden since the onset of captivity. If I was to make an escape, Monday would be my lone chance. But first, I would need warn the lady.

Tuesday, March 1, 1842 (evening)

I have found Mr. Dickens! And barely in time, for he and Catherine would have been departing today. I am presently in the home of his friend Mr. Johnson, where I am safe and able to rest.

But I must now relate how I came to be in this happy circumstance.

Monday morning, I awakened early having slept but little. What would this day bring? Suddenly recalling my dream, I sat upright.

I had been in the other city.

As dusk fell, I found myself riding in one of those horseless vehicles, sitting on a broad cushion of some dark, stiff material. A window separated me from the front compartment, where a man sat, manipulating a wheel that appeared to be the means of steering. He pulled it violently to his right, and we veered, my stomach lurching with the motion, then we accelerated, passing quickly through an intersection only to stop with a suddenness that threw me forward. I pulled a silvery lever on the panel to my right, and it swung outward. Before leaving, I handed the driver some bills of currency.

This setting quickly turned into Madame Burgundy's sitting room, the location of our first meeting. All I remembered of this part of the dream was her sincerity and grace, and my shame at allowing something horrible to befall her. Waking, I had found myself unable to return to sleep.

In the dream, I had been another person. One accustomed to life in this other city.

A short while later, Mr. Lilley called upon me to assist in something which turned out to be the transportation of the five new paintings to the basement of Mr. Bookman's house. There, in this subterranean locale, we set them on a marble-topped sideboard, one behind another, the outermost being the painting depicting the garrotter at his farthest point from Madame Burgundy.

Five into one, I thought.

Then it was time to visit the lady.

The three of us went, myself carrying the portrait, Bookman and Lilley walking on either side.

This house of Bookman was on a side street, Bond, scant blocks to the south of Madame Burgundy's.

What a relief to be away from the garrotter, whose face would be forever imprinted upon me.

But what a joy it was to see again the face of my dear lady, the flesh this time instead of the paint that had surrounded me in my place of captivity. And the delight she showed on seeing my creation. As she gazed at it, I spoke softly to her in French, attempting to speak urgently but in a tone of congeniality. I entreated her not to betray anything, in words or expression, no matter what she heard me say.

"These men are not your friends, nor friends of your worthy husband." I pointed to a part of the painting, as though explaining its nature.

"They intend harm.

"After we leave, you must burn the painting.

"The blood," I said, "the blood binds you to them."

I am sure she comprehended the seriousness.

Before leaving, I made one last request of her. "As we are going out, ask...the man with the name of the flower," —pausing, I waited to read the understanding on her face— "ask if he can assist you with something, call him back. I need a moment to separate myself from him."

As we descended the stairs, I had managed to keep Bookman ahead and Lilley behind. Bookman opened the door and stepped outside.

"Monsieur Lilley," the lady said. "My husband is soon to return from New Orleans. He sent ahead a trunk—could you come help Joseph carry it up the stairs? It is quite heavy."

Mr. Lilley stopped, then turned back toward her. I pulled the door shut behind me and shouldered Bookman aside.

I fled.

But Bookman, whose slowness I had depended on, lunged, clutching the tail of my coat, tripping me. We tussled, rolling into the street. The man's strength was far more than I had guessed from his comfortable appearance.

I had only a few moments before Lilley would exit the house, and I knew I had no chance overcoming the both of them.

Bookman pushed his weight down upon me. Then he screamed.

The other city had interceded.

One of the yellow vehicles rumbled toward us. I could hear it!

As could Bookman. He threw himself back in fright. While I, trusting the evidence of my days of observation, believing in the insubstantiality of these apparitions, jumped to my feet and ran straight into the onrushing machine.

Heat, quivering heat, and my vision blurred. Yet I kept moving. As though gazing up from the ocean's depths, I could see Bookman and the machine mingle, then separate, leaving the man gasping, wide-eyed yet unseeing.

I did not wait for his recovery.

Past the street on which stood the houses of Vanderkemp and Madame Burgundy, structures grew fewer in number, smaller, meaner, shacks and bits of land, no doubt soon to fall under the encroaching city. I came upon a wooded swath and made my way under the trees before stopping. My ankle, twisted that day upon the stairs, throbbed, aggravated during my fight with Bookman and my flight. I could go no further.

I would shelter here, I thought, among the protection of briar and branch. My clothes were torn, my right knee scraped raw and bloody. I found a brook and splashed my face with its chill water, then dipped my knee to cleanse it.

In the morning, I would strike off for downtown to locate my only friend on this wretched shore.

And when morning came, I found I had slept well, under the boughs of freedom.

Knowing that the island narrowed as it went southward, I kept to the trees for a time, passing a small dairy farm, then entered the zone of brick and timbers, streets leading to populated areas. I recognized Bowery. I found my former hotel.

But on entering, as I paused, taking in the busy lobby, which seemed alien to me after my ordeal, I found I was not yet safe. Mr. Lilley, unshakeable, stood at the counter talking to the clerk. I turned slowly back through the door and set off along the sidewalk, which had seemed such a gay promenade when first glimpsed from hotel window the day of my arrival.

Fearing that the others were near, dreading the sight of my shadow, the garrotter, I kept my face down. I passed an alley, then stopped, thinking to try for a rear entrance to the hotel, one that might take me through the kitchen or some other domestic region, and doing that, I made my way to Mr. Dickens's door and secreted myself therein.

I deplored becoming a burden to he and Catherine, but had no one else.

After explaining my situation to Mr. Dickens, he quickly settled upon the plan of requesting the assistance of Mr. Charles Johnson, the abolitionist who had dined with us. He forthwith composed a note to the man, which he sent by swiftest messenger, asking that Mr. Johnson might hasten here to consult upon my flight.

When evening came, Mr. Johnson led me back through the rear of the hotel, taking me to a house in the Five Points neighborhood nearby.

Tuesday, March 8, 1842 (morning)

There I stayed until March 5, on which day I traveled hidden with Charles and Catherine to Philadelphia.

I have booked passage from Philadelphia for Java in the Dutch Indies, for I feel Europe to be too close.

Today, my ship departs.

I have not yet heard how go Mr. Johnson's inquiries into the health or fate of Madame Burgundy. I must depart without knowing, but I hope she remains unharmed.

It was here, in Philadelphia, while waiting for my ship, that I completed this record, which I trust to my friend, Mr. Charles Dickens, that he may have it printed, in Dutch and English, for private distribution so that friends and family might know what events befell me in the City of New York in 1842.

May the whirligig of time carry me to peaceful lands.

Philip Schuyler, Philadelphia

A Postscript

Having spent the last several months traveling America, I am back in New York for a short time. Soon, Catherine and I will take ship for home. All these months, I have carried Philip Schuyler's journal, troubled by its weight. I wondered what had become of Philip's Madame Burgundy. Had she survived this plot only to succumb to another?

As I would only be stopping one night in the city before taking ship, I posted a letter from Montreal to Mr. Charles Johnson, a man described by Schuyler in these pages, asking that he update me on my return to New York. My hope was that he had been successful in delving into the identity of Madame Burgundy.

When I arrived at the hotel a message from him awaited, which I reprint here.

My Dear Charles,

As you know, I have not been long in the city of New York, having recently decided to devote (some might say squander) my family fortune to the cause of abolition. New York is the cross-roads. Here are the networks for hiding escapees and for aiding in the buying of sundered families that they may be reunited.

Much work is to be done here as well. The legal system is rampant with corruption. Did you know that a black man may be taken from the street, from his home even, and brought before a magistrate? And if witnesses claim that the man is an escaped slave, whether true or not, he will be taken to the South in bondage. I count on you to spread this news in England, that

World opinion may help sway that of America.

So as you might presume, I have met many people here, of circumstances high and low, of all races and nationalities. It is to these I turned in search of the identity and circumstances of the woman your friend described.

Having the street number made the first part quite simple. It is the home of a wealthy American family of Dutch extraction. I have also discovered that there is a very old and very powerful group of wealthy New Yorkers (both of the city and other parts of the state) who claim their lineage from the original Dutch inhabitants of then New Amsterdam. The Dutch were absorbed into the English population after the colony changed hands, losing their language but not their identity. The group goes under the name Stuyvesant Preservationist Society and comprises some of the wealthiest families in the region. Because of this, I have had to take care, as some of these people are also contributors to the cause.

The basic scenario is thus. A man by the name of Horace Nooteboom, eldest of a family of merchants and shipbuilders, met, in the course of his business, a woman from the island of St. Grillet, a lady of both French and African ancestry. They married, and he brought her to his newly-built home in a most fashionable block.

You can guess the consternation this caused. The mixing of races is not unknown here, but it is generally confined to the lower classes, and although she is not one hundred percent African in her heritage, her coloring is dark enough to cause notice.

In other parts of the nation, in the Western territories, where men and women alike toil in the fields of their farmsteads, I doubt her appearance would have attracted attention. But in New York the complexion of pale cream is the emblem of elegant society.

So you see, they would have experienced myriad difficulties even if left in peace. This Society, however, determined that one of their own should not embarrass them in such a manner, and it was they who contrived the scheme which embroiled your friend.

As might be expected, the husband is on the side of our cause, and has, through his business (which takes him often to the South, especially New Orleans), actively participated in aiding the flight of slaves, hiding them on his ships and bringing them to New York.

I have spoken to him, and I am happy to say that Madame Burgundy did survive the attempt. She did indeed destroy the painting. And whether or not you believe that some ill could be cast upon her by this odd series of paintings depicting a man approaching her with the aim of harm, it was enough for them to know that such had been intended.

They left the city, up the Hudson river on a steamboat. I believe their final destination was to be Canada.

These boats, as you know, are not the safest form of travel.

On the second day, at an early hour of the morning, perhaps before any passengers had awakened, an accident occurred. The starboard boiler exploded and the boat burst into flame. Few survived, and I am sorry to say Nooteboom and his wife were not among them.

I am afraid we shall never know whether such was a true accident, or another attempt by these persons, whose aim now included the husband, for he knew of their treachery. It is well that your friend the painter chose to separate himself by the gulf of oceans.

I toast your safe and speedy return journey.

Best wishes, as always,
Charles Johnson

I handed the letter to Catherine that she might read it too. I wish I could contact Philip to give him the sad news as well, but I expect I will hear from him when he is settled. For the moment, as Mr. Johnson said, it is well that he is far away.

Charles Dickens, aboard ship bound for Liverpool
Friday, June 10, 1842

Ataxia, The Wooden Continent

A Glossary of Terms Pertaining To Ataxia. Useful For Merchants, Naturalists, Trappers, Collectors, and Tourists.

Compiled and Translated By Stepan Chapman

Ataxia is a floating continent of no fixed address, often found in the Indian Ocean, sometimes in the South Pacific. It is usually accompanied by the Sailing Isles. Visitors to Ataxia immediately notice that everything and everyone there is made of wood. Ataxia's wooden terrain conceals a startling variety of the wooden creatures known as arboids. (See Arboids.)

The language of the local population registers on human ears merely as high-pitched squeaking. For this reason, a panoply of English-language argot terms have arisen to describe the colorful people and places of this unique seaborne continent. Until a reliable dictionary for the Ataxic tongue can be assembled, these phrases of argot must serve as humanity's only tools for the achievement of a deeper understanding of arboid culture.

A glossary follows. Both common nouns and proper names are included. All entries — whether arbographic, arbozoic, historical, ethnographic, or biographical — are arranged alphabetically for ease of reference.

THE ANGULAR COAST: The starboard coast of Ataxia extends into the haze of distance. The shore bends at exact angles, which are marked by beveled insets and lacquered lighthouses. Wooden gulls rake the dingy sky blinds with their squeals. Barnacle-encrusted scow men with ragged wives and rickety rowboat children huddle under tarpaulins on crooked plywood jetties. Stooped fishermen with cabriole legs drag ashore nets of twitching driftwood. Somewhere metal fly rods turn metal drive shafts. Somewhere steel axles turn wheels of purest rubber. Here we are poor. Here we have only wood.

ARBOIDS: Beings of living wood. A persistent enigma to the theorists of biology. Some are flea-sized. Some are big as bridges. Some are as simple as the Creeping Rail Ties, others as complex as the Ormolu Thumb Pianos of Osmosis Hollow. They construct themselves spontaneously in the wood pulp of Paper Swamp. (See Paper Swamp.) Botanists suppose that arboids evolved from trees. Arboids believe that the first trees grew on Ataxia, and that their descendants in the outer world have devolved into the senseless condition of *false wood*.

ATAXIA: A floating continent, entirely composed of wood. Populated by various races of arboids, celluloids, and laminates. Ruled by the priest cult of the Great Lectern at Shellac-Veneer. This magnificent city surrounds the sacred lectern's base. The cupolas and minarets of Shellac-Veneer rise from the Plain of Lath, Ataxia's central plateau. The Lectern's high priest administers the Holy Ataxic Empire from the Shrine of the Throne of Nails. Defended by armies of Drillers under the command of the Walking Barn Roof. (See The Drillers.) Major Cities: Shellac-Veneer, Cambium, Silo, and Wharftown. Main rivers: The Timber, the Pellet, and the Tanbark. Chief imports: screws, bolts, and brackets. Chief exports: Shovelers and toothpick hay. (See Shovelers.)

BASEMENT MARSH: A treacherous region, closed to tourists. Neither lagoon nor solid flooring. The stink of mildew hangs thick in the humid air. A bleached-out sun peers through the filthy window glass behind the chinks in the sky blinds. It drizzles a feeble twilight on the ruins of all intentionality. In the Marsh, the boundary between wood and mud dissolves into a foul black ooze, creeping with windup snails and scummed with the weakness and woe of a billion failed carpentry projects. Magazineville sank into the Marsh several twonks ago. The residues lend its muck the consistency of runny school paste. Basement Marsh is attached to no particular building. It moves restlessly from town to town. Sometimes the locals attack it with torches and sump pumps.

THE BEETLE MOUND OF '27: Heaps of chewed sawdust from the Boring Beetle Mound of 8927 FFG were first sighted by the Claw-foot Coffins of Distressed Maple County. Boring beetles soon consumed the Forest of Chair Legs and the Jungle of Dancing Bedposts. The Mound spread its beetles aft to the settlements of the Rococo Credenzas and even as far as the strongholds of the Awful Armoires. The Mound was destroyed by cleansing fire, thanks to the divine intervention of the Great Lectern and four divisions of his Combustion Controlmen. (See The Great Lectern.) To this day, the Beetle Mound is worshipped as an evil god by certain wandering tribes of tambour desks. In desk mythology, the Mound is described sometimes as an arbological outcropping and sometimes as a giant wooden robot.

THE BENTWOOD DESERT: A series of rectilinear terraces climb Ataxia's aft decks. The highest, hottest, and most arid of these is the Bentwood Desert. The sun that scorches the Desert can wither a traveler to dry roots and tangles in less time than it takes to die. Matchstick arthropods emerge at night and prey on the softer and wetter. In the sand dunes, Saguaro Trolls weave themselves from moonlit fish ribs of deadwood. They carry water buckets in blistered hands. With six arms each, they can carry many buckets. Ocotillo families tour the arroyos with their spears of teak and their herds of oars and barrels. They sell their head thorns to the needle factories and drink themselves blind on wood alcohol. Cholla People clump together any old way. They loiter under awnings and play accordions on foggy nights.

THE BLOSSOM FESTIVAL: In spring, all Ataxia blooms. Blossoms of all colors and descriptions erupt from every stable hand, every milk maid, every goat, fence post, and window frame—from the brows of elderly bureaus, from the ankles of toddling washstands, and from the loins of young settees in love. On the first squeakend of Mulch, Laminatia convenes its famous Blossom Festival on the pine cone fields of Rickshaw. Tourists are welcome to join the throngs of gleeful arboids on holiday and to eat the greasy wooden food sold by the vendors. The Festival climaxes with a thrilling race, wherein the fleetest spools of the realm compete for the Heartwood Spoolery Medallion. But the real business of the festival is the pollination of arboid pistils by the stamens of microscopic wood mites.

During the tweak that follows, the blossoms fall. Ambulatory Bins collect them for burial. Then life in Ataxia returns to its normal state of lethargy and numbness.

BRIAR SCORPIONS: Just what they sound like, and quite painful too. The venom from one briar scorpion can kill a house. They give off the stench of scorched linseed oil. Following copulation, the female eats the male and then spits him up again.

CONNECTOR TOYS: Before the weary traveler on the Plain of Lath can hike to the yurts of the Arrogant Building Blocks or the kivas of the Ugly Armrests, that traveler will surely stumble by starlight on the encampments of nomadic Connector Toys. They whiffle and snick in the brisk blue air of dawn. Their belly disks are ringed with peg holes. Their fingers are fins of green cardboard. Chains of Connector Toys climb the vines of Grape Wood Summit, subsisting on etched ferns and floral latticework. Eventually their waterlogged fibers sink below Croak's threshold and deconstruct. Their mortal remains are compacted by gavels and exported as breakfast cereal.

THE DRILLERS: Lumbering mechanisms that run on wood chips and waste paper. They begin as a dusty blur at the horizon line, where the Two-By-Four Prairie meets the grit-flecked louvers of the sky blinds. They ride their drills bareback, like a horde of nutmeg-crazed rolling pins. They disdain all pleasure and live only for hardship, glory, and pencil-chewing. Pray they don't notice you. The Drillers were once a tribe of hardwood warriors from the dustpans of Yew. Most of their race perished in the Outhouse Wars. Insanely loyal to the Great Lectern and his priest cult. Only the Drillers are permitted to wield the consecrated metal weapons which rend the infidel—the drill and the awl, the planer and the adze, the ripsaw and the belt sander.

QUEEN ELLEN, THE WICKERWORK GIRAFFE: Dowel of Eucalyptus, Baroness of Balustrades, and Countess of Caryatids. Pacifier of the Angry Teething Rings, liberator of the Tripod Tobacco Pipes, and Shah of the Trapezoidal Plinths. It was Queen Ellen who installed the palm escalators and the conveyer belts, who chiseled out the elevator shafts and hung the mangrove dumbwaiters. Hereditary monarch of Mortise, Tenon, Trestle, and Model Train Flats. Sole issue of Queen Buckboard the Tedious and Prince Creosote of Logjam. Queen Ellen was driven from Ataxia by the fourth dynasty of the Lectern Priests. She is under indictment for the usual high crimes — treason against the empire and so forth.

EYE KNOBS: These organs provide vision for the clans of the Ebony Dressers, the Acacia Tallboys, and the Sectional Cabinets. Eye knobs are still collected illegally by the Cannibal Pantries of the Off-True Archipelago and used in their hideous cork gumbos.

FFG: Abbreviation for Following First Growth. This acronym is tagged onto a numeral to indicate a particular squink within the standard time frame of Ataxic history. The continent was born, so the Pollen Elders tell us, on the first day of the squink 1 FFG, within the coils of a giant seaweed (or afterbirth) at the bottom of the ocean. During the first squonk of that squink, the continent attained buoyancy and bobbed to the surface. The Stuttering Monks of Smoke describe this primeval event as "the wooden world's release from mutterance to utterance." Before the squink 6976 FFG, no wood existed anywhere in the world, except on Ataxia, as trees are an exclusively Ataxic invention.

THE FLAMING WHEEL: Religious arboids believe that the sun is a fiery wheel. According to time-worn Ataxic legend, the earth is the cargo of an immense wooden-wheeled World Wagon. For millions of twinks, eleven upholstered zebras pulled the Wagon around the inner surface of a mammoth hamster wheel, gradually gaining speed. Eventually the Wagon rolled so fast that its right front wheel burst into flame. The Wagon took fright and kicked the blazing wheel loose with such force that it spun into orbit around the earth. The Flaming Wheel continues to circle, occasionally scorching the sky blinds. Meanwhile the Wagon's missing wheel has grown back crooked and rendered the Wagon lame, which accounts for the bumpy ride experienced by life on earth.

THE FOREDECK OVERLOOK: After days of cart travel on splintery roads with missing planks, one reaches the foremost promontory of the Egregious Clutter. There one finds a scenic observation point. Ataxia dwindles away behind one like a matchstick miniature, and the sea is a rumbling rumor in the mist and spray. From the Foredeck Overlook, clouds can be seen in detail, visibly condensing. The cloud mesas and cloud gullies shift and stretch like wood grain. Nothing can hold them still. They seem almost wooden. Then you realize that clouds are alive too. A sobering thought, when you consider the size of them. Or when you ask yourself why they look like cauliflowers. Or why cauliflowers look so much like brains.

THE FROSTY WHEEL: The Flaming Wheel of the sun grew lonely, as he traversed the sky blinds with no one but spindles for company. (See Sky Spindles.) The left front wheel of the World Wagon took pity on her radiant brother. She ditched the Wagon and joined the sun in orbit. As the moon, she pursues her brother constantly, but nonetheless spends much of her time benighted. Each squonk or so, she stops eating and pines away for him. Two tweaks later, she gorges herself on the yarn of the Pale Skein and regains her luminous rotundity.

THE GREAT LECTERN: Taller than the tallest redwood rises the Great Lectern. His satin-wood panels and mother-of-pearl inlays dazzle his loyal subjects' eye knobs. Sepia and beige are the Lectern's spires — ruddy at sunset, golden at dawn. Clockwork sparrows twitter on his cornices and preen their pasteboard wings. Sweet is the smell of the Lectern's cedar facings after the rain, and his pediments are carved with a vine motif. Supreme and invisible, he towers over the vast barge of Ataxia like a mainmast, with only the sky blinds for a sail.

KNOT GANGLIA: Current theories of wooden neurology lean heavily on the knot ganglion as the building block of celluloid consciousness. The knot ganglion was first theorized by pioneer glue doctor Cypress Plaque in his seminal *Comprehensive Arbology and Gratuitous Zoomorphics*. His theory is known as the Plaque system, Cypress's evasion, or the ganglionic fallacy.

THE MISMEASURED PEAKS: Cliff climbers, diagonalists, and staplemobilers all praise the unvarnished natural beauty of the Mismeasured Peaks. To starboard, the Peaks ascend to the Braced Platform. To port, they fall away toward Gouge Canyon. Sightseeing expeditions on calamander sawhorses leave from Baseboard, cross the Peaks, and disperse at Wedge Junction. Showers are available at the Clarinet Viola Quarry.

PAPER SWAMP: A body of wood pulp at the source of the Timber River. The womb of all life on Ataxia, unless you believe that old story about Xylem and Phloem. The Swamp is shallow but wide. The smell of fermenting mud is overpowering. Submerged proto-arboids claw the silt for waterproof silverfish and clothespin crabs. Ladders, ambries, Ottomans, surreys, and doorstops float past. Burbling pits of quickpulp menace navigation. Maps of the Swamp fall apart like wet paper towels. It's as if the place were cursed. These roots without stems, these limbs with no trunks—whence do they slither in such haste?

THE REALM OF LIVING ICE: A feature of Ataxic beliefs concerning the afterlife. According to *The Book of the Great Lectern*, the souls of useful arboids can look forward to a paradise called the Realm of Living Ice. The Realm occupies a shelving unit which the Great Lectern has extended from his upper reaches, high above the sky blinds. A land of lush orchards, gorgeous parks, and ample closet space. To get there, the Lectern's chosen souls must trudge across trackless expanses of snow, in search of the Frozen Lake of the Ice Sculptures. At the Lake, blizzards of ice needles strip away their wood to the last twig and etch their likenesses into figures of living ice. All of life's joys are felt postmortem by the chosen, while the damned in the Termite Realm feel all the pain. (See The Termite Realm.)

THE ROSEWOOD MINES: Far below the Bellows Works at Suffocation Hill lie the tunnel mazes of the Rosewood Mines. They operate day and night. There is no air in the deeper galleries—only winding darkness and the whimpers of the shoring timbers. The shafts descend almost to Ataxia's keel, and the continent's bowels groan in protest against its perforations. When a shift ends, winches drag up the miners on ropes. They emerge in clusters, stuck together with resin and tar. They hang, twisting in the wind. Spatulas pry them apart, and they stagger home to their families. The beautiful carvings from the rosewood shops are not for the likes of them.

THE SAILING ISLES: Independent in their movements, but joined to the floating continent by ancient alliances. The Isles accompany Ataxia wherever it wanders. Each Isle sets its own course by shifting the orientation of its sail trees and spinnaker weeds. Their hulls skim the crashing waves purposefully, while Ataxia merely drifts, its prow pointing east or west at random. Believed to be peninsular outriggings which detached themselves somewhere in the tangled thickets of history.

SANDPAPER FLIES: These ubiquitous pests self-generate from the slag heaps of particle board that surround the Dormer Ridge Mahogany Plant. Infestations of the larvae are difficult to eradicate from living structures, especially from buildings with allergies. Yet if there were no sandpaper flies and no sandpaper maggots, there would also be no government-issue maggot cheese on Rootdays, and arboids of the lower economic stratum would soon become brittle.

THE SCRAP BANDITS: An outlaw band that prowls the Shoddy Badlands. These casual assemblages of discarded lumber care little whether they live or die. They prey on the hickory farmers of Tornado Cranny and on the trappers of Mount Rakehandle. Created by the turpentine spill of 921 FFG, which eradicated scores of arboid species and instigated others. The Scrappers are bitter enemies of a rival collective of cutthroats known as the Nasty Coffers. The two gangs rumble periodically with letter openers, nail guns, and foul-mouthed briar scorpions.

SHOVELERS: Wrinkly tubular giants. They arise from mixed packing materials. Their limbs are corrugated cardboard. Their excelsior dreadlocks hang long and ratty. The government nationalized them last year. Now you see them digging trenches beside the highway or hollowing out foundations for new courthouses and prisons. Their dull gray silhouettes loom above the cities, blotting out the star spindles. Said to be somnambulant. Certainly their eyes are closed. Do they walk on two legs, or on four or six? Like sad old men in pajamas, they seem to be working in their sleep. They could crush us like ants, but they don't seem to notice us. I wonder can they speak. I wonder does anyone feed them.

SILO CITY: Nexus of a radial network of trade routes which connect the outer counties with the Plain of Lath. Extremely cosmopolitan. "Hot syrup music" drifts from the nightspots, enticing well-heeled tourists. Silo City serves as a refuge for large numbers of immigrant puppets, stateless dolls, and AWOL wooden soldiers. But on certain days, the shadow of the Great Lectern falls across the city at high noon. At such uncanny moments, shivering roof beams cling to their joists in mute apprehension. Balsa mice bite their own strings off, and shipworms vomit tiny tapioca puddings. Then the moment of intensity passes, and life becomes wooden again.

SKY SPINDLES: The Ataxic phrase for stars translates as sky spindles. Religious arboids believe that the stars are descended from the homeless spindles that balanced on wild coat trees during the dawn days of the First Growth. A typhoon swept them overboard, and they fell from Ataxia. Then the remorseful typhoon lifted them into the heavens, where they miraculously turned into stars. Now they spend the daylight hours busily spinning sunlight into white cotton yarn. They string this yarn into cat's cradles, thus adding layers to the Pale Skein, (known to mammals as the Milky Way.) During the night, they spin the cotton into starlight—all for the entertainment of the Frosty Wheel, whom they all adore.

THE SPLINTERHEAP RAVINES: Beware the Ravines. Sudden woodslides and predatory taborets imperil travelers there. Obstructed by impenetrable glades of croquet mallets, hook-billed canes, and bole-headed cudgels. Lianas of twine ensnare nocturnal kites, which are eaten by poisonous pagodas. Seductive arpeggios drift from the sunken packing crates of hungry harpsichords. Then there's nothing for miles but bare slanting floor, slimy with soapsuds and mop water. The dry rot soaks deep into your shoes and your hair. If a guide offers to take you there, he just wants to kill you and sell your bones for glue.

THE STORM ORCHARDS: Icy rain sluices down through the sky blinds. Flares of lightning turn gorse brush into coiled swarms of thorn snakes. Insane trees shake their branches at the maddened clouds, and the stink of charred wood and sizzling sap is everywhere. Sodden bark strips itself from waterlogged pith, like skin from fingers in a vat of lye. Falling tree limbs amputate your rain-numbed feet, and you stagger home through floodwater on your stumps and count yourself lucky. The stars rush in circles, like ladles with their heads cut off. They splash steaming star blood on the black-enameled night side of the sky slats.

DEACON SYCAMORE: Author of *Sycamore's Interminable Annals of Ataxia*. The honorable Deacon Boxcar Sycamore has served for many twonks as headmaster of the Birch Rod School at Woodstain. A venerated scholar of over two-hundred annual rings, but tragically dependent on injections of tropical bark extracts. Rumored to be a mummy, but remarkably well preserved and publishing steadily.

THE TEN TERRIBLE SISTERS: Torrential vine rivers. They run only at times of volcanic eruption and molten wood spills. The Sisters have devastated whole counties. Orchardists have nicknames for them, like Old Murder and the Cold Caress. The Pollen Elders say that the Sisters can turn the wood of drowned arboids into living flesh—surely a fate worse than death. When I think of this superstition, my brain nut clogs with pine tar, and tannin leaks from my eye knobs.

THE TERMITE REALM: According to Ataxic religious belief, death provides three possible destinations for recently-perished arboids. The Realm of Living Ice is described above. Another etheric domain is the Termite Realm, where the souls of heretics and other troublesome creatures suffer the torments of being eaten alive forever. For souls neither particularly useful nor especially troublesome, there is a third domain known simply as the Dump.

THE THRONE OF NAILS: The hereditary throne of the high priest of the Cult of the Great Lectern. Carved from a block of black locust in the squink 87 FFG, by the legendary sculptor Gingko Laurel. Modern high priests don't actually sit on the Throne, as the nails are still very sharp, and also as it is widely felt that the impaled corpse of the first high priest precludes the necessity for any of his successors to occupy the same chair.

THE TIKI WOMAN: (Sometimes the Tiki Man.) Escritoire of Bookcase and sole owner and operator of Cambium City. Protector of the Salad Spoons of Herringbone Valley and the Mashed Carton Riders of Birdhouse Cove. A respected tribal leader among the Box Wolves and the Knotted Rulers. The Tiki Woman's place of growth is unknown, and she has never been photographed. Falsely acclaimed as the rightful sovereign of Ataxia by certain half-mad refugees in the Burn Pile Zone—arboids with gnarled brains and bad table manners. The Tiki Woman is ostensibly loyal to the empire, but windup moles report her movements to hives of priestly filing cabinets.

TOOTHPICK GRASS: A common ground cover in Ataxia's river valleys. Grows around the roots of fluted columns, on the banks of slotted streams, and in the shade of mossy bench boulders. Harvested as food by the Stilt Walkers of the Adhesive Country. Used as cattle fodder by the table herders of Sandalbeech. The stems are hollow, and diving beetles use them for snorkel gear in times of Dutch elm disease. Comes back every year, just like it was invited. Crunches underfoot.

THE WALKING BARN ROOF: Absolute commander of the Drillers, the Telescoping Hat Racks, and the Furious Bassinets. Founder of the Armory Roots at Oaken Tor. The Roof is inexplicably impressive. A lopsided cascade of split-shake shingles, gray from squinks of weather. He walks abroad at the head of marching armies, amid the clumping of a thousand wooden boots. Nods to cheering throngs of stools, sheds, and tollbooths. The Walking Barn Roof is a loyal subject of the Great Lectern and has never had any problems with the priest cult.

WHARFTOWN: Poor disreputable Wharftown. Shame of the Angular Coast. Capital of crotch blight and crook corruption. The log drums pound all night there. Long a center for criminal, liminal, and fungal activities. A hotbed of the black market in foreign furniture waxes and unlicensed rags. Attracts a certain type of arboid. The wrong type.

WOOD RADAR: Can you feel it? Can you sense the detection waves as they ripple out from the Lectern's secret binnacle. The Lectern is always scanning us. His radar probes every dusty corner and exposes every crawl space. You can brush yourself with sealant or lock yourself in a trunk, but it's too late for any of that. The Radar can see inside your skull.

XYLEM AND PHLOEM: Arboids of various tribes relate various creation myths. The Lectern Priests relate the tale of Xylem the Willow Girl and Phloem the Bamboo Boy. This narrative derives from the following passage in *The Book of the Great Lectern.*

"Before the beginning, the Great Lectern descended from the sky blinds, and all that was about it was the sky blinds, nor did anything exist save for the sky blinds and the Lectern. At that time, the Lectern was filled with water, which didst cause him much swelling and discomfort, so that he didst release the water into the world. Thus were born the oceans. Following on this torrential event, untold eons passed unnoticed. The Lectern didst remodel his system of drawers without ceasing, and didst organize and reorganize his knickknacks. But still he was the only woodenness he knew that didst float upon the sea. And so, in his aching solitude, he didst fabricate a pair of upward-striving downward-rooted twins. And he named these twins Xylem and Phloem.

"Having no previous experience in arboculture, the Lectern didst transplant his mewling infants onto the surface of the ocean. But there they took no root, but rather sank. After lengthy thought, the all-father of trees didst cause his midsection to flange itself forth at sea level and to form a convenient shelving unit. And this shelving unit soon elaborated the decks, cabins, catwalks, gunnels, and holds of thrice-blessed Ataxia. Here didst the Willow Girl and the Bamboo Boy cross-graft themselves most fruitfully.

"Soon the groves of the trees begat the villages of the hut folk. The huts begat the buildings, and the buildings begat furniture, which then begat the debris people, who are disposable. And the Great Lectern saw that his world was good. For it is good to be wooden—to be hard and dense and numb. It is good to feel no pain."

TALES FROM THE CITY OF SEAMS

GREG VAN EEKHOUT

Lovers' Lookout

In the hills above the city, among the ruins of the old zoo, the kids come to screw. They cage themselves inside the animal enclosures and kick away the cigarette butts and the crushed beer cans and the brittle snake-skin condoms, and then, with the city glittering below, they fill the hot-smog nights with their whispers.

They are not alone.

There is a cave in the hillside behind the picnic grounds. It used to be the bear grotto, but over the decades, the cave has grown deeper. It goes far back, now, and down. Over the grotto's entrance hangs a sign that says something to the effect of *Abandon hope, all ye who enter*.

Understandably, this gives the dead pause. They tend to linger here.

Hearing the sighs and groans of the living young, the dead get ideas. They shed their frail uniforms and gossamer business suits and wispy club wear. They strip down to silver-moon flesh and lie in the grass one final time.

Like all lovers' lanes and modern ruins, the old zoo accumulates stories. One of these tales is that, when the zoo was shut down some three generations ago, most of the animals were sold to circuses and other zoos and private collections. A few escaped, however. There are jaguars in the hills, it is said, and vultures, and kudu. Sometimes at night, when the zoo reaches its height of passion, hyenas howl in ghostly sympathy.

Or so the tales go.

But the dead are wise, and they know these stories for the urban legends they are. They know the cries aren't from the descendents of escaped animals.

No, the cries are from the living, unknowingly exhorting the dead to abandon, but not to abandon hope.

Chinatown

When I worked for a plumbing supply wholesaler in Chinatown, the best part of my day was lunch. I'd walk by the window displays of tobacco-colored ducks strung up by their necks, the scents of grease and ginger trying to draw me in. But I was like a man passing a row of prostitutes without interest, secure in the knowledge that a more desirable lover awaits him at home. Lady Sze's Golden Crown Café was my destination, the only place in town where you could get a bowl of soup that had been simmering for a thousand years.

A thousand years was actually a bit of an exaggeration. A forgivable fib of marketing. Truthfully, the thousand-year soup had been cooking in its pot for only eight centuries, born in the latter days of Genghis Khan. The great Mongol warlord had been displeased by a subordinate, one Lu Ch'eng-Huan, in some small way forgotten to history (although the most recent Lady Sze once suggested to me that it had something to do with a concubine, a canary, and a paintbrush). Wishing to discipline Lu Ch'eng-Huan, the Khan had his head removed and boiled in a golden pot. The Khan kept the skull as a trophy, but, not realizing Lu Ch'eng-Huan was a sorcerer, permitted Lu's wife to claim the pot, the water, and the gray film floating on top. After taking it back to her home village, she added salt, leeks, onions, and garlic, and made a soup of her beloved husband's dissolved head. Every day she would add some more water, more vegetables and seasoning, and thus the soup was kept going.

Hundreds of years later, when Lu's descendents came to American shores, they brought the soup with them, keeping vigil over the cook fires on the deck of the brig *Prometheus*.

I had no idea how much of that was true, but the soup tasted wonderful and kept me cold-free, and Lady Sze (her actual name was Michelle) charged only three bucks a bowl.

One day as I sat in the restaurant savoring my lunch, a man in an ivory suit came into the place. His head was as white and hairless as an eggshell, and when he spoke, every syllable came out twisted into an odd shape. I think he was Belgian. "Daughter of Lu Ch'eng-Huan, far removed," he said, "I have grown impatient with your truculence. I have dealt with you in good faith. I have offered you riches—gems and antiques, property and estates, significant shares in profitable concerns—but you have mistaken my generosity for desperation. If you will not part with the soup in a fair exchange, I shall have to take it by force."

Michelle Sze was over at a corner table, taking care of some accounting matters. "Get lost," she said.

The white man smiled tightly. His blue eyes darkened as though glazed over by a layer of ice. "Boys?" he said, and, on cue, two men entered the restaurant and stood behind him. Their faces were broad, with mouths so wide their lips seemed to curve back behind their huge ears. Long-fingered hands twitched down low near their bowed knees. I somehow knew that these were not true men, but monkeys grown and reshaped to pass as men. They leered at Michelle Sze, rocking on their strange, short legs.

Michelle Sze barely glanced up at them. "Brothers," she said. And five men came out of the kitchen. They stood shoulder to shoulder, forming a wall. "To get to my soup," Michelle said, "you will first have to overcome my brothers. This will be more difficult than you might suppose. First brother is like stone. His flesh cannot be penetrated. Second brother has the strength of ten men concentrated in his right hand. Third brother is tireless and needs neither food nor water, neither sleep nor breath. Fourth brother can outrun a horse, a hawk, an arrow shot from a bow. Fifth brother, though he still walks among us, is already dead and cannot be harmed. Sixth brother can see a moth twitch its antennae from a hundred miles away. Seventh brother can hear the creak and groan of grass growing." Michelle wrote something on her spreadsheet. "Let's see your monkeys get past them."

The white man smiled as though Michelle Sze had said something cute but stupid. And then his smile faltered. "Wait a minute. Seven brothers? I count only five."

"Yes. Sixth and Seventh brothers took the soup out the back door as I was introducing you to First through Fifth." She scratched out something on the spreadsheet.

"Then you are defeated," the white man said, "for I had more monkeys posted in the alley."

"Yes," Michelle said, "and Eighth brother of the poison touch took care of them."

"Ah," said the white man, shutting his eyes. He rubbed the bridge of his nose. "Ah."

A silence followed. One of the monkeys scratched its ass and sniffed its fingers.

"Well, then," the white man said, finally, "another day."

"Another day," Michelle agreed.

And the white man took his leave with all the straight-backed dignity he could muster in the face of this setback, his monkeys ook-ooking behind him with disappointment and confusion.

The brothers stood around grinning at one another for a few moments until Michelle snapped at them to go back to work. Chagrined, they filed back into the kitchen.

I tipped my bowl to drink the last of my soup. "That turned out pretty well," I said.

She released a long, sad sigh. "Not really. We've been here for three generations, but now we're done with this city. We'll have to move the restaurant."

I choked on the broth. "Move? But ... Why? Your brothers ..."

"The Belgian will be back. And he can make monkeys faster than I can make brothers. So, we move." She got up and flipped the *Open* sign to *Closed.*

"But ... where will you go?" I asked, knowing I wouldn't like the answer.

"Far away. Across one ocean, perhaps two. Now, if you'll excuse me, sir, you've been a good customer, but I do have some arrangements to make ..."

And that was it. By the very next day, Lady Sze's Golden Crown Café had been abandoned. A week later, a donut shop had replaced it.

It took me months to find another regular lunch place, but I eventually settled on a Texas barbecue joint on the south 400 block of Milton. Their secret lay in the heated rocks that lined the bottom of the barbecue pit, brought here by way of Texas from Mexico. They were fragments of an Aztec pyramid and had been splashed with the blood of more than a thousand human sacrifices.

The ribs are pretty good, but I'm more a fan of the pulled pork sandwich.

Harbor District

I walked along the row of aquariums and pressed my nose against miniature worlds. Treasure chests spewed bubbles. Skeletal pirates gripped ship wheels. Fish nipped pink rocks.

Please Don't Tap The Glass, the signs said, so I refrained.

My kid's birthday was coming up. I'd been thinking about giving him an ant farm but changed my mind and decided he could do with some fish. When ants get out you've got them all over the house. When fish get out, they just die. Lots of arguments in favor of fish. The only question was, what kind? I had it in my head that goldfish die as soon as you get them home. They're programmed that way, with this little chip inside their bellies that somehow knows the second you've got them through the door, and then, *zap*, time to meet the Ty-D-Bol Man.

The shop was dark, hot and moist. Humming and gurgling filled the air. It was hard to breathe, and I loosened my tie. So many weird fish: ear-spot angels, convict tangs, chevroned butterflies, clown knives, blue-sided fairy wrasses. Near the back of the store, I paused before a 10-gallon tank with a porcelain castle. There was something different about the fish inside. About as long as my thumb, they weren't covered in scales, but rather in emerald-bright skin from their midsections to their tales, which ended in horizontal flukes, like a dolphin's. From the midsection forward, they were human-shaped: brown-skinned, with long, graceful arms; round breasts with little pencil-dot nipples; long, flowing black hair. Their eyes were like tiny diamond chips.

"Hey, what are these?" I called to the front of the store.

The shopkeeper—a tall hippy with a blurred U.S. Navy tattoo on his arm—sauntered over to me. "Mermaids," he said. "Pretty rare."

I spent a moment watching them swim. One broke the surface, arching her back and stretching. Another swam up to her and started braiding her hair. I felt a slight twitch in my crotch.

"How much?"

"Forty each," he said with the tone of someone trying to conceal the sound of hope in his voice. "And they go as a group."

There were six mermaids in the tank.

"Okay," I said. "I'll just take a couple of those Siamese fighting fish in the front of the store."

"More than one and they'll kill each other. That's why they call them *fighting* fish."

I got out my wallet. "How about three goldfish?"

As it turned out, my kid was pretty happy with his gift. I got him a nice little tank, some plastic plants for decoration, and only one of the goldfish died before we could get it all set up. It was nice to see him learning to take care of something, making sure the water didn't get too grimy, feeding the fish just the right pinch. I enjoyed going into his room when he was over at a friend's or at his mom's. I'd sit on the bed and watch the fish go back and forth. I could stare at them for hours. It was fun. Better than TV.

I figured the kid might enjoy some more fish, so I went back to the shop. The mermaids didn't look so good now. Their green tails were the color of wilted lettuce, and their hair was patchy, showing too much scalp. Their eyes had grown red. And one of the mermaids was gone. There were only five now.

Taped to the glass was a hand-written sign: *50% Off. Ask At Counter. Please Don't Tap On The Glass.*

I saw the shopkeeper's reflection in the tank. "What's wrong with them?" I asked.

"You're really not supposed to break up the group," he said, sheepishly. "But, you know, rent's climbing, economy's screwed ... I sold one of them. I thought they'd get over it."

I bent back down to the tank. Their eyes actually weren't red. They were gone. Just bloody sockets left, trailing threads of blood through the water.

"They grieve pretty dramatically," the shopkeeper explained.

I straightened and got out my wallet. "Think I'd like four neon tetras and three tiger barbs, please."

As he went off to net me my fish, I lingered a while longer by the mermaids. When I could stand it no more, I tapped lightly on the glass. They darted off in all directions, their mouths stretched in silent screams.

College Square

First of all, it's not a fetish; it's a preference.

Most guys have one. Maybe it's redheads, or poet chicks with tight sweaters and little round glasses, or girls who remind them of a their third grade teacher who was careless with her bra straps. Me, I like dangerous girls. Femme fatales. Exotic spies from foreign lands. Girls with knives who put you through your paces on the backs of their Harleys. I like being pursued by perilous women, and I don't mind if I get pounced on, or even roughed up a little. As long as I get away in the end.

I'm neither proud nor ashamed of this. I just know what makes me tick.

I watch them from across the street.

The tawny-haired one sweeps the walk in front of her café, her eyes green as a traffic light saying *go*. When she pauses, puts a hand against the small of her back and stretches, her dress draws taut against her curves. Then she catches me watching her. Her lips curl into a small smile and she goes back to her sweeping.

One door down, another café, and here a woman with black curls that fall over her shoulders waters hydrangeas in terra cotta pots. She bends forward, and water trickles from her watering can.

They don't look much alike, these two witches, but I'm sure they're sisters. And not the kind who stir the same pot and feed the same cats. These are sisters who, perhaps, shared the womb, and were it not for the intervention of calming teas drunk by their mother, they would have strangled each other with their own umbilical cords.

The broom stops moving. The water can stops trickling. The sister-witches tilt their heads, both giving me questioning looks, and go inside their respective cafés.

I choose the establishment of the tawny-haired one, because from where I'm standing, her place is on my left, and I read left to right. Through the doors I go, only to find that her café is disappointingly uninviting. Mismatched folding chairs are arranged haphazardly around wobbly tables. The prints on the walls are whatever was cheap at the mall poster shop.

With a scrape of metal legs against yellowing vinyl floor, I pull out a chair and take a seat.

The tawny witch is less attractive up close. Her arms are skinny, with thick blue veins pushing up the skin. And those once-amazing green eyes— contacts, surely—sit inside deep hollows.

It doesn't matter. The aromas will keep me here. Warm, buttery scents, with vanilla and light dancing over rich, dark coffee. My stomach rumbles, my mouth waters, my hamstrings tingle.

Eat not the food of witches, warn my thoughts, in an urgent voice of authority, like Ahab, or a Scottish preacher. *Eat not the food of witches.*

"A croissant and a large drip," I say, swallowing.

She sets a golden, pillowy croissant on a polystyrene plate, fills a paper cup with night, and sets both on my table. She tries to shake her hips as she returns to her place behind the counter.

I bite into the croissant.

Flaky crust gives way to soft wisps of pastry, soaking my tongue in a warmth that spreads to my chest and belly. Despite myself, I moan softly, and the tawny witch smiles now, a smile that softens the angles of her face and brings a glow to her cheeks. Her green eyes come to life.

She's got me, I realize with a panicky intake of breath. Caught. Trapped. No escape this time. Why, oh, why didn't I listen to Ahab?

I will come here every day for the rest of my life. I will have no meals other than what she makes for me.

Eventually, though, my plate is empty, even the crumbs gone, and I can see the bottom of my cup. And once more the tawny witch is too pale, too stretched out. Her smile reveals a bit too much gum. So, I put six dollars on the table and run out, her curses thrown at my back.

Outside, I catch my breath, craving a cigarette. My heart jackhammers in my chest, and this is the part I like best: The light-legged, dizzy buzz that follows an escape.

Is this how Harry Houdini felt after throwing off straightjacket and shackles and bursting naked through the surface of a half-frozen river?

What a great feeling. Nice going, Harry.

But I need more.

Only a few moments later I find myself moving toward the café next door.

Overstuffed chairs and throw pillows suggest long, rainy afternoons with steaming mugs and good books. The windows cast honey-colored light on warm wood floors.

The black-haired one has been waiting.

"Sit," she says. "Tell me what you want."

I take the chair nearest the counter, nearest her. "A croissant, please, and a large coffee."

"Cream and sugar?"

I like the way her lips form the word *cream*.

Not trusting my voice, I leave it at a mute nod.

She brings me a plate ringed with small green leaves and a cup painted with night sky and stars. Then she takes a seat in the chair opposite me. When I bite into the croissant, she moves her legs and exhales.

I chew. Hard, burnt crust gives way to something the texture of wood. I sip the coffee and get a mouthful of sour water and bitter grounds.

As I eat and drink, the witch's lips part and her chest rises and falls. I squirm in my seat, tension gathering in my thighs.

The awful taste of her food is no matter when she tilts her head back and shows me the exquisite long curve of her neck. For a moment, I even entertain the notion that I am seducing her.

But one does not seduce a witch. Not in her own café. Not when eating her food. And soon, I am in love with her, with her midnight forest of black curls, and her eyes, blue as glacial ice. And though I would be her captive lover, a pet of sorts, or a slave, I would not mind so much, because she has worked magic on my glands, and what is love but a product of pheromones and the promise of long, pleasant afternoons?

But is that what I want? Long, pleasant afternoons? Better loving through chemistry?

And, in the end, it is not. And I put down plate and cup, and leave six dollars on the table, and run out the door, plugging my ears against her strange, angry, hissed words.

I'm so good at this, this escaping thing. Two in one day. I am a young, virile, fleet-footed gazelle, and I'm still congratulating myself when I realize my legs are carrying me to a third door, one I hadn't noticed before, placed right between the two cafés. And that's where I go.

Inside, the tawny-haired witch smiles and grinds coffee beans by hand. The black-haired one makes slow circles on a table with a polishing cloth.

I have been in the houses of two witches, and I have eaten the food of two witches, and I have risked the ire of two witches. And today I have learned that I can resist witchcraft in matters of lust, and I can resist witchcraft in matters of breakfast.

But lust *and* breakfast?

That's a pretty damn good trap.

I close the door behind me.

The black-haired one polishes. The tawny-haired one grinds. Then, their hands fall motionless, and the witches come towards me, reaching.

Old Heights

Maybe he's a retired heavyweight who owns a cigar-stained Italian restaurant downtown and still spars with the kids when he runs his youth boxing camp. Or maybe he's a cowboy actor who exaggerates his Texas drawl when he does commercials for his Ford dealership. Possibly, he's an old news anchor who emcees the annual leukemia telethon and does a radio show early on Sunday mornings. Every town has one, the old local celebrity who represents the people in a way an elected politician never could. Whoever he is, you can be sure he's a raconteur, that he's been entertaining people for as long as anyone can remember. People agree that he's simply the nicest guy in town, though there are some faded rumors about womanizing, and some drunk driving allegations. But those happened so long ago, and anyway, they somehow make him human and better loved.

Around here, for my generation, at least, that guy was the Green Thunder.

The Green Thunder was the grand marshal in the Settler's Day parade.

The Green Thunder visited kids in the hospital.

.The Green Thunder judged the Daffodil Queen pageant.

You remember that commercial campaign the city did? A guy throws his fast food garbage out his car window, and a kid walks up, and he stares at the garbage, and he stares at the trash can across the street, and the voice-over says, "What would the Green Thunder do?" I still think of that commercial every time I see litter in the street.

The Green Thunder once had his cape pressed at my dry cleaner shop. Dropped it off himself, paid cash, and when I asked him for an autograph, he gave me that billion-dollar grin and got out an 8x10 glossy. He signed it, *To Sidney, My Dry Cleaning Hero. Thanks! Green Thunder*. Drew a little thunder bolt and everything.

His dry cleaning hero? It was the first time he'd ever been to my shop, and I hadn't even pressed his cape yet. He didn't have to do that for me, but that's the kind of guy he was.

And, look, I'm not defending what he said to that reporter. It was dead wrong. I think he was just trying to be funny, and that's how people talked in the neighborhood when guys like Green Thunder and me were growing up. When it comes right down to it, didn't he help a lot of people, no matter who they were? He didn't care if you were black or white or yellow or green. If you needed help of any kind, the Green Thunder was there.

On the other hand, I understand why people got upset. My wife, she's Korean, and when we were driving cross-country on our honeymoon, some of the looks we used to get ...

I keep telling people the Green Thunder was more than a remark made in a moment of bad judgment. He was a real part of this city for a long time.

They say he and that reporter had some history between them. They'd been friends back in the old days but had a falling out of sorts. Something about a signal watch, something trivial.

Anyway.

It's just sad.

I was sweeping in front of my shop the day he left. I heard the boom, the bang, the sound of the sky ripping apart that people who grew up when and where I did had come to associate with hope, and I looked to the sky, and there he was. Not the fast streak of green across the morning blue. Just an old man, slowly passing out of view.

He wasn't even wearing his cape.

Some people get a little upset when they see his photo hanging on my wall. I've had once-loyal customers stop coming in because I won't take it down.

Heck, sometimes I want to take it down myself.

What's the right thing to do?

I don't know.

I don't know what the Green Thunder would do.

Carnival Park

We knew there'd be trouble when the new balloon man showed up. Orange John had been working Carnival Park for as long as there'd been a Carnival Park, tying his balloon animals with rope-strong hands. He always had that far-away look in his eyes, as if expecting something to appear on the horizon. And one day, something did. A new balloon man.

You have guys like Orange John where you come from? You know what I mean. Guys who do one thing in one place, like the Knife Guy, or Mr. Rags and Mr. Rags, Jr.? They do their one thing, and you can't imagine them having a life outside that thing, like a home, or a family, or a bank account. These guys make a place what it is, as surely as pigeon-crapped statues and old buildings with columns and stone lions out front.

So there was Orange John near the war fountain in his oversized orange suit and Bozo hair, knotting himself up a real nice stegosaurus, when up came the young balloon man. He was a skinny boy in a black T-shirt, rainbow vest, and jeans painted like all the sample chips in a paint store. His uninflated balloons hung from his waistband like little tongues, and he stopped a dozen or so yards away from Orange John.

"Jack Many-Colors," he said, tipping an imaginary hat.

"Orange John," said Orange John, with a squint and a nod.

And so it began.

Many-Colors was the challenger, so he went first. He took out a brown balloon, put it to his lips, and blew. It extended like a time-lapse video of a growing vine, curving in on itself before he pinched the spout, grabbed the far end, and made a series of deft twists and knots. The end result: an odd sort of elephant with a weird, humped head, and squat, fat legs. Not terrible, but not a very good likeness. But then he took a white balloon from his waistband, and before we knew it, the elephant had huge, curving tusks. A mammoth, then. A good one.

A crowd had started gathering, and they *oohed* appreciatively around mouthfuls of hotdogs and soft pretzels. He handed the mammoth to a young boy who ran off, trumpeting mammoth sounds.

It was Orange John's turn. He gazed up at the sky, as if searching the clouds for inspiration. Then, after a few moments, he reached into his breast pocket and took out a red balloon and a yellow balloon. He put both to his mouth and blew into them, his eyes distant, like a smoker deep in thought. When the balloons were inflated to his satisfaction, he grabbed them roughly and wrestled them into a red hawk with yellow eyes and talons. He held it aloft and gave it a toss. The wind caught it, and it sailed over the fountain, over the trees, out of sight.

Many-Colors clapped his hands in silent applause, then went to work. One by one he inflated about a dozen orange and black balloons, storing them under his armpit until he'd accumulated an unwieldy bundle. There was a flurry of rubber squeaking against rubber, and then before him in the grass crouched a life-sized tiger.

He grabbed it by the scruff of the neck and tugged. It walked on articulated legs. The jaw fell open to reveal long fangs and a lolling tongue.

It was a fine balloon animal.

Orange John placed his palms flat against each other as if in prayer and bowed deeply toward Many-Colors. From his pocket he drew a number of black balloons, and when he was finished blowing them up, he panted, out of breath, his face red. With shaky hands, he made a spider and set it against Many-Colors' tiger. The spider grasped the tiger in its legs and squeezed, destroying the tiger with small pops. Then it slowly scuttled back to its maker, exhausted, and deflated itself empty.

Many-Colors' eyes went wide, and his mouth formed an *O*. But his expression of surprise wasn't genuine. He was mocking Orange John.

Reaching to his waist, Many-Colors pulled out every green balloon he had, and when he seemed to be looking for more, Orange John took out a handful of his own and held them out in offering. But Many-Colors just sneered at him and pulled more green balloons from the air until his sleight-of-hand had given him an adequate supply for his next sculpture. This one took a while. Sweat glistened on his brow, and his lips moved as though he were reading aloud as his hands did their work.

His dragon reared up on bulbous haunches, black claws gleaming. Its red eyes seemed lit from within, and from its great maw came long, sinuous twists of red and yellow balloon flame.

Orange John didn't waste time acknowledging his opponent, for the dragon was lurching towards him. With desperate speed, he tied and twisted and knotted. The dragon was almost on him, and Orange John's lattice of balloon-work had yet to take form. We could hear him release small grunts of pain or frustration as he worked. For the first time ever, we noticed the way his fingers curled, the knots in his knuckles. Orange John had arthritis.

The dragon stretched its jaws wide, revealing more rubber flame, and Orange John jumped back from his own animal—a large feline body with the head of a bird of prey and graceful back-swept wings. A griffin.

Well-chosen, we agreed among ourselves.

The two animals leapt at one-another, and for the next several minutes, an epic battle raged above Carnival Park. Flashes of color. Rubber squeaks drawn out into screams. Tiny pops of injury.

When the dragon of Many-Colors floated back down to earth, half its jaw was missing. One of its bat wings hung limp, barely attached.

But at least it was still recognizable.

Not so for Orange John's griffin. Shredded bits of rubber rained on us.

The contest was over. Orange John kept his back rigid with dignity, but he already looked half dead. Perhaps, long ago, he had humiliated an older, more fatigued balloon man in this very spot. Perhaps it was simply the way of things.

Many-Colors offered his dragon to a little girl, but she refused to take it. Tears streaming down her eyes, she crossed her arms and looked away from the younger balloon man. Then the rest of us exchanged glances, and we knew what was right.

"A giraffe, Orange John?" someone said.

"And after that, a big dinosaur with spikes," said someone else.

Many-Colors looked at us, not understanding. "But ... I defeated Orange John. I'm your balloon man now."

We told him he'd never be our balloon man. Carnival Park belonged to Orange John. Orange John was this place. This place was Orange John.

Many-Colors made a lot of noise—he never really wanted to be our balloon man anyway, he said; and Orange John's balloons smelled like cigarettes (which was true); and we wouldn't know a good balloon man if he blew a poodle up our asses. But it was no use. With more grumbling and curses, he left, going wherever balloon men with no parks go.

Orange John didn't thank us. He didn't need to. He just began working on a beautiful long-necked giraffe with spindly long legs, which was exactly what we needed of him.

To tie balloons. To be here. To always be here.

Those of us who live and work around Carnival Park had never asked for a champion.

All we'd ever wanted was a good balloon man.

The Strip

My hand reaches for the toilet stall door, and he says, "You ever hear of a zero room?"

Restroom attendants make me nervous. I've been going to the bathroom on my own since I was three, and I don't need help.

"Every city's got a zero room," he says, "but it's never in the same place. Not from city to city, not from moment to moment."

He sits over there on his little stool, his bottles of cologne gleaming in the spotlights over the mirror. The bright reflections hurt my eyes.

"They say zero rooms were built by the man who made all the cities. They connect places. Or, to put it another way, every door, every single one, connects to the same zero room. When you open a door, maybe it goes somewhere you didn't expect it to. Or maybe it goes to everywhere at once. Or maybe everywhere comes spilling through the door, like a great tidal wave, and all the places behind all the doors smash into each other and get mixed up and cancel each other out, and it's the end of everything." He moves some of his cologne bottles around as if they're chess pieces. "Or maybe nothing at all happens. You never know."

I stare at him a while longer, but he seems done with me. He arranges breath mints on a silver tray.

I turn back to the toilet stall. With my hand hovering near the door, I flirt nervously with godhood.

THE WINGS OF MEISTER WILHELM

THEODORA GOSS

My mother wanted me to play the piano. She had grown up in Boston, among the brownstones and the cobbled streets, in the hush of rooms where dust settled slowly, in the sunlight filtering through lace curtains, over the leaves of spider-plants and aspidistras. She had learned to play the piano sitting on a mahogany stool with a rotating top, her back straight, hair braided into decorous loops, knees covered by layers of summer gauze. Her fingers had moved with elegant patience over the keys. A lady, she told me, always looked graceful on a piano stool.

I did try. But my knees, covered mostly by scars from wading in the river by the Beauforts' and then falling into the blackberry bushes, sprawled and banged — into the bench, into the piano, into Mr. Henry, the Episcopal Church organist, who drew in the corners of his mouth when he saw me, forming a pink oval of distaste. No matter how often my mother brushed my hair, I ran my fingers through it so that I looked like an animated mop, and to her dismay I never sat up straight, stooping over the keys until I resembled, she said, "that dreadful creature from Victor Hugo — the hunchback of Notre Dame."

I suppose she took my failure as a sign of her own. When she married my father, the son of a North Carolina tobacco farmer, she left Boston and the house by the Common that the Winslows had inhabited since the Revolution. She arrived as a bride in Ashton expecting to be welcomed into a red brick mansion fronted by white columns and shaded by magnolias, perhaps a bit singed from the war her grandfather the General had won for the Union. Instead, she found herself in a house with only a front parlor, its white paint flaking, flanked by a set of ragged tulip poplars. My father rode off every morning to the tobacco fields that lay around the foundations of the red brick mansion, its remaining bricks still blackened from the fires of the Union army and covered through the summer with twining purple vetch.

A month after my first piano lesson with Mr. Henry, we were invited to a dinner party at the Beauforts'. At the bottom left corner of the invitation was written, "Violin Recital."

"Adeline Beaufort is so original," said my mother over her toast and eggs, the morning we received the invitation. "Imagine. Who in Balfour County plays the violin?" Her voice indicated the amused tolerance extended to Adeline Beaufort, who had once been Adeline Ashton, of the Ashtons who had given their name to the town.

Hannah began to disassemble the chafing dish. "I hear she's paying some foreign man to play for her. He arrived from Raleigh last week. He's staying at Slater's."

"Real-ly?" said my mother, lengthening the word as she said it to express the notion that Adeline Beaufort, who lived in the one red brick mansion in Ashton, fronted by white columns and shaded by magnolias, should know better than to allow some paid performer staying at Slater's, with its sagging porch and mixed-color clientele, to play at her dinner party.

My father pushed back his chair. "Well, it'll be a nice change from that damned organist." He was already in his work shirt and jodhpurs.

"Language, Cullen," said my mother.

"Rose doesn't mind my damns, does she?" He stopped as he passed and leaned down to kiss the top of my head.

I decided then that I would grow up just like my father. I would wear a blue shirt and leather boots up to my knees, and damn anything I pleased. I looked like him already, although the sandy hair so thick that no brush could tame it, the strong jaw and freckled nose that made him a handsome man made me a very plain girl indeed. I did not need to look in a mirror to realize my plainness. It was there, in my mother's perpetual look of disappointment, as though I were, to her, a symbol of the town with its unpaved streets where passing carriages kicked up dust in the summer, and the dull green of the tobacco fields stretching away to the mountains.

After breakfast I ran to the Beauforts' to find Emma. The two of us had been friends since our first year at Ashton Ladies' Academy. Together we had broken our dolls in intentional accidents, smuggled books like *Gulliver's Travels* out of the Ashton library, and devised secret codes that revealed exactly what we thought of the older girls at our school, who were already putting their hair up and chattering about beaux. I found her in the orchard below the house, stealing green apples. It was only the middle of June, and they were just beginning to be tinged with their eventual red.

"Aren't you bad," I said when I saw her. "You know those will only make you sick."

"I can't help it," she said, looking doleful. The expression did not suit her. Emma reminded me of the china doll Aunt Winslow had given me two summers ago, on my twelfth birthday. She had chestnut hair and blue eyes that always looked newly painted, above cheeks as smooth and white as porcelain, now round with the apple pieces she had stuffed into them. "Mama thinks I've grown too plump, so Caddy won't let me have more than toast and an egg for breakfast, and no sugar for my coffee. I get so hungry afterward!"

"Well, I'll steal you some bread and jam later if you'll tell me about the violin player from Slater's."

We walked to the cottage below the orchard, so close to the river at the bottom of the Beauforts' back garden that it flooded each spring. Emma felt above the low doorway, found the key we always kept there, and let us both in. The cottage had been used, as long as we could remember, for storing old furniture. It was filled with dressers gaping where their drawers had once been and chairs whose caned seats had long ago rotted through. We sat on a sofa whose springs sagged under its faded green upholstery, Emma munching her apple and me munching another although I knew it would give me a stomachache that afternoon.

"His name is Johann Wilhelm," she finally said through a mouthful of apple. "He's German, I think. He played the violin in Raleigh, and Aunt Otway heard him there, and said he was coming down here, and that we might want him to play for us. That's all I know."

"So why is he staying at Slater's?"

"I dunno. I guess he must be poor."

"My mother said your mother was orig-inal for having someone from

Slater's play at her house."

"Yeah? Well, your mother's a snobby Yankee."

I kicked Emma, and she kicked back, and then we had a regular kicking battle. Finally, I had to thump her on the back when she choked on an apple from laughing too hard. I was laughing too hard as well. We were only fourteen, but we were old enough to understand certain truths about the universe, and we both knew that mothers were ridiculous.

In the week that followed, I almost forgot about the scandalous violinist. I was too busy protesting against the dress Hannah was sewing for me to wear at the party, which was as uncomfortable as dresses were in those days of boning and horsehair.

"I'll tear it to bits before I wear it to the party," I said.

"Then you'll go in your nightgown, Miss Rose, because I'm not sewing you another party dress, that's for sure. And don't you sass your mother about it, either." Hannah put a pin in her mouth and muttered, "She's a good woman, who's done more for the colored folk in this town than some I could name. Now stand still or I'll stick you with this pin, see if I don't."

I shrugged to show my displeasure, and was stuck.

On the night of the party, after dinner off the Sèvres service that Judge Beaufort had ordered from Raleigh, we gathered in the back parlor, where chairs had been arranged in a circle around the piano. In front of the piano stood a man, not much taller than I was. Gray hair hung down to his collar, and his face seemed to be covered with wrinkles, which made him look like a dried-apple doll I had played with one autumn until its head was stolen by a squirrel. In his left hand he carried a violin.

"Come on, girl, sit by your Papa," said my father. We sat beside him although it placed Emma by Mr. Henry, who was complaining to Amelia Ashton, the town beauty, about the new custom of hiring paid performers.

The violinist waited while the dinner guests told each other to hush and be quiet. Then, when even the hushing had stopped, he said "Ladies and Gentlemen," bowed to the audience, and lifted his violin.

He began with a simple melody, like a bird singing on a tree branch in spring. Then came a series of notes, and then another, and I imagined the tree branch swaying in a rising wind, with the bird clinging to it. Then clouds rolled in, gray and filled with rain, and wind lashed the tree branch, so that the bird launched itself into the storm. It soared through turbulence, among the roiling clouds, sometimes enveloped in mist, sometimes with sunlight flashing on its wings, singing in fear of the storm, in defiance of it, in triumph. As this frenzy rose from the strings of the violin, which I thought must snap at any moment, the violinist began to sway, twisting with the force of the music as though he were the bird itself. Then, just as the music seemed almost unbearable, rain fell in a shower of notes, and the storm subsided. The bird returned to the branch and resumed its melody, then even it grew still. The violinist lifted his bow, and we sat in silence.

I sagged against my father, wondering if I had breathed since the music had started.

The violinist said "Thank you, ladies and gentlemen." The dinner guests clapped. He bowed again, drank from a glass of water Caddy had placed for him on the piano, and walked out of the room.

"Papa," I whispered, "Can I learn to play the violin?"

"Sure, sweetheart," he whispered back. "As long as your mother says you can."

It took an absolute refusal to touch the piano, and a hunger strike lasting through breakfast and dinner, to secure my violin lessons.

"You really are the most obstinate girl, Rose," said my mother. "If I had been anything like you, my father would have made me stay in my room all day."

"I'll stay in my room all day, but I won't eat, not even if you bring me moldy bread that's been gnawed by rats," I said.

"As though we had rats! And there's no need for that. You'll have your lessons with Meister Wilhelm."

"With what?"

"Johann Wilhelm studied music at a European university. In Berlin, I think, or was it Paris? You'll call him Meister Wilhelm. That means Master, in German. And don't expect him to put up with your willfulness. I'm sure he's accustomed to European children, who are polite and always do as they're told."

"I'm not a child."

"Real-ly?" she said with an unpleasant smile, stretching the word out as long as she had when questioning Adeline Beaufort's social arrangements. "Then stop behaving like one."

"Well," I said, nervous under that smile, "should I go down to Slater's for my lessons?" The thought of entering the disreputable boarding house was as attractive as it was frightening.

"Certainly not. The Beauforts are going to rent him their cottage while he stays in Ashton. You'll have your lessons there."

Meister Wilhelm looked even smaller than I remembered, when he opened the cottage door in answer to my knock. He wore a white smock covered with smudges where he had rubbed up against something dusty. From its hem hung a cobweb.

"Ah, come in, Fraulein," he said. "You must forgive me. This is no place to receive a young lady, with the dust and the dirt everywhere—and on myself also."

I looked around the cottage. It had changed little since the day Emma and I had eaten green apples on the sagging sofa, although a folded blanket now lay on the sofa, and I realized with surprise that the violinist must sleep there, on the broken springs. The furniture had been pushed farther toward the wall, leaving space in the center of the room for a large table cracked down the middle that had been banished from the Beauforts' dining room for at least a generation. On it were scattered pieces of bamboo, yards of unbleached canvas, tools I did not recognize, a roll of twine, a pot of glue with the handle of a brush sticking out of it, and a stack of papers written over in faded ink.

I did not know what to say, so I twisted the apron Hannah had made me wear between my fingers. My palms felt unpleasantly damp.

Meister Wilhelm peered at me from beneath gray eyebrows that seemed too thick for his face. "Your mother tells me you would like to play the violin?"

I nodded.

"And why the violin? It is not a graceful instrument. A young lady will not look attractive, playing Bach or Corelli. Would you not prefer the piano, or perhaps the harp?"

I shook my head, twisting the apron more tightly.

"No?" He frowned and leaned forward, as though to look at me more closely. "Then perhaps you are not one of those young ladies who cares only what the gentlemen think of her figure? Perhaps you truly wish to be a musician."

I scrunched damp fabric between my palms. I scarcely understood my motives for wanting to play the violin, but I wanted to be as honest with him as I could. "I don't think so. Mr. Henry says I have no musical talent at all. It's just that when I saw you playing the violin—at the Beauforts' dinner party, you know—it sounded, well, like you'd gone somewhere else while you were playing. Somewhere with a bird on a tree, and then a storm came. And I wanted to go there too." What a stupid thing to have said. He was going to think I was a complete idiot.

Meister Wilhelm leaned back against the table and rubbed the side of his nose with one finger. "It is perceptive of you to see a bird on a tree and a storm in my music. I call it *Der Sturmvogel*, the Stormbird. So you want to go somewhere else, Fraulein Rose. Where exactly is it you want to go?"

"I don't know." My words sounded angry. He did think I was an idiot, then. "Are you going to teach me to play the violin or not?"

He smiled, as though enjoying my discomfiture. "Of course I will teach you. Are not your kind parents paying me? Paying me well, so that I can buy food for myself, and pay for this bamboo, which has been brought from California, and glue, for the pot there, she is empty? But I am glad to hear, Fraulein, that you have a good reason for wanting to learn the violin. In this world, we all of us need somewhere else to go." From the top of one of the dressers, Meister Wilhelm lifted a violin. "Come," he said. "I will show you how to hold the instrument between your chin and shoulder."

"Is this your violin?" I asked.

"No, Fraulein. My violin, she was made by a man named Antonio Stradivari. Some day, if you are diligent, perhaps you shall play her."

I learned, that day, how to hold the violin and the bow, like holding a bird in your hands, with delicate firmness. The first time I put the bow to the strings I was startled by the sound, like a crow with a head cold, nothing like the tones Meister Wilhelm had drawn out of his instrument in the Beauforts' parlor.

"That will get better with time," he told me. "I think we have had enough for today, no?"

I nodded and put the violin down on the sofa. The fingers of my right hand were cramped, and the fingers of my left hand were crisscrossed with red lines where I had been holding the strings.

On a table by the sofa stood a photograph of a man with a beard and mustache, in a silver frame. "Who is this?" I asked.

"That is — was — a very good friend of mine, Herr Otto Lilienthal."

"Is he dead?" The question was rude, but my curiosity was stronger than any scruples I had with regard to politeness.

"Yes. He died last year." Meister Wilhelm lifted the violin from the sofa and put it back on top of the dresser.

"Was he ill?" This was ruder yet, and I dared to ask only because Meister Wilhelm now had his back to me, and I could not see his face.

"*Nein.* He fell from the sky, from a glider."

"A glider!" I sounded like a squawking violin myself. "That's what you're making with all that bamboo and twine and stuff. But this can't be all of it. Where do you keep the longer pieces? I know — in Slater's barn. From there you can take it to Slocumb's Bluff, where you can jump off the big rock." Then I frowned. "You know that's awfully dangerous."

Meister Wilhelm turned to face me. His smile was at once amused and sad.

"You are an excellent detective, *kleine* Rose. Someday you will learn that everything worth doing is dangerous."

Near the end of July, Emma left for Raleigh, escorted by her father, to spend a month with her Aunt Otway. Since I had no one to play with, I spent more time at the cottage with Meister Wilhelm, scraping away at the violin with ineffective ardor and bothering him while he built intricate structures of bamboo and twine.

One morning, as I was preparing to leave the house, still at least an hour before my scheduled lesson with the violinist, I heard two voices in the parlor. I crept down the hall to the doorway and listened.

"You're so fortunate to have a child like Emma," said my mother. "I really don't know what to do with Elizabeth Rose."

"Well, Eleanor, she's an obstinate girl, I won't deny that," said a voice I recognized as belonging to Adeline Beaufort. "It's a pity Cullen's so lax with her. You ought to send her to Boston for a year or two. Your sister Winslow would know how to improve a young girl's manners."

"I supposed you're right, Adeline. If she were pretty, that might be some excuse, but as it is . . . Well, you're lucky with your Emma, that's all."

I had heard enough. I ran out of the house, and ran stumbling down the street to the cottage by the river. I pounded on the door. No answer. Meister Wilhelm must still be at Slater's barn. I tried the doorknob, but the cottage was locked. I reached to the top of the door frame, pulled down the key, and let myself in. I banged the door shut behind me, threw myself onto the sagging sofa, and pressed my face into its faded upholstery.

Emma and I had discussed the possibility that our mothers did not love us. We had never expected it to be true.

The broken springs of the sofa creaked beneath me as I sobbed. I was the bird clinging to the tree branch, the tree bending and shaking in the storm Meister Wilhelm had played on his violin, and the storm itself, wanting to break things apart, to tear up roots and crack branches. At last my sobs subsided, and I lay with my cheek on the damp upholstery, staring at the maimed furniture standing against the cottage walls.

Slowly I realized that my left hip was lying on a hard edge. I pushed myself up and, looking under me, saw a book with a green leather cover. I opened it. The frontispiece was a photograph of a tired-looking man labeled "Lord Rutherford, Mountaineer." On the title page was written, "*The Island of Orillion: Its History and Inhabitants*, by Lord Rutherford." I turned the page. Beneath the words "A Brief History of Orillion" I read, "The Island of Orillion achieved levitation on the twenty-third day of June, the year of our Lord one thousand seven hundred and thirty-six."

I do not know how long I read. I did not hear when Meister Wilhelm entered the cottage.

"I see you have come early today," he said.

I looked up from a corner of the sofa, into which I had curled myself. Since I felt ashamed of having entered the cottage while he was away, ashamed of having read his book without asking, what I said sounded accusatory. "So that's why you're building a glider. You want to go to Orillion."

He sat down on the other end of the sofa. "And how much have you learned of Orillion, *liebling*?"

He was not angry with me then. This time, my voice sounded penitent. "Well, I know about the painters and musicians and poets who were kicked out of Spain by that Inquisition person, Torquesomething, when Columbus left to discover America. How did they find the island in that storm, after everyone thought they had drowned? And when the pirate came—Blackbeard or Bluebeard or whatever—how did they make it fly? Was it magic?"

"Magic, or a science we do not yet understand, which to us resembles magic," said Meister Wilhelm.

"Is that why they built all those towers on the tops of the houses, and put bells in them—to warn everyone if another pirate was coming?"

Meister Wilhelm smiled. "I see you've read the first chapter."

"I was just starting the second when you came in. About how Lord Rutherford fell and broke his leg on a mountain in the Alps, and he thought he was going to die when he heard the bells, all ringing together. I thought they were warning bells?"

"Orillion has not been attacked in so long that the bells are only rung once a day, when the sun rises."

"All of them together? That must make an awful racket."

"Ah, no, *liebling*. Remember that the citizens of Orillion are artists, the children and grandchildren of artists. Those bells are tuned by the greatest musicians of Orillion, so that when they are rung, no matter in what order, the sound produced is a great harmony. From possible disorder, the bells of Orillion create musical order. But I think one chapter is enough for you today."

At that moment I realized something. "That's how Otto Lilienwhatever died, didn't he? He was trying to get to Orillion."

Meister Wilhelm looked down at the dusty floor of the cottage. "You are right, in a sense, Rose. Otto was trying to test a new theory of flight that he thought would someday allow him to reach Orillion. He knew there was risk—it was the highest flight he had yet attempted. Before he went into the sky for the last time, he sent me that book, and all of his papers. 'If I do not reach Orillion, Johann,' he wrote to me, 'I depend upon you to reach it.' It had been our dream since he discovered Lord Rutherford's book at university. That is why I have come to America. During the three years he lived on Orillion, Lord Rutherford charted the island's movements. In July, it would have been to the north, over your city of Raleigh. I tried to finish my glider there, but was not able to complete it in time. So I came here, following the island—or rather, Lord Rutherford's charts."

"Will you complete it in time now?"

"I do not know. The island moves slowly, but it will remain over this area only during the first two weeks of August." He stood and walked to the table, then touched the yards of canvas scattered over it. "I have completed the frame of the glider, but the cloth for the wings—there is much sewing still to be done."

"I'll help you."

"You, *liebling*?" He looked at me with amusement. "You are very generous. But for this cloth, the stitches must be very small, like so." He brought over a piece of canvas and showed me his handiwork.

I smiled a superior smile. "Oh, I can make them even smaller than that, don't worry." When Aunt Winslow had visited two summers ago, she had insisted on teaching me to sew. "A lady always looks elegant holding a needle," she had said. I had spent hours sitting in the parlor making a set of clothes for the china doll she had given me, which I had broken as soon as she left. In consequence, I could make stitches a spider would be proud of.

"Very well," said Meister Wilhelm, handing me two pieces of canvas that had been half-joined with an intricate, overlapping seam. "Show me how you would finish this, and I will tell you if it is good enough."

I crossed my legs and settled back into the sofa with the pieces of canvas, waxed thread and a needle, and a pair of scissors. He took *The Island of Orillion* from where I had left it on the sofa and placed it back on the shelf where he kept the few books he owned, between *The Empire of the Air* and *Maimonides: Seine Philosophie*. Then he sat on a chair with a broken back, one of his knees crossed over the other. Draping another piece of canvas over the raised knee, he leaned down so he could see the seam he was sewing in the dim light that came through the dirty windows. I stared at him sewing like that, as though he were now the hunchback of Notre Dame.

"You know," I said, "if you're nearsighted you ought to buy a pair of spectacles."

"Ah, I had a very good pair from Germany," he answered without looking up from his work. "They were broken just before I left Raleigh. Since then, I have not been able to afford another."

I sewed in silence for a moment. Then I said, "Why do you want to go to Orillion, anyway? Do you think—things will be better there?"

His fingers continued to swoop down to the canvas, up from the canvas, like birds. "The citizens of Orillion are artists. I would like to play my *Sturmvogel* for them. I think they would understand it, as you do." Then he looked up and stared at the windows of the cottage, as though seeing beyond them to the hills around Ashton, to the mountains rising blue behind the hills. "I do not know if human beings are better anywhere. But I like to think, *liebling*, that in this sad world of ours, those who create do not destroy so often."

After the day on which I had discovered *The Island of Orillion*, when my lessons had been forgotten, Meister Wilhelm insisted that I continue practicing the violin, in spite of my protest that it took time away from constructing the glider. "If no learning, then no sewing — and no reading," he would say. After an hour of valiant effort on the instrument, I was allowed to sit with him, stitching triangles of canvas into bat-shaped wings. And then, if any time remained before dinner, I was allowed to read one, and never more than one, chapter of Lord Rutherford's book.

In spite of our sewing, the glider was not ready to be launched until the first week of August was nearly over. Once the pieces of canvas were sewn together, they had to be stretched over and attached to the bamboo frame, and then covered with three layers of wax, each of which required a day and a night to dry.

But finally, one morning before dawn, I crept down our creaking stairs and then out through the kitchen door, which was never locked. I ran through the silent streets of Ashton to Slater's barn and helped Meister Wilhelm carry the glider up the slope of the back pasture to Slocumb's Bluff, whose rock face rose above the waving grass. I had assumed we would carry the glider to the top of the bluff, where the winds from the rock face were strongest. But Meister Wilhelm called for me to halt halfway up, at a plateau formed by large, flat slabs of granite. There we set down the glider. In the gray light, it looked like a great black moth against the stones.

"Why aren't we going to the top?" I asked.

He looked over the edge of the plateau. Beyond the slope of the pasture lay the streets and houses of Ashton, as small as a dolls' town. Beyond them, a strip of yellow had appeared on the hilltops to the east. "That rock, he is high. I will die if the glider falls from such a height. Here we are not so high."

I stared at him in astonishment. "Do you think you could fall?" Such a possibility had never occurred to me.

"Others have," he answered, adjusting the strap that held a wooden case to his chest. He was taking his violin with him.

"Oh," I said, remembering the picture of Otto Lilienthal. Of course what had happened to Lilienthal could happen to him. I had simply never associated the idea of death with anyone I knew. I clenched and unclenched my hands.

"Help me to put on the glider," said Meister Wilhelm.

I held the glider at an angle as he crouched under it, fastened its strap over his chest, above the strap that held the violin case, and fitted his arms into the armrests.

"Rose," he said suddenly, "listen."

I listened, and heard nothing but the wind as it blew against the face of the bluff.

"You mean the wind?" I said.

"No, no," he answered, his voice high with excitement. "Not the wind. Don't you hear them? The bells, first one, then ten, and now a hundred, playing together."

I turned my head from side to side, trying to hear what he was hearing. I looked up at the sky, where the growing yellow was pushing away the gray. Nothing.

"Rose." He looked at me, his face both kind and solemn. In the horizontal light, his wrinkles seemed carved into his face, so that he looked like a part of the bluff. "I would like you to have my books, and my picture of Otto, and the violin on which you learned to play. I have nothing else to leave anyone in the world. And I leave you my gratitude, *liebling*. You have been to me a good friend."

He smiled at me, but turned away as he smiled. He walked back from the edge of the plateau and stood, poised with one foot behind the other, like a runner on a track. Then he sprang forward and began to sprint, more swiftly than I thought he could have, the great wings of the glider flapping awkwardly with each step.

He took one final leap, over the edge of the plateau, into the air. The great wings caught the sunlight, and the contraption of waxed canvas fastened on a bamboo frame became a moth covered with gold dust. It soared, wings outstretched, on the winds that blew up from the face of the bluff, and then out over the pasture, higher and farther into the golden regions of the sky.

My heart lifted within me, as when I had first heard Meister Wilhelm play the violin. What if I had heard no bells? Surely Orillion was there, and he would fly up above its houses of white stucco with their belltowers. The citizens of Orillion would watch this miracle, a man like a bird, soaring over them, and welcome him with glad shouts.

The right wing of the glider dipped. Suddenly it was spiraling down, at first slowly and then faster, like a maple seed falling, falling, to the pasture.

I heard a thin shriek, and realized it had come from my own throat. I ran as quickly as I could down the side of the bluff.

When I reached the glider, it was lying in an area of broken grass, the tip of its right wing twisted like an injured bird. Meister Wilhelm's legs stuck out from beneath it.

I lifted one side of the glider, afraid of what I might see underneath. How had Otto Lilienthal looked when he was found, crushed by his fall from the sky?

But I saw no blood, no intestines splattered over the grass—just Meister Wilhelm, with his right arm tangled in a broken armrest and twisted under him at an uncomfortable angle.

"Rose," he said in a weak voice. "Rose, is my violin safe?"

I lifted the glider off him, reaching under him to undo the strap across his chest. He rolled over on his back, the broken armrest still dangling from his arm. The violin case was intact.

"Are you going to die?" I asked, kneeling beside him, grass tickling my legs through my stockings. I could feel tears running down my nose, down to my neck, and wetting the collar of my dress.

"No, Rose," he said with a sigh, his fingers caressing the case as though making absolutely sure it was unbroken. "I think my arm is sprained, that is all. The glider acted like a helicopter and brought me down slowly. It saved my life." He pushed himself up with his left arm. "Is it much damaged?"

I rubbed the back of my hands over my face to wipe away tears.

"No. Just one corner of the wing."

"Good," he said. "Then it can be fixed quickly."

"You mean you're going to try this again?" I stared at him as though he had told me he was about to hang himself from the beam of Slater's barn.

With his left hand, he brushed back his hair, which had blown over his cheeks and forehead. "I have only one more week, Rose. And then the island will be gone."

Together we managed to carry the glider back to Slater's barn, and I snuck back into the house for breakfast.

Later that day, I sat on the broken chair in the cottage while Meister Wilhelm lay on the sofa with a bandage around his right wrist.

"So, what's wrong with your arm?" I asked.

"I think the wrist, it is broken. And there is much pain. But no more breaks."

His face looked pale and old against the green upholstery. I crossed my arms and looked at him accusingly. "I didn't hear any bells."

He tried to smile, but grimaced instead, as though the effort were painful. "I have been a musician for many years. It is natural for me to hear things that you are not yet capable of hearing."

"Well, I didn't see anything either."

"No, Rose. You would see nothing. Through the science—or the magic—of its inhabitants, the bottom of the island always appears the same color as the sky."

Was that true? Or was he just a crazy old man, trying to kill himself in an especially crazy way? I kicked the chair leg, wishing that he had never come to Ashton, wishing that I had never heard of Orillion, if it was going to be a lie. I stood up and walked over to the photograph of Otto Lilienthal.

"You know," I said, my voice sounding angry, "it would be safer to go up in a balloon instead of a glider. At a fair in Brickleford last year, I saw an acrobat go up under a balloon and perform all kinds of tricks hanging from a wooden bar."

"Yes, you are right, it would be safer. I spent many years in my own country studying with Count Von Zeppelin, the great balloonist. But your acrobat, he cannot tell the balloon where to go, can he?"

"No." I turned to face him again. "But at least he doesn't fall out of the sky and almost kill himself."

He turned away from me and stared up at the ceiling. "But your idea is a good one, Rose. I must consider what it is I did wrong. Will you bring me those papers upon the table?"

I walked over to the table, lifted the stack of papers, and brought it over to the sofa. "What is this, anyway?" I asked.

Meister Wilhelm took the stack from me with his left hand. "These are the papers my friend Otto left me." He looked at the paper on top of the stack. "And this is the letter he wrote to me before he died." Awkwardly, he placed the stack beside him on the sofa and lifted the letter to his nearsighted eyes.

"Let me read it to you," I said. "You'll make yourself blind doing that."

"You are generous, Rose," he said, "but I do not think you read German, eh?"

I shook my head.

"Then I will read it to you, or rather translate. Perhaps you will see in it another idea, like she of the balloon, that might help us. Or perhaps I will see in it something that I have not seen before."

He read the letter slowly, translating as he went, sometimes stumbling over words for which he did not know the English equivalent. It was nothing like the letters Emma and I were writing to each other while she stayed in Raleigh. There was no discussion of daily events, of the doings of family.

Instead, Otto Lilienthal had written about the papers he was leaving for his friend, which discussed his theories. He wrote admiringly of Besnier, the first to create a functional glider. He discussed the mistakes of Mouillard and Le Bris, and the difficulties of controlling a glider's flight. He praised Cayley, whose glider had achieved lift, and lamented Pénaud, who became so dispirited by his failures that he locked his papers into a coffin and committed suicide. Finally he wrote of his own ideas, their merits and drawbacks, and of how he had attempted to solve the two challenges of the glider, lift and lateral stability. He had solved the problem of lift early in his career. Now he would try to solve the other.

The letter ended, "My dear Johann, remember how we dreamed of gliding through the air, like the storks in our native Pomerania. I expect to succeed. But if I fail, do you continue my efforts. Surely one with your gifts will succeed, where I cannot. Always remember that you are a violinist." When he had finished the letter, Meister Wilhelm passed his hand, still holding a sheet of paper, over his eyes.

I looked away, out of the dirty window of the cottage. Then I asked, because curiosity had once again triumphed over politeness, "Why did he tell you to remember that you're a violinist?"

Meister Wilhelm answered in a tired voice, "He wanted to encourage me. To tell me, remember that you are worthy to mingle with the citizens of Orillion, to make music for them before the Monument of the Muse at the center of the city. He wanted—"

Suddenly he sat up, inadvertently putting his weight on his right hand. His face creased in pain, and he crumpled back against the seat of the sofa. But he said, in a voice filled with wonder, "No. I have been stupid. Always remember, Rose, that we cannot find the right answers until we ask the right questions. Tell me, what did the glider do just before it fell?"

I stared at him, puzzled. "It dipped to the right."

He waved his left forefinger in the air, as though to punctuate his point. "Because it lacked lateral stability!"

I continued to look puzzled.

He waved his finger again, at me this time. "That is the problem Otto was trying to solve."

I sat back down. "Yes, well he didn't solve it, did he?"

The finger waved once again, more frantically this time. "He solved it in principle. He knew that lateral stability is created with the legs, just as lift is controlled with the position of the body in the armrests. His final flight must have been intended to test which position would provide the greatest amount of control." Meister Wilhelm sat, pulling himself up this time with his left hand. "After his death, I lamented that Otto could never tell me his theory. But he has told me, and I was too stupid to see it!" He rose and began pacing, back and forth as he spoke, over the floor of the cottage. "I have been keeping my legs still, trying not to upset the glider's balance. Otto was telling me that I must use my body like a violinist, that I must not stay still, but respond to the rhythm of the wind, as I respond to the rhythm of music. He thought I would understand."

He turned to me. "Rose, we must begin to repair the glider tomorrow. And then, I will fly it again. But this time I will fly from the top of Slocumb's Bluff, where the winds are strongest. And I will become one with the winds, with the great music that they will play through me."

"Like the Stormbird," I said.

His face, so recently filled with pain, was now filled with hope. "Yes,

Rose. Like *Der Sturmvogel*."

Several days later, when I returned for dinner after a morning spent with Meister Wilhelm, Hannah handed me a letter from Emma.

"Did the post come early?" I asked.

"No, child. Judge Beaufort came back from Raleigh and brought it himself. He was smoking in the parlor with your Papa, and I'm gonna have to shake out them parlor curtains. So you get along, and don't bother me, hear?"

I walked up the stairs to my room and lay on top of the counterpane to read Emma's letter. "Dear Rose," it began. "Aunt Otway, who's been showing me an embroidery stitch, asks what I'm going to write." That meant her letter would be read. "Father is returning suddenly to Ashton, but I will remain here until school begins in September." She had told me she was returning at the end of August. And Emma never called Judge Beaufort "Father." Was she trying to show off for Aunt Otway? Under the F in "Father" was a spot of ink, and I noticed that Emma's handwriting was unusually spotty. Under the b and second e in "embroidery," for instance. "Be" what? The letters over the remaining spots spelled "careful." What did Emma mean? The rest of her letter described a visit to the Museum of Art.

Just then, my mother entered the room. "Rose," she said. Her voice was gentler than I had ever heard it. She sat down on the edge of my bed. "I'm afraid you can't continue your lessons with Meister Wilhelm."

I started at her in disbelief. "You don't want me to have anything I care about, do you? Because you hate me. You've hated me since I was born. I'll tell Papa, and he'll let me have my violin lessons, you'll see!"

She rose, and her voice was no longer gentle. "Very well, Elizabeth. Tell your father, exactly as you wish. Until he comes home from the Beauforts', however, you are to remain in this room." She walked out, closing the door with an implacable click behind her.

Was this what Emma had been trying to warn me about? Had she known that my mother would forbid me from continuing my lessons? But how could she have known, in Raleigh?

As the hours crept by, I stared at the ceiling and thought about what I had read in Lord Rutherford's book. I imagined the slave ship that had been wrecked in a storm, and the cries of the drowning slaves. How they must have wondered, to see Orillion descending from the sky, to walk through its city of stucco houses surrounded by rose gardens. How the captain must have cursed when he was imprisoned by the citizens of Orillion, and later imprisoned by the English as a madman. He had raved until the end of his life about an island in the clouds.

Hannah brought my dinner, saying to me as she set it down, "Ham sandwiches, Miss Rose. You always liked them, didn't you?" I didn't answer. I imagined myself walking between the belltowers of the city, to the Academy of Art. I would sit on the steps, beneath a frieze of the great poets from Sappho to Shakespeare, and listen to Meister Wilhelm playing his violin by the Monument of the Muse, the strains of his *Sturmvogel* drifting over the surface of the lake.

After it had grown dark, I heard the bang of the front door and the sound of voices. They came up the stairs, and as they passed my door I heard one word — "violin." Then the voices receded down the hall.

I opened my door, cautiously looking down the hall and then toward the staircase. I saw a light under the door of my father's study and no signs of my mother or Hannah.

Closing my bedroom door carefully behind me, I crept down the hall, stepping close to the wall where the floorboards were less likely to creak. I stopped by the door of the study and listened. The voices inside were raised, and I could hear them easily.

"To think that I let a damned Jew put his dirty fingers on my daughter." That was my father's voice. My knees suddenly felt strange, and I had to steady them with my hands. The hallway seemed to sway around me.

"We took care of him pretty good in Raleigh." That was a voice I did not recognize. "After Reverend Yancey made sure he was sacked from the orchestra, Mr. Empie and I visited him to get the money for all that bamboo he'd ordered on credit. He told us he hadn't got the money. So we reminded him of what was due to decent Christian folk, didn't we, Mr. Empie?"

"All right, Mr. Biggs," said another voice I had not heard before. "There was no need to break the man's spectacles."

"So I shook him a little," said Mr. Biggs. "Serves him right, I say."

"What's done is done," said a voice I knew to be Judge Beaufort's. "The issue before us is, what are we to do now? He has been living on my property, in close proximity to my family, for more than a month. He has been educating Mr. Caldwell's daughter, filling her head with who knows what dangerous ideas. Clearly he must be taken care of. Gentlemen, I'm open for suggestions."

"Burn his house down," said Mr. Biggs. "That's what we do when niggers get uppity in Raleigh."

"You forget, Mr. Biggs," said Judge Beaufort, "that his house is my house. And as the elected judge of this town, I will allow no violence that is not condoned by law."

"Than act like a damned judge, Edward," said my father, with anger in his voice. "He's defaulted on a debt. Let him practice his mumbo jumbo in the courthouse jail for a few days. Then you can send him on to Raleigh with Mr. Biggs and Mr. Empie. Just get him away from my daughter!"

There was silence, then the sound of footsteps, as though someone were pacing back and forth over the floor, and then a clink and gurgle, as though a decanter had been opened and liquid were tumbling into a glass.

"All right, gentlemen," said Judge Beaufort. I leaned closer to the door even though I could hear his voice perfectly well. "First thing tomorrow morning, we get this Wilhelm and take him to the courthouse. Mr. Empie, Mr. Biggs, I depend on you to assist us."

"Oh, I'll be there all right," said Mr. Biggs. "Me and Bessie." I head a metallic click.

My father spoke again. "Put that away, sir. I'll have no loaded firearms in my home."

"He'll put it away," said Mr. Empie. "Come on, Biggs, be sensible, man. Judge Beaufort, if I could have a touch more of that whiskey?"

I crept back down the hall with a sick feeling in my stomach, as though I had eaten a dozen green apples. So this was what Emma had warned me about. I wanted to lie down on my bed and sob, with the counterpane pulled over my head to muffle the sounds. I wanted to punch the pillows until feathers floated around the room. But as I reached my door, I realized there was something else I must do. I must warn Meister Wilhelm.

I crept down the stairs. As I entered the kitchen, lit only by the embers in the stove, I saw a figure sitting at the kitchen table. It was my mother, writing a note, with a leather wallet on the table beside her.

She looked up as I entered, and I could see, even in the dim light from the stove, that her face was puffed with crying. We stared at each other for a moment. Then she rose. "What are you doing down here?" she asked.

I was so startled that all I could say was, "I heard them in the study."

My mother stuffed the note she had been writing into the wallet, and held it toward me.

"I was waiting until they were drunk, and would not miss me," she said. "But they think you're already asleep, Rose. Run and give this to Meister Wilhelm."

I took the wallet from her. She reached out, hesitantly, to smooth down my mop of hair, but I turned and opened the kitchen door. I walked through the back garden, picking my way through the tomato plants, and ran down the streets of Ashton, trying not to twist my ankles on invisible stones.

When I reached the cottage, I knocked quietly but persistently on the door. After a few minutes I heard a muffled grumbling, and then a bang and a word that sounded like an oath. The door opened, and there stood Meister Wilhelm, in a white nightshirt and nightcap, like a ghost floating in the darkness. I slipped past him into the cabin, tossed the wallet on the table, where it landed with a clink of coins, and said, "You have to get out of here, as soon as you can. And there's a note from my mother."

He lit a candle, and by its light I saw his face, half-asleep and half-incredulous, as though he believed I were part of some strange dream. But he read the note. Then he turned to me and said, "Rose, I hesitate to ask of you, but will you help me one final time?"

I nodded eagerly. "You go south to Brickleford, and I'll tell them you've gone north to Raleigh."

He smiled at me. "Very heroic of you, but I cannot leave my glider, can I? Mr. Empie would find it and take it apart for its fine bamboo, and then I would be left with what? An oddly shaped parachute. No, Rose, I am asking you to help me carry the glider to Slocumb's Bluff."

"What do you mean?" I asked. "Are you going to fly it again?"

"My final flight, in which I either succeed, or— But have no fear, *liebling*. This time I will succeed."

"But what about the wing?" I asked.

"I finished the repairs this afternoon, and would have told you about it tomorrow, or rather today, since my pocket watch on the table here, she tells me it is after midnight. Well, Rose, will you help me?"

I nodded. "We'd better go now though, in case that Mr. Biggs decides to burn down the cottage after all."

"Burn down—? There are human beings in this world, Rose, who do not deserve the name. Come, then. Let us go."

The wind tugged at the glider as we carried it up past the plateau where it had begun its last flight, toward the top of Slocumb's Bluff. In the darkness it seemed an animated thing, as though it wanted to fly over the edge of the bluff, away into the night. A little below the top of the bluff, we set it down beneath a grove of pine trees, where no wind came. We sat down on a carpet of needles to wait for dawn.

Through the long, dark hours, Meister Wilhelm told me about his childhood in Pomerania and his days at the university. Although it was August, the top of the bluff was chilly, and I often wished for a coat to pull over my dress. At last, however, the edges of the sky looked brighter, and we stood, shaking out our cold, cramped legs.

"This morning I am an old man, *liebling*," said Meister Wilhelm, buckling the strap of the violin case around his chest. "I do not remember feeling this stiff, even after a night in the Black Forest. Perhaps I am too old, now, to fly as Otto would have me."

I looked at the town. In the brightening stillness, four small shapes were moving toward Judge Beaufort's house. "Well then, you'd better go down to the courthouse and give yourself up, because they're about to find out that you're not at the cottage."

Meister Wilhelm put his hand on my shoulder. "It is good that you have clear eyes, Rose. Help me to put on the glider."

I helped him lift the glider to his back and strap it around his chest, as I had done the week before. The four shapes below us were now moving from Judge Beaufort's house toward Slater's barn.

Meister Wilhelm looked at me sadly. "We have already said our goodbye, have we not? Perhaps we do not need to say it again." He smiled. "Or perhaps we will meet, someday, in Orillion."

I said, suddenly feeling lonelier than I had ever felt before, "I don't have a glider."

But he had already turned away, as though he were no longer thinking of me. He walked out from under the shelter of the trees and to the top of the bluff, where the wind lifted his gray hair into a nimbus around his head.

"Well, what are you waiting for?" I asked, raising my voice so he could hear it over the wind. Four shapes were making their way toward us, up the slope above Slater's barn.

"The sun, Rose," he answered. "She is not yet risen." He paused, as though listening, then added, "Do you know what day this is? It is the ninth of August, the day that my friend Otto died, exactly one year ago."

And then the edge of the sun rose over the horizon. As I had seen him do once before, Meister Wilhelm crouched into the stance of a runner. Then he sprang forward and sprinted toward the edge of the bluff. With a leap over the edge, he was riding on the wind, up, up, the wings of the glider outspread like the wings of a moth. But this time those wings did not rise stiffly. They turned and soared, as thought the wind were their natural element. Beneath them, Meister Wilhelm was twisting in intricate contortions, as though playing an invisible violin. Then the first rays of the sun were upon him, and he seemed a man of gold, flying on golden wings.

And then, I heard them. First one, then ten, then a hundred — the bells of Orillion, sounding in wild cacophony, in celestial harmony. I stood at the top of Slocumb's Bluff, the wind blowing cold through my dress, my chin lifted to the sky, where the bells of Orillion were ringing and ringing, and a golden man flying on golden wings was a speck rapidly disappearing into the blue.

"Rose! What in heaven's name are you doing here?" I turned to see my father climbing over the top of the bluff, with Judge Beaufort and two men, no doubt Mr. Biggs and Mr. Empie, puffing behind. I looked into his handsome face, which in its contours so closely resembled mine, so that looking at him was like looking into a mirror. And I answered, "Watching the dawn."

I managed to remove *The Island of Orillion* and the wallet containing my mother's note from the cottage before Mr. Empie returned to claim Meister Wilhelm's possessions in payment for his bamboo. They lie beside me now on my desk, as I write.

After my father died from what the Episcopal minister called "the demon Drink," I was sent to school in Boston because, as Aunt Winslow told my mother, "Rose may never marry, so she might as well do something useful." When I returned for Emma's wedding to James Balfour, who had joined his uncle's law practice in Raleigh, I read in the Herald that the Wrights had flown an airplane among the dunes near Kitty Hawk, on the winds rising from the Atlantic. As I arranged her veil, which had been handed down through generations of Ashton women and made her look even more like a china doll, except for the caramel in her right cheek, I wondered if they had been searching for Orillion.

And then, I did not leave Ashton again for a long time. One day, as I set the beef tea and toast that were all my mother could eat, with the cancer eating her from the inside like a serpent, on her bedside table, she opened her eyes and said, "I've left you all the money." I took her hand, which had grown so thin that blue veins seemed to cover it like a net, and said, "I'm going to buy an airplane. There's a man in Brickleford who can teach me how to fly." She looked at me as though I had just come home from the river by the Beauforts', my mouth stained with blackberries and my stockings covered with mud. She said, "You always were a troublesome child." Then she closed her eyes for the last time.

I have stored the airplane in Slocumb's barn, which still stands behind the remains of the boarding house. Sometimes I think, perhaps Orillion has changed its course since Lord Rutherford heard its bells echoing from the mountains. Perhaps now that airplanes are becoming common, it has found a way of disguising itself completely and can no longer be found. I do not know. I read Emma's letters from Washington, in which she complains about the tedium of being a congressman's wife and warns about a war in Europe. Even without a code, they transmit the words "be careful" to the world. Then I pick up the wallet, still filled a crumbling note and a handful of coins. And I consult Lord Rutherford's charts.

CRAZY RAIN

PIPER SELDEN

There's rain...and then there's crazy rain.

"It start off real slow maybe and den end up 'freaky—da whole house. Dass some kine bad spirit wen shake one big juju stick an fling plenny angry spit ova da whole place, yea? Da kine wen wake you up from dream las night. Then pau!—no mo. Eh, dis a big mess...and broke da sleep good, yea?"

I nod and stare with blank eyes into cold, blue-black sludge, strangely thankful for day old Kona blend—fuel for early morning exhaustion when the power's out. And thick is how you have to drink it after crazy rain, when the storms roll off the Pacific and slam into the small coastal town of Hilo. You drink your coffee thick and black... or you sleep off the day.

Waterlogged and weary before dawn, we are surprised at the knock on our front door. Auntie Kai from up the street stands like a wet rag on our front lanai, flower mu'u mu'u drenched and clinging to her bony frame. She has come to check on us, plenny worried about the new haole family, fresh from Oregon and still smelling like pine. Kai's gentle face is wrinkled and weathered from years in the sun, but there is magic and sparkle in her eyes. The spirit of aloha calls her urgently to our home in the wee hours, with extra flashlights, batteries and a good luck token that "jus' couldn't wait."

We invite her to join us at the kitchen table for talk-story and I check out the small green packet she has pressed into my hands. It is a tied bundle of ti leaves with something inside, probably Hawaiian crude salt, and still warm from Kai's small clenched hand. Kept in the house, it will ward off nightmares and bad spirits, or so we've been told by our Hawaiian friends. I hedge my bets and place the good luck bundle on the kitchen table between glow-in-the-dark praying hands and a small sandalwood Buddha, completing a multicultural, makeshift shrine. Looking for a little faith to spare, part of me wonders, Are my bases are covered yet?

"Thank you, Kai." Smiling, I look deep into her kind, warm eyes. I am choked with emotion — feeling blessed with such a neighbor and yet totally vulnerable and exposed, naked almost. I wonder if my husband feels the same, and it bothers me that I can't read him right now. God, how do we pick up the pieces? Tears are near again, silent and hot. The house isn't shaking anymore, but I feel it in my body now. Kleenex, where is the damn Kleenex?

Outside, the air is quiet and pregnant with uncertainty, like the breath before a scream. We are all tired, but sleep is out of the question — so we drink coffee. It is cold, but we drink it anyway and I pretend we are safe inside the house. Much is said at the table without speaking and when we do discuss the storm, it is in hushed tones. I'm half-worried it might hear us and pay a return, unwanted visit — a mother-in-law storm.

Good Lord! I can't imagine there is any water left in the sky and yet, it still falls. Last night seems ages ago. Like Kai, I remember the first rain, quiet in the afternoon — purring and calling out like a lover. Gentle and rhythmic, relaxing and peaceful, the rain wooed me like some funky kind of tropical Muzak. Thinking back, yea, Muzak didn't seem too far off — like the stuff they play at the dentist office to pleasantly distract you while a man in white pajamas makes meatloaf in your mouth. It's a nice distraction at first, then the drug wears off.

It was slow at first, tiny fingers drumming the metal roofs of Old Hilo Town into a magic sleep, a sound that dulls the senses like too much cheap, red wine. Not much on TV, so we called it an early night. To sleep we drift — to slumber, rain. That was what I thought then, before I knew what Crazy Rain was. And we had no warning.

"Who-eee!" is the local, high-pitched exclamation, when nothing else will do. Kinda like saying, "Damn!" except better somehow. It was fitting for the fury unleashed as the rain intensified, a lover spurned. Hot nails scraped metal skin and threatened to strip our roof or shoot right through it. If we had been in a plane, we would have seen the horror more clearly — collective clouds boiling and blackening the sky along East Hawaii, like a long pool of spilled ink soaking everything beneath it.

Furious from the mainland journey, the massive storm front approached shore along the Hamakua Coast. The angry and restless sky stretched from the tiny community of Hawi in the north, along Hawaii Belt Road to Hilo and down into the Puna lowlands, about 95 miles. High winds and surf dumped truck loads of debris onto the highway. Bayfront Highway in Hilo would be closed for days to clean up the mess. Whole roads in Puna disappeared, washed into the ocean by the pounding surf along with a few homes, laundry lines full of clothes, pets and a few ocean-front residents. Waves crested 25 feet in some areas, we were told. Maybe less, does it matter?

Our house was hit largely unprepared, the fate of new island arrivals. Fo Shame, stupid haoles! Nex time you betta wen watch out, an stay ready! So we searched by flashlight for water and supplies—power blinked out, instant night. Outside, wispy-thin power lines sparked, blowing in the gale like strings without kites, creating whole neighborhoods of darkness. We flew through the house taping star shapes on the windows—little tropical snowflakes we heard might keep the glass in tact. We hunkered down… just in case.

We were starting to wonder about our decision to move here. People imagine all sunsets and Mai Tais when they think about Hawaii. There's more too it than that, and we were hip-deep in that discovery—a cruel slap of reality, right in the kisser. And then the house began to shake, moaning and creaking on its pillars. Flimsy match sticks, probably from some Oregon forest, held our home just above the rising flood—alive and moving. Just hours ago it had been our back yard.

Waves and waves of hurricane rage tore holes in the earth and ripped great swatches from carefully planned gardens, replanting things topsy-turvy miles away. But what turned me icy with fear was the sound and power of the wind. Screeching - swirling - a chaise lounge lifted from a backyard barbecue, flapping through the air like a red, flowered bat and finally smashing into Verna's Drive In for an ill-fated, midnight snack. Downtown Hilo, Mother Banyan must have sighed—exhausted and defeated. Unable to bear the howling strength and after years of gusty trades, she lowered her ancient green head to the earth, releasing life energy back to the Aina, the land.

Sitting off-shore, the core pulsed raw and wild. Unsatisfied, it shot raw munitions into a helpless crowd of Big Island leeward residents. Beating rain was driven from the center of the storm, sideways and without relief, from the ocean front all the way mauka, mountainside, and back— drenching us, drowning us:

The car-jacking in LA, a bankrupt tax-attorney in Portland, the suicide in Pittsburgh, and the convenience store robbery in New York—darkness gathers. Drunks fought in a Dallas bar, a child was beaten in Detroit and a Seattle housewife surprised her husband and his lover, shooting and killing them both—it spreads.

Sadness, Anger, Jealousy and Violence — it builds.
Miami, Tulsa, Chicago, and Boise — it grows.
Clouds gather, mix, intensify and spread...
Pain, Greed, Frustration and Despair — it has to go somewhere.

Out over the ocean, the virus spreads. Sometimes to die, the storm evaporates and flies up to the heavens. Other times gaining new energy, it makes landfall—unleashing fury and dumping it's payload of human emotion on the island. Hurricane, tsunami, monsoon... Same, same water buffalo.

We drink the last of the coffee down to the crunchy bits, praying for day break and the storm's end. How many ti bundles in Hilo? How many praying hands? How many Buddhas? On each exhale, people in East Hawaii pray in their own tongue.

Finally, the siege retreats back to open ocean, quiet and spent. An early rainbow with first light, high and arching, calls us out—cautious relief. We emerge from hiding like shy forest animals, peel snowflakes and violence off our windows and bury the dead.

Three Days In A Border Town

Jeff VanderMeer

You remember the way he moved across the bedroom in the mornings, with a slow, stumbling stride. His black hair ruffled and matted. The sharp line down the middle of his back, the muscles arching out from it. The taut curve of his ass. The musky smell of him that kissed the sheets. The stutter-step as he put on his pants, the look back at you to see if you'd noticed his clumsiness. The way he stared at you sometimes before he left for work.

Day One

When you come out of the desert into the border town, you feel like a wisp of smoke rising into the cloudless sky. You're two eyes and a dry tongue. But you can't burn up; you've already passed through flame on your way to ash. Even the sweat between your breasts is ethereal, otherworldly. Not all the blue in the sky could moisten you.

The border town, as many of them did, manifested itself to you at the end of your second week in the desert. It began as a trickle of silver light off imagined metal, a suggestion of a curved sheen. You could have ignored it as false. You could have taken it for another of the desert's many tricks.

But *The Book of the City* corrected you, with an entry under "Other Towns":

> Often, you will find that these border towns, in unconscious echo of the City, are centered around a metal dome. This dome may be visible long before the rest of the town. These domes often prove to be the tops of ancient buildings long since buried beneath the sand.

Drifting closer, the blur of dome comes into focus. It is wide and high and damaged. It reflects the old building style, conforming to the realities of a lost religion, the workmanship of its metal predating the arrival of the desert.

Around the dome hunch the sand-and-rock-built houses and other structures of the typical border town. The buildings are nondescript, yellow-brown, rarely higher than three stories. Here and there, a solitary gaunt horse, some chickens, a rooting creature that resembles a pig. Above fly the sea gulls that have no sea to return to.

Every border town has given you something: information, a wound, a talisman, a trinket. At one, you bought the blank book you now call *The Book of the City*. At another, you discovered much of what is written in that book. The third took a gout of flesh from your left thigh. The fourth put a pulsing stone inside your head. When the City is near, the stone throbs and you feel the ache of a pain too distant to be of use.

It has been a long time since you felt that pain. You're beginning to think your quest is hopeless.

About the City, your book tells you this:

> There is but one City in all the world. Ever it travels across the face of the Earth, both as promise and as curse. None of us shall but glimpse It from the corner of one eye during our lifetimes. None of us shall ever fully see the Divine, in this life.
>
> It is said that border towns are ghosts of the City. If so, they are faint and tawdry ghosts, for those who have seen the City know that It has no Equal.

A preacher for a faith foreign to you quoted that from his own holy text, but you can't worship anything that has taken so much away from you.

He had green eyes and soft lips. He had calloused hands, a fiery red when he returned from work. His temper could be harsh and quick, but it never lasted. The moodiness in him he tried to keep from you. Most of the time he hid it well. The good humor, when he had it, he shared with you. It was a good life.

At the edge of town, you encounter the sentinel. He sits in his chair atop a tall tower, impassive and sand-worn, sun-soaked. An old man, wrinkled and white-bearded. You stand there and look up at him for a long time. Perhaps you recognize some part of yourself in him. Perhaps you trust him because of it.

The sentinel stares down at you, but you cannot tell if he recognizes you. There is about him an immutability, as if beneath the coursing red thirst of his flesh, the decaying arteries and veins, the heart that fights against its own inevitable stoppage, there is nothing but fissured stone. This quality comes out most vividly in the color of his eyes, which are like gray slate broken by flashes of the blue sky.

"Are you a ghost?" the sentinel asks. A half smile.

You laugh, shading your eyes against the sun. "A ghost?" There'd be more moisture in a ghost, and more hope. "I'm a traveler. Just passing through. I'm looking for the City."

You catch a hint of slippage in the sentinel's impassive features, a hint of disappointment at such an ordinary quest. Half the people of the world seek the City.

"You may enter," the sentinel says, and suddenly his gaze has shifted back to the horizon, and narrowed and deepened, no doubt due to some ancient binocular technology affixed to his eyes.

The town lies open to you. What will you make of it?

Your father didn't like him, and your mother didn't care. "He's shallow. He's not good enough for you," your father said, but you knew this wasn't true. He kept his own counsel. He got nervous in large groups. He didn't like small talk. These were all things that made him seem unapproachable at first. But, over time, they both grew to love him almost as much as you loved him.

Everyone eventually wanted to like him, even when he was unlikable. There was something about him--a presence that had nothing to do with words or mannerisms or the body. It followed him everywhere. Sometimes you think it must have been the presence of the City, the distant breath and heat of it.

In this border town, as the streets and the people on them come into focus, you realize the sentinel's question was not baseless: you are a ghost. As you reach the outskirts, the sand somehow finer and looser, you stop for a second, hands on your hips, like a runner who has reached the end of a race. Your solitude of two weeks has been broken. It's as if you have breached an invisible bubble. It's as if you have lunged through a portal into a different place. The desert is done with. You are no longer alone.

Although you might as well be. As you walk farther into the town, no one acknowledges you. These are short, dark-skinned people who wear brown or gray robes, some with a bracelet or necklace that reveals a sudden splash of color, some without. Their eyes are large and either brown or black. Small noses and thin lips, or wide noses and thick lips. Some of them have skin so black it almost looks blue. They speak to each other in the border town patois that has become the norm, but you catch a hint of other languages as well. A smell of spice encircles them. It prickles your nostrils, but not in the same way as a hint of lime. Lime would indicate the presence of the City.

For a moment, you think that perhaps your solitude has entered the town with you. That somehow you really have become a wisp of smoke. You are invisible and impervious, as unnoticeable as a speck of dust. You walk the streets watching others ignore you.

Soon, a procession dawdles down the street, slower then faster, to the beat of metal drums. As it approaches, you stand to one side. Twenty men and women, some with drums, some shouting, and in the middle four men holding a box that can only be a coffin. The coffin is as plain as the buildings in this place. The procession travels past you. Passersby do not acknowledge it. They keep walking. You cannot help feeling the oddness here. To ignore a stranger is one thing. To ignore twenty men and women banging on drums while shouting is another. Even the sea gulls rise at its approach, the chickens scattering to the side.

When the procession is thirty feet past you, an odd thing happens. The coffin opens and a man jumps out. He's naked, penis dangling like a shriveled pendulum, face painted white. He has a gray beard and wrinkled skin. He shouts once, then runs down the street, out of sight.

As he does so, the passersby stop and clap. Then they continue walking. The members of the procession recede into the side alleys. The empty coffin remains in the middle of the street.

What does it mean? Is it something you need to write down in your book? You ponder that for a moment, but decide this is not about the City. There is nothing about what you saw that involves the City.

Then dogs begin to gather at the coffin. This startles you. When they bark, you are alarmed. In *The Book of the City* it is written:

> Dogs will not be fooled. They will not live silent in the presence of the City--they will bark, they will whine, they will be ill-at-ease. And the closer the City approaches, the more these symptoms will manifest themselves.

Is a piece of the City nearby? An inkling of it? Your heart beats faster. Not the source, but a tributary. Otherwise, your head would be aching, trying to break apart.

But no: as they nose the coffin lid open, you see the red moistness of meat. There is raw meat inside the coffin for some reason. The dogs feast. You move on.

Above you, the silver dome seems even more enigmatic than before.

His name was Delorn. You were married in the summer, under the heat of the scorching sun, in front of your friends and family. You lived in a small town, centered around a true oasis and water hole. For this, your people needed a small army, to protect it against those marauders who might want to take it for themselves. You served in that army, while Delorn worked as a farmer, picking dates, planting vegetable seeds, fine-tuning the irrigation ditches.

You were in surveillance and sharp-shooting. You could handle a gun as well as anyone in the town. After a time, they put you in charge of a small band of other sharp-shooters. No one ever came to steal the land because the town was too well-prepared. Near the waterhole, your people had long ago found a stockpile of old weapons. Most of them worked. These weapons served as a deterrent.

Delorn and you had your own small home--three rooms that were part of his parents' compound at the edge of town. From your window, you could see the watch fires at night, along the perimeter. Some nights, you stared back at your house from that perimeter. On those nights, the air seemed especially cold as the desert receded further from the heat of the day.

When you came home, you would crawl into bed next to Delorn and bring yourself close to his body heat. He always ran hot; you could always use him as a hedge against the cold.

So you float like a ghost again. You let your footfalls be the barometer of your progress, and release the idea of solitude or no solitude.

As night approaches, you become convinced for a moment that the town is a mirage, and all the people in it. If so, you still have water in your backpack. You can make it another few days without a border town. But can you make it without company? The thirst for contact. The desiccation of only hearing your own voice.

Someone catches your eye — a messenger or courier, perhaps — weaving his way among the others like a sinuous snake, with a destination in mind. The movement is unique for a place so calm, so random.

You stand in front of him, force him to stop or run into you. He stops. You regard each other for a moment.

He is all tufts of black hair and dark skin and startling blue eyes. A pretty chin. A firm mouth. He could be thirty or forty-five. It's hard to tell. What does he think of you?

"You come out of the desert," he says in his patois, which you can just understand. "The sentinel told us. But he also said he thought you might be a ghost. You're not a ghost."

How has the sentinel told them already? But it doesn't matter…

"Could a ghost do this," you say, and pinch his cheek. You smile to reassure him.

People are staring.

He rubs his cheek. His hands are much paler than his face.

"Maybe," he says. "Ghosts from the desert can do many things."

You laugh. "Maybe you're right. Maybe I'm a ghost. But I'm a ghost who needs a room for the night. Where can I find one?"

He stares at you, appraises you. It's been a long time since anyone looked at you so intensely. You fight the urge to turn away.

Finally, he points down the street. "Walk that way two blocks. Turn left across from the bakery. Walk two more blocks. The tavern on the right has a room."

"Thank you." You touch his arm. You can't say why you do it, or why you ask him, "What do you know of the City?"

"The City?" he echoes. A wry, haunted smile. "The ghost of it passes by us, in the night." His eyes become wider, but you don't believe the thought frightens him. "Its ghost is so large it blocks the sky. It makes a sound. A sound no one can describe. Like…like sudden rain. Like…" As he searches for words, he is looking at the sky, as if imagining the City floating there, in front of him. "Like distant drum beats. Like weeping."

You're still holding his arm. Your grip is tight, but he doesn't notice.

"Thank you," you say, and release him.

As soon as you release him, it's as if the border town becomes real to you. The sounds of shoes on the street or pavement. The trickling tease of whispered conversations, loud and broad. It is a kind of illusion, of course: the border town comes alive at dusk, after the heat has left the air and before the cold creeps in.

What did the Book say about border towns?

Every border town is the same; in observing unspoken fealty to the City, it dare not replicate the City too closely. By necessity, every border town replicates its brothers and sisters. In speech. In habits. If every border town is most alive at dusk, then we may surmise that the City is most alive at dawn.

You find the tavern, pay the surly owner for a room, climb to the second floor, open the rickety wooden door, hurl your pack into a corner, and collapse on the bed with a sense of real relief. A bed, after so long in the desert, seems a ridiculous luxury, but also a necessity.

You lie there with your arms outstretched and stare at the ceiling.

What more do you know now? That the dogs in this place are uneasy. That a messenger-courier believes the ghost of the City haunts this border town. You have heard such rumors elsewhere, but never delivered with such conviction, hinting at such frequency. What does it mean?

What do you want it to mean?

You don't sleep well. You never do in enclosed spaces now, even though the desert harshness has expended your patience with open spaces, too. You keep seeing a ghost city superimposed over the border town. You see yourself flying invisible through the town, approaching ever closer to the phantom City, but becoming more and more corporeal, until by the time you reach its walls, you move right through them.

In your book, you have written down a joke that is not really a joke. A man in a bar told it to you right before he tried to grope you. It's the last thing you remember as you finally drift away.

Two men are fighting in the dust, in the sand, in the shadow of a mountain. One says the City exists. The other denies this truth. Neither has ever been there. They fight until they both die of exhaustion and thirst. Their bodies decay. Their bones reveal themselves. These bones fall in on each other. One day, the City rises over them like a new sun. But it is too late.

You loved Delorn. You loved his sly wit in the taverns, playing darts, joking with his friends. You loved the rough grace of his body. You loved the line of his jaw. You loved his hands on your breasts, between your legs. You loved the way he rubbed your back when you were sore from sentinel duty. You loved that he fought his impatience and his anger when he was with you, tried to turn them into something else. You loved him.

Day Two

On your second day in the border town, you wake from dreams of a nameless man to the sound of trumpets. Trumpets and…accordions? You sit up in bed. Your mouth feels sour. Your back is sore again. You're ravenous. But: trumpets! The thought of any musical instrument in this place more optimistic than a drum astounds you.

You quickly dress and walk out to the main street.

The sides of the streets are crowded and noisy—where have all these people come from?—and they are no longer drab and dull. Now they wear clothing in bright greens, reds, and blues. Some of them clap. Some of them whistle. Others stomp their feet. From the edge of the crowd it is hard to see, so you push through to the front. A man claps you on the back, another nudges you. A woman actually hugs you. Are you, then, suddenly accepted?

When you reach the curbside, you encounter yet another odd funeral procession. Six men dressed in black robes carry a coffin slowly down the street. In front and back come jugglers and a few horses, decorated with thin colored paper—streamers of pale purple, green, yellow. There is a scent like oranges.

To the sides stand children with boxy holographic devices in their hands. They are using these toys to generate the ghosts of clowns, fire eaters, bearded ladies, and the like. Because the devices are very old, the holograms are patchy, ethereal, worn away at the edges. The oldest holograms, of a m'kat and a fleshdog, are the most grainy and yet still make you shiver. Harbingers from the past. Ghosts with the very real ability to inflict harm.

But the most remarkable thing is that the man in the coffin is, again, not dead! He has been tied into the coffin this time, but is thrashing around.

"Put it back in my brain!" he screams, over and over again. "Put it back in my brain! Please. I'm begging you. Put it back!" His eyes are wide and moist, his scalp covered in a film of blood that looks like red sweat.

You stand there, stunned, and watch as the procession lurches by. Sometimes a person in the crowd will run out to the coffin, leap up, and hit the man in the head, after which he falls silent for a minute or two before resuming his agonized plea.

You watch the dogs. They growl at the man in the coffin. The coffin passes you, and you stare at the back of the man's neck as he tries to rise once again from "death." The large red circle you see there makes you forget to breathe for a moment.

You turn to the person on your left, a middle-aged man as thin as almost everyone else in town.

"What will happen to him?" you ask, hoping he will understand you.

The man leers at you. "Ghost, they will kill him and bury him out in the desert where he won't be found."

"What did he do?" you ask.

The man just stares at you for a moment, as if speaking to a child or an idiot, and then says, "He came from the outside—with a familiar."

Your body turns cold. A familiar. The taste of lime. The sudden chance. Perhaps this town does have something to add to the book. You have never seen a familiar, but an old woman gave you something her father had once written about familiars. You added it to the book:

> The tube of flesh is quite prophetic. The tube of flesh, the umbilical, is inserted at the base of the neck, although sometimes inserted by mistake toward the top of the head, which can result in unexpected visions. The umbilical feeds into the central nervous system. The nerves of the familiar's umbilical wind around the nerves in the person's neck. Above the recipient, the manta ray, the familiar, rises and grows full with the knowledge of the host. It makes itself larger. It elongates. The subject goes into shock, convulses, and becomes limp. Motor control passes over to the familiar, creating a moving yet utilitarian symbiosis. The neck becomes numb. A tingling forms on the tongue, and taste of lime. There is no release from this. There should be no release from this. Broken out from their slumber, hundreds are initiated at a time, the tubes glistening and churling in the elision of the steam, the continual need. Thus fitted, all go forth in their splendid ranks. The eye of the City opens and continues to open, wider and wider, until the eye is the world.

So it says in the *Book of the City*, the elusive city, the city that is forever moving across the desert, powered by...what? The sun? The moon? The stars? The sand? What? Sometimes you despair at how thoroughly the city has eluded you.

You stand in the crowd for a long time. You let the crowd hide you, although what are you hiding from? A hurt and a longing rise in your throat. Why should that be? It's not connected to the man who will be dead soon. No, not him—another man altogether. For a long, suffocating moment you seem so far away from your goal, from what you seek, that you want to scream as the man screamed: Give me back the familiar!

In this filthy, run-down backwater border town with its insultingly enigmatic dome, where people believe in the ghost of the City and kill men for having familiars—aren't you as far from the City as you have ever been? And still, as you turn and survey your fate, does it matter? Would it have been any different walking through the desert for another week? Would you have been happier out in the Nothing, in the Nowhere, without human voices to remind you of what human voices sound like?

Once, maybe six months before, you can't remember, a man said to you: "In the desert there are many other people. You walk by them all the time. Most all of them are dead, their flesh flapping off of them like little flags." A bitterness creeps into the back of your throat.

You look up at the blue sky—a mockery of a sky that, cloudless, could never give anyone what they really need.

"We should harvest the sky," Delorn said to you once. You remember because the day was so cool. Even the sand and the dull buildings of your town looked beautiful in the light that danced its way from the sun. "We should harvest the sky," he said again, as you sat together outside of your house, drinking date wine. It was near the end of another long day. You'd had guard duty since dawn and Delorn had been harvesting the last of the summer squash. "We should take the blue right out of the sky and turn it into water. I'm sure they had ways to do that in the old days."

You laughed. "You need more than blue for that. You need water."

"Water's overrated. Just give me the blue. Bring the blue down here, and put the sand up there. At least it would be a change."

He was smiling as he said it. It was nonsense, but a comforting kind of nonsense.

He had half-turned from you as he said this, looking out at something across the desert. His face was in half-shadow. You could see only the outline of his features.

"What are you looking at?" you asked him.

"Sometimes," he said. "Sometimes I think I can see something, just on the edge, just at the lip of the horizon. A gleam. A hint of movement. A kind of...presence."

Delorn turned to you then, laughed. "It's probably just my eyes. My eyes are betraying me. They're used to summer squash and date trees and you."

"Ha!" you said, and punched him lightly on the shoulder. The warmth you felt then was not from the sun.

The rest of the day you spend searching for the familiar. It might already be dead, but even dead, it could tell you things. It could speak to you. Besides, you have never seen one. To see something is to begin to understand it. To read about something is not the same.

You try the tavern owner first, but he, with a fine grasp of how information can be dangerous, refuses to speak to you. As you leave, he mutters, "Smile. Smile sometimes."

You go back to the street where you found the courier. He isn't there. You leave. You come back. You have nothing else to do, nowhere else to go. You still have enough money left from looting desert corpses to buy supplies, to stay at the tavern for awhile if you need to. But there's nothing like rifling through the pockets of dead bodies to make you appreciate the value of money.

Besides, what is there to squander money on these days? Even the Great Sea, rumored to exist so far to the West that it is East, is little more than a lake, the rivulets that tiredly trickle down into it long since bereft of fish. It's all old, exhausted, with only the City as a rumor of better.

You come back to the same street again and again. Eventually, near dusk, you see the courier. You plant yourself in front of him again. You show him your money. He has no choice but to stop.

"There is something you did not tell me yesterday," you say.

The courier grins. He is older than you thought—now you can see the wrinkles on his face, at the sides of his eyes.

"There are many things I will not tell a ghost," he says. "And because you did not ask."

"What if I were to ask you about a familiar?"

The grin slips. He probably would have run away by now if you hadn't shown him your money.

"It's dangerous."

"I'm sure. But for me, not for you."

"For me, too."

"It's dangerous for you to be seen talking to me at all, considering," you say. "It's too late now—shouldn't you at least get paid for the risk?"

Some border towns worship the City because they fear it. Some border towns fear the City but do not worship it. You cannot read this border town. Perhaps it will be your turn for the coffin ride tomorrow. Perhaps not.

The courier says, "Come back here tomorrow morning. I might have something for you."

"Do you want money now?"

"No. I don't want to be seen taking money from you."

"Then I'll leave it in my room, 2E, at the tavern, and leave the door unlocked when I come to meet you."

He nods.

You pull aside your robe so he can see the gun in your holster.

"It doesn't use bullets," you say. "It uses something much worse."

The man blanches, melts into the crowd.

He wanted a child. You didn't. You didn't want a child because of your job and your duty.

"You just want a child because you're so used to growing things," you said, teasing him. "You just want to grow something inside of me."

He laughed, but he wasn't happy.

Nightfall. Night. Hours ticking by. You still can't sleep. Your head aches. It's such a faint ache that you can't tell if it's from the stone in your head. This time the sense of claustrophobia and danger is so great that you get dressed and walk through the empty streets until you have reached the desert. Standing there, between the town and the open spaces, it reminds you of your home.

There's a certain relief, the sweat drying on your skin although there is no wind. You welcome the chill. And the smell of sand, almost like a spice. Your headache is worse, but your surroundings are better.

You walk for a fair distance—this is what you've become most used to: walking—and then turn and look back toward the town. There is a half-moon in the sky, and so many stars you can't count them. Looking at the lights in the sky, the sporadic dotting of light from the town, you think, with a hint of sadness, that the old stories, even those told by a holographic ghost, must be wrong. *If humans had made it to the stars we would not have come to this. If we had gone there, our collapse could not have been so complete.*

You fall asleep, then, or so you believe. Perhaps your headache makes you pass out. When you wake, it is still night, but your head pounds, and the stars are moving. At least, that is your first thought: The stars are moving. Then you realize there are too many lights. Then, with a sharp intake of breath, you know that you are looking at the ghost of the City.

For you have seen the City before, if only once and not for long, and you know it like you know your home. This sudden apparition that slides between you and the stars, that seems to envelop the border town, looks both like and unlike the City.

There were underground caverns near where you grew up. These caves led to an underground aquifer. In those caves, you and your friends would sometimes find phosphorescent jellyfish in the saltish water. By their light you would sometimes find and catch fish. They were like miniature lighted domes, their bodies translucent, so that you could see every detail of their organs, the lines of their boneless bodies.

This "City" you now see is much like that. You can see into and through it. You can examine every detail. Like a phantom. Like a wraith. Familiars and people transparent, gardens and walls, in so much detail it overwhelms you. The City-ghost rises over the border town ponderously but makes no sound. The edges of this vision, the edges of the City, crackle and spark, discharging energy. You can smell the overpowering scent of lime. You can taste it on your mouth, and your skull is filled with a hundred hammers as your headache spins out of control. You think you are screaming. You think you are throwing up.

The City sways back and forth, covering the same ground.

You start to run. You are running back toward the border town, toward this Apparition. And then, just as suddenly as it appeared, the City puts on speed—a great rush and flex of speed—and it either disappears into the distance or it disintegrates or…you cannot imagine what it might or might not have done.

Sometimes you argued because he was sick of being a farmer, because he was restless, because you were both human.

"I could do what you do," he said once. "I could join your team."

"No, you couldn't," you said. "You don't have the right kind of discipline."

He looked hurt.

"Just like I don't have the skills to do what you do," you said.

They seemed like little arguments at the time. They seemed like nothing.

When you reach the outskirts of the border town, you find no great commotion, no awe-struck hubbub. The streets are still empty. You spy a stray cat skulking around a corner. A nighthawk worships a lamppost.

You approach the sentinel's chair. He peers down at you from the raised platform. It's the same sentinel from the other day.

"Did you see it?" you ask him.

"See what?" he replies.

"The City! The phantom City."

"Yes. As usual."

"As usual?"

"Yes. Every two weeks, at the same time."

"What do you see? From inside the town."

He frowns. "See? A hologram, invading the streets. Just an old ghost. A molted skin—like the snakes out in the desert."

Your curiosity is aroused. You hardly know this man, but something about his dismissal of such a marvelous sight bothers you.

"Why aren't you excited?" you ask him.

A sad smile. "Should I be? It means nothing." He stands on his platform, looking down. "It doesn't bring me any closer to the City."

In his gaze, you see a hurt and a yearning that is mirrored in your own. You mistook his look when you first met him. He wasn't disappointed in you, but in himself.

Maybe all reasons are the same when examined closely.

You walk home through a border town so empty it might as well be a ghost town itself. No one to document the coming of the wraith-City. How had it manifested? For an instant, had the dome of the border town and the dome of the City been superimposed as one?

When people begin to ignore a miracle, does that mean it is no longer miraculous?

A man stands in your room. You put out your gun. It's the courier. He has a sad look on his face. Startled, you draw back, but he puts out a hand in a gesture of reassurance, and you're so tired you choose to believe it.

"It is not what you think," he says. "It's not what you think."

"What is it then?"

"I need a place. I need a place."

In his look you see a hundred reasons and explanations. But you don't need any of them. This is a man you will never know, that you will never come to know. It does not matter what his reasons are. Lonely, tired, lost. It's all the same.

"What's your name?" you ask.

"Benkaad," he tells you.

He sleeps on the bed with you, facing away from you. His skin is so dark, glinting black in the dim light from the street. His breathing is rapid and short. After a time, you put your arm around his chest. Sometime during the night, you reverse positions and he is curled at your back, his arm around your stomach.

It is innocent. It is different. It's not like before.

Once, you had to shoot a scavenger, a rogue—a man who would have killed someone in your community. He'd gone bad in the head. It was clear from his ranting. He had a gun. He came out of the desert like a curse or a blight. Had he been crazy before he went into the desert? You will never know. But he staggered toward the guard post, aiming his gun at you, and you had to shoot him. Because you let him get too close—you shouting at him to drop his weapon—you had to shoot to kill.

The man lay there, covered in sand and blood, arms crumpled underneath him. You stood there for several minutes as your team ran up to you. You stood there and looked out at the desert, wondering what else might come out of it.

They told Delorn, and he came to take you home, you dazed, staring but not seeing. Once inside, Delorn took off all of your clothes. He placed you in the tiny bathtub. He used precious water to calm you, massaging your skin. He rubbed your head. He cleaned the salt and sweat from your body. He toweled you dry. And then he laid you down on the bed and he made love to you.

You had been far away, watching the dead man in the sand. But Delorn's tongue on your skin brought you back to yourself. When you came, it was in a rush, like the water in the bath. It was a luxury he had given to you.

You remember looking at him as if he were unreal. He was selfless in that moment. He was a part of you.

Day Three

In the morning, Benkaad is gone, leaving just the imprint of his body on your bed. The money you promised him has been taken from what you left in your bag. You try to remember why you let him sleep next to you, but the thought behind the impulse has fled.

Out into the sun, past the tavern keeper, cursing at someone. The day is hot, almost oppressive. You can walk the desert for two weeks without faltering, but after two days of a bed, you've already lost some of your toughness. The sun finds you. It makes you uncomfortable.

Benkaad waits for you on the street. As soon as he sees you, he drops a piece of paper and walks away. His gaze lingers on you before he's lost around a corner, as if to remember you, for a time at least.

You pick up the paper. Unfold it. It is a map, showing where to find the familiar. A contact name and a password. Is it a trap? Perhaps, but you don't care. You have no choice.

You have woken refreshed for the first time in over a year, and somehow that makes you feel guilty as you follow the map's instructions — through a warren of streets you would not have believed could exist in so small a town, each one forgotten as soon as you leave it.

As you walk, a sense of calm settles over you. You're calm because everything you face is inevitable. You have no choice. This is the missing piece of the Book. This replaces the Book. You're afraid, yes, but also past caring.

Sometimes there's only one chance.

Finally, an hour later, you're there. You knock on a metal door in a run-down section of town. The directions had been needlessly complex, unless Benkaad meant to delay you.

You've got one hand on your gun as the door opens. An old woman stands there. You give her the password. She opens the door a little wider and you slip inside.

"Do you have the money?" she asks.

"Money? I paid the one who led me here."

"You need more money to see it and connect to it."

A surge of adrenalin. It is here. A familiar.

Two men appear behind the woman. Both are armed with bullet-fed guns. Ancient.

You walk past them to the room that holds the familiar.

"Only half an hour," the one man says. "It's dying. Any more and it'll be too much for you, and for it."

You stare past him. Someone is just finishing up with the familiar. He has detached from its umbilical, but there is still a look of stupefied wonder on his face.

The umbilical is capped by an odd cylindrical device.

"What's that?" you ask the old woman.

"The filter. If that thing gets all the way into your mind, you'd never get free."

"Strip," one of the men says.

"Strip? Why?"

"Just strip. We need to search you," the man says, and raises his gun.

"Strip?" you say again.

The old woman looks away.

That's when you shoot the two men, the old woman, and the customer. For some reason, none of them seemed to expect it. They fall with the same look of startled surprise on their faces.

You don't know if they'll wake up; the gun is unpredictable. Hopefully they will, but you don't much care at the moment. It surprises you that you don't care.

Your head is throbbing.

You enter the room.

There, in front of you, lies the familiar, its wings fluttering on the bed. It seems to both press down into the bed and try to float above it. Its wings are ragged. Instead of being black, it is dead white. It looks as if it has been drifting, content to travel wherever the air might take it.

You take the umbilical and bring it around to the back of your head. The umbilical slides through the filter. You feel a weak pressure, a probing presence, then a firm, more assured grasp, a prickling—then a wet piercing. The taste of lime enters your mouth. A scratchiness at the back of your throat. You gasp, take two deep breaths, and then you hear a voice inside your head.

You are different.

"Maybe," you say. "Maybe I'm the same."

I don't think you are the same. I think you are different. I think that you know why.

"Because I've actually seen the City."

No. Because of why you want to find it.

"Can you take me there?"

Do you know what you are asking?

"I attached myself to you."

True. But there is a filter weakening our connection.

"Yes, but that might change."

You don't know how I came to be here, do you?

"No."

I was cast out. I was defective. You see my color. You see my wings. I was created this way. I was meant to die in the desert. I let a man I found attach himself so that would not happen. Eventually, it killed him.

"I'm stronger than that."

Maybe. Maybe not.

"Do you know your way back to the City?"

In a way. I can feel the City. I can feel it sometimes, out there, moving...

"I have a piece of the City in my head."

I know. I can sense it. But it may not help. And how do you plan to leave this place? Do you know that even with the filter, in a short time, it will be too late to unhook yourself from me. Is that what you want? Do you want true symbiosis?

Is it what you want? You don't know. It seems a form of madness, to want this, to reach for it, but there is a passage in the *Book of the City* that reads:

Take whatever the City gives you. If it gives you a cane, take it and use it. If it gives you dust, take the dust and make a house of it. If it gives you wisdom, take wisdom. The City does not give gifts lightly. It is not that kind of City.

You're crying now. You've been strong for so long you've forgotten the relief of being weak. What if it's the wrong choice? What if you never get him back even after all of this?

Are you sure? the familiar says inside your mind. *It is different than connecting for a short while. It is a surrender of self.*

You wipe the tears from your face. You remember the smell of Delorn, the feel of his body, his laugh. The smell of lime is crushing.

"Yes," *I'm sure,* you say, and you find that it is true, even as you disconnect the filter, even as you begin to feel the tendrils of unfamiliar thoughts intertwining with your own thoughts.

You have chosen.

The most secret part of the *Book of the City*, which you have never reread, is hidden on the back pages. It reads:

I lived in a border town called Haart, where I served as a border guard and my husband Delorn worked as a farmer at the oasis that sustained our people. We loved each other. I still love him. One night, he was taken from me, and that is why I keep this book. One night, I woke and he was not beside me. At first, I thought he had gotten up for a glass of water or to use the bathroom. But I soon discovered he was not in the house. I searched every room. Then I saw the light, through the kitchen window, saw the light, flooding the darkness, and heard the quiet breath of the City. I ran outside. There it lay, in all its awful glory, just to the west. And there were the imprints of my husband's boots, illumined by the City—heading toward it. The City was spinning and hovering and gliding back and forth across the desert. Then it was gone.

In the morning, we followed my husband's tracks out into the desert. At a certain point, they stopped. The boot prints were gone. Delorn was gone. The City was gone. It was just me, screaming and shrieking, and the last set of tracks, and the friends who had come out with me.

And every day since I have had a question buried in my head along with my love for my husband.

Did he choose the City over me? Did he go because he wanted to, or because It called to him and he had no choice?

At dusk, you escape, the familiar wrapped around your body, under the robes you've stolen from a dead man. Your collar is high to disguise the place where it entered you and you entered it. Out into the desert, where, when the border town is far distant, you can release him from beneath your robes and he, unfurling, can rise above you, your familiar, crippled wings beating, and together you can seek out the City.

It is a cool night, and a long night, and you will be miles away by dawn.

ABOUT THE AUTHORS

FORREST AGUIRRE is a recent recipient of the World Fantasy Award for his editing of the *Leviathan 3* anthology. His fiction has appeared in *Flesh & Blood, Indigenous Fiction, The Earwig Flesh Factory, Redsine, 3rd Bed, Notre Dame Review, Exquisite Corpse,* and *The Journal of Experimental Fiction,* among others. He has work forthcoming in *3rd Bed, All Star Zeppelin Adventure Stories,* and *The MacGuffin.*

Locus Magazine calls Forrest ". . . an interesting writer, worth watching, whom I think could benefit from disciplining the wilder flights of his imagination a bit." Forrest spurns such disciplinary measures.

HOLLY ARROW is an associate professor of social psychology at the University of Oregon. With Jennifer L. Berdahl and Joseph E. McGrath, she is the author of *Small Groups as Complex Systems.* This is her first fiction publication.

MICHAEL BISHOP was born in Lincoln, Nebraska, at the end of WWII, and was raised all over the U.S., starting school, however, in Tokyo, Japan, at Yoyogi Elementary School, an educational plant for the dependents of American military and civil service personnel, and concluding his public schooling at the dependent high school in Santa Clara, Spain, the American housing enclave about eight miles south of Seville. He lived with his dad and stepmom, in Seville itself, though, "on the economy," and he rode a bus to Santa Clara for school. Once back in the States, Bishop found himself in Albany, Georgia, his stepdad's hometown, and wound up attending the University of Georgia.

Bishop's novels include *No Enemy But Time* (Nebula Award), *Ancient of Days, Unicorn Mountain* (Mythopoeic Fantasy Award), and *Brittle Innings* (Locus Award for Best Fantasy Novel of 1994), and he has published six or seven volumes of short stories, the most recent being *Brighten to Incandescence,* from Golden Gryphon Press.

STEPAN CHAPMAN has been composing fantasy fiction since the days of Damon Knight's *Orbit* anthologies. His major publications are *The Troika*, a novel, and *Dossier*, a story collection. *The Troika* won the Philip K. Dick Award and will soon be translated into Russian.

Stepan and his wife Kia live in Cottonwood, Arizona, where he is currently preparing his second novel, *Burger Creature*, an epic American tale of love and androids.

Stepan tells us that "Ataxia, the Wooden Continent" forms a thematic triad with "State Secrets of Aphasia", which appeared in *Leviathan 3*, and "The Revenge of the Calico Cat", which will appear in *Leviathan 4*. He seems to be assembling some sort of modern geography of Toyland.

ELIOT FINTUSHEL lives in quiet dignity near the Sonoma County Fairgrounds between the horse stables and the transmission shops. He earns his living as an itinerant showman. Eliot's current touring how is a solo performance of *The Book of Revelation* called "APOCALYPSE: The Pentagon Papers of the Religious Right," which he'll be performing at the Vancouver Fringe Festival and at Chicago's Single File Fest this autumn. Check out his performance work and a bunch of short fiction for free at fintushel.com.

THEODORA GOSS was born in Hungary, and spoke Italian and French before she spoke English. She can still count in those languages. At various points in her childhood she remembers rice fields filled with frogs, a market square selling parrots, and nuns. She has gone under the Alps in a train too many times. She spent a significant amount of time trying to escape reality, mostly by reading about dragons. After a brief internment in law school and a law firm in Boston, where there were no dragons to speak of, she returned to school to study for a Ph.D. in English literature. She has taught college courses on fantasy, as well as fantasy and science fiction writing workshops.

Her stories have been published in magazines and anthologies including *Realms of Fantasy*, *Alchemy*, *Lady Churchill's Rosebud Wristlet*, and *Mythic Delirium*, and online at *Strange Horizons*, *Fantastic Metropolis*, and *The Journal of Mythic Arts*. They have been reprinted in *Year's Best Fantasy* and *The Year's Best Fantasy and Horror*.

GAVIN J. GRANT does not write everyday. He does not have a writing schedule—nor a writing hat, particular pen, nor chair. He does not enjoy definitions. Anecdotal evidence on occasion suffices. He runs (with Kelly Link) Small Beer Press and edits and publishes the 'zine, *Lady Churchill's Rosebud Wristlet*. He and Kelly now edit the fantasy section of *The Year's Best Fantasy & Horror*. His fiction publications include *The Third Alternative*, *Strange Horizons*, *Journal of Pulse Pounding Narratives*, and *Scifiction*. After trying various coastal metropolises, he has settled for slightly higher ground in an old farmhouse in Northampton, MA. He looks forward to living in a democracy.

ALEX IRVINE's first novel, *A Scattering of Jades*, won the Locus, Crawford and International Horror Guild first-novel awards. It has been translated into four languages. His short fiction, collected in *Unintended Consequences*, has appeared in *Salon*, *Scifiction*, *Magazine of Fantasy and Science Fiction*, *Asimov's*, *Vestal Review*, *Lady Churchill's Rosebud Wristlet* and elsewhere. His next novel, *One King, One Soldier*, is due any minute. He lives in Portland, Maine with his wife, Beth, children Emma and Ian, and dog Rooney.

KEN LIU's fiction has appeared in *Empire of Dreams and Miracles*, *Writers of the Future XIX*, and *Strange Horizons*. More information about him can be found at his web site: *http://people.deas.harvard.edu/~liu51/*

    A native of Lanzhou, China, Ken Liu wrote his first novel, a technological utopian adventure set in the year 2000 complete with illustrations, in Chinese, when he was in the third grade. He can no longer locate that manuscript, which saves him from a lot of embarrassment. Currently, he is studying to be a lawyer in Boston, Massachusetts, and he would like to write a surrealistic story some day about the Internal Revenue Code.

STEVEN MOHAN, JR. lives in Pueblo, Colorado where he works as a manufacturing engineer. When not writing, he helps his wife keep track of their three small children. Steve's short fiction has appeared in *Writers of the Future*, *On Spec*, *Talebones*, *Extremes 4: Darkest Africa*, and *Aboriginal Science Fiction* and has won honorable mention in both *The Year's Best*

Fantasy and Horror and *The Year's Best Science Fiction*.

JERRY OLTION is the author of *Abandon in Place*, *The Getaway Special*, and the forthcoming novels *Anywhere But Here* and *Paradise Passed* plus several Star Trek books and over a hundred short stories. He won the Nebula award in 1997 for the novella version of *Abandon in Place*. He lives in Eugene, Oregon, with his wife Kathy, who also writes science fiction, and who had a story in *Polyphony 3*.

Jerry grew up in Wyoming, where "Bagging the Peak" is set. The story is partially autobiographical, based on a climb in July of 2003 in which his niece, who was going up for the first time, said that the surprising thing wasn't that Jerry had climbed the peak twice already, but that he was doing it a third time. They began speculating what makes people push themselves so hard for so little apparent gain, and by the time lightning chased them down off the mountain, they had brainstormed the entire story. This one's for Marlo, who went to the top.

TIM PRATT has been nominated for a Nebula Award and for the John W. Campbell Award for Best New Writer. He has published (or has stories upcoming) in *Realms of Fantasy*, *Asimov's*, *The Year's Best Fantasy*, and other nice places.

Concerning "Hart and Boot", Tim warns, "the bare historical facts of this story are true, though I can't guarantee that it all happened *exactly* the way I've described."

KIT REED's new novel is *Thinner Than Thou*, about a diet evangelist in body-conscious America, where physical perfection is the new religion. Kirkus calls it "sometimes appalling" which she considers high praise. Her previous novels include *@expectations*, *Captain Grownup*, *Fort Privilege*, *Catholic Girls*, *J. Eden*, and *Little Sisters of the Apocalypse*. As Kit Craig she is the author of *Gone*, *Twice Burned* and other psychological thrillers. Her books *Weird Women, Wired Women* and *Little Sisters of the Apocalypse* were finalists for the Tiptree Prize. Of the short fiction, *The New York Times Book Review* says, "most of these stories shine with the incisive edginess of brilliant cartoons...they are less fantastic than visionary."

JENN REESE's work has appeared in *Strange Horizons*, *Flytrap*, and various speculative fiction anthologies such as DAW's *Rotten Relations* and *Sword & Sorceress XXI*. Over the years, she has earned a living doing desktop publishing, database programming, and Web design, among other things. Most recently, she wrote books on American slang for people trying to learn English. Jenn currently lives in Los Angeles, where she studies martial arts, plays strategy games, and keeps an online journal: *www.memoryandreason.com*.

BRUCE HOLLAND ROGERS' stories have appeared in *The North American Review*, *Realms of Fantasy*, *Descant*, and *Quarterly West*. He lives in Eugene, Oregon. "The Train There's No Getting Off," co-authored with Ray Vukcevich and Holly Arrow, is a symmetrina, a fixed form of prose or poetry. Other examples of the form appeared in *Polyphony* and *Polyphony 2*.

PIPER SELDEN is a writer, artist, activist and self-proclaimed "worm wrestler." She currently lives in Hilo, on the Big Island of Hawaii, with her two children, husband and geriatric cat. She is a member of HIWA, Hawaii Island Writers Association, and is currently working on a variety of projects including a collection of letters and short stories, a book on composting in Hawaii, and a self-help guide on simplicity and spirituality.

The story "Crazy Rain" is based in part on Piper's first hurricane experience in the Hawaiian Islands. When not monitoring the weather channel or dodging lava flows, Piper enjoys playing in the dirt, either gardening or tending her compost pile. She takes Hula to practice humility and collects recipes for the perfect Mai Tai. This is her first published story.

LUCIUS SHEPARD has been one of the most honored writers in science fiction, fantasy, horror and beyond, winning each of the World Fantasy Award, Hugo, Nebula and International Horror Guild Awards.

His recent publications include *Two Trains Running*, *Louisiana Breakdown*, *Aztechs*, and *Floater*. Forthcoming in 2004 will be *Trujillo* (a collection of short works from P.S. Publishing), *The Handbook of American Prayer* (a novel) and *Viator* (a novel from Night Shade Books).

Born in Virginia and raised in Florida, Shepard has lived in the

Midwest, New England, New York and most recently the West Coast. His travels throughout the world are reflected in the exotic settings of much of his work, especially Latin America. He currently lives near a strip mall in Vancouver, Washington.

DIANA SHERMAN started out as a playwright before she began writing science fiction and fantasy. She has had eight plays in various festivals, a story in *Talebones*, and has a play forthcoming in *Exquisite Corpuscle* edited by Jay Lake and Frank Wu. That play is also getting a staged reading with Moving Arts in Los Angeles. She has taught composition at USC and creative writing at Scripps College, and has no idea where she'll be teaching next semester. Other than that, she has two great cats, one awesome brother, and a pretty cool family overall.

JEREMIAH TOLBERT lives with wife and felines in the mountains of Wyoming. He is the co-editor-in-chief of the *Fortean Bureau*, an online speculative fiction magazine for the weird and strange. He spends 14 hours a day behind a keyboard, a small fraction of which are spent writing. In the remaining hours, he takes photographs, and, occasionally, he sleeps.

MIKAL TRIMM writes stories and poems in many genres—even genres that don't exist yet. He has sold to publications in three countries, although he has been told that he is not encouraged to actually *visit* those places. His work has littered the pages of magazines that really should have known better, including *Gothic.net*, *SAY...Was That A Kiss?*, *Flytrap*, *NFG*, and *Andromeda Spaceways Inflight Magazine*. He currently lives in Lockhart, Texas. This marks his first appearance in a professional anthology, and he's quite sure that a mistake has been made somewhere.

JEFF VANDERMEER's latest books include *City of Saints & Madmen*, *Veniss Underground*, and the story collection *Secret Life*. Pan MacMillan will release *The Thackery T. Lambshead Pocket Guide to Eccentric & Discredited Diseases*, co-edited by Jeff, in November 2004. His books have made the best-of-year lists of *Amazon.com*, *Publishers Weekly*, *Publishers' News*, *The San Francisco Chronicle*, and many more. He is a two-time winner of the World Fantasy Award.

410

Concerning this story, Jeff writes, "'Three Days in a Border Town'" came out of a story I'd written earlier in 2003 called 'The City,' which is in my Golden Gryphon collection *Secret Life*. 'The City' is a kaleidoscopic, surreal tale about the search for a mythical city in a parched possibly far-far future world. It more or less introduces the city, but there isn't much of a plot to it. I didn't expect to write more stories with the same setting, but the images from 'Three Days' just came to me one evening and within a week I'd written the story. I like it because I've had to modify my style, taking a more stripped-down approach in keeping with the setting, and I've totally fallen in love with the main character. I'm now working on more stories set in the same milieu, the next one called 'The Circus on the Bridge,' continuing the tale of our heroine's quest."

GREG VAN EEKHOUT's work has appeared in *STARLIGHT 3*, *Magazine of Fantasy & Science Fiction*, and *Asimov's Science Fiction*, among other places. He lives in Tempe, Arizona, where he is currently at work on a novel or two. He maintains a web site at *http://www.sff.net/people/greg* and an online journal at *http://www.journalscape.com/greg*.

RAY VUKCEVICH's latest book is a collection of stories called *Meet Me in the Moon Room* from Small Beer Press.

DON WEBB has published fiction in a variety of venues and languages. His most recent fiction collections include *A Spell for the Fulfillment of Desire* (Black Ice Books), *Stealing My Rules* (CPAOD Books), and *The Explanation and Other Good Advice* (Wordcraft of Oregon). His first book, *Uncle Ovid's Exercise Book*, won the 1988 Illinois State University/Fiction Collective fiction contest. His 2nd book, *Marchenland ist abgebrannt*, appeared in Austria in 1990

His short fiction has appeared in nearly 200 large and small magazines in the United States, Great Britain, Canada, Australia, France, India, Japan, and Norway (including *Isaac Asimov's Science Fiction Magazine*, *Science Fiction Age*, *Amazing*, *Interzone*, *Semiotext(e) SF*, *Back Brain Recluse*, *Fear*, *Prakalpana Literature*, etc).

Don Webb is an expert on the magical practices of Late Antiquity, his most recent occult book is The Seven Faces of Darkness: Practical Typhonian

Magic from Runa Raven Press. He has lectured on Left Hand Path theology, Egyptian magic, Sadeanism. Don lives in Austin. Texas.

ROBERT FREEMAN WEXLER's first novel, *Circus of the Grand Design*, is just out from Prime Books. His 2003 novella, *In Springdale Town* (PS Publishing) was reprinted in the *Best Short Novels 2004*. "Valley of the Falling Clouds," appeared in *Polyphony 3*.

ERIC M. WITCHEY is an award-winning writer who lurks amid ferns in the Northwest. When not teaching or writing, he stands in streams flipping flies at mythical fish and wondering in awe at the complexity of a universe in which a man can easily spend a thousand dollars to trick a finned creature whose brain is the size of a pea. His fiction has appeared nationally and internationally in magazines and anthologies. He has published short fiction in seven genres under four names and has won recognition from *Writers of the Future, New Century Writers, ralan.com*, and *Writers Digest*. He has sold how-to articles to *Writer's Digest Magazine, Writer's Northwest Magazine*, and *Northwest Ink Magazine*.

ABOUT THE EDITORS

DEBORAH LAYNE founded Wheatland Press in 2002 and has been co-editing the *Polyphony* series ever since. Her own fiction has appeared at *Clean Sheets, The Fortean Bureau* and will soon appear in *Flytrap 3*. She is a member of the Wordos Writers Workshop of Eugene, Oregon. Having earned degrees in history, philosophy, history and philosophy of science and law, she is content to focus on speculative literature. Deborah lives in deepest, darkest Oregon with her family.

JAY LAKE is a 2004 Hugo Nominee (for his novelette "Into the Gardens of Sweet Night") and a 2004 John W. Campbell Award for Best New Writer nominee. His stories have appeared in places too numerous to mention including *Realms of Fantasy, Strange Horizons* and *Asimov's*. He has three collections in print: *Greetings From Lake Wu, Green Grow the Rushes*, and *American Sorrows*. In addition to his work on the Polyphony series, he is the co-editor with David Moles of *All Star Zeppelin Adventure Stories* and the editor of *TEL: Stories*. He is a member of the Wordos Writers Workshop of Eugene, Oregon. Jay lives in Portland, Oregon.

OTHER TITLES AVAILABLE FROM
WHEATLAND PRESS

ANTHOLOGIES

POLYPHONY 1, Deborah Layne and Jay Lake, Eds. Volume one in the critically acclaimed slipstream/cross-genre series will feature stories from Maureen McHugh, Andy Duncan, Carol Emshwiller, Lucius Shepard and others.

POLYPHONY 2, Deborah Layne and Jay Lake, Eds. Volume two in the critically acclaimed slipstream/cross-genre series will feature stories from Alex Irvine, Theodora Goss, Jack Dann, Michael Bishop and others.

POLYPHONY 3, Deborah Layne and Jay Lake, Eds. Volume three in the critically acclaimed slipstream/cross-genre series will feature stories from Jeff Ford, Bruce Holland Rogers, Ray Vukcevich, Robert Freeman Wexler and others.

TEL: STORIES, Jay Lake Ed. An anthology of experimental fiction with authors to be announced.

EXQUISITE CORPUSCLE, Frank Wu and Jay Lake Eds. Stories, poems, illustrations, even a play; an elaborate game of literary telephone featuring Gary Shockley, Benjamin Rosenbaum, Bruce Holland Rogers, Kristin Livdahl, Maggie Hogarth, and others.

ALL STAR ZEPPELIN ADVENTURE STORIES, David Moles and Jay Lake Eds. Original zeppelin stories by Jim Van Pelt, Leslie What, and others; one reprint, "You Could Go Home Again" by Howard Waldrop.

SINGLE-AUTHOR COLLECTIONS

DREAM FACTORIES AND RADIO PICTURES, Howard Waldrop. Waldrop's stories about early film and television reprinted in one volume.

GREETINGS FROM LAKE WU, Jay Lake and Frank Wu. Collection of stories by Jay Lake with original illustrations by Frank Wu.

TWENTY QUESTIONS, Jerry Oltion. Twenty brilliant works by the Nebula Award-winning author of "Abandon in Place."

THE BEASTS OF LOVE, Steven Utley, Intro. by Lisa Tuttle. Utley's "love" stories spanning the past twenty years; a brilliant mixture of science fiction, fantasy and horror.

AMERICAN SORROWS, Jay Lake. Four longer works by the Hugo and Campbell nominated author; includes his Hugo nominated novelette, "Into the Gardens of Sweet Night."

NONFICTION

WEAPONS OF MASS SEDUCTION, Lucius Shepard. A collection of Shepard's film reviews. Some have previously appeared in print in the *Magazine of Fantasy and Science Fiction*; most have only appeared online at *Electric Story*.

POETRY

KNUCKLE SANDWICHES, Tom Smario, Intro. by Lucius Shepard. Poems about boxing by a long-time poet and cut-man.

NOVEL

PARADISE PASSED, Jerry Oltion. The crew of a colony ship must choose between a ready-made paradise and one they create for themselves.

FOR ORDERING INFORMATION VISIT:

WWW.WHEATLANDPRESS.COM

Printed in the United States
34620LVS00006B/9